The Elvish Prophecy

Book 1
The Paladin Chronicles

Neil Port

Dedication

This book is dedicated to my wife and family with especial thanks to my grandmother, who believed in me. I need to give thanks to my "team" of volunteer reviewers: Meryl, Alison, Ralph, Shirley, Ainie, Fiona and Linda, to name just a few.

This describes a world with similarities to our own, commencing just before three and a half centuries BC. There are differences, some obvious, some less obvious. Some historical names, places and characters are used to provide a setting for this book, but it is a work of imagination and the events described and characters described should not be taken as an historical or accurate account. Any resemblance to any person now living or living in more recent times is purely accidental. War and battle is not glorious and it is not depicted as such, so this book and those that follow are not intended as children's books.

ISBN: 978-0-9873845-0-8

The Elvish Prophecy, Book 1 of the Paladin Chronicles

Copyright © Neil Port, August 2012, all rights reserved

Neil Port Independent Press, Newcastle Australia.

First edition August 2012.

Second Edition, March 2020.

Editor: Jeff Palley (https://www.upwork.com/fl/jeffpalley),

Conversion to eBook: mailto:ebooksspecialist@gmail.com

Cover design: Paul Kimber (http://www.angelheartdesign.org)

Maps Radana Pavelkov (Nivues@yahoo.com)

Reviews (Readers Favorite): "First rate. brilliant. fascinating characters...truly memorable." A.DiNizo ."Intriguing.incredible. wonderful.intricate....a delight to read."S.Dagg

Contents

Author's Notes V

About the Author V

Chapter 1: Hakeem of the Shantawi 1

Chapter 2: Mules, a Runaway, and Pergamon 12

Chapter 3: The King's Game, an Elf, a Lesson, and
the Men's Latrine 46

Chapter 4: An Inexperienced Man, a Trap, and a Plan 74

Chapter 5: Leaving Malea 84

Chapter 6: Conducting a War, and Summoned Home 100

Chapter 7: A Reluctant Princess, a Coming of Age,
and Leaving Elgard 103

Chapter 8: A Man of Integrity, Girl-Talk, and a Loving Family ... 135

Chapter 9: A New Horse, a Widow, and a Poisonous Drink .. 143

Chapter 10: A Fearsome Warrior and a Young Gypsy Girl ... 166

Chapter 11: Shopping For a Girl, and a Troublesome
Young Slave 181

Chapter 12: Meeting God, and a Most Determined Pupil 203

Chapter 13: Paladins, Lady's Choice, and a Visit to
a Caravanserai 224

Chapter 14: The Western Chapterhouse and a
Troubled Novice 246

Chapter 15: A Tribesman's Daughter 268

Chapter 16: Assassins, Prophecy, and an Elf Princess
in Danger 298

Chapter 17: Desperation, and a Dying Elf 341

Chapter 18: Hakeem's Lady and Her Reluctant Ally 355

Chapter 19: The Wedding of Kassandra 368

Chapter 20: Flight, and Anything You Can Do an Elf Can Do Better! 378

Chapter 21: Peasants, a Great Lady, a Pig, and Fighting a Post... 389

Chapter 22: Gypsies, and a Desperate Battle 398

Chapter 23: A Gypsy Family, an Angry Princess, and the Shocking Truth 408

Chapter 24: An Impossible Dream, and a Gypsy Wedding ... 425

Chapter 25: The Hunt for Elana, the Bādiyah, and Wādī Karsh.. 433

Chapter 26: A Memorable Entrance 453

Chapter 27: The New Warlord 463

Chapter 28: An Elf in a Hurry... 473

Chapter 29: Seléne, her Torturer, and a Dying King 489

Chapter 30: An Unexpected Return, Apologies, and Monsters... 518

Chapter 31: A Catastrophe only a Woman Could Understand.. 530

Chapter 32: Hakeem, Other Mad Scientists, and the Holy Mother 540

Chapter 33: Jacinta's Clever Parents 549

Book 2 of The Paladin Chronicles.................................**574**

The Defence of Troia..574

**Excerpt: Book 2 The Paladin Chronicles.
The Defence of Troia** **576**

Chapter 1: A Desperate Race, a City in Peril, the Elf Queen ...576

Author's Notes

Spelling I have tried to use Greek and Aramaic names into the phonetic equivalent in our ("Roman") alphabet (transliteration rather than translation into the English equivalent. Hence we have "Aléxandros" ("our defender"), "Philippos" ("lover of horses"), and "Troia.". I also use Australian English and Australian spellings.

Gypsies For 'poetic' reasons I have used this incorrect term for the Romani. It has some derogatory connotations in certain parts of our world. I most certainly mean no offence by using it.

About the Author

Neil Port lives with his wife in Port Stephens, Australia. He has three grown children and four grandchildren. He has retired from medical practice to write. The Elvish Prophecy is the first of seven books in The Paladin Chronicles series.

2020 Revision After eight years, and finishing the last book in the Paladin Chronicles Series, I returned, not to re-write book 1 but make some simple changes to improve it's readability.

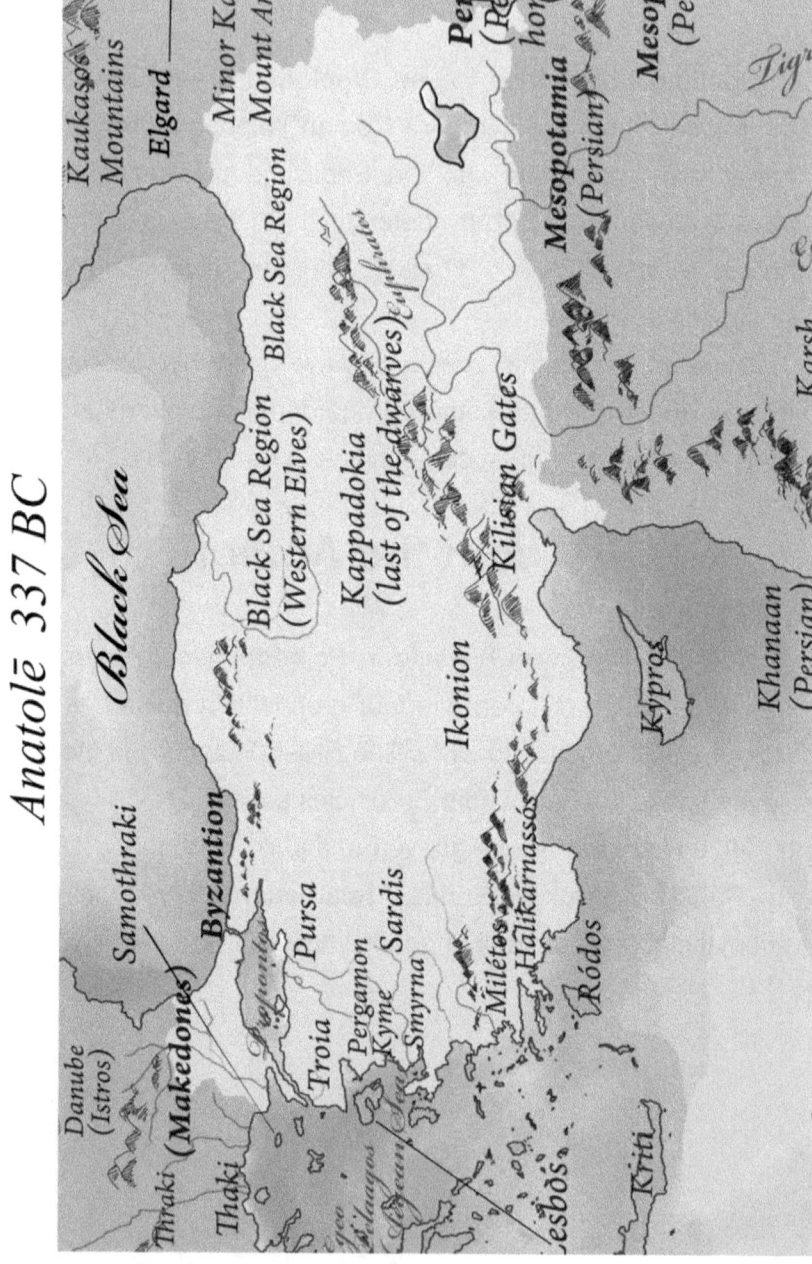

Anatolē 337 BC

Black Sea

Danube (Istros)
Thraki (Makedones)
Samothraki
Byzantion
Troia
Pursa
Pergamon
Kyme
Sardis
Smyrna
Milétos
Halikarnassos
Ikonion
Ródos
Lesbós
Kríti
Kypros
Khamaan (Persian)
Black Sea Region (Western Elves)
Black Sea Region
Kappadokia (last of the dwarves)
Kilikian Gates
Euphrates
Kaukasos Mountains
Elgard
Minor Kau
Mount Ara
Pers
Mesopotamia (Persian)
Karsh
Tigri
Meso (Pers

Chapter 1: Hakeem of the Shantawi

Samit burned with rage when he heard the distant trumpet call and saw Hakeem's small force crest the faraway hill. It was as if molten lead flowed throughout his body, never in his 60 years had the veteran commander felt such fury!

Victory was already theirs. The Troians were beginning to fall back in disarray. Hakeem was ordered to skirmish and harass from a distance, not join the main fight.

The young pup!

He had been seen as the most promising of all their legendary Shantawi mercenaries. Samit had given him a full command of 120 of the desert horsemen, despite his young age.

Now good Shantawi men would die so that Hakeem could make a gesture, so that he could join in routing the enemy. The penalty for him would be swift, but it would bring shame on Samit and those under his command.

Samit paused on a small hillock, his eyes sweeping the battleground. Below him was a chaos of men fighting and dying. The Troians had made a surprise attack on the northern defences and broke through to march on Pergamon, the great Aiol fortress-city.

Samit's forces had joined the Aiol King Helios in a desperate dash to stop them here, in this valley. Defeat had seemed inevitable for their smaller Aiol force, but then the Troians attempted to advance with much less cavalry than expected and the Aiols managed to attack their flanks.

The Troians had taken heavy losses and were now attempting the most difficult of all tasks, an orderly withdrawal in the middle of a battle. The Aiol forces had been pressing them back for more than a turn of the glass. The small size of the enemy cavalry was incomprehensible, but it seemed that at last the crafty Troians were caught.

The Aiols were pressing their advantage and Samit's main command had joined them in harrying the Troian vanguard.

Samit glanced back at Hakeem's men and felt a surge of blessed relief. Hakeem's small command hadn't turned to join the battle. His trust in the young tribesman had not been misplaced.

But what were they doing? They were rapidly skirting the main fighting, staying parallel to a distant ridge. Samit smiled in pride as he watched them gallop. Few could ride like the Shantawi! But what could be the cause of their urgent ride?

They seemed to be headed straight for the Aiol royal party on a hillock, well back from the main battle.

A sudden horror gripped Samit as a thought came to him. He glanced at the ridge that ran the length of the battlefield. Could that ridge conceal an enemy detachment, planning to attack the King and flank the main force? Was the Troian retreat a clever trap?

He cursed, where were the missing Troian horse?

It was then he heard something carry across the wind that made his blood freeze, the Berserker chant! It was the most sacred of all the Shantawi battle hymns. It had not been heard in over a hundred years.

Hakeem and his men called on their God. They didn't offer their lives to this coming battle, they believed them lost. They pledged their very souls that they would give glory to their God.

They pledged to fight to the death, but they asked God to give them inhuman strength and, in their rage, no thought for their safety. The Shantawi Berserker Chant was a final prayer by the Shantawi warriors as certain death approached.

It meant only one thing.

"Hold this flank!" he yelled to the surprised General, Evagoras.

Spinning round, he screamed in his own tongue. "To me! To me!" as his trumpeters took up the call.

Treachery! Evagoras thought, but knew it was impossible. Honour was very literally a religion amongst these tribesmen.

In the confusion, the flank began to fall apart but Samit didn't care. If he was wrong, he was a dead man.

He spurred his horse, not waiting for his men, who were raggedly disengaging and galloping like the wind to catch their leader. Careless of his horse, at full gallop over the uneven ground, he was only halfway to the distant Aiol royal standard when the enemy boiled over the ridge like ants from a nest that had been kicked. He was too late.

Evagoras had fallen for a clever trap. His main army had been drawn further and further away, leaving the royal party isolated at the rear. The enemy cavalry would take the Aiol King and would fall on the Aiol army from behind. A fresh cavalry outflanking a battle-weary centre who'd just lost their king.

Few would survive this day.

The King led a score of heavily armoured Lancers in his guard. Formidable in combat, their heavy armour made flight impossible. The rest of the King's personal guard was composed of eighty Latin mercenaries, all heavy infantry. They quickly formed a square around the King and his mounted escort. Their large rectangular shields formed a solid wall, but they were handicapped against cavalry by their short swords. Each carried two heavy *pila* (javelins) on the underside of their shields, but the tight formation protecting the King, and the speed of the cavalry, prevented them from using them.

Samit watched as the infantry met a cavalry charge of superior numbers as best they could. Just as the enemy threatened to overwhelm the royal party, Hakeem's charge hit the enemy van and, incredibly, it swept it away.

* * *

In the short pause afforded them, Hakeem nudged his horse up to the King and his loud voice rang out. "Great King of Aiolía, it is thus that we of the Shantawi come to fulfil our oath to you!

"If we fail, we will gladly die at your feet. But should that prove to be our fate, we will build such a burial mound from the bodies of your enemies, that you need never feel shame amongst the greatest of your ancestors, or the mightiest Warrior Kings of old."

With these grim words the small knot of remaining defenders cheered and bashed sword against shield. They were eager for the fight.

The young King Helios nodded gravely, and then gave a great shout.

"It is here, that we will stand!" He grabbed his standard himself and thrust it into the soil with a great blow.

Hakeem ordered his men to form up on either side of the infantry and they turned to face the second wave of Troians that were galloping towards them.

The Latins held the centre and the Shantawi in the wings were ready to encircle the Troians as their enemies attacked.

What a cavalry they were! They were heavily outnumbered and yet the Troians had no chance against them.

* * *

As he rode, Samit laughed. His heart was bursting with pride and joy. This was the essence of the Shantawi warrior. If any survived, what songs would be sung? If they died, who could not wish for such an ending as they would make?

Behind him the desert mercenaries sang their own battle songs as they rode. Horns sounded as they thundered on. In the front was the growing clamour of fighting.

A desperate plan had come to him, but it would require the King and Hakeem to hold out longer than anyone had any right to ask of them.

* * *

Just then, Hakeem saw a frightening sight that foreshadowed the end. The Troian advance guard were swift and lightly armoured like Hakeem's men, but they seemed to be falling back.

Behind them, he could see a large company of lancers gathering for a charge. The Troians had three or more of these companies and they formed a formidable force. Heavily armoured, they carried long heavy wooden lances tipped with iron. Their shields were broad and half the height of a man. Their helmets had feathery plumes that bobbed as they arranged themselves in formation.

Their horses were heavy and strong. They lacked the speed and stamina of the desert-bred horses, but they could ram their enemies with brute strength. Their saddles had a wooden brace, like a chair, at the back of the rider, to steady their rider from the impact of his lance and their horses were also armoured with leather. A powerful slash could get through, but it would take a direct hit with an arrow or a solid thrusting stab to cause sure damage.

The lancers would charge in formation, as a unit, where each man supported the man on either side of him. From the front, in formation and crouched behind their heavy shields, they were almost invulnerable.

The desert fighters were the finest mounted skirmishers in the known world. They would gallop up to their enemies and shoot their wickedly accurate and powerful recurved horse-bows and then ride away before they could be engaged in a stand-up fight. Guiding their small wiry horses with their knees, they could fire at full gallop and even fire backwards when galloping away. Any unprotected infantry that came against them in the open would be rapidly diminished without much loss to the horsemen.

They did not fight in tight formation, instead relying on speed, agility and individual prowess. If they could employ their greater speed and agility, they could likely defeat a heavy cavalry unit, but it would take time. It would be a deadly cat and mouse game, and against so many they would need a great deal of room.

They were were not going to get it. They had to defend the King.

The heavy lancers would be front on, in proper formation, and with time to build up the speed of their charge. If Hakeem's men got in their way, they would simply roll over them.

Samit's force was swelling in numbers, but he was separated from Hakeem by the Troians. Whatever Hakeem did, he would have to do it without help.

There was only one chance for Hakeem's small force, but it would require a great deal of luck. If Hakeem's men could break up the lancer's formation somehow, they could attack from the vulnerable sides or perhaps get close enough to render their lances useless, but this required the lancers being diverted from their charge at the Aiol King.

If he could hit them hard from the sides early in their charge, they might be induced to pause and try to mop up Hakeem's men first.

He only had a short space to try this. Once they got too close to the King, the Shantawi would need to face them; the Latin infantry could not be expected to meet a charge of heavy lancers unaided.

So to do this, Hakeem would have to ride well out to meet them. At the very best, it would be at great cost. Only a madman would try this knowing he had such a short distance, was hindered by the need to defend the King, and he and his men were outnumbered two to one.

Madman or desperate, he would take as many of the Troians with him them as possible, before he and his men were cut down. It was better than waiting.

Hakeem nudged his horse close to the King and nodded to the disaster they faced. Conversationally, as if remarking on the weather, he said "I'm intending to ride down and meet them. It will likely not go well for us."

Then Helios, the young King of the Aiol, nodded solemnly. "And so the time for all of us now comes." He reached forward and clasped the large mercenary's hand. King to mercenary, they farewelled like equals, like brothers.

Leaving his wounded and sixteen mounted bowmen with the King, Hakeem took less than 80 men down to meet the charge of twice that number.

* * *

Samit pulled his horse to a sudden halt. He would not try to reach Hakeem and the King. Such an attempt would only lead to defeat. He glanced back. The main battle seemed to be turning against them, so he'd get no help from their army.

He needed to do something fast with the small force at his disposal.

If Samit could avoid a direct engagement, there may be a chance. He hoped the Troians would remain focused on Hakeem and the King. It meant, in a way, using them as bait. If things went wrong, which was likely, Samit would not live to face the aftermath. To leave the King at peril would be seen as cowardice. The tribesmen's reputation for honour would be gone forever.

Samit used the same concealing ridge to gather his force just across from and behind where the enemy were pouring out. On his order, over 600 arrows struck the enemy's unprotected rear.

Chaos broke out.

Some Troians galloped forward, whether to commence the charge or escape this new threat was unclear. A few galloped back towards Samit's men but when they realised they were doing it alone, they tried to turn back. Many milled around, unsure of what to do.

Whoever was left in charge on the enemy side seemed to continue to try to get his men to form up for a charge at the King, but they were being decimated from a vulnerable rear, making it impossible to organise.

At the same time, Hakeem's small force used their bows to harry from the front. The Troians seemed frozen in horror and indecision, and then it was too late for them.

Samit's forces sent wave after wave of arrows into the enemy. Dead and dying men and horses obstructed the Troians from going forward and the crush of men coming behind prevented them from retreating. The walls of the gully prevented them from escaping to the side.

Samit began to work back along the ridge to mercilessly rain death down on the trapped Troian reinforcements. Troian wounded and their deserters fleeing from the battle claimed that daimôns had joined the Aiol side in attacking them.

The King led his knights against the few lancers who managed to come forward as a unit, taking them from the side.

It was just then that Hakeem heard a gurgling scream. It was his dearest friend, the elf-scout Elwan, struggling in vain to keep mounted with a great lance embedded in his chest.

Anguish and rage hit Hakeem like the exploding of a volcano. To this day, Hakeem can't recall what happened next.

He came back to himself, hearing the King's voice, as if from a distance, "Hakeem! Steady man! It's over."

He found himself on foot with blood, not his own, splashed all over his clothes and body. His friends were giving him a very wide space, as he looked wildly around. His sword was ruined. He cautiously looked around for a replacement.

As Hakeem tried to clear his confusion and chase down a horse, a message from Samit requested the King to join him to lead the attack. A victory owed to the desert tribesmen would be resented. It had to be an Aiol victory.

The King led the tribesmen into the exposed flank of the enemy. "Aiolía! ... Aiolía!" they chanted as they rode. The Troians broke. Not a careful retreat, but a rout.

Soldiers who turn their back and flee throw down their heavy shield and tall spear so they can run faster. They become an easy target, especially for horsemen. The main Troian force was decimated that day. A great legend of the Aiol King and his mercenaries was formed, and grew in the telling.

* * *

Hakeem never found out what really happened before he came to his senses. He heard exaggerated tales by awestruck Aiol soldiers of his fighting with superhuman strength. His own men refused to correct these. In fact, one gave an oath that the whole force withdrew and simply let Hakeem fight the Troians alone.

If he seemed frustrated by their teasing, they would pull away in mock alarm saying, "Careful, don't make him angry!" Sometimes he would seem to catch them whispering to one another 'Berserker' just loud enough to be sure he could hear.

Other men would have felt exalted by the hero worship growing around him. Hakeem didn't like it. That he seemed embarrassed earned him greater respect, but it encouraged the teasing.

He understood the need of his men to take pleasure in victory, and enjoyed their good mood. He knew it was good natured, and often could not resist smiling or playing along, but underneath it all he felt sad and lonely without his friend. That he was seen as a hero was just another barrier between him and the rest of the men.

Samit and King Helios began befriending him and the friendship of the older men helped.

Chapter 2: Mules, a Runaway, and Pergamon

Hakeem had been orphaned soon after birth. Having no close relative, he was raised by others of the Shantawi *Badawiyyūn* (Bedouins) before being accepted at age five into the abbey in the desert city of Karsh. Only the Grand Abbot knew why he accepted a boy at such an unusually young age. Hakeem never betrayed that trust.

Hakeem could recall little of his life before the abbey and never asked about it. The only family he ever had was his teachers and mentors, yet about all other things he was endlessly curious. The next youngest child at the abbey was twice his age, but Hakeem showed great promise and by seven he could join the classes designed for the older boys.

The monks at the Abbey were followers of the mystic religion called Shayvism. It taught love of others and a cycle of reincarnation to reach enlightenment.

Karma (fate), for the Shayvists, was not a reward or punishment for good or bad deeds done in a previous life, it was 'chosen' by lessons one needed to learn. The poor and humble were not seen as inferior in their spiritual journey compared to the rich and powerful.

Mediation and extensive training in the martial arts was used by the Shayvist monks to discipline their minds and bodies. Hakeem excelled at almost everything he was taught, which included armed and unarmed combat, military tactics and horsemanship, but his greatest love was the religious texts. His only desire was to become a religious monk and study the mysteries of their sect.

He didn't feel part of the group of older boys and was too much in advance of those his own age. So he was always solitary, quiet, serious and hardworking, but shy and naïve.

None could doubt that he had a good heart. If an animal or a boy needed help, he always seemed to be at hand. He was always polite to his superiors and a good-natured teacher of the younger boys. He was the favourite of the monks and the younger novices alike.

On the day of his coming of age (18), Hakeem made an appointment with the Grand Abbot to formally ask to become a monk. The memory of that meeting is forever burnt into Hakeem's mind.

He gave a respectful bow and looked at the kindly old man, *Gavri'el* (Gabriel). Gavri'el was the closest thing to a parent he had ever had.

"Father Gavri'el, today is my coming of age."

"So soon? Truly?" Gavri'el looked unsettled. "I was meaning to talk to you before this, but the time has slipped away."

"Father, as I am now of age, I wish to apply to be a monk."

Gavri'el smiled at him with gentle fondness. "You will have to forgive an old man, Hakeem. I really meant to talk to you before this."

It felt as if a large rock of ice had settled into Hakeem's chest, his breath caught in his throat. Hakeem had never even a moment of doubt, why the need for a talk?

"Talk about what, master?" He managed, his mouth was dry, his heart pumping. "All I have ever wanted is to be a monk and remain here like you and all the others."

The abbot shifted awkwardly in his seat. "It was what I had meant to talk to you about. It is not your path.

"You will join the company of Shantawi mercenaries led by Samit in Aiolía. There are some monks leaving for there in ten days, I want you to travel with them. You are to train as a paladin."

Hakeem never considered he would be refused. It was all he ever wanted. He had thought he was their best student. He had always worked so hard. How had this happened? It was if his world had dropped out from under him.

He knew little about the paladins. There had only been four in all the history of Shayvism and that was so long ago now. He did know that to be a paladin was to become a warrior, not a monk. Monks can defend themselves and assist with local security but the 'life path' of a warrior was very different.

The spiritual dangers of being a soldier or mercenary are many and obvious.

While the Shayvists officially teach that all life paths are equal, most have greatest respect for scholars, and most think that becoming a monk is the highest calling of all.

They seemed to accept monks so easily. Why not him?

He burned with shame. The abbot was recreating an archaic tradition, just for him. It was offered out of pity, for a fault he could not see.

With tears falling down his cheeks and sobs wracking his body, he begged, "Please. Please... this is my home .... to be a monk ... it's all I've ever wanted "

The Grand Abbot waited patiently, until his tears ceased. It took a long time no matter how he struggled to control them.

"We are proud of you, but it is not your path."

"But what am I to do?" Hakeem asked in despair.

"Go to Aeolia. Have faith. Come to me tomorrow and we will talk on this."

There was no use arguing. Hakeem gathered himself to bow respectfully. "Thank you father, I will go now and meditate on why I am not to become a monk."

The abbot opened his mouth to say something more, but Hakeem was already walking away. Wise old men, they say, can see the blindness of the young, but old and powerful men can sometimes forget what it is like to be young. The abbot was so sure that he was right that it caused his wisdom to fail. He had put off what would be an awkward and difficult discussion with his favourite novice. He was not given another chance.

Hakeem left, feeling wretched.

He gathered his few possessions and the little money he had and left within the hour. The only weapons he took were a belt knife and one of the heavy wooden staves the monks used when walking.

He did not take provisions, not wanting to feel he owed the monastery anything. He didn't know what else to do, so he would go to Aeolia and become a mercenary, but they couldn't expect him to face his shame by staying in the monastery till then!

He said goodbye to no one. He was challenged by the old monk guarding the gate. When he said he was leaving the elderly monk hesitated, "but that's impossible," before allowing Hakeem to pass, as was his right.

Hakeem closed his mind to avoid dwelling on the pain. He slipped through the dark back streets of the city and searched out the cheap boarding houses and taverns for a caravan owner headed for Anatolē. It was not too late and in the third tavern he visited, he had a stroke of luck. The man serving was blind in one eye and limped badly.

Hakeem approached him diffidently. "Sir, I take you for a veteran."

The old man smiled at him, seeming amused. "Well you would be right, lad, and I take you as a young lad looking for a favour."

Hakeem laughed and nodded. "I wish to make for Aeolia, on the West coast of Anatolē and wish to work my passage."

"I know where Aeolia is, you young pup!" scolded the old man, but he smiled in a friendly enough way. "You choose a long journey for yourself, so I wish you luck. That man against the wall over there, his name is Gennadios. The other man he is sitting with is his brother, Agapetos. They are going to Ikónion. Gennadios wouldn't pay you much but he just lost a man to the grippe, so it won't hurt to ask."

Several lamps caste their dim light through the room and shadows moved as people opened and closed the door. Hakeem thanked the old man and moved past several tables of men drinking to reach the rough-cut table where the two big teamsters sat half in gloom, drinking from double-handled mugs and quietly talking.

Hakeem gave a short bow, palms held together in front, as was his habit. "Gennadios, sir, my name is Hakeem. I wish to work my passage to Ikónion."

Gennadios's brother grunted. "You're too young. Go away, boy."

Hakeem didn't move. "I am strong, I am good with animals and I can fight."

Agapetos snorted and looked him up and down. "Perhaps you would like to prove that against me."

Hakeem shrugged, willing enough. "If you will give me the job and promise no grudge if I beat you."

"Leave him alone, Agapetos." Gennadios interrupted. "You don't know who you are offering to fight, boy. I'll pay you one silver *obolos* (a sixth of a drachma) per day and all you can eat, be at the stables near the south gate in the morning."

Hakeem smiled gratefully. "If you have no objection, sir, I will sleep with your animals."

At the stables he got a friendlier reception. Their teamster, Origenes was Greek but fluent in Aramaic, Hakeem's native tongue.

"An obolos for a boy!" he said, clearly impressed. "He must have liked you, I only get two. He will expect you to work for that though. You look a strong lad, I hope you are."

The two of them had one end of the large stables to themselves. They were lying on straw and blankets. Origenes positioned them in the middle so they could get a view of the stalls on either side. Gennadios had eighteen mules in three teams. They were medium size, less than fourteen hands high. which Hakeem later found out was the best size for team mules.

The mules were tied by a long lead so their rumps faced outwards. Mules need less sleep than men, so most were still awake and standing, one turned its head to study Hakeem curiously. Its eyes glinted faintly in the shadowy light of the small lamp. It looked intelligent with its long ears standing up alertly.

Origenes started giving Hakeem an education about mules. Hakeem found he enjoyed the old man's company and Origenes found him an attentive listener.

"Give me a mule any day, Hakeem," Origenes was saying with great relish, gesturing at the animals half-seen in the light. "They are even-tempered, smart and will outlast any horse."

"I hear they kick," Hakeem said, a bit doubtful. He had no experience with mules.

"Ungelded males can be troublesome, but horses are worse! Mules are only trouble when they need to be, " Origenes claimed. "Shows how intelligent they are. Did you know a good mule is worth seven times the cost of a donkey or three times the cost of a horse? They can travel twice the distance of oxen at twice the speed."

Hakeem looked at the shadowy figures with a new respect.

"Believe me, boy," Origenes finished as they were bedding down to sleep, "if you want to be happy in your life, all you have to do is choose your mules with more care than you'd choose a wife." Hakeem nodded, his young face serious.

He'd try to remember that.

* * *

They were up at first light. Once Hakeem understood what was needed, the work of harnessing the three teams went quickly enough. He still needed Origenes to tell him which mules were paired with which and in what position.

Each mule had its own individual harness adjusted for its size and a heavy collar individually fitted by moulding when wet and then trimming and stitching, so it didn't rub. Origenes was very fussy with his mules.

"You work well, boy!" said Origenes as Hakeem lifted and carefully positioned the heavy harness. Hakeem grinned at the compliment as they finished with last-minute adjustments and walked the pair to their position on the shaft. He was used to harnessing horses to wagons, it wasn't a lot different. He and Origenes worked well together.

With the morning sun shining in their eyes, they finished tying the coverings over the wagons. They were made from hemp-cloth waterproofed by linseed oil. Origenes said to leave them loose on one side so Gennadios could check the load. Agapetos and Gennadios had been drinking late and there wasn't much more to do till they arrived. Origenes tossed a *chalkos* (copper) to a young boy to fetch them.

It was then that they had a problem. Their three wagons were blocking the exit from the marshalling yard. It hadn't mattered at first, as Hakeem and Origenes were first up and made good time, but the other teams had more men helping and now were ready. They immediately became impatient.

"Move your loads!" said a burly teamster, he walked right up to Hakeem and stood close to intimidate him. It was not pleasant, the man had sour breath and hadn't bathed recently. Other teamsters had gathered behind and were starting to complain loudly.

Hakeem very felt nervous, these men weren't known for their patience.

Origenes called down from his seat on the wagon, "I'm really sorry *Binyamin* (Benjamin). Gennadios has let us down."

"I'm sorry, sir," Hakeem added. "We have sent for him and his brother. They will be here any moment."

The man gave Hakeem a push designed to unbalance him. "Move your teams, now *boy!*" He said with emphasis, "or we will move them for you."

Hakeem rolled with the push and moved gracefully to the side as he did so. "There are only two of us and there are three teams, we will move as soon as our owner or his brother arrives." Checking the load could be done later!

The man wouldn't wait. "I'll show you." he grunted and swung hard at Hakeem. He was shorter than Hakeem but a powerfully built teamster. His swing was easily strong enough to knock Hakeem down.

Without thought, Hakeem ducked under the punch, and rapidly responded. He hit Binyamin hard in the stomach with his right fist. As the man's swing missed, he trapped the man's arm against his body pushing with his left hand and moved forward to block a kick with his knee. His right fist pumped back and then forward to hit the man in the mouth.

As the man grunted and bent over, Hakeem grabbed the back of his head and kneed him hard into the nose as he came down. Binyamin dropped at Hakeem's feet as if he had been hit by an axe. Hakeem danced smoothly back to keep his distance and waited, ready for any more.

It had taken seconds.

Binyamin's men and the others were shocked by the abrupt violence, and the ease with which a mere lad had disabled such a strong man, but they wouldn't hesitate for long. Hakeem, satisfied that Binyamin was staying still, ran back to the wagon and slid out his quarter staff.

He moved to face the crowd in a slight crouch, his staff held pointing forward like a spear held underarm. Origenes was shouting something or other. Hakeem yelled loudly over his shoulder. "Stay back, Origenes. I'll handle this!"

He was astounded to see Binyamin getting to his feet, admittedly unsteadily. Blood was flowing freely from the man's nose and mouth. He wasn't up to saying anything but he drew a Xiphos, the sharp pointed Greek short-sword for stabbing and slashing.

The other three from his team had moved in front of their leader and had their Xiphoi at the ready.

"Can we stop this fight?" Hakeem pleaded. "I don't want to hurt any of you."

"Too late for that, boy!" one of the men snarled, starting to circle around. "You tricked our boss somehow, but you dream if you think you can hurt us. We will make that stick of yours into firewood and then we will cut you up real bad like."

Hakeem could hear Agapetos and Gennadios shouting from far behind him but he couldn't spare them any attention. He brought his stave up and ran the short distance between himself and the men. He simply punched the end of his staff at the man on his right.

He was utterly astonished to find the man wasn't expecting it. All he did was to try a flimsy block and arch backwards, trying to get out of the way without even moving his feet.

He couldn't really be expecting Hakeem to wait for them to come to him, could he? That was preposterous!

The staff made a crunching "whack" as he hit him in the chest. The man bent over, unable to breathe, clutching his chest with pain. Hakeem hoped it wasn't hard enough to kill him.

He mentally shrugged, he doubted it.

Now to concentrate on the other two.

He pulled his staff back and made a quick feint for the face of the next man. The man looked frightened and raised his sword in an equally ineffectual parry. Hakeem spun the staff around and brought the other end whistling around to crack him really hard across the shins. The man collapsed, screaming. These men knew nothing about fighting against a man with a quarter staff.

"Enough!" Hakeem demanded of the last man who was still uninjured. Just then Agapetos, Gennadios and Origenes joined Hakeem, with their own Xiphoi at the ready. The man nodded and lowered his sword and stepped back, looking a bit pale. The fight had lasted less than a minute.

"My Lord," Hakeem said urgently. "We need to move our wagons before the town guards are called or there is more trouble. There are some in this city I do not wish to meet."

"Well, I can imagine that, Hakeem, now I have seen you fight," said Gennadios, stunned by the lad's ability. "Have you killed a man?"

"No sir, and there is no accusation against me." Hakeem drew himself up with dignity.

"We'd better go then. You really can fight," Gennadios said, shaking his head in amazement.

"Those men had no idea what they were doing," Hakeem said simply.

"Tell that to all those men Binyamin and his boys have bloodied over the years," said Agapetos, feelingly.

* * *

Origenes and Hakeem were sharing a wagon. Origenes loved to talk, which was not a problem because Hakeem liked to listen. The Greek was telling him about *Anatolē* (Turkey) and was incredulous at how little Hakeem knew.

"Don't you know anything, Boy?"

Hakeem shrugged, "It didn't seem important."

He had never intended to leave the monastery, he thought, glumly.

Anatolē 337 BC

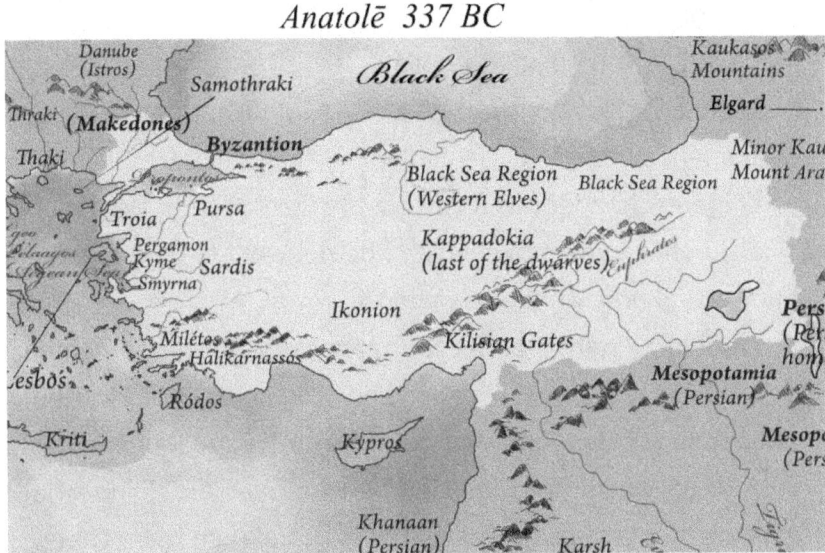

They were leaving Karsh, Anatolē lay to the north and west of where they were.

The name comes from Greek 'the rising of the sun', referring to its easterly position from Greece. According to Origenes, it is a large box-shaped bridge, connecting the West and the East with land traffic funnelled across the narrow straits that form the entrance to the Black Sea.

Hakeem was headed for Pergamon on the West coast. It would be a long journey.

The three mule teams were making their way through the wādī (valley) where Hakeem's home city lay and had joined the road that zigzagged out of the valley to head north.

Hakeem and Origenes were in the third wagon in line and while Origenes tried to hang back, they travelled in a dense cloud of dust. Origenes wore a faded *pilos* (Greek felt cap) and a cloth tied over his nose and mouth and Hakeem wore an old *keffiyeh* (headscarf) with a faded white and *woad* (blue) pattern, tied so only his eyes were showing.

"Why are you going to Aeolia?"

Hakeem had no real answer. "Some of my people are mercenaries there."

Origenes nodded, "Did you always want to be a mercenary?"

Hakeem's eyes grew bleak. "I do not want to be a mercenary. I just don't know what else to do."

He told Origenes about the monastery. Origenes confessed he had trained to be a priest and worked in a library, but he refused to tell Hakeem which God he had served, or why he had left. All he would say was that he was happiest doing what he was doing. Maybe that was comforting. Hakeem wasn't sure.

Origenes regarded the young man warily. He had seemed such a nice young man, respectful, keen to please and eager to learn, but under that surface lay something very dark. When it was triggered as it had been, it was terrifying. He was terrifying.

He was sure something had happened causing him to have to leave, something the young man wasn't saying. Anyone could see why a group of monks wouldn't want someone like Hakeem in their monastery.

The army was a good idea, the young man needed to learn how to control his temper or he would murder someone one day.

"Can you tell me about Aeolia, Origenes?"

Origenes was jerked out of his reverie. "It's 'Aiolía' in the local dialect. It's on the western coast of Anatolē. I'll start at the beginning. You know about the elves and the Aryans don't you?"

"I have heard about them," Hakeem said gesturing vaguely.

Origenes sighed. "You're lucky it is a long trip, my young friend.

"I'll tell you what I know. I don't know everything. For that you'd have to ask an elf, though I doubt you'd get an answer."

The heavy wagon entered a level part half way up the road that climbed out of the Wadi Karsh. Origenes paused to allow Hakeem to look down on the oasis say goodbye to the only home he had ever known.

It was a truly beautiful sight, especially compared to the dreary land they were moving into. Hakeem was impressed by how strongly the mules pulled for their size. Origenes was right, mules were better.

"No human knows when the elves first came to Anatolē but it was many thousands of years ago. When humans first met them, they worshipped them. It was said that all of them had some form of magic back then, either big or small." He took a breath. "If so, the elves are not as they were, but you know what legends are like and elves won't talk about it.

"The Western Elves ruled the native humans of Anatolē. If you ever meet an elf now, you might wonder how a human could tolerate them for a week, let alone thousands of years but there is something about the elves that is hard to describe, and their humans were very loyal."

"Aren't the Eastern Elves the greater ones?"

"What? The Eastern Elves only ever had one city, and each of the cities of the Western Elves were greater than it, but let me come to that.

"The greatest and holiest city of the Western Elves was Troia (Troy). It was said to be a place of many wonders and the city of their great seafarers. The old races of *Hellás* (Greece) and the many islands, the ones that we call the 'Pelasgoí' were also great sailors and builders and were on good terms with the elves. I think it was the elves that taught them, but both were mostly peaceful."

Hakeem looked at Origenes in surprise, "Different Greeks?"

Origenes nodded. "There are still some Pelasgoí settlements left, mainly villages. They were darker than the later Greeks but now the races are mingling. We don't know much about how they were back then, it was a long time ago and soon you'll understand why we don't have much of the old records. The Pelasgoí weren't united into one kingdom of course. Their greatest cities were on *Kriti* (Crete) but they were all through the islands and mainland.

"Centuries before the time of the Aryans, a savage warlike race began to conquer the Pelasgoí. We call them the Mykēnai (Myceneans), after their greatest city."

"They sacked Elvish Troia." Even Hakeem knew that tale!

Origenes nodded and paused as the wagon reached a big dip. Origenes didn't need a whip, he didn't need to scream and curse. Hakeem didn't need to leap off and run to lead the mules from the front.

All Origenes did was "cluck" several times, make some "Yee-harr" noises and shake the reins lightly. The mules gingerly allowed the wagon to roll into the hollow and, with a jingling of the harnesses they deftly pulled at exactly the right instant and in the right way, allowing it to rock out. They *were* smart animals!

Origenes paused to think where he was up to.

"Compared to the elves and the Pelasgoí, the time of the Mykēnai seems short. It took them five hundred years before they conquered all the old Greeks. The Pelasgoí of Crete (the Minoans) and their allies had navies that proved too strong for them but then there was a terrible eruption on the island of *Thera* (Santorini). It shook the whole world and darkened the sky for a very long time.

"There were great waves moving over the ocean, destroying all in their path. Well, you can imagine the effect on a nearby maritime culture. It was a terrible disaster and it allowed the Mykēnai to conquer the last of the Pelasgoí."

"I heard there was a Greek story about something like that," Hakeem murmured.

"Atlantis?" Origenes snorted. "9,000 years ago, that could only be a story." He thought some more. "It was one of Plato's stories. If he had said 900 years before his time, that would have been right. Athēnai was a Mykēnai city then, but of course Plato makes the Athēnai the brave heroes of the tale, better for the Athenian theatre.

"Anyway, once the Mykēnai had defeated the last of the Pelasgoí they turned their attention to the elves. It took them two hundred years, and the Mykēnai were at the height of their power then. They say King Agamémnonas led a thousand ships to sack Elvish Troia. It is one of the reasons why many elves hate humans so much.

"Some Greeks will tell you differently, but the elves never stole anything. It was greed, pure and simple, and the need to conquer, that drove the Mykēnai. Even then they only defeated the elves through treachery, by offering peace and then betraying them."

Hakeem counted himself lucky to be travelling with such a great storyteller. He noticed Origenes had a faraway look in his eyes as he spoke of Elvish Troia.

Origenes was from the Greek city of Troia, built by the Athēnai more than five hundred years after the burning of the elf capital, but the Greek Troians always felt a very special connection with the elves of old.

"After they had finally conquered Kriti, Troia and the coast of Kanaan, Aígyptos was the last great maritime power that could oppose them. The Mykēnai had a fearsome reputation back then, the Aígyptoi called them and those allied with them the 'sea people'.

Your people called them *Plištim* (Philistines) but that was only a remnant of them. Within decades of the sacking of Troia, all their great cities were no more. Only a small fraction of them survived the destruction and the famine that followed."

"The Aryan Hordes," Hakeem said softly.

Origenes nodded. "They came in wave after wave in numbers too many to count, there seemed no end to them. They didn't just kill people and burn cities, they took everything. The countryside was stripped bare, and just when things had started to recover, there were more of them. After they had gone, many strong kingdoms, empires and cities – some that had stood for thousands of years, were simply no more.

"They say the Western elves and their allies fought bravely against them, but it finished them. Now only a few Western Elves remain in the woodlands just south of the Black Sea.

"The Eastern Elves fared better. Their mountainous kingdom and forests were better suited to their way of fighting and poorly suited to the Aryan chariots. They renamed their city Elgard to celebrate its survival.

"Two or three hundred years passed and a new people came to Hellás from the north, related to the Mykēnai but not them. They built on the remnants of the Mykēnai and Pelasgoí. They are the greatest and cleverest humans that have ever set foot upon the earth."

He winked at Hakeem. "My Greeks!"

Hakeem couldn't help but laugh. He grabbed a goatskin of water from an overhead hook and passed it to Origenes. Origenes smiled and spat and then took a swig and rinsed his mouth before swallowing and passed it back.

Origenes was right yet again, Hakeem decided. His ignorance of anything outside of Karsh was almost complete. He was going to try to enlist as a mercenary, but he didn't even know if there was a war on. He didn't think there was.

"You frightened me back there." Origenes said softly.

"I'm sorry, Origenes, I didn't want to fight."

"What about that temper of yours?"

"Origenes I wasn't angry." Hakeem looked at Origenes steadily. "I was trying not to hurt them. It was such a silly reason to fight."

Origenes looked at his big companion in confusion. Then, as he thought back, he realised Hakeem *had* tried to avoid a fight. He shuddered slightly ... that was what this boy could do when he *wasn't* angry!

"Who taught you?"

"The monks."

"Would you know how to use this, then?" Origenes pulled a battered gorytos from behind him in the wagon. "It was owned by Philandros, who died of colic. I was his friend so it's mine to give. You can have it if you can use it. If you don't take it, Agapetos will, and he doesn't use a bow."

Hakeem looked at the old gorytos. *Gorytos* is the Greek name for the holster of the shorter (composite) bow that many call 'Scythian' bows. It has space for the quiver, a hood to keep the inside dry and slots for beeswax, oil if used, spare bow-strings and arrowheads. It was usually carried over the shoulder but can be attached to a saddle.

Hakeem slid out the bow and quiver and his expression of pure delight said it all to Origenes. He took one of the arrows out, checked its length, sighted along it, and then frowning in concentration very carefully rolled it along the wooden corner of the cart, his wide grin returning as he did so.

Then he took out one of the hemp bow strings and warming a dab of wax between his thumb and forefinger, carefully waxed it.

Placing the bow carefully on some cloth and rising to a half crouch, he attached one side of the bow string and levered his weight to finish stringing it. He grunted and coloured with the effort.

"It's easier to do that on the ground, but this really is a heavy bow!" he said with appreciation.

Hakeem fumbled around in the gorytos. "Is there a thumb ring or a glove?" he asked.

"I wondered what these were." Origenes passed two odd shaped rings across. They were like rings but with long flattened tails at an angle a bit like a helmet.

Hakeem laughed, "These aren't for decoration. These are made from polished cow's horn. You really need to make your own, I can show you how. I'm sorry I didn't meet Philandros.

"This is a nice bow but I really can't take it. It is too valuable. I'll show you how it is used. A heavy battle bow has to be drawn by a thumb with a thumb ring, or three-fingered grip with a leather guard or glove. Using the thumb grip is far easier and it gives you a cleaner release, so it is more accurate," he explained.

"You put the ring just over the joint of your right thumb, the flat tail of the ring protects the end pad of the thumb … see the nock on string, that's where the arrow fits." Hakeem continued.

"You take the string just below the nock with your thumb. You bend your thumb completely into an angle. There is a very shallow groove on the ring … there … that's where the string goes when you pull on it. Now you grip the nail of the thumb with your big finger, which helps the thumb. You use two fingers of the same hand to make sure the arrow stays securely in place."

He demonstrated with an arrow then put the arrow to one side. Then he pulled the bow a few times and then held it for a while at full draw. "It is a very heavy battle bow," he repeated, grinning with appreciation.

He passed it to Origenes and showed him how to wear the thumb ring and how to use it. Origenes grunted and tugged as hard as he could while Hakeem took the reins of the mules. Origenes swore profusely and went red in the face but couldn't get it even to half draw.

"It's not like a long bow. It's harder at half draw than at full draw," Hakeem said, encouraging him. Origenes took a deep breath and pulled harder and, lost control. The bow string hit his forearm hard with a loud "Whack!"

Origenes bent over in agony, he was monotonously swearing in Greek.

"Oh!" Hakeem said wincing sympathetically. "I should have warned you. Your left arm was all wrong. I didn't think you were going to release it."

Origenes gave him a look of disgust. "I didn't think I was going to release it either," he said through gritted teeth.

It is very bad to 'dry shoot' a Scythian bow (shoot it without an arrow) Hakeem decided not to mention this at this particular moment.

In fact he was quite alarmed at the vengeful look Origenes was directing at the expensive bow and hastily placed it well out of his reach.

"It's far too heavy for you. You should learn with a hunting bow first."

"I think you had better keep it," Origenes said nursing his arm, still red in the face.

Hakeem looked uncertain but his eyes were sparkling. Origenes didn't understand why he was so impressed with it, it looked rather plain. "It's a horse bow, isn't it?"

"I think this might have been made for infantry," Hakeem said slowly. "It would be too heavy for most, but I could use it on horseback." He smiled. "I'd need to practice with it, but it's as if it were made for me."

"It's yours," Origenes said through clenched teeth. He was gingerly fingering a welt on his forearm.

"Are you sure, Origenes? Do you have any idea how long it takes to make a bow like this and what it would cost? I can't ever pay you for it," Hakeem gestured helplessly.

Origenes nodded. "Just don't ask me to try it again," he said firmly. "Now let's try to work on your terrible Greek, so I don't have to think of my arm."

Origenes explained that there were wild mountainous regions to the north of the Hellás and that's where the influx of new Greeks came from, first the Mykēnai and then later his Greeks. It was this that allowed the Hellás (Greece) to be one of the first great regions to recover after the Aryan hordes.

Indeed for a time Hellás with its limited farmland had became crowded and the young Greeks needed to make their fortune far from home. It meant the new Greeks had built a mighty maritime civilisation that stretched over all of the north of the Mediterranean, the adjacent seas and lands.

They dominated much of *Anatolē* (Turkey), especially along the Aegean coast and the entrance to the Black sea. The Athēnai rebuilt Troia as a Greek city. With the prevailing trade winds favouring its sheltered harbour and its control over the entrance to the Black Sea, it became the greatest of all their colonies. Hakeem found out he was headed for the Greek (Aegean) coast of Anatolē, south of Troia.

The greatest rivals of the modern Greeks were another great seafaring race. Distant cousins of the Hakeem's Aramaeans, the Greeks called them *Phoiníkē* (Phoenicians). They came from the coastal region Hakeem called *Knaʿn* (Canaan) and also their ancient colony *Qarṭāj* (Carthage). They dominated the southern Mediterranean coast, while the Greeks dominated the northern coast. But the greatest enemy of the Greeks was really the Greeks themselves.

"If you have two Greeks from different parts of the Hellás in the one room, you immediately have an argument. Leave them for a turn of the glass and they'll be trying to kill each other."

It was an exaggeration, but while the Greeks of the Hellás endlessly fought amongst themselves and lost control of their maritime empires, a King called Philippos brought his barbarian kingdom of Makedonía from the point of collapse to conquer all of his neighbours.

The famous narrow pass of *Thermopylae* (it was called the "hot gateway" because of its springs) was still occupied by an Athenian garrison to prevent him reaching the central Hellás but Philippos held all of the land to the north.

When Hakeem had started his journey, Philippos was campaigning in Thraki (Thrace), and the Athenians and Troians were in the process of sending desperately needed help to Perinthos and Byzántion on the entrance to the Black Sea. They were the last cities on that side of the straights that were not under Makedóne control.

Hakeem didn't know it then, but Philippos was destined to be a name that he would know very well.

* * *

It was six moons later that Hakeem finally found himself, dusty and travel weary, walking through the gates of lower Pergamon. During his journey he had gained great knowledge of Anatolē and its history, and his Greek was greatly improved. He had as his most precious possessions, a somewhat battered gorytos, and a small hoard of coins.

The royal Aiol city is Kyme, but Hakeem had made for the mercenary barracks at Pergamon, Aiolía's great fortress-city in the north. Pergamon stood between Aiolía and the most dangerous of their neighbours, the Greek Troians. South of Aiol lies the Ionian league and east is the Lydian city (*Sardeis or* 'Sfard' in Lydian).

Since the loss of tribute from the wealthy coastal city of Smyrna, which switched to join the Ionian league fifty years earlier, and loss of land to the Troians, the royal Aiol dynasty was only holding on tenuously while surrounded by powerful neighbours. Always hanging over it was the threat of further war with the Troians.

King Helios was rebuilding the kingdom his father and his father's father had allowed to run down. Bandits, pirates and deserters had become very numerous and bold under the old kings. There were many roads and surrounding areas of the country that had become unsafe. A number of local warlords declared independence. Trade had dried up. The cities were impoverished and its army run down. It was why he had employed a mercenary force. It was expensive but as his kingdom started to recover, it was paying for itself.

Hakeem waited to wave to his latest travelling companions, who had stopped at the guard station in front of the gate. They had business in the lower part of the city.

With a lot of "mooing," shouting and swearing, the cracking of a whip and a great cloud of dust, the bullock drivers slowly got their team moving. As they inched off, Hakeem was absolutely sure, after a fortnight of travelling with them, that he definitely preferred horses or mules, almost anything other than cattle as a means of travel!

He started to trudge in another direction, along the road and over a stone bridge (across a small river) that lead to the lowermost gates and fortification of the akropolis (from *akron* 'summit' and *polis* 'city').

Pergamon means 'castle' in an ancient native tongue. It had started life as a fortified hilltop in the misty time before the arrival of the Greeks.

The base of the hill was surrounded by the junction of two tributaries that joined at Pergamon to form the river Kaïkos, so it was naturally fortified on all but the south side, which was also the only entrance.

The river Kaïkos had long silted up and Greek ships were larger now, so the river was no longer navigable to the sea. Even so, no one was likely to want to abandon a site this good.

As he came closer to the hill, far above he could see the palace complex, barracks, and storage areas surrounded by the upper defensive walls. He could also make out the roof and the upper parts of the columns that marked the temple to the Goddess Athēnā.

One of the guards at the gate directed him to the administrative barracks housed in the akropolis itself, so Hakeem, feeling nervous now that the end was in sight, continued to trudge up the curving path past the crowded *agora* (market), baths, gymnasia, and various minor temples before joining the foot traffic up the steep, broad steps which led to the great gates guarding the final entrance to the upper-most fortress.

A surprise awaited him at the top. He was ushered in to await an audience with the Shantawi commander, Samit, himself. Apparently he had received a letter from Father Gavri'el and the situation was such an unusual one that Samit wanted to question him personally.

Hakeem found himself seated in an empty room, anxiously waiting for no less than the most senior warrior of all the Shantawi.

He wondered what was in the letter, but the file leader who ushered him in would give him no clue.

When Samit had finished his morning's work, he hurried to question the young man. The letter made no sense at all. It was very complimentary and said the lad had applied to be a monk. If the abbot thought so well of Hakeem, why was he in Aiolía, instead of the monastery in Karsh? The monks never sent one of their own to join the mercenaries.

Did Hakeem have some fault? But a Grand Abbot of the Shayvists would *not* have neglected to mention such a thing. The correction of fault was a Shayvist article of faith. Samit, like most of the Shantawi, was brought up on Shayvist teachings.

To get him expelled from the order, it would have to be a serious matter and yet the the young man had *not* been expelled.

As he met with Hakeem and tried unsuccessfully to put him at his ease, Samit became more and more puzzled. Hakeem had wanted to become a monk since he was a child and he had been rejected. The large lad was polite and softly spoken, he seemed earnest. He had strong religious views and was distinctly naïve, exactly as one might expect.

He wasn't a bully. He said he liked training the younger novices. He was interested in caring for animals. He was self-effacing, but had a scholarly grasp of Shayvism. He was clearly intelligent.

He would make a perfect monk.

He looked like he could handle any violence that came his way, but that wasn't unusual in a Shayvist monk. Why send him to be a mercenary?

Hakeem had joined the Monastery at five as an orphan. It was a cruel thing to send this young man away; the monastery had been his whole life. It certainly wasn't going to be easy for him adjusting to a soldier's life in the barracks. He couldn't afford a horse, so he would be in the infantry and separated from the other Shantawi.

The young man was deeply wounded by his rejection, as one would expect. The reasons had never been explained to him. Samit hoped it didn't leave him bitter. He hoped it wouldn't cause the ruin of such a promising young man.

The only explanation that Samit could find was something to do with 'paladins', but they didn't have those anymore. The abbot had some plan involving re-creating the idea of religious knights and wished to use Hakeem in some way, but Hakeem had to be free to choose his own path.

It was one of the central tenets of their faith.

Samit felt a strong stir of anger. That old man was a complete fool, even if he was a Grand Abbot. There was no valid reason for refusing this young man's request to become a monk.

Well, the abbot was not so powerful, or so beyond reproach, as he might believe!

For the moment, there wasn't much else he could do. Samit welcomed Hakeem as kindly as he could and sent him to get kitted and settled into the infantry barracks. He made a mental note to keep a watch on the progress of this young man, after that, he put it from his mind. He had many other things to worry about. It was Hakeem's karma and he needed to face it.

* * *

The first weeks in Aiolía were the most miserable of Hakeem's life. He was shy, reserved, and religious. Many didn't know how to take him. Some thought he was aloof.

Others mistakenly saw him as a target for bullying. That was one impression they found was most definitely wrong. Responding to bullies was the one area where the young lad was not given to any great subtlety.

Hakeem didn't expect to fit in or be liked, and so he kept to himself. Most of all, he was lonely and ached for the only home he ever known. A few made an effort to befriend him and were pleasantly surprised. Hakeem didn't drink, gamble or go whoring, but he was slow to anger, he made a good friend and he was certainly a good man to have at your side in any trouble.

* * *

When Hakeem was called to see the *Lochagos* (infantry captain), not much more than one moon after his arrival, he assumed he was in serious trouble, but he didn't know why. The Captain was a God compared to a new recruit!

Pallas was busy when Hakeem's escort had him wait outside and went in to announce him. Hakeem was alarmed when Pallas dismissed his other visitor and asked that Hakeem be shown in immediately.

"Ah Hakeem!" Pallas said as Hakeem was ushered in. "At ease," he added, as Hakeem automatically dropped to his right knee, head bowed and right hand across his chest.

"Deimos speaks very well of you, but I suppose you know that."

"I'm certain I don't know that, sir," Hakeem replied stiffly, standing alert and ready.

"After three days, he had you training new recruits," Pallas said dryly.

"Is that unusual, sir? It's what I had been doing at the monastery for three years. What the recruits are learning is simple, sir." He paused. "He gives me extra attention, and learning and teaching is something I like, if I may say, sir. Dekadarchos (Sargent) Deimos never said whether he was pleased with me or not, sir."

"It's about the monastery I wanted to talk to you," Pallas said changing the topic. Hakeem felt a familiar icy lump inside.

"There is someone from the monastery that has come here, who wishes to see you," Pallas finished, watching Hakeem closely.

Hakeem felt a wave of shame and agony, but he simply stood and waited.

"Do you wish to see him?"

Hakeem was surprised to be asked. "Sir, I see no point. I asked to become a monk and I was not found suitable. I have no wish at all to look back on that time, or talk to anyone from that place. My wish is that I be left alone, they have made their decision and I have no place amongst them."

Hakeem was even further surprised when Pallas spoke kindly to him. He could have sworn his face showed no clue as to the pain this request caused him.

"Hakeem that is your right, try to not let this distract you. Those monks were a bunch of fools. I expect you to have an early promotion, so make sure you don't disappoint me!"

Hakeem straightened himself up and took a deep breath, but he couldn't prevent a smile. "Yes, sir! Thank you, sir!"

That was it, Hakeem was dismissed, and he heard no more for many days.

* * *

The monk, Brother Cephas, was one of the senior-most monks of the order, junior only to a full abbot. All he wanted was to talk to one of the junior recruits and no one would let him.

He had made the long journey from Karsh and was bearing a letter from the Grand Abbot himself! He was forced to become increasingly insistent, until finally he was brought to talk with Samit the Shantawi commander. As he was led to see the commander, he felt relieved. This 'misunderstanding' could now be corrected. An order from Hakeem's superior would immediately solve the problem.

"Brother Cephas, did you wish to see me?" Samit said pleasantly enough, as the elderly monk in his white robes was ushered in.

Cephas was a little taken aback. Samit was a grey haired man in his early sixties, but still fit looking. He was sitting in battle armour with his sword drawn and lying across his lap. He had a whole stichos of fifteen men, also in full armour, standing behind him, seemingly at the ready. Then Cephas laughed to himself at his own reaction. This couldn't be for *his* visit, now could it?

"Well, my Lord. It's a very simple matter. I wish to see one of your men, Hakeem, who has left our monastery to come here," he explained.

"And he doesn't want to see you," Samit finished for him.

He seemed to be familiar with the matter. Cephas smiled with relief, he knew Samit would understand.

Samit gave him a slow smile in return. It was hard to know how friendly it was.

Then Samit waited. The time started to stretch out, though Samit and his men showed no sign of discomfort or impatience.

Cephas eventually shook himself a little. "I wish to talk to him," he smiled as he explained.

None of the men responded, they simply waited. They could have been carved of stone. Cephas was becoming increasingly unsettled by their lack of reaction. Samit still sat impassively, waiting.

"He won't see me," Cephas mumbled uncertainly.

No one else in the room moved a muscle.

Samit waited a long time and then asked, "And was there anything else you wished to talk to me about?" with a distinctly wolfish smile at the monk.

"Well," Cephas was getting a distinct sense of unreality. "I came all the way from Karsh to speak to the lad, and he doesn't want to talk to me. I have spoken to those in charge but they won't give me permission. When I insist, they refer me to someone else, and now I have had to talk to you."

Samit looked surprised. "Hakeem, has he stolen something or committed some crime? It wasn't mentioned in the letter Father Gavri'el sent me." He held up a piece of parchment.

"Hakeem? No!" Cephas was utterly appalled.

"I understand he applied to be a monk, and he was refused. Is that true?" Samit eyes were flashing angrily, as he looked at the increasingly uncomfortable monk.

"Yes, but ..." Cephas started.

"Silence!" Samit shouted angrily. He leapt to his feet, striking the arm of his chair with a slap like thunder.

"You rejected that man, though I can find no fault in him. So he is *not* part of your order. He has a right not to want to talk to you, under the very laws of your own order! You will leave this camp!"

"You don't understand!" Cephas spluttered desperately. "There has been a misunderstanding."

Samit towered over the old monk, and held his sword forward, at the ready.

"I understand perfectly!" Samit shouted loudly, his face flushed and his breathing rapid. "An injustice has been done. That young man wanted to become a monk and he was refused." He pointed at Cephas with his naked sword, "not because he was unworthy, but because someone with power over him wanted him to become something else. And now, you refuse to leave him alone.

"Let your superiors know he is here under *my* protection, and I will *not* permit *anyone* else to come here to harass him."

As he finished, he nodded over his shoulder to the leader of his guard with a smile. "Sampson, could you ensure Brother Cephas finds his way out of the city? I forbid him from interfering with any of my troops. If he still finds this difficult to understand, you may arrest him and hold him until I have time to attend to the matter."

"My lord, you exceed your authority!" Cephas was more shocked than angry. "I am a special envoy of the Grand Abbot."

"So I exceed my authority, do I?" Samit paused, as if considering. "You seem to have forgotten who I am." He said this gently and smiled dangerously at the monk, glancing almost idly at his sword, held ready.

Cephas's head jerked up in recognition, his mouth hung open. The men in the room could almost see him thinking. Samit was the senior-most warrior of the Shantawi! If war threatened their homes, it was Samit who would lead them. He had a role and title, but by tradition it was *never* spoken of, and it had hardly ever been invoked in peacetime.

Yet it was his unquestioned *right* to invoke it at *any time* he perceived a threat, no matter how distant, to the war readiness of the Shantawi. The Abbot intruding on one of their mercenaries under Samit's command, in such a matter Samit's authority was absolute. He could go to any length necessary to enforce his decision and it would be accepted as a matter of course.

Would he invoke his authority now? Looking at Samit's face, the monk realised he would. That was exactly what he meant! For Cephas, it was as shocking and frightening as if he were running hard across an empty field and a precipice suddenly appeared in front of him.

If Cephas made any more fuss, Samit could take this as far as he wished. It would become public knowledge what the brotherhood had done. Cephas bowed and mumbled his apologies and, fled as quickly as he was able. His escort had to scramble to keep up with him.

Once he was out of earshot, Samit sat down, laughing. He had thoroughly enjoyed that.

He knew something almost unprecedented was going on. Why would the Grand Abbot dismiss Hakeem and yet send someone so senior all the way from Karsh to speak to a mere recruit?

Samit had already talked to Pallas, the captain in charge of Hakeem. The lad was as unhappy as Samit had expected him to be. He was also very talented, as expected, probably more so, but this didn't explain what was going on.

The Shayvist Grand Abbot had had some sort of plan for Hakeem, and it had fallen apart when Hakeem left the monastery so suddenly. This was very unusual behaviour for Shayvist monks!

It didn't matter, he wouldn't let the order do this to one of his men.

* * *

Hakeem was passed the letter from the Grand Abbot but he stored it, unread. It was only a moon and a half later that Hakeem received a message saying the old man had died. The great old man had never stopped asking after Hakeem, and had left another letter and a book to him. Overcome by grief and remorse, Hakeem could open neither.

He knew the old man regretted what had happened.

Hakeem had forgiven him.

He had given the abbot no chance to explain. What would the old man have said? Somehow he preferred not to know. It was all too painful.

The Grand Abbot was the closest he ever had to a father. That day, he asked for some time to himself and went into a nearby forest. When he returned the next afternoon, he didn't mention it again. The final link to his childhood was broken.

Chapter 3: The King's Game, an Elf, a Lesson, and the Men's Latrine

Hakeem produced his new orders to Niketas, the grizzled old recruiting *dekadarchos* (sergeant), in a room crowded with beeswax tablets and papyrus.

He remained at attention with a barely supressed smile on his face and his chest proudly puffed up while the old veteran read them.

Then Niketas looked up at Hakeem, leaned back, and laughed. Hakeem had just received a promotion, after only two moons of service. He saw nothing funny about it. He remained stiffly at attention, the smile dropped from his face and his eyes looked bleak.

"Oh, good, they have sent me another new *dimoiria* (corporal)!" Niketas called out to his aide in the small office. "I hope he can play the King's Game!"

The Aide laughed at the jest. The 'King's Game' was a dice and board game from Aígyptos.

"You have no position for me," Hakeem said darkly, as he realised what was happening. "I won't be playing the King's Game."

"I'm sorry," Niketas apologised. "I suppose I should be congratulating you." He sighed gloomily. "They keep sending me seconds. I already have nine waiting for a post already. One has been waiting for three moons ... What a way to run an army!"

Until he was attached to a dekadarchos (sergeant), Hakeem's promotion wasn't effected. He would be paid as a common soldier, but he couldn't return to his previous *stichos* (file). He was stuck nowhere, just like nine other men.

"I'm sorry, 'Akeem. They give our best soldiers a promotion and then send them to *fae skata* in the barracks." Niketas swore. "I can't find a new dekadarchos out of my *kolos*!"

Hakeem's initial impression of Niketas softened. He was rough and foul mouthed but not deliberately spiteful. Hakeem knew Niketas could hardly pull a dekadarchos out of his '*kolos*', but he didn't intend to '*fae skata*' (eat shit) in the barracks either!

The decadarchoi, literally meaning 'leaders of ten,' each commanded a *stichos* (file), mostly fifteen or sixteen men. They were, in many ways, the real backbone of the army.

In war, they led from the front so attrition was high, but there were enough hardened veterans to replace them. In peace, though, there simply weren't enough suitable soldiers with the sort of experience and now King Helios was expanding his army as well.

"You can complain to Pallas, but you may as well *skipse kai glipse*."

Hakeem frowned, the last obscenity made no sense, 'bend over and lick'? He would *really* rather it wasn't explained to him.

He had the idea, complaining to his *lochagos* (captain) would do no good.

"Look at this!" Niketas he waved a parchment in front of Hakeem. "A fort that is a lump of *skata* has been waiting for a file leader for four moons. So what, I say?

"Some *malakas* (masturbator) who got sent there demands another file leader. Where am I supposed to find one? I wanted to say '*pare mou pipa*'." Hakeem had to chuckle at that, he very much doubted the sergeant would actually say "suck my pipe" to anyone, let alone a superior officer.

"He is an *anthypolochagos* (junior lieutenant). To get sent there, he couldn't be too popular, I say. Now his father turns out to be some sort of *archimalakas* (head and important wanker) and I have received his letter as well.

"I will have to show this to Pallas, and tell him we must take a file leader from an existing file and send it to this flea-ridden place. You can imagine how he will react!"

"Well," Hakeem said, lifting up the letter. It was brief, but there was no mistaking the message. "I plan to see Pallas so I am happy to carry this good news for you as well."

"It can't possibly help you," Niketas said, looking very uncertain as he looked up at Hakeem holding the letter.

* * *

Pallas stared at the parchment written by the lieutenant's father. The father had been a lochagos who had retired after coming up through the ranks. He had recently bought a commission for his son.

The father would be furious about where his son had been posted: the fort at Malea had an ill reputation. There was no mention of this, nor would there be.

The fort had three understrength files, each of eleven men. The sensible thing was to merge them into two files but his son had a bought commission, this entitled him to lead three files and this meant three file leaders. The message was short and blunt. His son had a legal entitlement and his father was not without friends.

Pallas looked up. He looked like he wanted to smash things. "I can't conjure men capable of being proper file leaders out of the air!" he said to himself.

Hakeem managed to supress a grin, Pallas had not said out of his 'kolos', like Niketas, but this was not a good time to show amusement.

Then Pallas noticed Hakeem was still waiting at attention, his face expressionless. "I suppose you have come to complain to me too. Did you bring this to put me in a good mood first?"

"No sir," Hakeem said respectfully "I merely came to deliver your mail, sir."

He produced a papyrus document and placed it carefully on top of the other one.

"What's this? It's from Deimos!" Pallas cried in surprise. He squinted. Then he moved the paper back and forward. He turned it upside down and then turned it around and held it up to the light. "He actually wrote something himself. I didn't know he could do that."

He eventually flopped back, defeated and threw the paper from his hoplomachos (drill sergeant) back on the desk. "How does he expect me to read something like this?"

"It's about me sir." Hakeem said. "It's a recommendation for promotion."

"Hakeem, we already received this verbally," Pallas said. "We have accepted it. I'm just sorry we have no position for you."

"Well, sir, that's not exactly true. Deimos has agreed to take me as his second. In fact, he says I have been his acting second for two moons."

Pallas was impressed, Hakeem had no combat experience yet Deimos had agreed to keep him training recruits!

"But that's not what this is about, sir. You will see that the letter is dated today."

It was so outrageously cheeky that it took a moment for Pallas to comprehend what Hakeem was actually suggesting.

"You got Deimos to recommend you for file leader!" Pallas surged from his chair and struck the table loudly in disbelief. "Was he drunk?" he said laughing. "You're not even a second yet, you don't have a position!"

"Yes, sir I agree, *normally* that would be the case. I have checked the rules with the pay master. With Deimos saying I was his acting second for two moons, I am entitled to be a second waiting a new assignment, not a soldier waiting to become a second. I already have a place to go as a second, in case there is any dispute.

"So I have two moons experience which is the minimum, before I can be legally recommended for file leader and I have the recommendation of my dekadarchos." Hakeem concluded.

Pallas dropped back in his chair laughing. The sheer audacity of it all!

"All, right, very clever, Hakeem. Maybe you are not as naïve as we all thought.

"I can't let you get away with it, of course, but with Deimos's recommendation and some more experience, you will make file leader in a couple of moons. Believe me, you would rather wait and have a proper command than go to Malea."

"I wouldn't mind sir," Hakeem said quietly. "I take it you have another solution, sir?" He stood waiting, his face expressionless.

"I admire your nerve, Hakeem." Pallas said levelly. "I just can't let you get away with something like this." His last few words trailed off in a weak fashion.

He paused for a long while completely motionless and then finally he shook his head in disgust. He looked like a man swallowing something distasteful. "You'll regret this, Hakeem. If you were Greek, I couldn't promote you like this, you know that."

Hakeem nodded. "Yes sir, thank you, sir. I'm a Shantawi, sir."

* * *

The time Hakeem was in Malea passed very quickly, for him and all those around him. The tribesmen have a saying, "it was almost over before it began." It was the events of Malea that convinced Samit to make what seemed an extraordinary gamble, putting Hakeem in charge of a full century of Shantawi cavalry. Yet Hakeem could have been forgiven if he found his introduction to Malea decidedly discouraging. Not that he expected any better.

It was on the way there that he first met Elwan. Elwan had been sent there to escort Hakeem on the last leg of his journey from the village of Aigiriossa to Malea. Hakeem was delivered there early in the morning and he found the elf already waiting.

He had heard about elves from Origenes but he had never met one. He was intrigued by the subtle 'otherness' of his companion.

The elf was tall, no taller than Hakeem, but he was slender as all elves are. That could be deceiving, Hakeem knew: even strong elf warriors looked slender and all of them had a speed and balance that was hard to match.

The elf's complexion was inhumanly fair. His face was smooth (elves do not grow facial hair). His red silky hair was tied in a warriors knot to reveal the pointed ears of an elf which were said to be able to hear the fall of a leaf at scores of paces. When he turned his gaze on Hakeem his intense green eyes seemed to shine.

He was dressed in the green and brown leathers of an elf scout and armed with a heavy elf-knife with an exquisitely carved ivory handle. He had a long sword with an equally beautifully decorated hilt and he carried a composite bow.

All elvish weapons are not only exquisitely beautiful; they are of a quality even the best human weapons could not meet. Yet Elwan's marked him out as an elf noble.

Hakeem was only carrying his weapons, a light pack, and the sealed orders that would allow him to assume his first command.

His other meagre possessions would follow in due course.

Elwan didn't bother to offer his name. As soon as he thought Hakeem was ready, he turned without a further word, and began walking out of the village, Hakeem realised he was supposed to follow. When they reached the open road, without a glance at Hakeem behind him, the elf simply began running.

Hakeem grinned as he saw his guide take off. The elf was making a point! He could outrun Hakeem, but that would be too obvious. Instead, he was maintaining what for an elf was a relaxed lope. Hakeem had been trained to endurance and mental discipline. He would find this more comfortable than the elf expected.

The elf maintained a rhythm that would rapidly eat the distance between them and the fort and Hakeem managed to match him without any strain. At this pace, they would easily arrive on the morning of the third day rather than the evening of the fourth.

Hakeem reached into the discipline of his mind that allowed him to merge with the rhythm of his body, Hakeem ran as one trained for endurance, but he could not match the grace of an elf!

His rhythm varied over the uneven ground. The elf ran as if he were somehow flying through the forest; the dappled morning sunlight flickering through the trees almost made him seem to disappear or blur as he ran.

It was as if Hakeem, for all his training and mental discipline, reached blindly for something that elves could do so easily as breathing. They could merge with their surroundings by their very nature. "You sound like an elephant!" the elf called back to him in a musical voice.

Compared to you, I am, Hakeem thought, but he didn't bother to reply.

The elf had his war-bow strung and Hakeem cursed his own foolishness, but he didn't pause to string it till he noticed a change in the behaviour of his companion and softly called to him. The elf waited a little ahead, scanning the forest while Hakeem crouched down and quickly and efficiently strung his heavy bow and extracted his quiver. He turned to acknowledge Hakeem who cautiously moved up.

He had expected the human to have trouble keeping pace but the big lad wasn't even out of breath. He felt more inclined to talk to him now, but he allowed his eyes to continue to scan the forest, alert to any changes as he spoke.

"Perhaps there is one of you humans, who is not completely deaf and blind," he said grudgingly.

Hakeem favoured the elf with a sheepish grin. "I am, compared to an elf. I only watched you. You kept glancing at that ridge beyond the trees. Will they attack?"

"No, they only watch," Elwan said. "That looks a proper bow, do you know how to use it?"

"I would say 'yes' in any other company but not in front of an elf," Hakeem returned politely.

Elwan smiled, greatly pleased by the reply. "You are a Shantawi, how does a Shantawi end up not only on foot, but going to a neglected outpost in this Godforsaken land?"

Hakeem smiled, his own eyes automatically scanning the bushes.

"I argued with the Grand Abbot, and had to leave abruptly. It left no time to steal a horse."

Elwan laughed and whistled in surprise. This stranger argued with the most powerful man in Karsh! "Can you fight on foot?"

"In that, I think I am safe to say 'yes' in your company or any other, but why are you here, elf? Why would they waste a full blood elf-scout by sending him to Malea?"

"I told the truth!" Elwan spat.

"To the Grand Abbot?" Hakeem asked with his eye brows raised.

Elwan looked at him suspiciously, and then suddenly threw his head back and laughed.

"No, it was a lochagos. He was the son of a noble," he admitted. "By the way, my name is Elwan from C file. Our file leader got himself killed in the woods, like the damn fool he was. We all wait impatiently to see what they trawl from out of the sewer to send us. I will have to play nursemaid to another *daufi* (stupid) human who knows nothing and acts like he knows everything."

"Well, all I can say is that the daufi human will be fortunate if he has a full blood elf scout," Hakeem suggested mildly.

Elwan snorted.

Hakeem extended his hand. "By the way, my name is Hakeem. I would feel privileged, if you have some time to instruct me in how *not* to get killed in the woods."

Elwan was touched by the courteous request. The elves had an almost magical ability in what they called 'woods-craft' (the art of reading the wood and moving through it, leaving little sign of their passing). It made them terrifyingly efficient in the woods.

"Well, agreed then, Hakeem. They say the Shantawi are the only humans worth knowing! I like you, even though you are a human. Are you coming to C platoon too?"

"I am, my tactful friend," Hakeem agreed. "I am the one they have at last trawled up from the sewer. You said I will be daufi in the woods, and that is my thought also. I will freely admit it and hope to hold you to your promise to train me and our men in woods-craft."

Elwan looked at him in shock.

"You can't be," he said, incredulous. "You are only a boy! You cannot be fit to be a file leader!"

Hakeem looked back at him and laughed. "It seems if I want an honest opinion, I only need ask an elf. I know little of the Elfkin but I had heard they are usually not so hasty a people."

Elwan had nothing to say to that. He gave Hakeem a long searching look, up and down. Then he nodded and they were back running.

* * *

As they emerged from the trees, Hakeem could view the fort, about a mile distant. Elwan motioned him to silence. Without a word, the elf led Hakeem to one side, and settled himself down behind a bush. As Hakeem carefully joined his new friend, they were able to get a good view of the village and the nearby fort without being seen. *So we are to observe*, Hakeem concluded. Hakeem was beginning to suspect that elves were not great ones for idle chatter.

After about five minutes, Elwan led him back out of sight behind the trees and waited till they were both settled comfortably. "So, human, what did you see?" the elf asked, his face unreadable. Hakeem decided that his first lesson had started.

"It's not what I expected," Hakeem started. "What I see most of is what I *don't* see. It's called a fort, but there are no proper fortifications, not even field fortifications or a simple watch tower. The fort is little more than a permanent camp, a collection of wooden buildings forming a rectangle on a small hill."

"That is good," Elwan nodded. "What else *don't* you see?"

"There are two sentries on the roof but they are resting comfortably and not alert. The forest has been allowed to grow back too closely, but recently there has been an attempt to cut it back."

"Our new lieutenant, Aeton," Elwan informed him. "He has been here two moons."

"Not much progress for thirty men in two moons," Hakeem commented dryly. "No stockade, despite the ready timber, no barriers, ditches or even water barrels for defence against fire. The town too, is wide open."

"Now you know," Elwan said simply. "It is a depressing place. It has never been attacked and it will never be attacked."

"At least there is a well, is it a good one?"

"The well is good," the elf said sardonically.

"What happened to the previous lieutenant?"

"He drank wine without adding water," Elwan said simply. "This place had no lieutenant for a year, and not much of one before that. In case you are not yet convinced about the place you have come to, my large friend, let's see how close we can get you before we are both noticed!"

* * *

Hakeem's first meeting with Aeton the *anthypolochagos* (junior lieutenant) of the fort could not be described as promising. When Hakeem and Elwan entered the room, Aeton stared at him in utter horror.

The pair fell in unison to kneel on their right knees, their right hand across their chests and heads bowed in salute. Aeton was utterly appalled.

His father had come up through the ranks to retire as lochagos. It was a struggle for his father to purchase commissions for his two older brothers and Aeton never imagined he would be able to do the same for him. It must have near impoverished his parents.

Aeton *should* have been attached as an aide to a senior *lochagos* (captain) and further promotion would then be on merit. As soon as he received his posting orders, he realised that his father had enemies and they had set a trap for his youngest son.

He was sent to a fort at Malea, a tiny village in thinly populated foothills. Malea *had* belonged to Smyrna, before Smyrna switched to paying their tribute to the Ionian league fifty years earlier. Aiolía had decided to lay claim to Malea, as punishment to Smyrna.

Neither side took it as a serious move. Smyrna was not really an enemy of Aiolía, they were too interdependent, and now Smyrna had powerful protection from their new friends.

Malea was a place of no great importance in a small section of wilderness that no one really wanted. The only paths to Malea were side tracks, one off the main road leading from Smyrna to Prusa in Bithynia, and another off the main trade route from Aiolía to Ikónion.

The roads to Malea were narrow and impassable to carts after even the slightest of rains. Yet a collection of wooden buildings was duly built just outside the village of Malea and called a fort.

Aeton would be the most senior officer there. He would be deprived of the help of a senior experienced officer or any chance to make important contacts. Worse, he would never be noticed in such a posting.

Yet it was only after Aeton had arrived that he realised just how diabolical the trap was. There was one export from the hills around Malea that was both well-known and plentiful ... bandits! It was an ideal base for attacking traffic on several major trade routes!

Aeton, due to his rank, supposedly had three *stichos* (files) at his disposal. The minimum for a stichos was ten, though most had fifteen to eighteen. His *stichoi* were understrength at eleven men each.

If he included himself and three file leaders, he had 37 fighting men, two cooks and a stable hand. Most of the soldiers he was given were lazy, corrupt, or petty criminals.

No one wanted to come here. There were several bandit leaders not far away with bigger and better commands than he had.

He could do nothing effective against the bandits without two or three times the men he had. He was doomed to irrelevance and failure, at a time when the new king was transforming his kingdom and there was so much opportunity.

Now there was the suspicious delay in replacing one of the *dekadarchos* (sergeants) who had been killed. His father even had to write a letter.

As he looked at Hakeem, he realised with a shock the true extent and power of the malice he faced. They had sent him a boy! It was impossible! It was incredible!

Hakeem looked up and announced his name in a clear voice "*Kyrie* (Lord) Anthypolochagos, my name is Hakeem." He passed his sealed orders to the lieutenant.

Aeton felt a sinking feeling as he accepted the orders. He studied Hakeem out of the corner of his eye.

The lad obviously had little or no money. He was dressed in the army issue Greek three-quarter length chiton and laced sandals. Over this, he had brown leather armour which left his arms and legs bare, not regulation, but neither expensive nor new.

He had an army issue *peltastēs* (light leather and wicker shield) over his shoulder and *xiphos* (short sword) at his hip. He had a distinctly battered gorytos slung over one shoulder as well.

His unadorned helmet had a small dint and was lined inside with linen. It was swinging from a strap he had attached to his gear. Aeton could see a woollen *chlamys* (short-cloak/blanket) bundled into his small pack.

He was certainly big for his age, and muscular. He moved with grace suggesting some training. His tanned face was handsome and he had dark curly hair. He had a full beard and moustache, neatly trimmed and his brown eyes met Aeton's gaze evenly.

Aeton looked warily at the dispatch and then chewed his lip as he opened it. He still hoped it was some mistake, he hoped this wasn't his new dekadarchos. As he read it, he felt like screwing it up and angrily throwing it in the lad's face. This was preposterous!

A Greek at eighteen had to serve two years' compulsory military service and training, before he was a citizen. Hakeem wasn't old enough to be a Greek citizen let alone a Greek officer. This didn't apply to Shantawi mercenaries, but Aeton still hadn't heard of a sergeant anywhere near as young as Hakeem.

The lad might look big, but he was just a boy. The hard men of file C would eat him alive.

He was described as highly recommended. Did they think Aeton was stupid?

He sighed, he would have to register a complaint, but he had better wait till this boy slipped up. He felt so helpless! Even if he knew who was doing this to him, there wouldn't be anything he or his family could do.

"Well, Hakeem, you come very highly recommended," he said dryly, waiting to see how the young man would respond. Elwan started to rise, but quickly resumed his kneeling position when he noticed Hakeem hadn't moved a muscle.

"At ease!" Aeton called impatiently. The two men rose to stand, looking alert and respectful.

"Hakeem, can you tell me why a Shantawi is in the *infantry*? Or why he would come here where no one else wants to be?"

"Yes sir, I volunteered," Hakeem replied quietly.

Aeton paused. "You, what?" he asked, incredulous. "For a moment, I thought you said you volunteered."

"Yes sir, I had to insist. I had two reasons, sir.

"The first is that I am not nobly born. I could be a second in a stichos which is very good after joining not yet a season ago, but the position here was for a dekadarchos. No one else wanted to come, and they didn't want to lose anyone to this post. I managed to get recommended for an additional promotion."

Very clever! Aeton thought with complete disgust. Did anyone think of what *I* might think of that? Well, congratulations, boy! Wait till you find out what you got with your clever bargaining.

What a mess.

"The second reason is," Hakeem was continuing, smiling with relish, "… I hear you have a lot of bandits!"

Aeton looked at Hakeem as if he had gone mad. "So you're not sent here by my enemies and you hate bandits."

Hakeem looked puzzled. "Sir, no one pushed me to come here … but why do you say I hate bandits?"

"Because I thought you were saying you wanted to kill them, wasn't that what you meant to say?" Aeton snapped at him irritably.

"Yes, sir! They certainly have to be stopped, and that's the only way I know of," Hakeem said and then he paused, "but it would be very wrong for me to hate them. I hope you understand that, sir?" The big lad looked at him earnestly.

Aeton stared at him disbelievingly, almost lost for a reply. "So you want to kill them, but it's nothing personal," he suggested.

Hakeem nodded enthusiastically and visibly relaxed, the lieutenant really did understand!

It was then that Aeton remembered something about Hakeem he hadn't thought through till then. Hakeem was brought up in a monastery from the age of five. He was likely to be strange and religious. What on earth was he doing as a soldier?

Aeton tried to force himself to finish with a friendly smile and a small chuckle.

"Well perhaps you aren't here to stir up trouble. I suppose you wish to rest after the elf has run you into the ground. I didn't expect you till late tomorrow. I'm surprised you're still standing."

"Oh no, sir!" Hakeem returned enthusiastically, "It wasn't too bad, and Elwan has agreed to show me the rest of the men, so I'll start right away if I may. I have no second in command, and Elwan is qualified; would it be alright, if I selected him?" he asked, looking at Aeton.

Aeton was shocked by the idiocy of the request. "Are you sure that's wise?" he said, barely managing to be polite. "Elwan himself will tell you that he is hardly popular."

"I understand how that might be, sir," Hakeem nodded in acknowledgement. "But he is exactly what I need. I think you will be surprised."

"Alright, I'll let you try it." Elwan was qualified to be second in command and there was no one else suitable in the file. There was no official reason he could refuse ... but there was a reason Elwan was never put in a position of command. Meet him and you instantly understood. Didn't this young fool from the desert see the obvious?

"I promise we won't stir up trouble, except on your behalf, sir," Hakeem had finished cheerfully.

After they had stepped out of the hut that was the lieutenant's and were walking away, Elwan turned to Hakeem. "He didn't like your choice for second," he said with a wry smile.

Hakeem shrugged. "He didn't like me much either. He thought one of his enemies sent me." He chuckled.

"Well what do we do now, my big friend?"

"I'm going to suggest to the men that we should do some regular training."

"Suggest?" Elwan looked at him quizzically. "May *I* 'suggest' you make that an order if you really want it done?"

"Oh, no!" Hakeem laughed. "We wouldn't want to upset them now would we? I think I'll just explain to them I think it is a good idea. I'm sure they will agree." He smiled confidently.

Elwan looked at the young man in disbelief. "You don't want to upset them by ordering them to train. You expect them to agree it is a good idea?"

"That's the way!" Hakeem said slapping his new friend on the shoulder.

As Hakeem strode purposely towards the men's barracks, Elwan followed, shaking his head.

* * *

Aeton had remained sitting at his desk, his head in his hands. He hadn't thought things could get any worse but they had. He had a boy as his new sergeant, a religious fanatic who wanted to charge out and kill people ... but it was nothing personal! Please don't think that, sir, it would be wrong to dislike anyone you are killing!

What infernal madness was that?

How the lad would react when he met the motley collection of troops they had in this godless fort, Aeton couldn't imagine. Would he preach to them, or want to convert them?

The men would defeat Hakeem, though. They had defeated Aeton and it had only taken two months. They had done it, not by open defiance, but wearing him down, resisting him every step of the way.

No matter what he suggested, it couldn't be done, or shouldn't be done, or it wasn't wise … or they tried it and made sure it failed. The men had done it with the barely concealed support of the two sergeants. There seemed no way out from the trap he found himself in.

He just hoped Hakeem didn't start fighting them when they started to do that to him. He sighed. He would find out what would happen between Hakeem and his men soon enough.

He never imagined he would be finding out the very same morning.

* * *

It could not have been more than two turns of the hour-glass when Damianos and Hesiod, the other sergeants came hurrying in. They told him Hakeem was physically attacking his own men for disobeying his orders.

"Bring him and the men involved to me!" Aeton snarled, his stomach sinking. This was exactly the sort of thing he was worried about. An officer attacking soldiers who couldn't strike him back.

Any discipline and punishments had to be applied formally in Helios's army and a record of punishments kept. The King insisted on it.

Aeton bent his head. Who had sent this mad horror to him? Then he straightened up. Perhaps this was better, if he could have Hakeem on report within hours of arriving, he could show what they were doing to him.

Soon he was glaring at Hakeem, who stood impassively at attention. He didn't look concerned in the slightest. Yet if he was one of these religious fanatics; he wouldn't see that he had done anything wrong, would he?

Next to him was Elwan, standing silent, motionless, his face a mask of elvish reserve. Behind them were three of Hakeem's men: Nikodemos, Isokrates and their ringleader Saul. They were known for their unsavoury reputation, but now they were looking in very poor shape!

Their clothes were dirty and their hair all over the place. Nikodemos was tenderly fingering a broken nose which was clogged with blood, forcing him to breathe through his mouth. His face and hair had dirt and bits of grass through it, his ear had been bleeding but had stopped and his tunic was ripped and had blood all down the front. Saul had a cut lip and his cheek below his right eye was puffy and bruised. He was supporting Isokrates, who was hopping about with a neatly bandaged ankle.

Hakeem appeared untouched, his clothes were still as neat as when he arrived, his curly black hair and beard nicely combed and trimmed. He flashed his bright white teeth in a friendly smile at his lieutenant.

"Well, Hakeem," Aeton shouted angrily. "You only left my presence two hours ago and already you are accused of physically attacking these men, when they disobeyed your orders."

Hakeem nodded.

"So you admit it?" Aeton sputtered, in angry disbelief.

"Of course not, sir," Hakeem answered respectfully. "I was just agreeing with you that the other file leaders had accused me. I was awaiting permission to speak."

"You were awaiting permission to speak," Aeton repeated slowly. "What is this about disobeying orders then, you should have put them on report, not attacked them."

Hakeem looked puzzled. "I have no idea what that is supposed to be about, sir. I issued no orders. I told the men I thought we should be doing daily training. These gentlemen," he waved his hand to indicate the trio, who had tried to smile winningly as they bobbed their heads at their lieutenant, "felt they didn't need further training. I merely gave them the chance to show me what they could do. No one was seriously hurt."

Aeton surveyed the three. Nikodemos's nose and Isokrates's ankle would keep them both out of heavy action for weeks. "Saul, what is your version of this?"

"Well sir, the Sergeant was showing us some techniques."

Aeton had to lean back and smile. Despite himself … he really had to smile. Of course that is what happened! Hakeem claimed he hadn't *ordered* all his men to train and some refused. It was a philosophical discussion between him and his men!

Aeton could imagine the scene. The rest of the squad would be assembled and Hakeem would invite any man who wished, to come forward, one at a time …

This was a surprise.

His opinion of the young tribesman rose tremendously. Despite his youth and inexperience, he had chosen to pit himself against possibly the three toughest men in the whole fort and he had beaten them. Not only did he know how to gain the men's respect, but despite his age, he really was a skilled fighter. Perhaps there was something to the claims about him, after all.

He noted the look of admiration they were all giving Hakeem. They didn't feel abused! Hakeem wasn't all orders and rule books at least. He may be young but he was acting like a seasoned file leader.

"Nikodemos attacked the sergeant first, who tripped him and pushed him," Saul continued. "He fell hard, face-forward onto the ground, that's how he broke his nose, but the Sergeant reset it straight for him. It will be as good as new in a few weeks, the Sergeant says.

"That's when I collided with Isokrates while we were trying to close on the Sergeant, and he was able to tangle us both up together and trip us up. It was because he dodged too quickly for us. The Sergeant bandaged his ankle for him, did a good job too, sir. The Sergeant is right, sir, we have a lot to learn, sir!"

Aeton held up his hand quickly to stop the explanation and looked at the men before him. He was confused. "Hold on," he said slowly, trying to understand what happened. "Do I understand this correctly, you were fighting *all three* at the same time?" he carefully checked Hakeem again, who didn't seem in the slightest ruffled.

Hakeem nodded quickly. "Yes sir, there were only three of them, sir, and they weren't well trained in that sort of fighting."

"Only three of them," Aeton said softly, almost to himself. He realised he was starting to echo in disbelief whatever this man said to him. "After racing an elf for two full days to get here, but there were only three men to deal with." Three tough and experienced veterans, probably the toughest men in the fort!

Hakeem took a big breath. "That was just the point I was making, sir!" he said with obvious enthusiasm. "These men have had basic Hoplitai training. They don't know how to cooperate in a mêlée. They just got in each other's way."

Aeton nodded. He felt a bit numb, stunned. Soldier training concentrated on fighting in formation, and individual fighting when the formations broke up (the *mêlée*).

Cooperation in the chaos of the mêlée was considered too hard to teach.

There was something that had been nagging at the back of Aeton's mind since he met Hakeem. He was struggling to remember the little he knew about the Shayvist monks. He had never met one, but he remembered the Shantawi mercenaries spoke about their fighting skills with the greatest respect. Hakeem had grown up in a Shayvist monastery since he was five.

Great Zeus! What sort of training had Hakeem gotten from those monks? Aeton was just beginning to get an idea of the level to which Hakeem had been trained … "Only three," Hakeem had said.

It was *just* like the Shantawi to have their religious monks as dangerous warriors! The monks were far worse, by the sound of things, than their respected mercenary cavalry, and that was saying a very great deal indeed.

"Is there any cause for complaint?" he asked.

The five replied smartly in unison, "No, sir!"

"I'm sorry, sir," Hakeem said a little regretfully, as he made ready to leave. "It will be two or three moons before I can get the men into the shape they need to be in, but I think you will be very pleased with the results. They will make good soldiers."

Aeton had struggled unsuccessfully, not to repeat, "They will make good soldiers." He was shaking his head in admiration and, for the first time since he arrived, he was smiling.

* * *

Aeton almost felt dizzy when Damianos stormed in looking furious, it was only early in the afternoon of the same day. How long was Hakeem going to keep this up? he wondered.

"Sir! You have to stop that man. He just pushed one of my men into the cess pit and then threatened me."

Aeton had difficulty imagining what had happened, but he nonetheless eyed Damianos unsympathetically. Damianos would be trying to cause trouble for the new file leader. "Perhaps we should hear Hakeem's version of all this, I imagine he is waiting outside."

He called out and Hakeem knocked and duly entered. The Hakeem in question seemed to be having trouble supressing a wide grin.

"Hakeem, did you push one of Damianos's men into the cess pit?" Aeton was having a distinct sense of unreality.

"Yes, sir, I couldn't restrain myself, sir." Hakeem was trying to stop himself from laughing. "I had to remove the wooden boards on either side, of course; he wouldn't fit otherwise. I'm sure you understand that part, sir."

"Was there any reason for that, or did you just pick a victim at random?" Aeton enquired, trying to maintain a straight face.

"Well sir," Hakeem relaxed his stance, settling himself as if ready to make a story of it for his lieutenant. "The trench used by the men smells terribly, not too surprisingly I might add. I will see to that problem, when I have a chance, sir. It's in an awful state.

"Well, anyway, some men have gotten into the habit of making their mess short of the pit and leaving it for others to clean up. I found one of those men and I suggested he clean up his mess and that of some of the others.

"He told me I wasn't his sergeant and seemed rather smug about it … and then, well I just couldn't help myself. I, er… *assisted* him into the pit sir.

"I didn't hit him or anything. I know that's not allowed. He *has* got a sore shoulder though but that was from where I was stopping him from hitting *me.* He was also trying to get away and then later it was a tight fit and he didn't seem to *want* to get into the trench, you understand. I told him to stop struggling, but he just wouldn't listen, sir.

"His shoulder will be as good as new in a week." Then he paused, "Well, perhaps it will be two weeks … well, it might even be more, but it *will* heal completely! I was very careful not to hurt him, sir.

"I think he wanted to make a complaint about me himself, but I believe he is having a problem getting rid of the smell, sir. I think you can understand.

"I do think he will be more careful in the future, the pit was rather full and I think well overdue to be re-dug."

"He was my man!" Damianos muttered angrily. "And this man's file prevented me from getting in to help him. When I protested later, Hakeem said he would put me in the same place."

"It's simply not true, Damianos!" Hakeem patiently explained. "They were just crowded around to see what was happening. No one anywhere near could hear what you were saying, your man was screaming so loudly. My ears are still ringing." Hakeem paused and moved his head around as if to clear his hearing. "All *I* said to you was 'come here and I'll show you.'"

"Damianos," Aeton said tiredly, holding up his hand to stop the two men bickering. "If you were doing your own job, you would have less time to complain about others doing theirs. You should be grateful Hakeem has saved you the problem of dealing with this. Not only are you dismissed, tell your man if he comes anywhere near me to complain whether he is smelly or not, he will only find himself in more trouble!"

Damianos paused and looked like he was going to argue, but then he shot a furious glare at Hakeem and left, slamming the door.

Aeton looked at his newest file leader. "Is there really a way to make the pit smell less?"

"Of course there is sir, there are several ways.

"For the simple trench-pit like the men use, we need to add a layer of ashes and sand every day and twice a day in summer. Lime, made from baking sea-shells or limestone, mixed with ashes is really the best, if we can get that.

"They all know that, sir, and haven't done it. The whole thing is disgusting and dangerous to the health of the men." He looked angry. "The men's pit should have been filled in a moon ago and another re-dug. You dig them that deep to bury them, not to keep using them till they are full.

"The officer's pit is designed for permanence and privacy. It's even simpler; all it needs is a properly designed vent-pipe. You put a fine cloth filter to prevent flies getting in.

"The vent sucks the bad smells out by drawing air in through the holes we sit over inside the shed. The flies cause the worst of the smell. Any flies that do get in go up the pipe to the light, so they can't get in and out, and they die inside. Don't worry about it, sir; leave it all to me, sir."

"You'll order your men to dig a new pit?"

Hakeem seemed unconcerned. "I'll do it myself, if they don't want to help, it won't take too long and the exercise will do me good. That way, I know it's done properly. Could you get the other two files to fill in the old one after that?"

Aeton realised Hakeem meant it. He would invite his men to help, but would do it himself if they didn't want to help. Aeton would bet a year's pay that *every single man* in his file would be out helping their sergeant before he finished. Hakeem was the sort of leader that wouldn't ask his men to do something he wasn't prepared to do himself.

Let the other file-leaders deal with the old pit

… he would give the order himself.

"Hakeem, you seem to know a lot about pit latrines, did they teach you that in the monastery ?" He was surprised Hakeem had learned something so practical from a group of monks.

Hakeem nodded cheerfully. "That and a lot of other things. You have to know these things, sir, if you don't like the smell." he laughed a little. "But it's a sergeant's job, sir, not a lieutenant's job."

"Thank you, Hakeem," Aeton said quietly. He was getting an idea of why Hakeem was promoted so quickly. He wondered what else Hakeem had learned at the Monastery. The Shayvists seemed to be remarkably practical for monks.

For the first time since he had come to this place, Aeton felt a surge of hope; perhaps things could be different with this strange young ex-monk here. "Hakeem, do you plan to do anything else today?" he asked, half hopefully and half fearfully.

"Yes sir, I'm going with Saul and a couple of my men and check the food preparation and the condition of the food stores."

"I see. It might be better if I ordered you to do that."

"Thank you, sir." Hakeem turned to leave.

"Hakeem, do I need to warn you that now is a good time to start watching your back?"

Hakeem laughed. "No sir, you don't have to tell me that, sir."

Chapter 4: An Inexperienced Man, a Trap, and a Plan

It happened only three days later .

Aeton looked at his new friend sadly. Hakeem was looking as serene as ever, as he stood at attention. He obviously didn't understand just how much trouble he really was in. In the room with Aeton were the two other file leaders and two armed guards stationed behind Hakeem (who had been ordered to surrender his weapons). The windows were shuttered for what was to be a private hearing.

Aeton really had grown to like the young man in the short time he had been here. He was beginning to think that things could be better at the fort but Hakeem's military career had just ended.

"You know this is a very serious charge," Aeton said heavily to Damianos and Hesiod who were looking smug with ill-concealed triumph. He felt boiling with anger. He knew they had set a trap for Hakeem and the inexperienced young man had fallen for it. For the first time, he felt real hatred for them.

He nodded to Hakeem. "What they say, is it true?"

"Yes sir, I issued a formal challenge to Damianos and Hesiod. I offered to fight them today, one after the other. I suggested we fight unarmed or with staves. I don't really want to damage them too much."

Aeton felt a wrench inside himself. "What on earth has got into you, man?" he cried, almost imploringly.

"Well sir," Hakeem took a breath. "They said I was currying favour with you, sir; which of course is true. They said I wished to show them up, which is not true at all.

"They reminded me they were both experienced fighters and then they told me in some detail what they would do to me, sir, if I continued. I just thought it simpler to get it over and done with, so I offered a formal challenge."

"He lies!" Hesiod snarled, furious. "We don't know what he is talking about, sir. We never threatened him!" He flashed Hakeem a smug look. It their word against his and there were two of them.

"Oh, I was worried they might not remember. They seemed so upset, sir," Hakeem said looking at the other two with what seemed like concern.

"Sometimes people don't remember things, when they are upset," he explained, as he passed a parchment sheet to Aeton. "I have produced a record of what they said to remind them. I'm not sure why they would really want to cook and eat my testicles and I don't understand that other thing with my head and my kolos, it didn't seem possible … physically I mean sir."

"That is ridiculous!" Damianos looked like he would almost burst with indignation. "Just because he wrote it, doesn't mean it's true!"

Hakeem sighed, and shook his head ruefully. "I knew this might happen, they were just so upset. It's lucky that Elwan and four of my men just happened to be around the corner, and they heard everything these men said *very* clearly. Do you want me to call them?"

Aeton almost dropped the parchment and shouted in surprise. He looked at Hakeem sharply but Hakeem was busy giving

Damianos and Hesiod a completely innocent look. The pair had suddenly gone very pale. No, Aeton realised, he didn't have to warn Hakeem to watch his back.

"Sir!" Damianos protested, desperately. "It was only a hypothetical threat. No one would take it seriously."

Aeton looked at him unsympathetically, and then resumed reading the parchment.

"Sir," Hakeem interrupted. "I really must apologise. Greek isn't native to me, what does Damianos mean by a hypothetical threat?" He inclined his head politely to a now thoroughly frightened Damianos.

"Yes, Damianos," Aeton invited and favoured him with a slow smile. "I don't really understand either, but I happen to be Greek and had what I thought was a thorough education. When is a threat not a threat? Perhaps you can enlighten both of us."

Damianos seemed stuck for words.

"Well then," Aeton said, passing the parchment to Damianos who took it as if it would burn his fingers. "Hakeem, the evidence seems to be clear enough. You have a right to issue a challenge to two fellow officers who threaten you in this way, but this gives us a serious problem. This region is unsettled, so technically we are on a war setting. I cannot let you fight them, and any other situation is intolerable."

"It seems I misunderstood sir," Hakeem said politely. "Damianos and Hesiod did not mean to threaten me. In that case, I apologise. If they will give me permission, I will withdraw my challenge."

Damianos and Hesiod hesitated, and looked at each other and then nodded sourly in agreement.

"Thank you, Hakeem; under the circumstances I really am grateful," Aeton said, eyeing the other two distastefully. He realised Hakeem only wanted to warn them off.

But Aeton wasn't finished; he wasn't nearly finished.

What they had done was not at all unusual, older men warning off new ones they thought were too young and too enthusiastic. It got out of hand when he offered a formal challenge. And he would have fought them, too. Aeton had no doubt.

Then they refused to back down and saw it as a chance to get rid of Hakeem. Unfortunately the harder they tried with Hakeem, the deeper in they got.

What they had done, threatening Hakeem and blocking Aeton's efforts may not have been unusual, but they had done something that was completely and utterly unforgiveable.

They had been caught doing it.

These two had secretly blocked every attempt Aeton made to get the fort and the men in shape. When Hakeem tried to warn them off, they didn't back off. They made an official complaint knowing it would completely destroy the young man

No, Aeton wasn't finished with them at all.

He looked at them grimly. "Damianos and Hesiod I am not satisfied with your behaviour, not since I first arrived here, and this document, which I can get witnessed by no less than two officers and four of the men, gives me all the proof I need. Do you know what that means for the two of you?"

He gave them a satisfied smile. The looks they gave him back suggested that, whatever else they lacked, it wasn't imagination.

It wasn't quite open mutiny. Short of a capital offence, perhaps, but it was hard to see how they could be in much more trouble. The room had gone unnaturally silent. Outside, they could hear the soldiers going about their chores. A small amount of light came through the shuttered window.

He had them! He really had them! Had Hakeem only been here a few days?

He smiled at them wolfishly. 'It seems that the two of you have put me in a difficult position." He paused delicately, considering. "I could, of course, have you both *scourged* (flogged*)* and discharged. Any back pay would be forfeit, naturally." He looked at them, inviting them to agree with him. After their endless barracks level complaints, they had suddenly lost the urge to talk.

He stretched the moment out, as if thinking.

He well knew how terribly unpopular he would be with his superiors if he got rid of two sergeants, but *they* wouldn't be thinking about that just now, they would be watching him too closely for that, with the sort of horrified fascination a man would have for his own executioner.

"It just so happens, another solution occurs to me. Being a small garrison, we have never needed a senior sergeant, but if we have one, this will stop any squabbling amongst the three of you. If you would kindly support my recommendation, I think I can appoint Hakeem as acting senior sergeant, while I am awaiting official confirmation.

"And then we can all forget about this unpleasant matter, don't you agree?" Aeton enjoyed the looks of dismay on their faces.

"You understand of course that neither of you will want to cross me again."

He gave them a careful smile … and they wouldn't. He might not press charges against them but news of this would spread like wildfire through the *whole* army, even though this hearing was supposedly behind closed doors.

A young inexperienced dekadarchos, only eighteen years old, an orphan raised in a monastery in the middle of the desert, besting two experienced veteran sergeants who ganged up on him.

The two men were frozen. They looked like he had just asked them to agree to their own hanging. Then their shoulders slumped and they gave quick jerky nods of surrender. There was a look of profound disbelief on their faces about what had just happened.

"Dismissed you two, I will have the paperwork drawn up. Hakeem, remain."

After they had left, Hakeem was returning his short sword and knife to their sheaths. "Sir, you will not regret this, I promise."

"You know," Aeton laughed, "I don't think I will.

"I suppose congratulations are in order. I really cannot believe it, though I was part of it. Moving from a common soldier to a senior dekadarchos is quite something for a man to do in a whole career! You have done it in a few days, I doubt that has ever happened anywhere in this world. I must confess I feel somewhat awed by what you have done here, my young friend. If you have any pretentions at being king, perhaps I should warn Helios."

Hakeem laughed at that. "Thank you, sir. No, I won't be becoming a king. Besides, I was acting 'second' before, not just a soldier."

Aeton caught himself muttering "you were acting second" under his breath and then shook his head and laughed again.

"Sir, may I suggest you give them that parchment I wrote, as soon as they sign for me to become senior sergeant?"

"Are you sure?" Aeton asked. "You have just made some serious enemies here."

Hakeem shrugged and smiled. "Sir, I'll be safe for a good while now, and even after that, they will be too cautious of me and too busy wondering what I have planned for them."

Aeton studied his new friend very closely. "What do you plan to do to them?"

Hakeem laughed. "Absolutely nothing, and that's the beauty of it all!" Hakeem finished triumphantly.

Aeton waited for Hakeem to explain.

"Or I should say," Hakeem amended, "very little. We will get this fort and the defences of the town in order. Then I am going to offer to train them and their men."

Aeton snorted in surprise, "Hakeem, they will refuse."

Hakeem's laughed softly and nodded. "Of course they will, sir, I want them to refuse. They will be surprised at how little I ask of them.

"They will hardly believe they got off so lightly, after what we *could* have done to them. Their men will see me taking my own file away from the fort for training, while they are taking it easy. They will think they are lucky that I am not their file leader, but they will feel uneasy.

"It's human nature not to want to miss out on something, and they will know we are up to something. After that, we will go about discouraging some of the local bandits."

"I know, Hakeem! You won't share the bandit's loot with them." Aeton clapped his hands in delight. That would really serve them right!

"No, sir, you don't understand, that's not what I mean to do." Hakeem was speaking very intently. "My men will be under strict orders not to talk about their training or the raids. The other files will be under orders not to ask. Otherwise my men are to remain perfectly polite and courteous to the men of the other files, to the extent it will seem suspicious. Any problems they will refer to me. There will be no taunting and no bragging.

"If you agree sir, you and I will act as if nothing is wrong.

"Any plunder must be divided properly. We must be absolutely fastidious about that. A proper accounting will be made in front of yourself and the other two sergeants, and any accusation of cheating properly dealt with.

"A tenth share of any money will go to the King, a tenth share will be set aside for equipment and the soldier's fund, and a tenth share will go to the town and local peasants. You will get a Captain's share and the rest will be distributed in *exactly* the right proportions from the stable boy and cooks right up to the sergeants.

"The money will start to appear, but where it comes from and how we obtained it will be a secret. I can easily explain the need for secrecy.

"We will not push it in their faces but we will tell them nothing. They must have no real excuse, whatsoever, to focus their anger on us."

Aeton thought for a long while, and then he nodded doubtfully in understanding. "A bit like digging the trench, I suppose. That certainly worked, but are you sure it will work this time?" he said a little doubtfully.

Hakeem grinned. "Believe me, sir. This will drive them completely crazy. I absolutely guarantee it.

"After the second successful raid, they will be almost where we want them, and by the third they will be falling over themselves to join us. If they are not ready by the third raid, I don't want them, but don't worry, they will be. They will make good soldiers and fighters if they just let themselves."

Aeton smiled at the big man's confidence. The words "they will make good soldiers and fighters if they just let themselves" were echoing in his mind.

"One thing, I don't understand: why do we have to give such large bribes?"

Hakeem took a big breath. "Sir, most of the townspeople are more loyal to Smyrna than Aiolía. In the hills, a lot of them have family members and friends who are bandits. This is very poor country.

"We won't spend *any of it* on bribes … or rewards for information. We don't need information, we have Elwan. The last thing I want is civilians putting themselves in any danger of reprisals from the bandits.

"If there are widows or orphans, farmers who have fallen on bad times, money for building an altar, a temple, or a barn, someone who needs a small gift to replace a few chickens or a goat, or build up a herd or buy an ox, … anything worthwhile, that is what we will do.

"Small amounts, but for any good cause and we will also help in other ways too, provide physical help and expertise wherever we can.

"It might even stop some from becoming bandits, or mean that some bandits can go back to honest work, if we can make being a bandit dangerous enough.

"I wouldn't like to promise that, though. People will start to be happy to see us when we come to help them in any way we can, and not expect anything in return."

"'Do good works and they will praise you', it's easy to tell you grew up in a monastery," Aeton said. "Alright, Hakeem, you have been right so far, so we will do this your way. But the bandits outnumber us and you are only going to use a third of our strength."

Hakeem smiled and nodded. "We will make this fort and town secure, so we can't be raided here. Then we will train my men. After that, Elwan and I will pick our fights. If the bandits have any real chance against us, we won't fight them. I don't want to lose any of my men if I possibly can avoid it."

Chapter 5: Leaving Malea

Hakeem was standing on the walkway overlooking the newly constructed wooden palisade when Aeton went searching for him. It had been over a year since Hakeem had come to Malea and now it would be only a few days before he would have to go.

Aeton joined him in looking out towards the forest, waiting for one of their patrols to return. The brush beyond had been cleared and proper field fortifications dug on all parts of the hill except the road up the small hill to the fort.

"I had expected you to come in search of me after the courier arrived," Aeton said quietly.

"We both knew what the news would be," Hakeem said looking out. "I was trying to put all of this in my mind. I will miss this place, has it only been not much more than a year?" he sighed.

In the last six moons they had all been so busy, waging a virtual all-out war on any of the remaining bandits.

"You don't want to leave, do you?"

"Aeton I have to, I have been offered a position as *hipparchos* (cavalry captain) with the Shantawi horse and I am not yet twenty."

Aeton nodded. Hakeem couldn't become a captain and stay at Malea and he was a Shantawi, he would want to join their famous cavalry.

"You'll be happier there."

"Will I? It seems all of my life is about endings." Hakeem sighed. Then he mentally shook himself. The mood was past. "And I hear it's all because someone's been spreading terrible lies about me back at Pergamon. I don't know who, but I suspect it's been you, my friend. I hardly credit they have been believed."

Aeton laughed. "Someone has to, you won't boast about yourself!"

"Are you still refusing to leave?"

Aeton laughed. "It also came with the orders. They finally agreed. I will be a *lochagos* (infantry captain) and can stay here.

"I will have a full lochos, though it will be scattered between here and the other nearby forts. It will be much easier to hunt out bandits with that number of men. I will have four times the area, as well, which is not such a bad thing." He smiled, before including what had become the standing joke at the fort.

"It is starting to get hard to find bandits around here anymore," he laughed, "I never dreamed I would refuse to leave. When I was sent here I thought it was a trap set by my father's enemies."

"Congratulations as well, then. We will be captains together." Hakeem put his arm on his friend's shoulder, now their rank would be equal.

"If this place *was* a trap for you, it would have been a good one," Hakeem laughed. "But you have sent a very clear message back to whomever, don't you think?"

"My father wrote to me too." For a moment Aeton couldn't continue, tears came to his eyes.

"He's so proud," Aeton said hoarsely. "Did you know he sold almost everything? They are comfortable again, now. I won't be the only member of my family who will never forget you, Hakeem."

Hakeem coloured, but looked very pleased.

"You know it is you that I have you to thank for this miracle."

Hakeem shook his head. "Every man did their part. Elwan is most responsible. It was him, and your leadership."

"I know he is your best friend and your blood brother, but before you came he was just another elf-faced *malaka*. Now there isn't a man here who wouldn't lay down their life for him."

Hakeem laughed. Aeton did not normally use obscenities. He was saved from answering by a horn from the sentry tower, loudly sounding the challenge. Someone had keen eyes!

Damianos's file had just emerged from the forest.

Damianos's signaller answered, the "all clear" and his stichos began to marching back, singing as they marched. Hesiod ran out of his office and called for the report. He gave a sharp command, and the duty detail ran to open the gate.

"There's another two that never stop boasting about you and will be sad to see you go." Aeton said, meaning Damianos and Hesiod.

Their men had already joined with Hakeem's men in helping build a wooden temple when the two other dekadarchoi approached Hakeem, to ask to be trained.

They were hesitant, anxious about how Hakeem would react.

And what did Hakeem do? All he did was to clasp them both firmly in a warm handshake. "Well, I won't pretend you won't be most welcome!" It was exactly the right thing to say.

Some of the town's folk had already been waiting for the returning patrol, and more were hurrying to cheer them in. The town's folk loved their soldiers.

The help they gave was deeply appreciated and they always had plenty of money to spend in town. Every single one was meticulously polite around the town's folk, especially women.

Hakeem had had to talk to only a small handful, and being Hakeem, he only had to do it once.

Their good behaviour was unusual in a group of soldiers brought from outside a region. The soldiers knew now what it was like to be loved and admired rather than hated and feared by those they were supposed to protect.

There was more than one wife and sweetheart in the enthusiastic crowd.

As they approached, each of the warriors looked smart with their new leather armour. Each carried the powerful composite war-bows and short Greek swords that had become the standard armament at the fort.

They marched proudly, their eyes fixed ahead, pretending they weren't pleased with the reception.

They had been brought up to full strength and another file was to be added soon. They each had their own full blood elf scouts. Now men were asking to come to the fort.

"You will have to go around and say goodbye properly now."

"Hemera!" Hakeem said in alarm.

"She knows," Aeton said, giving the men a salute as they marched smartly in. "She saw the courier and was one of the first to come and ask. What will you do about her?" he asked, hiding a smile.

Hakeem looked discomforted and blushed. "I think she and the other women will be alright now. They have the trading post and the guest house and the laundry business to the fort, some of the women are even getting married. That they see life can be good again warms my heart more than I can say." His eyes became moist.

"They are very grateful to you," Aeton said. Hakeem had spent his own money helping the women he had rescued.

"Hemera thinks she owes me something, but she doesn't! She was my responsibility. All the women were, but especially her and her sister. I'm just glad they don't hate me, especially Artemisia." He chuckled a little. "You know, they seem to think it is *me* that can't manage on my own. They all want to cook and sew and do things for me. I can sew myself." (Hakeem deliberately didn't mention his cooking.)

He had met Hemera and her sister Artemisia during his very first raid. The first raid was not the most difficult one, but Hakeem and all his men still remembered it vividly, even now.

* * *

"Every second man should rest," Elwan had murmured ...

Hakeem knew Elwan enough to know he was nervous. It was their first raid. None of their men would ever match an elf, yet by human standards their stichos was already silent and deadly in the forest. Within twelve moons they would have something quite remarkable with this group.

Elwan's name meant "elf friend" in the old elf tongue. The stichos had called themselves 'the Elf Friends' and now it was time to show they were worthy of that title!

Hakeem and Elwan's men were spying the camp of the same group that had killed their last file leader and several others. If Elwan was satisfied that their small force could attack with an overwhelming advantage, they would. If not, they would quietly leave, and think of something else. Hakeem and Elwan suspected they would have their chance after the moon rose.

There was more than a score of bandit warriors, but they hadn't detected Hakeem's soldiers. Hakeem settled comfortably to observe the mountain cabins the bandits operated out of. They seemed confident and made no attempt to hide their coming and goings or the change of their guards. He was getting an idea as to who was in what cottage.

Most of the men stayed outdoors gathered around a great open fire to cook and talk and drink. The sound of their laughter echoed back to the silent, grim, men watching.

One of them began to sing a song in one of the native dialects, and many of the others joined in. It was a light jaunty tune and from the reaction of the audience, Hakeem knew it was almost certainly rude. They would have a couple of turns of the glass before the moon would be well risen, then Hakeem and his men would attack.

Hakeem and Elwan had taught the men to all aim their bows like true warriors. A hunter sights their bow along the arrow and then makes allowance for distance or wind. This is too clumsy to be used for a moving target or rapid fire and it completely useless on the back of a galloping horse or in poor light.

An archer training for battle must learn to aim a bow like he would aim a rock for throwing. Someone experienced with throwing rocks looks at a point and then hits it with the rock. He doesn't try to sight along the rock. That's because he can judge the weight of the rock and the distance, and knows that if he uses his body in a certain way, which way the rock will go.

An archer training for battle must learn when he holds the bow a certain way and draws it with a certain force at a certain distance, where the arrow will go. He hits targets just by looking at the spot where he wants the arrow to go.

They had all trained at this and Elwan had taught them how to shoot arrows in darkness when all they could see was the target. Just look at the target and the training takes over.

Once the moon rose. The bandits would not be ready for the attack. They would be outlined against the fire, and the bandit's night vision would be ruined. What was coming should be a one-sided fight.

Hakeem had made it *very* clear to his men that any women and children were not to be touched unless they made a credible attack with a weapon. There were four women and two children. Two of the women were unkempt, miserable creatures, little better than slaves.

As he waited, Hakeem found himself willing the bandits to drink more; they didn't seem to add water to their wine and the party was getting louder. One of the men tried to grab one of the women Hakeem had decided were slaves. She squealed as she escaped, much to the amusement of the bandit men. One of the other women who was better dressed looked cross but she didn't say anything.

When the three quarter moon rose, Hakeem could have sworn half the night had passed in waiting but he knew it hadn't. They needed to wait just a bit longer ...

Elwan finally signalled to Hakeem and he carefully crawled over and they left to circle around for the guards. It was Hakeem's turn to show what he had learned. The remainder of the men waited, clutching their bows. If anything went wrong, the attack would be aborted.

There was no noise from the guards and Hakeem and Elwan carefully crept back to re-join the men.

At a gesture from Elwan, the men spread out to choose their targets.

* * *

The four women would never forget that night also. Two had been stolen from a local village and the two others were sisters, Artemisia and Hemera.

When Artemisia and Hemera were captured by the bandits, all their travelling companions killed, their safe, pampered, world as daughters of a wealthy merchant had come to an end. Hemera was almost sixteen and Artemisia was fourteen. It had been a brutal time, but they had survived, and they were more fortunate than the other two.

Hemera had been chosen by the leader and Artemisia by his second in command, Atys. They had a child each and loved their children. They had adapted themselves to their fate. That night, the new life the sisters had made for themselves also abruptly and violently came to an end.

Without warning, arrows began shooting out of the darkness and the men were running, crying and dying. It took moments to realise what was happening … they were under attack! The four women quickly grabbed the children and hid in the rough shack Amynta and Hêbê shared. They didn't know who was attacking the camp or why or what would happen to any women and small children.

The men of the camp were unprepared and surrounded on all sides. They wore no armour and most only carried their *xiphoi* (short swords). They couldn't see their attackers and could do little but cower under cover.

From inside the hut, the women could hear men screaming and shouting in pain and rage, , the "prrt" of short bows and the noise of the arrows finding targets.

Atys gave a mighty call to charge, and the women could hear the sound of running feet and the clash of weapons and yelling.

Then, for a time, there was silence.

They had managed to quiet the two children to sleep when they heard a loud voice giving orders in Greek and men calling out to each other. The attackers were systematically checking the camp. They were taking their time. They could hear a big man approaching the cottage. They would be found!

"Persus, stop!" their leader called out. "Women and children are hiding in there. Wait for me to come."

The two sisters, Artemisia and Hemera motioned for the others to be silent. Hearts racing, they moved to place themselves between the others and the door. They were allowed belt knives, they drew them and waited.

Then there was a gentle knock to the door. "Hello inside! Is any man in there with you?"

Hemera considered what to say and decided on the truth. "No, but who are you?"

"Soldiers from Malea, Lady. My name is Dekadarchos Hakeem. May I come in and talk to you?"

"You're going to anyway."

"That is true." As the door opened cautiously, by the light of the campfire they could make out the shadowy outline of a bearded face, which peered tentatively from cover. When he was satisfied, the soldier moved slowly and cautiously into the doorway, crouched behind his shield as he scanned for enemies. He braced himself as he pushed the door flat against the wall with his hand. Then he stealthily moved in, checking each corner for signs of ambush. Satisfied, he left his shield by the door.

"What is going to happen to us?" Artemisia asked, her voice quivering, as the man carefully inspected them and the hut.

"If you cooperate with us, nothing bad, I promise. You and your children are under my protection. Please put your knives away."

Behind the big man, another brought a lamp. They saw in surprise that the new man was an elf.

"Elwan, let the men know we will be staying here tonight. Secure the camp and set watches. I want a guard sleeping outside this door, someone you trust." He turned to the women, "If you have any wants, let him know, but wake him gently."

"What happened to Atys?" Artemisia asked her voice flat, and face expressionless; she knew the answer. Hemera placed a hand on her sister's shoulder.

"A bandit? I'm sorry Lady, they are all dead."

Artemisia held herself stiffly in Hemera's arms, the tears would come later.

"I am sorry for your losses, even though I ..." His words hung awkwardly.

"My sister loved her man," Hemera looked at the large man in the light of the lamp. "But you will find the rest of us shed few tears for these men."

"Then glad I am that I could rescue you." He said. "I will see that you are united with your families and will give you all the assistance you need."

"Are you making fun of us?"

The dekadarchos looked stunned.

"We have been gone for years. You know it is too late. How can you even talk of *families*? They will curse us, call us sluts. Our children will be called bastards. Most likely, they will beat us and cast us out! Better you had left us or killed us if you are going to send us to our families."

"A pox on your families then!" The man shouted. In an instant he became terrifying. His face was murderously angry in the shadowy light cast by the lamp. He looked around jerkily, his fists clenched, as if looking for something to strike. The children woke and began screaming.

With difficulty he calmed himself and lowered his voice.

"I apologise, Ladies. My anger is not with you or your children. You must think me a fool. I had an *unusual* upbringing." He sighed heavily, blushing deeply. "I should know. I do know … that it is the way, even amongst my own people. If you allow, I vow to do all in my power to help."

"Why?" Hemera asked, taken aback.

The man drew himself up stiffly. "I killed your men. Your family will not help. I am honour-bound, of course," he said indignantly. "I will not fail you."

Hemera was too surprised to reply, but as she looked closer in the light of the lamp and it came to her. The sergeant was dressed as a Greek but he was a Shantawi!

She had heard of their obsession with honour. In a happier time, she would refuse his help, but pride was something she had long forgotten.

"How many of men have you, Sergeant?"

"I have eleven men, Lady. We are fortunate to have taken no casualties."

"Eleven men!" Hemera was incredulous. "There were twenty five of them."

"Yes ma'am, I know. Please stay in here for your own protection till the morning. We will be making a late start after breakfasting." With that, he turned and was gone.

* * *

Hakeem's men also would never forget that night.

It had been decided by Hakeem and Elwan that they would spend the night at the bandit camp rather than moving through the forest in the dark with women and children and plunder.

The main group was in the next cabin congratulating each other. Two of the men were sharing out the remains of the bandit's food. Isokrates's was counting the coins the men had found. His eyes were sparkling in the lamp light, as he arranged the money into neat piles. It was a fortune and there was a lot of other plunder ... wagons, animals and kit.

"It is so much money!" Isokrates said breathlessly as he counted.

"And there are women next door as well." Nikodemos nodded with approval.

"No one will touch those women," Hakeem said loudly from behind. He had appeared suddenly behind Nikodemos.

"They are bandit's whores! What does it matter? And why do we have to divide this money up with the others at the fort?" Nikodemos complained, twisting around.

"Nikodemos, do you have any complaints about my leadership so far?" Hakeem asked softly.

He stepped back and crouched a little, ready. His eyes were cold, carefully watching the man.

"No sir!" A thoroughly frightened Nikodemos replied loudly, springing to attention.

"Good," Hakeem smiled, straightening up, but the smile didn't touch his eyes. "You all will do exactly as I say. I hope to make you rich, but this is not why we are here. Remember, this and you'll get on fine with me."

He gestured to the pile. "Now, isn't it good of these nice bandits to put all their loot together so we can take it from them?"

The other men laughed a bit shakily, grateful to break the tension.

"If those women are whores, which I doubt, you will have more than enough money to afford whores, but when you get back to town, not here, and not when you are on duty." He looked around the room balefully searching for dissent. "Or you can try your charm, but all of you will treat *all* women, whether they are whores or not, whether in the hills or in the town, *properly*." He paused "Am I understood?"

Everyone rose to attention, shouting loudly, "Yes sir!" in unison.

Hakeem turned his back and went to check the sentries.

Isokrates smiled at Nikodemos who looked thoroughly chastened.

"Careful around Hakeem, you know what he's like!"

Nikodemos had nodded ruefully.

Hakeem had done more than his share of the fighting. He had silently killed both the bandit sentries. He had shot three or perhaps more, and killed three others quickly and efficiently in the brief hand to hand fighting.

That was more than enough to make them fear him, if they didn't already but what had happened next, none of them would ever forget.

Hakeem hadn't allowed any to surrender and then, without hesitation or any obvious concern, he had efficiently and mercilessly went from one of the bandit wounded that had survived to the next.

Now Hakeem left the hut to check on Persus who was on sentry duty. The young man was hidden in the shadow, staring out into the night.

"Are you all right?" Hakeem asked Persus gently. He was said to have had a Persian grandfather, hence his name. He was Hakeem's age and almost as big. He would make a good sergeant one day.

Persus looked back at him. His eyes had a haunted look.

"I couldn't do that, what you did. Will it always be like that?"

"Persus, you did fine," Hakeem said earnestly. "It was my decision not to take prisoners. I was happy to take care of it myself."

"Take *care* of it?" Persus shuddered. "How can you talk like that?"

Hakeem sat in silence for a long time till Persus thought he wasn't going to answer.

"Persus, what would happen to any that we took as a prisoner?" he asked softly.

Persus let out a big breath and grinned at his own foolishness. "They would hang," he admitted.

Hakeem nodded. "There are two reasons to capture bandits. One is to get information through torture. We have Elwan, and I won't allow torture.

"The second reason is entertainment. It entertains people to watch criminals be judged and condemned and then hung. The bandits might face their deaths with courage and defiance or not, but in the end everyone will see their lifeless bodies on the scaffold, and know all of their bravado was futile. It makes the judges feel important and powerful. They are treated like trophies.

"Keeping a wounded bandit alive just to hang him as soon as he can stand is not a kindness, and I won't pretend it is. I won't pretend there is less blood on my hands if I bring a man for someone else to kill.

"I won't *play* with men … *bandits or no.*

"I know how to make it quick. No, it was better for them."

He looked at Persus, his face and voice expressionless.

"If there was any chance for them, I wouldn't have done it, but once we fought them, the decision was already made. I do my own killing, Persus."

"I suppose you are used to it by now."

"I have only killed animals before tonight, Persus." Hakeem shrugged. "Now Elwan and I are going to scout around. When we return, we say 'elf' and you say 'friend' and please try not to kill us, if you can."

Persus tried to summon a weak chuckle. "I suppose it's what they deserved."

Hakeem paused. "Deserve? I don't know what they deserved, because I don't know their story. Judging them is not our job. Bandits kill and steal and rape. Our job is to stop that, and so we did."

He gestured out to where the pile of bodies was, a little away from the encampment.

Persus looked back at Hakeem as he moved away. Hakeem could not be faulted for the care, even the love he showed to his men, and yet he could be absolutely terrifying.

* * *

Aeton watched his friend lost in thought. "Hemera and the other girls have sent an invitation for you to go to their house for dinner," Aeton said, carefully watching Hakeem's reaction. "They were very specific. You are to come by yourself."

"Don't look at me!" Aeton laughed as Hakeem's looked at him with panic in his eyes. "It's just women! Surely you don't need someone along to protect you."

"No," Hakeem said, laughing weakly. "Of course not."

Hemera, by tacit agreement, was 'off limits' while Hakeem was around. Hakeem probably had never realised it.

Aeton would be one of the first to go calling on Hemera, once Hakeem had left.

It was sometimes easy to forget Hakeem was still so young and he had been raised well away from women. Aeton was fairly sure that all the women had given up on Hakeem by now, but they were all very fond of the shy young man. They would definitely wish to say goodbye and they were not above teasing him while they still had the chance.

* * *

The events of the time in Malea already seemed so long ago. Hakeem's friendship with the elf went beyond anything Hakeem had ever experienced, and now he would not see him in this life again.

Chapter 6: Conducting a War, and Summoned Home

After their catastrophic defeat at Pergamon, a serious blow had been struck against Troian strength. Troia had conquests and numerous satellite holdings which now stood vulnerable. Many of the nearby smaller holdings were keen to pledge loyalty to Helios.

Helios's plan was simple: push his advantage rapidly. He didn't expect to be able to successfully hold large tracts of Troian territory or besiege her strong points. He would push the Troians as far as he could, and then offer them a generous peace. This would be a peace he hoped they would feel honour-bound to accept without the sort of bitterness that would trigger endless wars. For Helios, there was more profit in peace with Troia than in a war.

To fight a war and show mercy changed greatly the way the war was fought and paid for. Most kings can only afford a small standing force of professional soldiers.

A militia could be raised for defence, but the simplest way to pay a large attacking force is through plunder and extortion. Using plunder, money from selling slaves and also drafting peasants from villages to fight, a conqueror can raise an enormous army.

As he shows success, others join from near and far for a share in the booty. A victorious army can become like a landslide. It gathers men and wealth as it travels, unless the defenders can somehow stop them or start to make the victories costly.

If Helios wanted to preserve and liberate what he had conquered, his campaign could soon exceed his resources. If his men thought they wouldn't be paid, his army would simply fall apart.

Except that the Troians had not shown a light touch on those they conquered. They had maintained control with their formidable army. Once the army was defeated, what the Troians believed was a fledgling empire fell apart with terrifying speed.

Helios was seen as a liberator and the oppressed gave whatever they could to help his campaign. Many cities and towns fell without a fight, joining Helios and his allies. New allies joined to regain land, to seek revenge, or to end the menace of Troia, so they did not need to be paid.

His army was able to reclaim the plunder that the Troians had accumulated, and there was wealth for all without sacking those he hoped would become friends.

He could pay for supplies and didn't have to strip the countryside bare. By the time Helios entered the Troad, he rode at the head of a large force and the Troians were in complete disarray.

Samit had taken over the command of the army from Evagoras. Hakeem became Captain of the Royal guard, which was not just a great honour. It was a great opportunity.

He got to work with Samit, Helios and their advisers. He learned about armies, morale, money, logistics, intelligence-gathering, strategy, momentum and the diplomacy that made up such a campaign.

He learned how to take a stronghold without a fight or with minimum loss of men. He learned the strategies of surrounding and neutralising a strongly held position, or outflanking a defence. He had access to libraries and maps of old campaigns.

Hakeem loved to learn and had a natural grasp of anything military. Helios found him a valued aide, despite his youth.

After the declaration of peace, Hakeem was sent as the military advisor accompanying the ambassador to the Troian court. He continued to learn more of the complex strategy and politics that brought the miracle of peace to the troubled region.

Hakeem would have liked to be able to make even a brief trip to bring the news of Elwan's death to his family. As Elwan's blood brother, he had a sworn duty to make sure Elwan's wife and daughter were cared for. He had met them on visits to his friend's home, and while he had written to them, he longed to see them again.

It was eighteen moons after his friend's death before Hakeem was able to travel. He received a formal summons to appear before the new Grand Abbot in Karsh, Father Maluch. Omar, the abbot of the nearest chapterhouse, also requested to meet with him for some unknown reason.

A summons from the Grand Abbot could not be ignored, and this time King Helios and Samit ordered him to go. He was put on leave for a year and Helios proclaimed he would be promoted to the *taxisarchos* (commander) in charge of the Shantawi and allied mercenaries on his return.

Chapter 7: A Reluctant Princess, a Coming of Age, and Leaving Elgard

Elana slammed the door, threw herself on her bed and wept. The pain was almost physical.

The door was opened tentatively by her maid, but before Iona asked anything, Elana yelled, "Leave me!" and buried her face deeper into her pillow. She mustn't let anyone else know they had gotten to her.

Elana, soon to be of age, was a princess of the fabulously wealthy kingdom of the Eastern Elves. She was her father's heir, destined to be a queen. She was mentioned in the ancient Elvish Prophecy as the one who would be a great queen and destined to give birth to a daughter who would lead a resurgence of elvish power.

She could look out of her window and see the richness of her lands and the majesty of the vast city-fortress. She could wander the palace and see the exquisite tapestries, the mosaics, the huge gilded statues and rich decorations. She could see the halls thronged with richly clad elves: merchants, servants, soldiers and dignitaries. She was born into almost unimaginable wealth and power.

And yet she was so desperately unhappy. She must not let her stepmother know the poisoned words had found their mark, it would give the Queen another way to hurt her.

The feeling came over her again. It felt she was drowning in shame and anguish. The intensity, she knew, was a memory of how her stepmother had hurt her when she was so little and helpless.

She was an adult now, she had been taught that every time she faced the feelings and defeated them, she got stronger. She knew all that, but still she struggled with the power of her stepmother to give her pain.

All she could do for the moment was grit her teeth and wait for the feeling to pass, like a great wave, as she knew it would. She was no longer a small elf-child of four, she was no longer so vulnerable, but still, by the Great Mother, it hurt.

She had overheard, as she was supposed to overhear, her stepmother saying to her friends that she had the body of a boy.

Xanthe gleefully said that if she wasn't the Princess, no man would be interested in her. It was exactly what Elana feared and she burned with shame.

Some said Elana looked more like her mother as she grew, yet Elana knew she would never be as beautiful as her mother. She had heard so many stories about how beautiful and loving her mother, Hera, was.

It was Elana who had killed her.

Elana was only six when Xanthe had told her. She remembered not knowing where to run or where to hide. Xanthe said her father hated her because she had killed her mother.

And Xanthe was so hard and cold when she said it!

At the time, the small girl, Elana, had thought she deserved such horrible treatment. Now she realised Xanthe had plotted to do it in this way and had chosen her moment when she could hurt her little stepdaughter the most.

Her mother had wanted to give her husband, King Cyron, a child, but Hera had a weakness of the heart. Her healers advised her it would be very dangerous, as elves are wise in such matters. They wanted to give her medicine to prevent this, but Hera, named after the beautiful Goddess, Queen of Heaven, would not hear of such a thing.

As her pregnancy progressed, it became obvious that her life was in serious peril but by that stage the pregnancy was advanced. She refused to end her pregnancy and kill the baby she felt quicken inside her. Hera died giving birth to Elana.

Hera, known for her beauty and loving nature, gave her life for the child she bore.

Perhaps finding out she killed her mother was worse, if anything *could* be worse, than when Elana first met her father.

From small, Elana knew her father didn't like her, but never knew why.

Her earliest memories were from when she was four. She knew that she had no mother, and her father had never seen her, not even once. He did not live at Elgard then.

She was told he was busy extending his kingdom, but she also heard he visited the city several times but had never come to see his daughter. She knew that there was something shameful about having a father who didn't want to see you. As a small child, she only knew she was bad, but she never knew why.

Her father had only one living relative, his half-brother who was a soldier and had never married, so she was alone in the royal quarters and was raised by servants. Ailya, the servant in charge of the little princess, was the closest she had to a parent. All the servants doted on her, she loved them, and she was happy for a while.

The memory of the return of her father was burnt like a wound deep in her soul.

She was playing hide and seek, she remembered, with one of her favourite young maids. She couldn't remember much else about the maid as she never saw her again.

They were both laughing and running around excitedly. The maid was calling her by her pet name, "Elly the eel" … she remembered that. She was called that because they said she was quick and cunning in chasing games, even for a small girl-elf.

Out of nowhere, a great angry warrior came in bronze armour. Only later, Elana guessed he had come to her quarters unannounced. Everyone stopped whatever they were doing, frozen, and bowed to the King in fear.

To the four year old girl, he looked huge. She remembered she was so frightened it took her a few moments to remember the King was also her father … she knew that.

He was in such a rage! He shouted something about "princess" and her "being his daughter." He said something about how he wanted her treated, she remembered that. She thought her father would hit the maid she loved.

The maid had thrown herself trembling at the King's feet. Elana felt it *she* who was wrong, yet it was the maid who was going to be punished. Was it her playing and making noise? Was the maid supposed to stop her?

She was overcome with terror, unable to move. When he turned his anger on Ailya she wanted to run to Ailya's defence, this was her Ailya! To her abiding shame, she ran to her room and hid behind a couch.

Eventually a shadow appeared at the door. The King came to the doorway. She cringed away, behind the couch up against the wall. Cyron didn't enter; he just stood at the doorway and measured her with his piercing eyes.

"Well daughter, have you grown so wild you have no greeting for your father?"

She thought he would come in and hit her then, and her heart was racing.

"No words for me, I see," he said. "Not much of a homecoming then."

She had felt like begging and begging, "please tell me what I have done wrong!" but he turned his back and walked away.

It was only later that the little child understood. As Elana thought back now, she felt the drowning wave of shame and anguish at the thoughts of that small child.

The King didn't love her. Elana knew she was bad in some way. He was angry at anyone else who loved her. That was the reason.

He was forbidding the maids to love her.

From that day on, most became aloof and formal. There were still some, those closest to her, who were brave enough to love her and she loved them in return, but the little girl understood now, it had to be a secret.

In public, she had to seem aloof and they too had to act their part. Only in private could they show their feelings. Elana had learned that a princess, even a very small one, had to hide her feelings.

The next day she was summoned to her father's presence. She had to wear her best dress which was a light blue. Her soft yellow hair was brushed and brushed till it was silky and glistened. Everyone had told her that her hair was her best feature. She remembered it was tied with a gold bow at the back, and she was allowed to wear the small silver elf-tiara that was one of her favourites.

She had to enter and curtsy and murmur "my King" and not look up till spoken to.

She remembered there was a strange dark haired woman sitting next to the King. She was in a beautiful dress, with lots of jewels. The woman held a small bundle wrapped in a blanket, and behind them stood a dark haired boy-elf about eleven or twelve. She had never seen dark haired elves before and she stared at them before she realised she was being rude.

That was the day she met her stepmother, Xanthe and Xanthe's son, Nikan.

"Are you well daughter?" the King asked. Elana was too frightened to speak. Beside, she didn't know what the question meant. She later found out it was a meaningless question that adults asked of each other, and she was supposed to say that she was 'well'.

As the time stretched, she heard her new stepmother sneer. "What a stupid child!" and the boy standing behind their chairs sniggered. She felt then what was to become a very familiar wave of shame.

"This is your new mother," the King said. Elana didn't know what to do, so she curtsied to Xanthe and bowed her head.

"We are coming to live here in the Palace."

"Does that mean I have to go away, now?" the little girl asked, frightened by the idea. She knew her father didn't like to be near her.

"What a silly question," she heard Xanthe say. "I told you she was stupid."

Elana managed to look up at the King, despite her fear. "My King, can Ailya come to live with me when I have to go, so I won't be so lonely?"

Cyron never answered her and Xanthe ordered her led away. She remembered seeing Nikan glaring at her, with a sneer on his face.

Now Elana was almost eighteen and she felt again the shame of that small child, but now she felt pity for that little girl who was also her and, not for the first time, she felt anger.

She knelt and said a prayer to the Great Earth Mother, Erya for strength. After that she felt better and managed to assume her cool, haughty mask enough to call for her servant, Iona.

"I heard what they said," said the young girl, bustling in with water for Elana to wash her face. "It's horrible and it's not true! You're beautiful! You don't look like a boy at all! There's nothing wrong with your breasts, you are tall and slim, and that's all. They shouldn't be so mean to you all the time, it's not fair!" she said indignantly and breathlessly.

"Well, I thank you." Elana was amused despite herself, for all Iona's opinion was worth. Yet somehow the silly girl helped her feel better.

Ailya, Elana's nursemaid and governess was dead these last two years. Elana's stepmother, Xanthe, had deliberately given her Iona, who no one listened to and was known to be inept.

Elana was determined to be forbearing with the girl. She would prove Xanthe wrong! Besides, she had no need for more people to dislike her, even if it was only a silly and clumsy servant.

Elana couldn't help but smile back at her maid. She certainly couldn't fault Iona over loyalty. And she could be company, whatever her other faults, and often helped cheer her up.

She knew that was what others would say. What a princess she was! She was so friendless that she valued the company of servants.

Her father, when he returned, had brought Xanthe, a widow. His marriage to Xanthe had brought the last of the Eastern Elvish land's under his control and a duchy that gave him open access to the Black Sea. Xanthe and Cyron did not seem to love each other. Elana as a child assumed this was normal in a marriage.

Xanthe also brought Nikan, her son. Elana shuddered as her thoughts turned to Nikan. Cyron wanted a son and was pleased to at least have a stepson. Nikan was clever enough to know how to flatter and impress the King.

But it was the small bundle in a blanket that her stepmother carried that was to capture Elana's heart more than she could ever have imagined. No one bothered to tell her what it was. She remembered her sense of awe as the maids introduced her for the first time to her new baby half-sister, Seléne.

Seléne was tiny and perfect. She was fair, like every elf-child, but had dark hair, unusual in an Eastern Elf. The newest Princess of the Eastern Elves was busily engaged in sucking her thumb and as Elana looked down at her baby sister in wonder, the tiny little princess looked back and smiled at her.

Xanthe was not interested in being a mother of small girls. She preferred parties, gossip and all the frivolous trimmings of royal life, but Elana had found someone who she was allowed to love.

She spent every moment she could with her sister; she loved her, she protected her, and she told her over and over that she was pretty, that she was smart and that she was, above all else, a good girl and that everyone loved her.

Elana never wanted Seléne to feel the way she felt.

Elana smiled to herself as she cleaned herself up and her thoughts turned to Seléne. If it weren't for her sister, she didn't know how she would have survived! Dear Seléne!

Elana was the substitute mother for her half-sister, more than four years younger. They were sisters and best friends. Seléne always seemed more confident and outgoing even though she was younger. It was Seléne who gathered around her a small group of true friends.

The control always seemed tighter on Elana. She was required to learn music instruments, elf history, languages and etiquette. They controlled who could be her friends; after all she would be the Queen one day!

Elana felt that was only an excuse to make her life miserable. The only true friends Elana could have were Seléne's.

Elana would so often come to her sister, down and dispirited. Soon they were both in hysterics over Seléne's imitations of the members of the court.

Dark of hair, as Elana was fair; Seléne would be shorter and fuller when she grew into womanhood. She was just fourteen and already fuller in the important area of breasts, which her lanky sister was so lacking in.

Seléne was the best thing that her stepmother and father brought. For all that happened, after Xanthe and Cyron and Nikan came, she could not say she regretted their coming … because they brought Seléne.

Elana, as she got ready, thought of her stepmother. It took a long time for her to understand Xanthe and how subtle she could be. Elana felt inherently full of shame. Xanthe merely confirmed her shame and pretended to be forbearing of the hopeless stepdaughter she was burdened with.

She never seemed to tire of telling her friends and Elana how awkward, ugly and stupid she was. Elana, back then, thought Xanthe was showing good-natured tolerance towards her.

One day, Xanthe over-played her hand. While Ailya was away, Elana was so pleased to hear from Xanthe that there was to be a children's fancy dress party. Xanthe even supplied her with a village girl costume! When she arrived in excited anticipation, she walked in to find herself in a grand function and Xanthe was ready to pounce. She claimed she had told Elana the child's party was cancelled. She said Elana looked so cute and insisted on parading her around in front of the guests, while Elana, in anguish and shame, was completely humiliated.

But Elana's memory was better than that. She was perplexed, she couldn't resolve it with Xanthe, who seemed to delight in the 'silly' girl's mistake. Finally a maid told Elana there was never any plans for a children's party. Elana didn't have to be told to keep *that* a secret.

Elana realised then that it was fortunate that her father insisted Ailya remained in charge of her care. Behind the scenes, Xanthe would have given her unfashionable clothes, incompetent maids and stupid tutors. She realised her 'friends', the children of Xanthe's friends that Xanthe had chosen for her, were secretly taught to despise her, and her stepmother who pretended to be her friend, was really her enemy.

It was a very subtle game they all played and it took Elana a while to understand how it was possible for Xanthe to hate her so much and why. Xanthe doted on her son Nikan, who could do no wrong. She planned to have Nikan as king. But what was she to do with her stepdaughter, who was named the heir?

Elana had one weapon and for a while, she used it. She was the Princess! She was the Heir! She was the One Foretold!

In the end, they could do nothing to this, or so she thought.

They tried to look down on her, but she could turn the disdain back on them. Pretending it didn't hurt, she withdrew behind her mask. She went through a period of being the spoilt princess, made worse by the deep unhappiness within.

Only a few knew Elana's arrogance was pretence, a weapon against her enemies.

Elana learned to become a player in the Queen's court with its diversions for the bored aristocracy. She even started to gain some of the other player's admiration, but in the end it felt shallow and pointless. For someone spending their whole life hoping for approval, it was a shock to find so many people whose approval she despised.

The more her father saw her spoilt behaviour, the more he disliked her, never for one minute suspecting his own role and he gave her no chance to join with him in the more serious business of the Court.

Elana didn't expect her father to like her. From very young, she became clever at avoiding him. She learned his habits, his visits on holy feast days. She knew when there would be small family dinners and she had found lots of secret hiding places. To her relief, she would hear Xanthe telling the maids not to bother, as they tried to look for her.

If she heard his voice, she would melt away. A few times she accidently walked in to catch her father enjoying spending time with Seléne, chatting with her, both of them smiling and laughing.

If she could, she would leave before she was noticed, otherwise her father and Seléne would both became stiff and awkward in her presence, and seem relieved when she left.

On the few occasions she met her father outside of formal occasions, he might ask her an awkward question about her studies or horse riding or archery which everyone knew she loved, but she had learned early how to give her father polite and meaningless replies.

Occasionally when she was riding or practicing her bow, she caught him staring at her from some distance. She didn't know why he would do something like that. Perhaps it was to make her feel uncomfortable.

Her father had most time for Nikan. Nikan knew how to flatter and impress his stepfather. Nikan was seven years older than Elana. He started out as a bully, and as his behaviour was tolerated, he transformed into a secret dark sadist, a young man who felt pleasure and arousal when he had others in his power, especially young girls.

Whenever he could, he made Elana's life miserable. When Elana was small, a maid had caught him trying to fondle her. Elana remembered being beside herself with shame and terror.

It was to Xanthe she tried to explain what happened, but was simply told not to be silly. Soon after, Nikan 'found' the maid 'stealing'. He was delighted to watch the maid get whipped and sent from the castle.

* * *

In a few weeks, now, it would be Elana's eighteenth birthday.

The very last thing she wanted was the sickening pretence of a celebration. She hoped Xanthe and her father would agree.

"No, child!" Xanthe smiled at her. Her stepmother seemed to be in a friendly mood at the mention of a grand ball. "You are the heir to a powerful kingdom. This is your coming of age! It is a big event and many important people will be called. Don't worry, Elana. I have a surprise for you."

Elana's confidants, Iona and Seléne, the maids she liked, all her tutors, Seléne's friends and even the Great Priestess of the temple would not agree with her. Not even one would support her. Of course her eighteenth had to be celebrated!

The palace was abuzz with excitement for weeks. Everyone wanted to be invited. Elana, at the very centre of it, felt sick in the stomach at the thought of it. She wished they would all go off and have their wonderful party without her.

But when a gown was sent to her from Xanthe, it was exquisite. It was red, the design was unfamiliar, but the quality was in no doubt.

Seléne and Iona confirmed how pretty she looked in it. Elana was surprised by the generosity, as she had received no new clothes since Ailya had died, and there was not much she had that she hadn't outgrown.

Perhaps Xanthe wanted her to look her best after all. She felt the beginning of excitement over the ball and hurried to thank Xanthe.

Xanthe was talking to Cyron. Cyron saw Elana uncharacteristically happy and was struck by the resemblance to Hera, but on this occasion it brought a smile to his lips. He looked forward to seeing her in whatever dress she seemed to be so excited about. Elana had grown into a beautiful woman, he realised.

On the afternoon of the celebration Elana, Seléne and two of Xanthe's nieces from Seléne's circle were getting themselves ready and doing Elana's hair. Iona hurried in looking very troubled.

The dress was Hera's!

Xanthe's maid was hurrying to tell Elana.

This was unbelievable! To give Elana a dead woman's dress! Not even a human peasant would wear a dead woman's dress under any circumstances, and this was such an important occasion.

How clever! Elana had no money till she was 18. She had no other dress suitable to wear, Xanthe had seen to that. She *couldn't* wear the only suitable dress she had.

Seléne was shocked and angry at her mother's wickedness. "What are you going to do?"

Elana felt elated and somehow dizzy. "Make sure that our 'mother' or her maid cannot pass a message to me without witnesses. I *will* wear the dress!"

Seléne and her friends were scandalised but excited. This would really blow up in the face of the Queen. Everyone knew the Queen had given Elana the dress.

The maid came in with an 'important message' while Elana was surrounded by the other girls. When Elana coldly demanded she pass the message in front of everyone, the maid turned and fled.

After a while, Xanthe herself came with demands to see Elana on her own.

Elana refused, there wasn't enough time to get ready as it was, and the other girls backed her up. If it was urgent, tell her now in front of everyone, or it could wait. Xanthe's bluster didn't work in getting Elana alone.

The banquet was laid, the guests all seated, and the time had come for her father and mother to lead her into the hall and present her as an adult. Cyron waited with a pale Xanthe. Elana swept into the hall, looking the image of Hera.

Elana came up to Cyron and offered a tentative smile. "Is something wrong Father? You surely must love the dress Mother gave me. Exquisite isn't it?"

"What is the meaning of this?" Cyron, demanded angrily.

"I tried to tell her," Xanthe started.

"What, Mother?" Elana enquired innocently.

"It's your mother's dress," Xanthe hissed, appalled.

"What! It's my mother's dress!" Elana shouted. "You make me wear a dead woman's dress to my coming of age?"

She made sure her voice would carry clearly into the large banquet hall just beyond them.

"You have given me no other clothes to wear. Is this another of your cruel jokes?" Elana demanded loudly.

Cyron tried to hush his daughter. "I was not aware of this," he said, looking furiously at Xanthe. Elana simply looked coldly at her father, her tone quieter, almost menacing. "And were you not, my Father? Ever have you raised a hand to protect me?"

Cyron looked abashed. "This is not the time, Elana. You will shame me in front of my guests."

"No, Father, you shame *me*. You let that slug try to rape me when I was seven, and what did you do? You made him your favourite and whipped the maid who protected me. You forced me to watch as I 'needed to learn how to dispense justice', or will you say that was Xanthe's idea, father?

"Oh of course, I dreamed all that up! Have you asked the maids? Have you asked my young cousin what he's like? For that matter, have you asked your own daughter, Seléne, what dear Nikan attempted to do to her?"

Xanthe tried to say, "Don't talk to your father like a spoilt child. You're a princess!"

"Thank you, Mother," Elana replied, starting to raise her voice again so she could be heard. "Remember the fancy dress you made me wear in front of everyone? There was never a plan to have a fancy dress party! It was another of your cruel tricks to make a small girl feel humiliated. You take every chance. You try every trick against me! When I got this lovely dress, I thought you had changed.

"To think I loved you once. Well, you planned this, so I will not be ashamed to wear this dress of my mother's. Let's meet our guests!"

She marched forward quickly, not waiting for them.

Protocol meant the parents must precede her and present her to the guests. By her being the last to enter, they gave her honour, on the occasion of her coming of age. Elana continued gracefully into the room without pause, and moved to stand waiting at the table of honour.

The guests were stunned. She was not announced. She had been tricked to wear the dress of a dead woman. This was unbelievable! She was the heir! This was a dreadful scandal!

Worse still, time stretched agonisingly as the audience waited for her parents to follow. The guests looked increasingly uncomfortable. A murmur started and was getting louder and louder. Why did they delay? What were they doing? Raised voices could be heard outside, arguing.

Elana stood by her chair waiting, impassively. Finally the royal couple entered stony faced, pointedly not looking at each other. Elana took a breath and her voice carried clearly across the great ball room.

"Ladies and gentlemen, I present to you the King and Queen!" she announced.

Everyone stood, though they should have stood for her.

"Well it seems I must announce myself. Thank you all for coming to this occasion of my coming of age. Let us begin," Elana concluded and, smiling serenely, she sat.

Her parents were not given the chance to introduce her. But for the moment, her parents were stunned speechless by what had happened. They couldn't do anything in front of the audience, lest they appear to argue in public.

The servants scurried to serve, the musicians tried their best, but the grand party could only regain a strained air.

Elana, looking radiant, sat at the head table, beside the discomforted king and queen. Elana was the perfect hostess, caring for the guests in any breaks, getting up to circulate and make small talk between the courses. The fact that she didn't eat a mouthful or drink even a sip of water was lost on no one. Only Seléne and her cousins knew they had smuggled fruit from the kitchen earlier.

Back at the table with her parents, she made no conversation. She had a fixed half smile on her lips. She sat there, staring ahead, beautiful and proud, like a queen, but it was as if she were a queen made of ice.

Once the last dessert was served, the speeches would be made, starting with her father. But as the desserts were still being put on the tables, Elana rose to her feet.

"Well, my parents may not wish to speak at this time, but I have an announcement. Today, I celebrate my coming of age. I must leave the court soon to take up residence on my mother's estate which I now inherit. The lodging will be modest, but for the first time, I will have an income."

There was a loud murmur. The estate was nowhere near suitable for a princess! Does she mean she has no allowance?

"It seems that my mother's clothes were preserved at her death, including this exquisite dress. I now realise how sensible this is in a case such as mine, as I have been given none other. I look forward to receiving the rest of her effects, as is my right. I apologise for wearing such a fine dress poorly. I have been told I am awkward and boyish."

Amongst the confusion, there were shouts of denial and Elana smiled warmly to each one.

"While I didn't know the origin of this dress before today, my parents did. It only confirms what they have said many times. I nonetheless, accept its ancient meaning."

There was a din of confused murmurings. What was this? Many were looking around puzzled.

The ancient High Priestess struggled to rise, a look of horror on her face. Suddenly it was very clear, to the old lady. "No! It was never your fault!" she shouted loudly, appalled.

"Dear Reverent Mother, I thank you for your kindness," Elana smiled at the old woman. "Please don't anyone be distressed. This is a burden that I long have carried. I will return to my parents the cost of raising me, as soon as I can afford to do so."

Her father stood up with a shout but Elana merely raised her hand and her voice rang out. "Please Father; it pains me to be reminded so, at this time, but let me answer while my courage lasts.

"And last, I am my father's heir.

"I know this has never been the wish of either my father or his wife. So let it not be so. In full honour in front of these witnesses, I release my father from this. Father, in front of these witnesses, name who you wish to be your heir. On my honour, I will abide by your wish."

Pandemonium broke out. Everyone was talking at once.

"It has to be you, because of the Prophecy," Cyron growled still standing, looking shocked.

"Dear Father," Elana laughed. "Is this not my second sin? I will make amends. Why, I only need be Queen for one hour. I will sign the papers now. You are free to choose."

Xanthe was whispering urgently. "No … not him," Cyron said irritably. He sat, as if tired. "….It will be… Elana." He said heavily.

Elana was stunned by her father's reply. She shook her head, bewildered, as people left their tables to gather around her jostling and shouting encouragement. The noise was rising to a tumult. She raised her hand again, drawing herself up to be every inch the princess she was.

"My friends, Lords and Ladies, I am touched by your confidence. This was not the outcome I expected, but I am no coward to avoid my duty to our people. My father is the greatest ruler of his time. I promise, you will never find his daughter lacking!"

Everyone stood clapping enthusiastically. By clapping harder they wanted to make up for how she had been just treated. When the applause died down, she smiled and surveyed the sea of faces.

"I'm sorry to bring such solemnity to such a joyous occasion. It is time to dance! Who will dance with me?" Behind her, her father started to get up but Elana never saw him. She pointed to the Persian ambassador "Mr Ambassador, you are a diplomat to say I am beautiful. For that, would you do me the honour of the first dance?" As she walked with him to the dance floor, she reached up and kissed him on the forehead.

Cyron plonked himself down, it was as if she slapped him in the face, but why would his daughter want to dance with him? He was stunned. On this one night he was faced with how cruel he had been.

Worse, he had left her at the mercy of Xanthe and Nikan. The intensity of their hostility to Elana would have been only too apparent, if he only cared to look.

He was a busy king and had reunited the ancient land of the Eastern Elves. So it was too easy to say he had no time to think about her. But he made time for Seléne, he had time for Nikan. He had time for his subjects, but not his eldest daughter, his heir.

He hadn't been able to reconcile his feelings towards Elana. It was simpler to blame her. Any prejudice was fed by subtle poison from Xanthe. He now presumed Xanthe had poisoned Elana against him. He had dismissed his wife as frivolous, but failed to see how devious she was. He looked to enemies beyond his borders, and neglected the state of his own house.

He only had himself to blame.

Now the party was in full swing and there was Elana, beautiful, gracious and glowing. He saw some of the quality he had been blind to. He saw his daughter, now a beautiful woman and yet a stranger. He was a great king, but suddenly he came face to face with an appalling folly.

Xanthe's clever scheme had blown up in her face. She sat and wondered how it could go so far wrong. It started as a clever trick to get Elana to wear an old and unsuitable dress. She remembered Elana coming almost pathetically grateful to thank her, but it was in front of Cyron. Poor foolish child! She was like a lamb to the slaughter, what chance did she have?

And now, Xanthe was publicly branded as wicked and spiteful to the heir and her influence would be seriously diminished. Her son's 'weakness' was revealed and Elana was reconfirmed as the future Queen. Surely Elana couldn't have done this knowingly?

But there was more to come, the ancient High Priestess limped painfully to their table. "Are you wicked? How could you do this?"

Xanthe was shocked to be spoken to like that. "I will do as I please!" she said, looking angrily at the old woman.

The old crone fixed her eye on the Queen. "So you admit it!"

Xanthe smiled and nodded; it was silly to deny it. She knew Cyron had kept much of Hera's clothes and possessions. There was a large portrait of Hera in that very dress in Cyron's study. It looked so much like Elana that it had given her the idea.

"I admit it, and I don't care."

"Do you not? You know she is the one foretold. You utter fool!" Xanthe was about to explode, but the priestess hadn't finished. "It was almost 1500 years ago when Penelope saw herself responsible for the death of her mother. On her coming of age, she wore her dead mother's dress, as a sign of her shame. She banished herself from the palace, renounced the right of being a daughter to her father, and repaid her father what he had spent raising her.

"You have tricked Elana into the same thing.

"You have shown to the world how you both have been treating Elana. You will divide our kingdom, one against the other. I warn you!" she said fixing Xanthe with an angry stare.

"She is favoured by the Goddess. For your own sake, do not dare to raise your hand against her. Elana may not return now until Cyron has died, but when she does, you as her accuser must be the one who is exiled. Didn't you think?"

Xanthe was aghast when the meaning sank home, but Cyron exploded loudly at his wife. "You evil woman, leave my sight! You have plotted against me and my heir. Leave now, before I strike you!"

The guests were caught frozen, half way through the celebrations, at his shout.

Elana herself paused, and then announced in her clear voice. "I'm sorry. It seems my celebration is doomed to be spoiled. I would have liked to have a little longer. After this, I am banished; didn't you know?

"My mother's death in childbirth is seen as my fault, so I was given my mother's dress to wear at my coming of age. I didn't know this was my mother's dress, but my parents did.

"I have to leave the palace till my father dies, and I have to return to him the cost of raising me. That's the great surprise they planned for my coming of age. I feel very sad, but I must accept such things.

"Best I go quickly. Sorry I won't see you again."

Elana turned and almost ran out, leaving everyone in confusion. Her guests stood in shock, horrified. It was impossible to believe what had been done to her, but they had all been witnesses.

Her father had no chance to talk to her.

From that moment Xanthe and Nikan were in disgrace.

* * *

If Elana was interested in power, she would have stayed. Instead, Elana made plans to leave the palace as soon as she could.

The quantity she would take, even with Hera's belongings, was pathetic. It was another sign of Cyron's shame. He tried to send gifts for her, but they were all returned. Nor would she take any expensive items of her mother's. She refused all other offers of help and was waiting for a motley escort from her mother's holdings. Before marriage, her mother had not been a rich woman. She decided to take Iona, the incompetent maid that had been foisted on her by Xanthe.

It was three days later when Cyron summoned his daughter. He had with him his half-brother, Hector. Hector was in command of the legions, the second most powerful man in the kingdom. He was a good part of the reason for Cyron's success.

Hector was also devoted to both of his nieces, and was one of Elana's greatest supporters, second only to Seléne.

"You wished to see me, my King!" she announced as she swept in. She was wearing a well-remembered dress of her mother's. Cyron felt a lurch as if in Hera's presence, but this 'Hera' was as cold as ice.

"What have you done to your beautiful hair?" he asked, shocked.

"Oh, my King, do you like it? I'm told by everyone that I look like a boy. I think you would have preferred a son, so I cut my hair to please you.

"It was an ancient custom for royals to cut their hair short at the loss of a King. While I never knew my mother, I can grieve the loss of both my parents now."

"Please sit." Cyron indicated the chair, not knowing how to respond.

"Why, I prefer to stand," Elana replied brightly. "What business do you have of me?"

"I thought we could talk." Cyron started.

"Well, that's nice. That's what we are doing now. When will we finish talking? I know you dislike my company, and I don't want to trouble you unnecessarily."

"Elana, I'm your father," Cyron tried to say.

"So you have called me to tell me that! Well, you said you regretted having me as your daughter. Do you think that Xanthe didn't delight in telling a small girl such deeply hurtful words? I suppose you want an apology. You know, I find it difficult to apologise for being born.

"At least, though, in this we agree. I'm sorry I'm your daughter too, but wait! Don't we forget? It is corrected! We can move on."

"Put that nonsense about not being my daughter aside."

"Nonsense is it?" Elana shouted. "I am publicly shamed at my coming of age. Don't say it was none of your doing! Mother dearest has never tired of quoting how often you have blamed me for my mother's death. Do you think she would have dared such a thing otherwise?

"I have accepted the punishment. Why a newborn baby, so young, to be condemned for murder! And my own mother, too, how black my crime, you are right to find me so disgusting.

"What do you want of me now, to go back on my sworn word? Great Holy Mother, do you never tire of humiliating me?"

"Elana, I've made an awful mistake." Cyron said.

"What a cruel trick you play. You wish to make this exile harder for me." Elana drew herself up and looked at him coldly, her eyes glittering with tears. "But somehow your words fail to touch me."

"Elana, I'm sorry!" Cyron cried out, clutching at his desk.

Elana looked at him coldly. "You can't be serious!"

"The other night, you looked so beautiful; you looked like your mother." His voice caught in his throat.

"I'm sorry to look like my mother. Xanthe told me it's another reason you hate me. But you see it's difficult, because I never met my mother. As for beautiful, I think we understand one another perfectly. I am an adult now, I don't appreciate lies."

"Don't call me a liar!" Cyron growled.

"Then don't lie." Elana's eyes flashed "My whole life you have avoided me, why the interest now when I'm leaving?"

Cyron bowed his head. He looked broken. For once he looked his age, tears started in his eyes. "I have a picture of her ... in that dress ... I've always loved it ... I loved her ... I can show you."

"Well! Good! Keep the picture then. You have made portraits of the others but none of me. That can be your portrait of me, old man.

"You won't see me again in this life. I will never let either you or your wife humiliate me again." She turned, a maiden made of ice. "Why did you call me here? Do you hate me so much that you won't let me be? Don't you understand you have won? You don't have me as a daughter. I will go away. I have offered to renounce all my inheritance." Tears began streaming down her cheeks.

"Elana, I am sorry, I've been wrong," Cyron pleaded.

"So what must I do now, feel sorry for you? Well, seeing you only gives me pain. I remember hurt on hurt. Did you know ... I once loved you both? What a fool I was, but of course I was only a small child.

"Now seeing you, being here, brings back to me all the pain you've caused. Did you know that the sight of you brings me pain? Did you not wish I was never born? Did you not hate me? Did you not blame me? And now you want me to feel sorry for you as well? May I go now?" She turned to leave.

"Elana, please don't go."

"No, King, as I will never call you Father again. Will only my death please you?

"Deny that you blamed me time after time for my mother's death. I can't see what I did, yet I was blamed. No matter, I wore my mother's dress at my coming of age, I accept the punishment. Don't ask me for pity as well. Just let me go." With that, she left.

"Well," Hector turned to his older half-brother, who was also his best friend. He was one of the few people who could criticise Cyron with impunity. "Don't say I didn't warn you again and again. She was such a sweet and trusting girl. I must say, you and your wife did some amazing work."

"Is it too late, do you think?" Cyron asked his friend.

"What, for you and her? For the sake of the Gods, she is a woman now! Do you wish to return milk that has spilt or repair a jug shattered into a hundred pieces?

"Is it too late for her? I believe deep down there remains still that lovely, trusting child that you and your wonderful wife have tried so hard to utterly destroy.

"But you haven't told her! She will find out from the wrong people, despite how secret you think it is."

Just as they were speaking, Elana was outside, finding out from the wrong people.

Xanthe and Nikan and some of their few remaining friends lay in wait for the princess as she left her audience with her father. "So what do you think?" Nikan asked with a nasty smile. Gone was even a superficial pretence of friendship.

Elana looked at him blankly. Nikan and Xanthe turned to each other with incredulous smiles "He hasn't told you, has he? This is so delicious!"

"Told me what?" Elana, confused, found herself surrounded by a circle of leering faces.

She had done great damage to them and Xanthe relished this chance at spite.

"Well, darling daughter. It's the moment you have waited for. At last, the Prophecy is invoked and you are to travel to meet the father of your child to be, the identity of this charming prince has been revealed."

Elana felt a lurch inside herself. She had somehow put the Prophecy out of her mind, there was no sign it was ever going to be fulfilled, yet this was the most important of all elvish prophecies.

As a child, she had dreamed of who her prince might be. He was to be a lost prince of the Western Empire. He was to be a great warrior. She and Seléne would often play a game describing what wonderful men they would save themselves for.

Now, ringed by the grinning faces of her worst enemies, she had an awful sinking feeling. She went pale and desperately steeled herself not to show a reaction. Then, they gave her the name.

It hit her like a blow. She barely prevented herself asking if it were true.

She managed to say levelly, "I see, thank you for telling me. Now, if you'll excuse me I mean to discuss this with my father." She tried to sound as if the news was only of mild interest, rather than being absolutely crushing.

Disappointed at her reaction, they nonetheless howled with laughter. It was going to happen to her and there was nothing she could do about it.

Hector heard the 'click, click' of her boots down the hall. Uh, oh, he thought. She was making a lot of noise for an elf walking. The door burst open. Elana was trembling with rage as she faced her father.

"I thought you could never humiliate me again. I was wrong! Now I'm eighteen, you send me off like a lump of meat. Djorn the Grey! I'm to be sent like a brood cow to become pregnant to a man almost three times my age. He has a wife, so I'm not to marry him and he's only a local landowner. Then I'm to return here to have the baby, to prove my shame to all.

"I am to be Queen and have no chance to hide my humiliation. You seek to totally destroy me, am I to be given no chance? I will be despised! You want my rule to fail!

"No one will marry me after that and then what? Am I to kill myself? Well, I won't give you that satisfaction. You were playing me before. I clearly underestimated the depth of your hatred. Why do you hate me so?

"Congratulations old man, I almost believed you."

Cyron could only shake his head helplessly. She spun on her heel and slammed the door.

Cyron was appalled, "She hates me!"

Hector paused before hurrying after his niece whom he loved. "Yes, she does hate you, my king and my brother. I think you have given her good cause.

"All I can say is she is good at it, don't you think?"

Hector had to make haste. He noticed with pride that Elana kept control as she marched to the privacy of her quarters. It seemed everyone knew what was happening, and was watching her intently.

Hector pushed past the maid who tried to bar him entry into Elana's private quarters. He called "Elana!" and she whirled to face him, her face white with fury. "You know it's not your father's doing. It was an event triggered by your coming of age," Hector started.

"Liar!" She screamed at him, beside herself with rage.

"Elana!" he called sharply. "Neither I nor your father are lying to you. Do you forget that I am your friend?"

Elana stopped, frozen, for an instant, then with an "Oh", her hard cold manner dissolved into tears.

Like a small child, she ran and flung herself into his arms. She clutched desperately at his shoulders and buried her face into his chest.

"Please, please, don't you hate me too, Uncle! Oh what am I to do?" He stood there and comforted the young girl. Her tears went on and on and he found himself crying too.

Always busy with the King's wars, Hector was named after the hero of the final desperate defence of Troia. He had never married, he had no children of his own, but he loved Elana and her sister Seléne deeply.

Unfortunately, he could not talk sense into Cyron who was mad with grief over the death of Hera. When news of Hera's death reached them, they were on campaign. Something in Cyron died that day.

Cyron buried himself in his work. He refused permission for Hera's room to be cleaned out. It became like a mausoleum. The first few times they returned to the palace, Cyron would sit there by himself for unknown hours. Hector once came in search of him in the middle of the night, to find him just sitting there in the dark, not making a sound.

Hector wondered about Xanthe. Her offer of a marriage of alliance was too good to refuse. She wanted to be Queen, and hoped her son could be the King. Did she come determined not to love Cyron, or was she given no chance?

Whenever Hector could, which was not often enough; he spent time with the two girls. He took Elana and Seléne camping, hunting, fishing and swimming. Whenever he visited, he brought presents, things little girls would love. Remembering all this, Elana knew that here was someone else who loved her.

Hector stayed with Elana until she was cried out and ready to sleep. He tucked her in her bed and kissed her. As he left, he saw Seléne waiting, distraught, outside Elana's room.

He hugged the young princess and murmured, "She's better than I would have thought, but she's sleeping. Her maid's with her. Don't let her be alone for the next few days."

Seléne guiltily told him about her complicity with Elana's plan. She and her friends had no idea all this would happen, it seemed a bit of a game.

Hector shook his head. "It's not your fault. She decided to fight back in the only way she could. It cost her dearly, but consider what she accomplished all in one stroke: Xanthe's power is all but broken. Nikan is revealed for the snake he always was. Your father has come to his senses, though far too late. She is seen as a brave heroine and has been confirmed as the future Queen.

"She's a lot smarter than most realise. She knew exactly what she was doing. Now, some empty-headed fools will despise her, for what her duty demands of her. I doubt she will ever be able to marry.

"She has been so strong for so long, now she has to face far worse. Those that really matter though, will see her as the princess who was given nothing, yet sacrificed everything. I think she will make a great, if somewhat tragic queen."

* * *

Elana conducted herself with formal dignity in the days before she was to depart. Now she would be travelling, not to her mother's home, but to the region of Anatolē adjoining the Black Sea. One day, she would be the Queen. She was determined to show herself to be worthy in every inch of her being.

She would have to face one of the worse humiliations a woman could be asked to undergo. Then she would have to return to the reactions of others. All that was left to her was to act in dignity.

Soon after she re-emerged, from her room that day, she was ambushed by Nikan. In front of an audience, he asked her what she intended to do. She looked at him coldly and spoke loudly and firmly. "Are you simple? I will do whatever is required of me for the good of my people."

Before she left, she had to attend an official dinner, held in honour of the event, where the High Astrologer would announce his findings. When she came in and tried to sit at one of the lesser tables, her father himself came down to shepherd her to a seat at his right hand.

When she hesitated, he asked, "Do I have to beg?" He even got a small smile. "No, my Lord, at least not in front of all these people." She paused. "You meant what you said?" The king nodded. She felt a little better.

Unfortunately, she had also meant what she had said to him.

Cyron gave a speech, publicly admitting she was blameless, and saying she must always be treated as his heir and his daughter, no matter what she said. He couldn't prevent eventual self-imposed exile, but she had agreed to return whenever the kingdom needed her.

Public sympathy for the princess was intense. Elana was surprised at the number who gathered to offer support. Some she didn't know, for most it seemed heartfelt.

She was grateful, but a bit shy and surprised, that so many thought well of her. Some she was more cautious of, such as past members of her stepmother's court, who were rapidly distancing themselves from Xanthe. But to all, she was perfectly gracious and polite.

Chapter 8: A Man of Integrity, Girl-Talk, and a Loving Family

Elana decided to depart almost immediately. It was too early for a pleasant journey, but she couldn't face putting it off.

Also, to fulfil the timing of the Prophecy, she needed to have her daughter in her arms and present at the palace by a certain date. She didn't want to take any chances.

So they had already crossed the snow-clogged mountains too early in the season, enduring snow storms so fierce that even a party of elves, even well provisioned, felt chilled and miserable.

Now they were making their way west, deeper into the north eastern corner of Anatolē, in the beautiful area just south of the sea coast. The Black Sea region of Anatolē is known for its stunning beauty, a region of charming mountain scenery, lush green forests, bays and rivers and waterfalls.

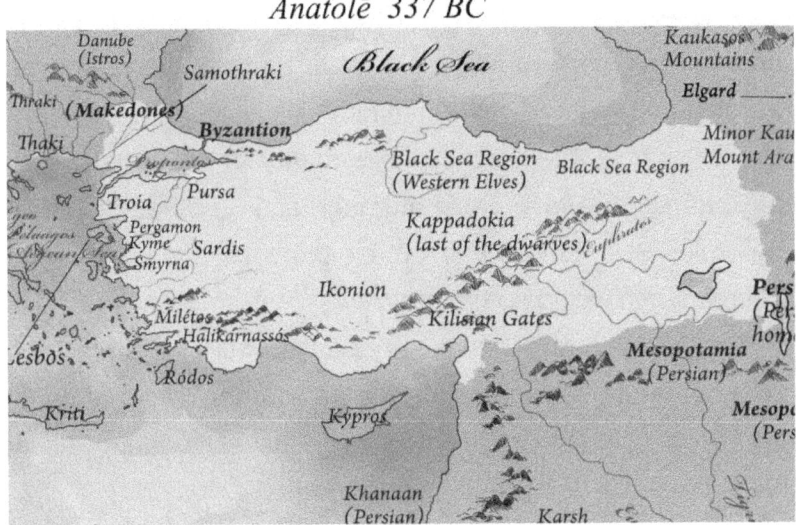

Anatolē 337 BC

Except in winter.

The rain kept up day after day. It trickled down the neck of her coat. Nothing would dry. Even the elves had trouble lighting a fire. Many times, the travellers had to climb off to lead the horses, struggling through the mud and slush.

Even going to relieve herself would leave her feeling like a cold, bedraggled rat.

Elana was sick of it all, sick of the smell of wet horses, sick of the rain, sick of her companions and especially sick of her empty-headed maid! As the journey progressed, she fell deeper and deeper into bitter brooding.

She was the heir to the kingdom of the Eastern Elves. She was fated to be the great Queen whose coming was foretold in ancient Prophecy. She was to give birth to a daughter intimately tied to a resurgence of elvish prosperity and power. She was born into power and privilege, and yet her life was a bitterly unhappy one. Now she was being forced into prostitution of her body.

She was sent to become pregnant to a minor chieftain somewhere deep in this god-forsaken forest. She was a virgin and her first man would be almost three times her age, already married and she had never met him!

Her shame would be a public matter. It would spoil forever any chance of a favourable marriage and be an eternal stain on her rule. Still, Elana was an elf princess and whatever fate decreed, she would do her duty.

She had felt a brief sense of release, with her coming of age. Just as she hoped to escape the palace, the trap had snapped shut again, firmly and horribly. The deeply unhappy life that seemed to be the fate of Princess Elana simply wouldn't let her go.

There was a lot of sympathy for the princess amongst her battle-hardened soldiers and small retinue. Noble families act as if their servants are deaf and stupid, but there is many a sharp mind and a long memory behind an impassive expression.

Elana was reserved, but always fair and considerate in her treatment of servants. She certainly had a temper and a sharp tongue, but mostly saved it for her enemies. It was widely known how she had been treated over time.

Since the crisis of her coming of age party, she was increasingly seen by the palace staff as 'our princess'. To know what Elana had faced, and to see how bravely she went to her disgrace, broke their hearts.

They rode as if to a funeral.

So, Black Sea, black mood, Elana was not in a mood to be tolerant and each and every one of her companions heard her bitter complaints, and felt the lash of her tongue over the slightest problem, as if they were personally to blame.

They sympathised, even felt some guilt, but there was little they could do. Elana just wanted this sorry period in her life over. They for their part longed to leave their charge in the care of the Western Elves and get as far away as they could.

It was a gloomy trip.

* * *

Elana felt better after a warm bath, dry clothes and some stew, but she found no matter how hard she tried, she couldn't be gracious to these people.

She had only just arrived and already she could hear herself offending Djorn's family. They were her hosts and they seemed lovely people. At any other time she might be delighted to have them as friends. It wasn't their doing, she desperately told herself.

She had dreaded this moment and now her heart was hammering, her breathing was rapid and her mouth dry. She felt like disappearing into the ground, but being a princess she showed no outward sign of her agitation.

"I didn't want an official welcome but it seems you give me no choice," she said, addressing Djorn.

What she really wanted to do was to run and hide, far away from anyone; far away from her sad awful life; far away from her shame. She felt desperate, frantic, but no matter how fast her mind raced, there was no way out.

Djorn was by no means an unattractive man. He still moved like a warrior and had maintained his fitness. In his youth, he had cleansed the surrounding hill country of bandits and thieves. He had attractive silky hair, dark as was not unknown in the Western Elves, though it was peppered with grey. For elves in rustic surrounds, he and his family were well-spoken and carried themselves well and they seemed to be knowledgeable about events in Elgard.

"I don't *need* to spend time getting to know you. I am here to be serviced. You have agreed. I don't wish to pretend; for me this is not about love or pleasure." Her courage was almost giving out, even to herself she sounded cold.

Djorn coloured, but he maintained politeness. "My Lady, you are tired. You have had a long and difficult journey. I suggest we talk on this later."

"Very well," Elana stood up, businesslike. "If you just show me to your bed, so we can get this over and done with. The delay for me will only make things worse."

Djorn drew himself up and looked at her coldly. "Such an offer! Well, I must decline. As I said, we will talk on this later."

Elana went pale, and tears started in her eyes. She had gone too far! What was she to do? She hesitated, head bowed, uncertain what to do, and then her courage broke and she fled to her room.

It was only moments later that Elana was sitting on the bed head bowed, feeling completely wretched and she was receiving what was a very rare scolding from her maid!

"What do you expect?" Iona demanded. "You were so cold and rude. I'm certain you caused his manhood to shrivel. Keep that up and you get no performance from him."

Elana burned with shame, but she was also amazed. She had no experience of men, and no mother to guide her. All she had heard told her men were always ready to have sex with almost anything, any time and under any circumstances.

She didn't know such a thing was possible.

Now she sat humbly, while Iona tried to tell her about male egos and how scorn from a woman could cause men, especially older men, to lose potency.

If he finds me so repulsive, what then? She felt a sense of rising panic. She would fail! Her mission would fail! It was unthinkable.

Yet in a very small corner of her mind, it was almost funny. After all her despair and trepidation, Djorn was too bashful to start.

* * *

The next morning Djorn's wife, Eugenia was supervising the preparation of breakfast, with her maids. Elana walked into the kitchen to talk to her, moving reluctantly, as if to her own hanging. She felt terrified of the older woman.

Eugenia glared at Elana, but her cold anger turned to confusion as she took in Elana's appearance. She expected to see a haughty, proud princess. Elana looked dreadful. It was obvious she had been crying and hadn't slept. Her head was bowed and she spoke in a small, desperate voice.

"Lady, I'm sorry; please forgive me." Elana tried to keep her voice steady and failed, bursting into tears instead. "What must I do?" she finished, sounding small and lost.

Eugenia's heart melted. It was hard for all. It was hard for Djorn. It was hard for Eugenia, having her husband sleep with another, younger woman. It was hard for their children, some of whom were older than Elana. It was hard to welcome this young lady into her house, and not see her as an enemy, rather than this brave young woman.

But what was it like for this young girl, a princess, barely old enough to be a woman? She had saved herself for marriage or love, and now must lose her purity, under circumstances that would forever leave her shamed. Who were they to judge her for a little burst of anger?

She took Elana in her arms and comforted the young girl. Elana clung to the older woman, and sobbed and sobbed.

From that moment, they saw another Elana. Not the arrogant princess, but a shy young girl that hid beneath a mask: uncertain, polite and grateful for the smallest of kindnesses.

They felt guilty for contributing to her shaming, but there was no choice.

A shameful incapacity arose for Djorn, which he had never had with his wife. He didn't want to talk about it and became sullen and angry. It was the final irony.

Elana had been determined to be the cold haughty princess to protect her pride. She planned to be completely passive, but this would do her no good!

Somehow, very strangely, it made her feel better about the whole thing. She realised it was also difficult for Djorn and his family. She felt less ill-used.

She expected Djorn would enjoy her humiliation, and gain extra pleasure from it. That would be truly horrible. Her respect for Djorn increased, though this didn't solve the problem.

Eugenia couldn't believe Elana took it all so lightly.

"It's because I'm so ugly. Perhaps we can use my face to scare the crows, or curdle the milk," Elana suggested.

Once, Elana caught Eugenia in the kitchen explaining to the other women how Djorn was finding it hard. "But it's not hard at all, and that's the problem!" Elana insisted with a mischievous smile.

The ladies broke into giggles that kept surfacing for the rest of the day, whenever they looked at each other. It was the sort of frank girl-talk that most men never guess happens.

Nothing could have been stranger than Eugenia teaching the younger woman how to appeal to her husband. Or Elana determined not to develop any affection for Djorn, yet at the same time having to almost seduce him.

She found it was simply impossible not to feel increasing affection for Djorn, he being the man he was.

To elves, the union of a man and a woman is a deeply spiritual thing capable of creating new life. As a result the time of losing her virginity is a special time in a woman's relationship with the Great Earth Goddess. Not that an elf-woman always lays with whom they would choose. Especially not if they are noble-born or wealthy.

Djorn was a man of the deepest integrity. Many would not have thought this way, but to him, to do this to Elana was abhorrent, despite the importance of a prophecy two thousand years old.

He became in the end fond of this lovely shy young woman, but still did not to want to sleep with her. It had to be right for her, for him and for his family.

Elana, who had no mother of her own, could not complain about the education she was gaining in the ways of men and women.

In the end she loved her time with Djorn's family. She loved them all: Djorn, Eugenia, all their family and even their servants.

In the end she just wished that she could stay there. She would have been content to be a much loved junior wife to a minor noble in the forests of the Western Elves. She hated the thought of returning home to be the despised Princess of the mighty kingdom of the Eastern Elves.

But it could never be, because her father said that one day she would be the Queen!

Chapter 9: A New Horse, a Widow, and a Poisonous Drink

It wasn't till summer that Hakeem was able to finally set out from Kyme, the royal city of Aiolía.

To avoid seeing the devastation caused by the recent war, Hakeem decided he would go east of Aiolía, past the Lydian city of Sardis, and then on to a small enclave of Aioli holdings to join the main trade route which finished climbing the coastal mountains before heading across the central Anatolian plateau.

From there, he would follow the main trade route to Ikónion and the easternmost chapterhouse of his order, where he would meet with Father Omar.

After that, he swing north and east to Mazaka, in Kappadokia and then on to the Black Sea region where the widow of his blood brother lived. After visiting her, he would head south across the breadth of Anatolē to the Kilisian pass that led through the Taurus Mountains to Tarsos, the last outpost of Anatolē on the Kilisian coastal plain.

Tarsos was the entrance to the fertile west coast of the Mediterranean which was currently held by the Persians. After travelling parallel to the Mediterranean Coast for a relatively short while, he would head west into the desert, the place of his birth.

Hakeem planned 30 miles per day or more of leisurely riding. With several long stops he would take a large part of the year allowed just to reach his desert city home. His return journey would be quicker, he would board a ship from the Mediterranean coast.

He looked forward to the journey and the long periods of solitude, after his experiences in the war and its aftermath and he declined an escort. He was travelling in summer, and avoiding the really dangerous sections caused by the recent war.

In the few remaining dangerous stretches, he would stick to well-travelled paths and travel with caravans, which were always glad of an extra swordsman. He should easily avoid any serious trouble, or so he thought.

For a Shantawi tribesman, it was a great irony that the first problem Hakeem faced concerned his horse.

Horses, to the Shantawi tribesmen are not just transport. They are intelligent loyal travelling companions, each with their own personality. Nadeer was one of a number of overly-generous last minute surprises Helios had for him. Hakeem's protests were ignored. Nadeer was big, strong and confident. He was trained as a war horse in the Keltoi region of southern Ibēría.

Perhaps Hakeem should have delayed his start, and given them both a chance to get familiar with each other but a Shantawi would never expect to have a problem with a horse!

Hakeem had two horses. His pack horse, Farah was one of the smaller desert bred horses known for speed and endurance. He spoiled himself by getting a good one, and Farah was a warhorse in her own right.

Part of the problem was the horse expected Hakeem to give him commands in some unknown Keltish dialect, and to use body signals completely unknown to the tribesman.

Nadeer was also used to a rider who held the reins in two hands. All this together convinced Nadeer that his new owner was a novice.

Then there was the question of dominance. With trained horses, the leader is supposed to be the rider. In the wild, it was usually am older mare.

For some reason Nadeer, big and completely inexperienced in such things saw himself as the natural leader of his small 'herd', moving across Anatolē.

To make trouble more certain, Nadeer was ungelded, a stallion, bred for strength and spirit and he was travelling in close proximity to a mare. He just had to dominate and impress!

They were not long into the journey when Nadeer, at the worst possible time, set out to show Hakeem that Nadeer was really in charge, whatever Hakeem may have thought about it.

He went out of his way to misunderstand, even commands given with two hands on the reins. 'Go forward' meant prance sideways, 'turn left' meant take your rider and his pack horse to the right through those prickly shrubs or the weeds that clung to your clothes, or try to wipe him from the saddle using that low hanging branch!

'Be careful' down this slope was a chance to show off. You don't really want me to slow down now do you? I've only just got a chance to gallop!

It got worse as Farah became increasingly unsettled by the big horse's antics.

Despite Hakeem being an excellent horseman, Nadeer was easily strong enough to throw or seriously injure him if he chose to. He was a big, strong heavy warhorse 700 kg or more, over three quarters of a ton.

Nadeer's excursions through various shrubs and foliage were more playful, not the vindictive actions of an unbroken horse that truly hated being ridden.

Hakeem found the behaviour of his young horse amusing. He was dealing with a spirited horse, one that possessed a sense of humour.

As Nadeer tried to wipe him off against a tree trunk for the third time in a row, he leant forward and stroked Nadeer's neck for a while, as if contemplating.

"Nadeer, is all this young horseplay *really* necessary?" he asked quietly. "Haven't you grown out of this sort of thing?

"It's going to be a very long trip if you keep this up, don't you think? I know you're not nearly as bad as you would like me to believe."

Nadeer looked back at him and snorted in disgust. His attempts to scare or annoy his rider weren't working.

Finally, Farah the old experienced mare showed she would only put up with so much from the youngster. She gave Nadeer a *very* firm and *very* painful nip on his rump.

Nadeer looked shocked, and bowed his head and flattened his ears in submission. After this he toned down the worst of his excesses. He was also starting to realise that Hakeem was an excellent rider.

He still continued some of his bad behaviour on the next day. This was partly to show he didn't give in too easily and partly for fun. He played up a few times on the second and third day, just to show all was not forgotten.

For strength and courage, a stallion (ungelded) is the best, but the gain is only slight and they are certainly a great deal more trouble. Most riders would chose a mare or geld their horses (at two years old) for the discipline required in a war horse.

The last thing a warrior needs is for a horse to play up at the wrong time, or want to 'announce' his presence to the enemy's mares when stealth is required. Some Iberian horse master recognised something special in Nadeer and decided not to geld him.

To train a war horse, the rider and his horse need to form an especially close bond. Horses are prey, not predators. They are superbly designed to run *away* from danger, and as swiftly as possible.

To get them to charge *into* battle needs superb training, and they need to have absolute trust in their rider. Hakeem patiently showed Nadeer his use of the reins two handed and then one handed. Then he started to teach him his own version of hands-free riding, guiding him with his knees.

He took many breaks and spoiled his horses with apples, grain, and regular brushing. Horses, like most animals, love to be brushed, and will sometimes gently nibble each other affectionately in the paddock.

Nadeer pretended disdain at each turn.

It was an act. In truth he was loyal and affectionate. As Hakeem was brushing him, he seemed to say, "Alright, if you really want to brush me, that's nice ... a bit more towards the back, ah ... that's better."

Hakeem was nonetheless surprised and touched on the fourth day to wake to a fine morning drizzle with Nadeer standing over him in the light rain. He got up and gave the horse a huge hug.

Nadeer looked at him as if to say, "You don't think I was standing there to shelter you do you? Of course I wasn't! No, no need to hug me, no need at all."

For a rider, to journey a long way with horses binds you to them with a special bond: they are your closest and sometimes your *only* companions. Most Shantawi tribesmen grow up in a saddle. They spend more time with their horses than with their family. The reverence with which they treat horses has been the substance of many famous jokes.

* * *

The central part of Anatolē is an uneven plateau surrounded by coastal mountains. As the road crested a coastal mountain path and began descending, Hakeem left the cool air. The stately teak forest gradually gave way at first to scrubby pine and then orchards of olives and many other fruits. The rocky crags gave way to grey dusty volcanic soil, long cleared. This land had the Mediterranean climate with hot dry summers.

Hakeem didn't mind the sun but it was really hot in mid-day, so he changed out of his Greek uniform to don the robes of the *Badawiyyūn* (Bedouin) with his *keffiyeh* (head scarf).

On the seventh day, he had been up early, it was especially hot, and Nadeer and Farah had been climbing all day. He stopped at one of the small way-houses in a village at the base of a hill, to get some tea and give his horses a rest.

A smiling old grandma and her daughter, Sara, served him the strong black local tea under a large hemp cloth awning. Several tables and chairs were set up, but Hakeem and a wizened old toothless man were the only customers.

For a couple of coppers, Sara's son, Petros, watered and fed his two horses while he rested.

It was like most of the villages in this rich land: wealthy and well kept. The main street was cobbled and banked very steeply up the hill, then branched. He could see almost a dozen of the pleasant houses made of sun-dried mudbrick.

Their shaded small compounds were enclosed by mud, stone or brush fences, beyond which he could see plum and orange trees. A nearby, single story house had hay drying on its flat roof.

Most of the adults were away working in the fields or up ladders dealing with the plum harvest, but there was a continual din of chickens, children, dogs, lambs and goats. Along the main road was a steady trickle of pedestrians and hand drawn carts but also donkeys, donkey carts, and the occasional horseman.

It seemed a long time since he could rest like this, and he felt no hurry to move. It was too soon to stop for his evening meal so he drowsed in the sun, sipping more tea, his mind wandering. He felt better than he had for some time.

The voice of the boy, Petros, startled him. "That's a nice horse sir!"

He smiled "His name is Nadeer, the rare one. He is a gift from a wealthy friend."

"Nadeer indeed, I've never seen his like. A gift fit for a king!"

"I wouldn't say as much. He looks far better than he is," Hakeem lied. "His size means he can't gallop very far. One of his legs is a little weak." Nadeer snorted and looked at him reproachfully. If any horse was smart enough to learn speech, this would be the one.

The boy smiled. A single traveller would do well not to appear too rich, though the land around Petros's village was now peaceful thanks to the King. "Well you could have fooled me, Lord. I would have thought he was a fine war horse." Hakeem merely nodded, absently.

And what a magnificent horse he had!

Dappled grey with darker hind quarters, he was huge, all of 17 hands high, full of sleek muscle.

He had a great muscular neck and a thick mane and tail. Enormous hindquarters and strong forequarters allowed him the agility of a much smaller horse to stop and turn, but in galloping he was truly the king of all horses. He had an unusually large and strong heart giving him the rare combination of power, speed and great endurance.

He was quick to learn and, despite pretending not to be, he was eager to please. He was a large strong war horse but Hakeem was told he was good natured and tolerant around children.

He was now prancing back and forwards and lifting his feet high, as if he wanted to give lie to his master's claim of fault. The old man, who had overheard, chuckled at the joke the horse played on his master. Hakeem tried to ignore his antics but eventually had to laugh.

"Enough! Enough! You've won your point, Nadeer!"

A small crowd of children had gathered to watch Hakeem and Nadeer. He tossed a few coppers to them and said to the boy, "He's gentle enough to carry them, if you'll walk him."

The horse looked at Hakeem reproachfully, but soon Nadeer was plodding backwards and forwards with two or three excited children on his back and a look of long-suffering on his face.

True to word, he was patient and gentle. Soon little children were patting his face and sides and hugging him. One fed him an apple which he took with exaggerated delicacy, so as not to bite, causing all to laugh. Hakeem suspected Nadeer was very fond of children, despite his doleful expression.

When this was over, the woman shooed the laughing children away, to give Hakeem peace.

Her son, despite his mother, came shyly back to talk to Hakeem.

"Were you in the war, sir?" Hakeem simply nodded, hoping he would not be asked to tell some tale of glory. The boy seemed to be too shy to continue.

"My father was in the war, in the infantry. They say he died in a great battle against Troians." His eyes were moist and his voice broke with sadness.

Then Hakeem understood. He made enquires but as he expected he didn't know the boy's father at all.

"Your father was *that* Bora!" he exclaimed, leaning back and smiling broadly, as if in delighted remembrance. "Of course I knew him! Did you know that name means hurricane?

"I was *so* sorry to hear he died. What a mighty fighter he was! He fought very bravely!

"Did you know earlier he saved me and several of my men? I'll tell you the story of some of his deeds. I can really see your father in you. I think you will be strong and brave just like him.

"He named you *Petros* (Peter) . Did you know that is a Greek version of a name from my tongue, *Cephas*? It means solid and strong, like a rock."

Like magic, an audience of small faces appeared. The afternoon wore on, as Hakeem recounted story after story. Some had an element of truth, several were completely fanciful. Hakeem cunningly dug for details, and was careful not to depart too far from the plausible. At the end of it he reached into his saddle bag and gave the boy three small Troian silver coins. "Here, your father would want you to have these." Petros's eyes were huge with wonder as he stared at them in disbelief, unwilling to close his hand around them in case they disappeared.

At that his mother, Sara, bustled up. "I know what you are doing and it's kindly done. I'll still thank you not to spoil my son and fill his head with your grand stories."

The handsome tribesman brushed off the offence and smiled, "and how do you know it's not true?"

"And what was your role, stranger, in the war? You've mentioned little of that."

Hakeem laughed heartily. "Me? I was a guard on a supply train. I kept as far away from any fighting as I could!"

"You tell some wonderful tales but you tell poor lies about yourself, sir. I don't take you for a simple soldier. But you fill my son's head with dreams of glory. I have lost my husband to war. Must I lose my only son?" Sara's eyes sparkled dangerously, as she turned angrily on him.

Petros piped up, "She wants me to learn to read and be a scribe. I would be ashamed if I didn't become a great fighter like my father!"

"Listen to me very carefully," Hakeem said, staring deeply into the young boy's eyes. "There is nothing glorious in fighting. Great evil is done in war."

He then spoke gently to Sara. "War stole your love, but don't be angry with him for going. In the lands where Troians crossed over, they were not kind to women, children, or old men. There are things I saw there that I wish I hadn't. Your husband gave his life to protect you from that."

"And Petros," he said to her son. "Where I come from, we value learning, above all else. Those who read and study are seen as greater than warriors. I had to learn to read before they would teach me to fight." There was a gasp from the small audience: this warrior could read and write!

"We sometimes have to fight," Hakeem continued to Petros. "But there is little glory in it. Never despise peace. Your father died to give it to you."

"Well," said Sara, wiping a tear from her eye. "I see you are a philosopher as well. Thank you for your words, they ease my heart somewhat. I suppose I shouldn't be so angry with Bora. I'm just angry with all you men and your wars.

"You are modest and much younger than I thought, but you must think we country folk are stupid not to recognise the great warrior, Hakeem. It's said you are kind and fair of speech, and I find it so."

There was a sudden commotion! People started to shout to their friends. There was an important man in their village!

Hakeem blushed deeply, and desperately tried to hush her to silence. "As you can see, I'm not so great," he said quickly. "I hoped to travel quietly and my name becomes a burden. I hope there aren't many more on my path as clever as Petros's mother, Sara!"

It was too late for him! Sara smiled at the mischief she had played on her self-effacing guest, as people began to run back and forwards shouting in excitement. Soon there was a crowd of villagers wanting to shake his hand. There was no question of his leaving before the morning as the villagers readied a feast.

The men sat down with him to discuss the tactics of new and old campaigns, they soon found their guest as knowledgeable as his reputation claimed, but deeply courteous. Hakeem had studied many old campaigns in the libraries of Pergamon and Troia, but here was a chance to hear eyewitness accounts and opinions from some of those who were there!

Soon there was a large bench set up with cups, glasses, pebbles, salt and fish sauce containers set up as opposing units, there was learned discussions on terrain, tactics and equipment.

The old men were thoroughly charmed to have their memories found to be so important, and to have a senior commander hanging on the words of old soldiers. They had given little credit to the horsemen before. After Hakeem's visit, it would be impossible to say anything in the village against the courage and fine qualities of the desert horsemen.

He was coaxed to show the famous sword the King had given him. It was passed around with a reverence approaching awe.

There is a mystique surrounding a good long sword, it is because they are so difficult to make.

Human iron is hardened ('wrought' or 'tempered') by hammering and heat, using charcoal and bellows to get the fire as hot as possible. The problem is, getting iron hard enough tends to make it brittle and it could snap in battle.

This would be, at the very least, unfortunate.

So spears (and shields) are the mainstay of an army and common secondary weapons are long knives or short-swords.

But the Shantawi are horse-mounted skirmishers. They need their swords to be long enough for use on horseback.

The cheaper long-swords are made softer so they can easily be straightened or repaired. The Keltoi weapon-smiths make the best human long swords. They make the iron into rods. Some rods they make harder by laying them in burning charcoal and then tempering them more. The remaining rods are kept out of the charcoal and are less tempered so they are softer. Then the hard and soft rods are welded and hammered together in a precise way to form a sword that is hard where it is needed and yet soft where it is needed. The length and balance has to be just right.

It can take a week of precise work to produce just one sword for a great noble or senior commander and then it might be ruined at the last moment.

No wonder a perfect human long-sword or the master craftsmen who can reliably produce them are rare, and have achieved legendary status.

The elves have a technique they learned from the dwarves, but a fine elf-sword is prohibitively expensive. Hakeem almost fainted when he found that King Helios had commissioned a sword for him, but not from the elves but from the dwarves.

Dwarves made axes and hammers, not swords! He never found out how much the sword cost or why the dwarves agreed, yet Helios was *most* insistent. He believed Hakeem had saved his life.

Most long swords are designed for stabbing with the point or slashing with the blade. Stabbing (the torso) is more lethal but if you are galloping past, it may cause you to lose your weapon. The least consequence would be looking silly as you gallop into battle unarmed.

A good slash to a limb or torso would be just as effective in neutralising an opponent and slashing is better suited for a cavalry charge, but the Shantawi also do close-in fighting with shields so they need a sword that can stab as well as slash.

When Hakeem first drew his sword, he almost dropped it in surprise. It was *so* perfect for him! Some unknown dwarf master craftsman had somehow made the perfect sword for Hakeem and his fighting style.

The hilt was of a hard wood clamped to the metal and covered by an unknown skin, glued and sewn. It fitted his hand exactly and was not slippery, even when damp. There was a pommel to improve the grip and balance. There was a horizontal metal guard at the end of the handle, just like an elf sword.

The balance was perfect. The blade's cross section was lens shaped. There was a central channel in the middle of the upper part for balance, making the point lighter and also allowing the sword to be withdrawn from the enemy's flesh more easily. It kept a beautiful edge with little attention. It didn't show rust, and it was long and thin but virtually unbendable.

The dwarves did not make things as beautiful as the elves, but this sword had the beauty of perfection. One side had Hakeem's name in dwarvish runes and the other side the name of the sword, 'peace', spelt in dwarvish runes. Hakeem called his sword 'Mir' which means 'peace' in his own language.

Other dwarfish runes had been added, which he was told gave it magical properties, but he didn't know whether this was true or not.

It was the best sword he had ever seen. Hakeem could not help but grin with pleasure whenever he thought of his sword, and whenever he drew it. He loved to swing it and hear it whistle slightly. His horse, his blade and a holding of land in the Troad were unexpected presents given when he renewed his vow to King Helios.

Eventually, Sara had to shoo the other men away so she and the women were able to prepare for the feast. She showed Hakeem to her wash room. Sara at times rented a room to travellers, and had a full wash room with a tiled floor, an uncommon luxury in a small village. It included a sunken drain that was connected to the street.

The roof was a flat roof of overlapping fired-clay tiles on a wooden frame. Between the wall and the overhung roof, there was a gap of about a foot which gave light and ventilation but maintained privacy. In winter, shutters closed this gap, and a simple hearth on the floor provided warmth when needed.

A traveller could have a tiled bath but for those, like Hakeem, who preferred quicker or more frequent bathing, there was a stall, separated from a tall copper cauldron by a short wall of bricks. The caldron stood on a single three-quarter circle of bricks and Sara had lit a small fire underneath to make the water warm and comfortable.

Hakeem could easily reach over into the cauldron and bail jug after jug full of warm water over himself. He was luxuriating in thoroughly washing the road grime of many days from his head and body.

Meanwhile, Sara was musing on her surprise guest. She shook her head in amazement. Where was that anger she felt towards Bora and all men? She felt grateful towards Hakeem, and admiration for him, that she had hid with her usual teasing manner.

Also there was re-awakening of feelings that bitterness had long suppressed. She found herself powerfully drawn to the handsome tribesman. His easy smile, kindness and friendly manner gave her warm tingly feelings, in the areas of the body that a man might touch. She wondered what it would be like to be held in his strong arms.

She had last seen her husband more than two years ago. It was a long time since she had lain with a man. She longed for her husband, his strength, his touch, the sound of his laughter.

She had no one to make her feel special, no one to make her feel beautiful and attractive. She had resigned herself to grow old without again having the feel of a man's touch and his love. She felt lonely, despite her family and friends around her.

Sara as a child was the leader amongst her friends. She was always the bold and adventurous one. As a young woman, she was exceptionally sharp witted and loved teasing first boys, and then any suitors. It had taken a strong man, like Bora, to capture her heart and tame her as much as anyone could have done.

She was now a widow in a village and had to be careful with her reputation. This didn't mean her sense of mischief had disappeared!

She brought scented oil to rub on her guest's back. This was quite acceptable for an honoured guest but she definitely had other possibilities on her mind.

Greeks are more relaxed about nudity than Shantawi tribesmen … evidently. Hakeem's reaction when he saw her walk in while he was standing naked, bathing was dramatic!

He yelped and dropped the soap, which went skidding across the floor. He dived for the towel, almost knocking over the nearby oil lamp. He missed the towel and finally retrieved it from the floor, where it had fallen in the water.

He stood there with soap suds from his hair draining into his eyes; his towel was miserably wet and wrapped around his waist. He reached for the dipper and rinsed his hair, only getting the last little bit of the towel completely saturated.

Wet and dripping, he looked a sorry sight.

Sara could hardly contain her amusement. "I brought some scented oil to rub on your body."

"Thank you." Hakeem said as he recovered himself, and came forward to collect it.

Oh my, he was tall, built like a wrestler and very handsome. "No. When you're finished, I'll help you put it on your back. Here, I'll get a fresh towel and help you dry off."

As she grabbed a dry towel and moved towards him, he blushed furiously and tried to back away. He flinched as if burnt, when she touched him, trying his best to relax. She struggled not to burst out laughing.

She directed him to sit, and began rubbing the oil on his back and chest, enjoying the feel and smell of him. When she went to rub his legs, he shot up and danced out of her way and firmly took the bottle with a husky, "thank you."

He tried unsuccessfully to be unobtrusive as he struggled to hide his swelling manhood. It was insisting on trying to push up against the towel.

In the end he was forced to turn his back to undo the towel and quickly tuck himself in and retie it. He turned back, trying to pretend nothing was wrong and hoping she wouldn't notice.

"You'll be sleeping in my house tonight," Sara was saying. "I sense you're not familiar with the ways of women, whereas I'm older and an experienced woman. The nights can be cold so close to the mountains and we don't lock our doors. I don't think anyone will mind which bed you woke up in, as long as we were discreet."

Hakeem couldn't believe what he was hearing. Sara was in her thirties but beautiful, desirable. He admitted he found himself powerfully attracted to her dark hair, brown eyes and sharp wit. She moved closer and he felt aroused by the promise hidden by her dress. He felt dizzy with her perfume, but he also felt panicked.

It wasn't as if he didn't want what was being offered, but he was terrified. Hakeem had strict moral views on 'easy' sex, or the use of prostitutes and he had no experience. He was still a virgin at twenty two. He was scared he would be inadequate, and his first lover would be left disappointed. His heart was racing and hands were shaking.

She glanced at a bulge in his towel wrap and smiled. She certainly hadn't lost her touch. She was aware of his agitation but there seemed to be something else.

He sputtered, "L-L-Lady you have me at a d-disadvantage. You are such a beautiful woman and so desirable."

She looked at him incredulously, and a bit dangerously, "But?"

Now he was truly scared of the situation. Would she fly into a rage? He was beyond being scared of that which he so strongly desired. He knew it was not going to happen … or so he believed!

"Men where I come from don't do certain things in a casual way," he said breathlessly. "You have a child! You need help. I'm not sure I can be what you need."

Sara relaxed and laughed, in a pleasant musical way. "Is that all? Sorry I don't mean to seem like such a *seirēn* (siren). I mean no ties, no obligations." She moved close enough to press her body against his. Her leg slid between his and she started to rub his chest very lightly. She could feel the pressure of his erection. He was panting, jammed up against the table, unable to retreat further.

"I-I c-can't. Please don't be angry." Suddenly, she stepped back and looked at him in surprise.

"You're a ...I mean you haven't, have you?" she gasped.

A virgin! This was perfect! Built like a god, shy, gentle and thoughtful. She would love to help him with his little problem of virginity!

"I-I c-can't do this without t-ties. Please don't be angry."

"Don't look so frightened! There's no force, though I'd love to change your mind. Hakeem, you act more like a monk than a soldier!" She spoke the last in an intimate, husky voice and gave his penis a light squeeze as she moved regretfully away. She was delighted, when he jumped, followed by a shuddering reaction.

"Remember, you can change your mind," she said, swaying her hips as she moved to the door.

She paused at the door, looking back and gave him a seductive smile. "I promise to make it worth your while. Now, for both our sakes, I'll need to let you get ready.

"I mean it, don't look so frightened! You're not in any trouble, from me or anyone. This is the first time I've done this sort of thing. I didn't think I would! In case you haven't noticed, I like you. I like you a lot. Even though nothing happened, I think you're nice, and I'm glad you came." She gave him an affectionate look and left.

Hakeem made his shaky way to the guest room, and sat on the bed, flummoxed. He felt as if he had been run over by a herd of horses!

Then he quickly got some pants on, in case she came back. He tried too quickly and became tangled in his pants so he had to stop himself and deliberately take his time.

He dressed in his best white pants and light cotton top. He attached the three golden and one silver sickles to his belt, indicating his Shayvist mastery level and then pulled the gold medallion, from the Aiol king, over his head.

Then he took a deep breath, and sat down again to gather himself. He sighed. Sara didn't seem too angry with him, and he hoped that was so. He had practiced discipline most of his life, but she had torn him almost beyond his will to resist.

He couldn't have sex without any obligation to her and her son. Perhaps he was a prude. No, he chuckled, no *perhaps* about it! Well, only the weak reed bends easily in the wind, as they say.

He shook his head, smiling wryly. He had no experience of women, he always hung well back. He feared he wasn't attractive, being big and feeling awkward. Well that explodes that theory at least.

Sara also smiled, as she hurried about her chores. Well, so much for life ending once she was a widow! She had missed out on one handsome tribesman, but was in no doubt about her effect on him. She now felt more attractive and alive than she had for a long time. Perhaps there may be another man for her, one day.

The evening started with a magnificent feast. Then there was singing and some dancing. Hakeem didn't dance but he sang a sad, haunting melody in his own tongue.

While there was no prohibition on alcohol and drugs in Hakeem's religion, it was generally discouraged. To be polite he sipped some of the local 'distilled' wine. It was made from their cheaper wine, frozen in the mountains in winter and the ice removed by a sieve to make it concentrated, and then it was flavoured with anise.

It had a ghastly taste! Like sickly medicine for a cough.

Sara was as good as her word. She sat by his side smiling, laughing and talking pleasantly; though there was still a twinkle of mischief in her eye, when she smiled at him.

After the meal, she politely asked him the purpose of his journey. On impulse, he told her about his blood brother. As he talked, Hakeem felt again how desperately he missed his friend. Tears welled in his eyes. He bowed his head in misery and his voice faltered. Sara rested her hand on his shoulder and said sympathetically, "we each have our loss."

The room fell silent, many murmured their sympathy. In his mourning, Hakeem seemed even closer to them, more human. The respect and affection they had for the tribesman swelled.

Then one of the old war veterans stood up solemnly and raised his glass. "To old friends ... to Elwan!" Everyone in the room repeated this and many drained their glass.

They all looked expectantly at Hakeem, smiling. Out of the corner of his eye Sara gestured that he should drink. With a fixed smile in his face he downed the remainder of the foul drink, with only a slight shudder and coughing. Everyone clapped and someone moved quickly to fill his cup. He remembered that next there was another old man, giving a solemn toast, "to those we have lost."

They toasted other lost friends, both his and those from the village, they toasted the village, they toasted the King, they toasted Samit, they toasted the Shantawi, they toasted Hakeem, he toasted them and then they toasted ... in fact, Hakeem had no idea who or what they toasted after that!

He did remember that it all felt *very* emotional and solemn. The rest of the night got increasingly hazy as he drained cup after cup. He couldn't recall exactly when he passed out under the table, but he awoke in the heat of the morning, feeling absolutely terrible!

His head was pounding, his mouth was dry and his body was weak and aching all over. And yet, somehow, his grief was easier. He wondered if it was like going through some sort of purging ceremony.

When he went in search of Sara and found her in her kitchen she was sympathetic, though she couldn't help laughing at his suffering. She gave him a breakfast of *staititas* (pancakes) and cheese, olives and yesterday's barley bread soaked in wine. He was surprised he could eat at all.

They had a brief moment alone as he was preparing to leave.

"Thank you, Hakeem for all you have done for us, for me and Petros." She said, her eyes a little moist.

"No," he replied. "Thank you! You ... all of you here, have helped me with things that have been hurting for a long time. I just wish it didn't feel like you poisoned me in the process."

Sara laughed, an easy open laugh. She asked if he would come back this way and he looked at her lovely face.

"I'd like to. Maybe I'll even come back with a very different proposition. A man could only be proud with a woman like you, and a boy like Petros, at his side."

"Then I would refuse! I said no ties and I meant it," Sara said, smiling.

"What do you mean?"

"You're young and don't have experience, we both would have to be sure. At least I didn't scare you away, though. You'd better go now, hero, before I drag you inside, despite all your protests."

He laughed, "Hero? Sara, don't you ever stop with your teasing?"

She smiled back, looking thoroughly desirable. Then she spoke very carefully and earnestly, "Hakeem, this time I *am* serious. Being a hero is not only about strength of arms. You leave this village, as our hero.

Goodbye, Hakeem!"

She leant forward and gave him a kiss on the cheek. He could feel her lips there, where she had kissed him for a long time after he rode away.

Chapter 10: A Fearsome Warrior and a Young Gypsy Girl

Hakeem's sleeping and waking dreams were filled with Sara, mainly on what might have been. When he passed back this way, he didn't dismiss the chance that he might collect a certain lovely someone and her son.

Then something happened that drove even Sara out of his mind. Five days on from Sara's village, as he rounded a bend he spotted trouble a good way ahead.

The wheat harvest was mostly finished. The sun was casting tall afternoon shadows. In the distance he could see something burning … a small caravan. Its horse lay shot by an arrow, still left in its traces. Perhaps half a dozen men milled around nearby.

Hakeem could see four bodies on the ground, they looked like Gypsies. Two were women lying face down, murdered from the back as they tried to flee. There was a dog barking loudly. After a high yelp, it was silenced. A bit closer he could see a man riding a horse back and forward, chasing a child.

Hakeem must have arrived just after it was happened!

The sensible thing was to give this trouble and the band of men a wide berth, but the thought of a child being run down by a horse after such murder, filled Hakeem with such a rage he could not ride on.

He tied Farah to a small tree, and quickly donned his armour, lifted his shield with his left arm and loosened his sword in its sheath. Soon he and Nadeer were galloping swiftly to intercept the other man on the horse.

Coming closer, he slowed to a canter, surprised that the man on horseback seemed to pay him little heed. The man seemed to be totally focused on running down the little Gypsy boy ... no a girl of about eleven.

Nudging his horse up between the man and the girl, Hakeem smiled dangerously at the stranger. "You seem such a big man on such a big horse to run down such a little girl."

"Mind your own business, you filthy desert rat," the man sneered at him, looking him up and down. "Haven't you heard that the new king's sorting out such as you? I'm in charge here, so just run off before you get into real trouble!"

He smiled as his men arrived and fanned out nearby.

Hakeem automatically noted there was only one bowman. He had an arrow nocked, but his bow was slack and pointed to the ground. He didn't stand well back as he should have, not trusting his aim or worse, he was a fool.

The men were poorly kitted out. None bore shields, none had proper armour, they carried crude looking swords, but one had a staff. If the bowman or the man with the staff were any good, they could still give him some nasty trouble but at first glance, they were simple ruffians, good for bullying peasants only.

"Well, you're the foreman but why are you chasing this girl? Has she committed a crime?"

The tribesman spoke with authority, and was not cowed by the presence of armed men. His horse and kit all spoke of senior rank. He spoke like he expected to be obeyed.

The foreman looked a bit discomforted and he searched for an answer. "No, but her family stole my goat. I came to check and found they'd eaten half of it."

"You lie. It was ours!" the young girl screamed in impotent rage. "We had to eat it, you never paid us!"

"I see," said Hakeem, drawing Mir with a flourish, and pointing it at the man. "You didn't pay wages and you claim it was your goat. Even if it was your goat, killing their horse is more than an exchange, and they may have been justified, if there were unpaid wages.

"There are four bodies, damage to their home, and you're chasing this girl. I carry the seal of your King!" He took a big breath, and his voice carried loudly and clearly. "I suggest you pay a sizable blood debt, now! Or it will be you finding yourself in serious trouble!"

He hoped if he moved things along quickly, he just might cow the bully, and fixed his gaze on him grimly. He automatically kept the bowman in view, out of the corner of his eye.

He didn't have any real hopes of avoiding a fight, and after a few seconds he saw the foreman tense.

As the foreman went for his sword, Hakeem spun Mir in powerful circle. He brought his sword whistling back with such speed that he caught the foreman across the neck before he had the chance to bare more than a few inches of his blade!

He heard one of the ruffians screaming hysterically, "Kill him!"

In the ensuing shock and confusion, one of their men jumped in front of their own bowman. Hakeem charged his horse forward at the man and hacked him out of the way. The bowman was trying to get a clear shot, but was too panicked and trying to half-run backwards at the same time. Hakeem cut him down.

Turning quickly, Hakeem raised his shield to block a blow from the staff. He pushed his horse hard up against the nearby men, managing to overbalance three who were trying to fight together and quickly cut them down.

The last man threw his weapon down and turned to run. Hakeem nudged Nadeer into a trot after him. As he drew level with the desperately fleeing man he leaned out and slashed him hard across the back of his neck. The man pitched face forward with an agonised cry and was still.

It was over in moments. When Hakeem killed, he was ruthlessly efficient.

He felt some regret that he had to kill, but it was inevitable when he decided to intervene. As for taking a defenceless man from behind, it didn't bother him at all. He could not leave a witness, however false, to accuse him of murder.

He tied his helmet to the saddle and dismounted and quickly and efficiently performed the task of ensuring they were all dead.

He thought that the murdered Gypsies would be unlikely to understand the regret he had at killing the men, as he carefully cleaned his weapons on one of the men's clothing, but he was a Shayvist.

The little girl stood frozen on the spot. Her eyes were staring at him in mute terror, as he finally approached her. He moved slowly and gave her what he hoped was a kindly smile.

"What is your name?" he asked, squatting down nearby.

Her mouth moved, but no sound came out. He held his hand out and she flinched away.

"I'm not going to hurt you." Hakeem said gently. "I'm sorry about your family." Even to him it sounded such an empty thing to say. The girl made no response; she just stood there breathing fast, her eyes wide, watching every move he made. Hakeem shrugged to himself. He wouldn't rush her.

* * *

The small girl was trapped in a waking nightmare. Her family had worked so hard, even she had worked. The foreman was saying they hadn't worked properly and he wouldn't pay them. He threatened them if they didn't leave.

It was an excuse, even she knew it. Their wages were poor but the foreman wanted to keep the little that was theirs for himself.

Her father was arguing with him and the foreman's men had gathered around threateningly. She was frightened of the angry voices so had hid under their wagon.

Then her father was suddenly tired and wanted to sit down. She saw him clutching at his stomach and his clothes showed a spreading stain.

In horror, she realised they had stabbed him.

Her brother had moved to catch his father, and they had murdered him too, stabbing him in the back. Then her mother and sister tried to escape but they shot them from behind and they jeered at them as they lay dying.

And then they found her.

She ran, in mindless terror, no idea where she was running to. The man ran her down with his horse and then he was playing with her, cheering and taunting her attempts get away, letting her go and then riding after her. It was a game to him!

Her heart leapt in relief when out of nowhere a big man came. He was in armour and sat a great war-horse. He looked a fearsome warrior. He seemed very angry, but then the men ran up to surround him too. They were going to kill him too. What could one man do against so many?

And then he moved.

It was shockingly violent. His sword was a blur. He hit so hard, he almost cut the bad man's head off! Blood sprayed everywhere! The bad man fell from the horse … he was dead! His eyes were staring!

The warrior spurred his horse with such strength and speed. All those men, they had terrified her but they didn't have a chance.

Was he even human?

And then he had walked up to her, his clothes and armour covered in blood and with his hair all over the place. He would kill her too!

* * *

Hakeem found water and cut some cloth from one of the men's bodies. He carefully cleaned himself and his kit as well as he could, and then quenched the fire and picked anything of value off the corpses. He figured that anything left belonged to the girl. The Gypsies had nothing of value, but all the men had money and the foreman had a very heavy purse!

Where was the owner of this land? Probably something to do with the war.

He removed the tack from the foreman's horse but let it run free. He could not afford anything that might tie him to this place. As he worked, he checked the small girl out of the corner of his eye. She still stood where he had left her, a forlorn figure, staring over the devastation of her family's encampment.

To the little girl, it was incomprehensible. It could *not* have happened. In moments her family, her world, was no longer there. It was not possible. What was going to happen to her?

As Hakeem was digging a shallow grave for the Gypsies and laying their bodies out as nicely as he could, the little girl came closer, to watch. Her tears had dried.

"My name is Hakeem. I really am very sorry for your loss. I mean you no harm, I promise. You had better come with me now," he said kindly.

She looked at him solemnly, her dark brown eyes still wide with shock and slowly nodded. "I'm glad you killed them," she said in a faint voice. She paused, her tears began again. Then a sob wracked her body. She hiccoughed and turned to the large warrior.

"They k-killed my f-family," she explained, as if he, too, would not be able to understand. "...f-for n-no reason they k-killed them! My f-father, my mother, my sister and my b-brother. They are all d-dead!"

Her small voice was filled with disbelief.

She sobbed again, staring at the destruction the murderers had caused, and the bodies of those who loved her, who only moments ago were alive.

"Jacinta...." she managed. "My name is Jacinta."

Jacinta was maybe 11 or 12. She had started her stage of growth, but showed no sign of change into womanhood. There was no doubt, through the dust and tears, what a great dark beauty she would become.

Hakeem finished preparing her family in the shallow graves he had dug. Their murderers could lie where they had fallen.

As he started to say words of comfort over the graves and fill them in with soil, Jacinta emitted an empty, agonised cry. She put her hand hard across her mouth and bit her hand to stifle it. He came closer and held her, she was trembling violently and he could feel her small heart hammering.

He gave her time to say goodbye. She would not see the graves of her family again.

She had stopped crying and stood staring at the graves, unseeing, for a while. He waited with her, and then she nodded slightly.

She didn't resist as he lifted her up onto Nadeer, and then mounted behind her. She twisted to look back as they rode away to get Farah. While he repacked his gear, Jacinta waited, sitting listlessly on Nadeer, and then they were off, Hakeem giving the scene of slaughter a wide birth, trotting the horses to get quickly past.

Jacinta was biting her lip to try to hold back the tears. Hakeem bundled her into his arms, laying her sideways across the saddle, and gently hugged her to him, guiding Nadeer with his knees with Farah on a lead rope.

For a long time she was lay stiff and silent, shivering, but then she emitted a great cry of anguish and her small frame was racked again and again with sobbing. Hakeem found tears touching his own eyes as he clutched the little girl to him.

Jacinta had cried herself out again and slept in his arms for a time. When Hakeem felt they were far enough away, he turned off the main road to set up camp for the evening. He risked a small fire, and forced her to eat a little bread and olives and drink some water. She lay listlessly on her side staring into space.

He then told her she should sleep, but when he approached her with his blanket she cringed away, shuddering. She looked like a small animal with terror in her eyes. He smiled to reassure her and moving slowly he gently tucked her in. What in the name of the Gods did she expect he would do to her?

She feared he might do something bad to her. He felt a dark surge of anger at the thought. She was only a little girl and had just lost all her family.

He sat beside her, caressing her face and hair and gently patting her shoulder. Eventually she relaxed and quietened to sleep. He spent a long time that night staring into the flames of the fire and watching the girl sleeping restlessly, moaning in her sleep. He was thinking about the evil men do, and worrying what to do with the little girl.

Dawn found the tribesman with her finally sleeping peacefully on his shoulder and his arm around her. Nadeer and Farah had come close by, instinctively guarding the small girl. As he felt her small head on his shoulder and her arms across his chest Hakeem felt a strong surge of protectiveness for this gypsy girl.

* * *

Jacinta was silent and glum for many days. Hakeem decided she was a rather quiet, young girl. Only later he found out just how wrong he could be sometimes!

Slowly Jacinta relaxed and began to trust the mysterious and dangerous stranger. Hakeem admitted how much he was enjoying her company, though his heart ached for her. He could have got her to ride his smaller pack horse, but the great horse Nadeer carried them both without any trouble. For the time, instinct told him that human contact was important for the Gypsy girl.

He also felt pleasure having the young girl ride in his arms. Slowly she started to notice things around her and she started to chat with her huge companion. Her pleasant accented Greek and the way she pronounced "Hakeem" was an absolute delight.

It was on their fourth day that they had their first argument.

It started when they were approaching a river, he said he planned to wash all their clothes and blankets and bathe. Hakeem loved to bathe. Also he had noticed his scalp was decidedly itchy since he met Jacinta. He needed to free them both of some small unwanted travelling companions.

Hakeem was fastidious in looking after his troops, as much as his horses, and knew a lot about common ailments. Human head lice were for him easy to treat but in a group of men more keep hatching, so you need to keep at it for a long time. Soap, vinegar, scented oil and plant extracts were included in just some of the remedies for lice that he knew.

Hakeem was also very accustomed to arguments, especially when he suggested anything to do with hygiene to his 'men', and his little Gypsy girl wasn't about to disappoint him.

"I don't need to bathe. My family didn't bathe. It's bad for you. You lose oils from your skin." Jacinta seemed shocked at the very idea!

"Nonetheless, you *will* bathe," Hakeem stated flatly.

"No I *won't*! You're not my father and you can't make me!" Jacinta, a Gypsy girl, was certainly used to holding her own with strangers.

"Oh, Jacinta won't bathe!" said Hakeem solemnly, as if considering the fact. He started to gently tickle her. Fortunately he found her delightfully ticklish.

"Oh I can't make her!" he continued, tickling her and turning her upside down.

Soon they were both laughing and attacking one another as they tried to remain seated on the horse. When it came to the river there was a hilarious splashing competition which ended in them helplessly laughing and hugging on the bank.

She looked fondly at him, "I love you, Hakeem."

"I love you too, Jacinta." He returned, surprised at the strength of his feeling.

* * *

There was barely a moment since he met Jacinta that Hakeem didn't worry about what was best for this little girl.

He wanted a normal childhood for her, something he certainly hadn't had and he couldn't give her. The sensible thing was to find people of her own kind, a good family who would foster her.

There was the matter of the money from the foreman. He wanted to set it aside for her, for when she grew up but the only safe way he could think of was if he kept it and gave it to her when she came of age.

Jacinta wanted to stay with him. "Aren't you an officer of some sort? You must have quarters. I can keep house for you and cook."

Hakeem felt heartbroken when she said this. He already loved the young girl, but it wouldn't be fair to her. He would be away too much and too busy with other duties.

As he tried to explain this to her, Jacinta would just say, "but I *want* to stay with you!"

It made him feel terribly guilty. He was all she had. He knew, though, if he could find her a proper family, she'd soon forget him.

It wasn't long before they came against a sizeable camp of Gypsies outside a village, and Hakeem made careful enquiries. A lady called Moira had lost a girl child of illness, thirteen moons ago. It had been hard for her to have children and she yearned for another little girl.

He spent some time talking to Moira and her husband, Andreas. They seemed a lovely, caring couple. He saw Jacinta shyly making friends with their younger daughter. When it all seemed agreed, he gave Moira some money and got final approval from the head man, a fat and coarse man, called Gyorgy.

He wouldn't like to do much business with Gyorgy. He had initially wanted to refuse. Jacinta belonged to another tribe, and he didn't see why he should make her his problem. Finally, for a largish bribe, he consented.

Hakeem made arrangements to meet Moira and Andreas's family whenever they were near Aiolía and he gave Jacinta a letter in case she ever needed help.

Jacinta clung to the big tribesman at first, and had to be pulled off, crying. He squatted down and gave her time, talking to her gently, and she finally quietened. After a difficult goodbye, Hakeem rode slowly away.

Jacinta felt a great wrench as Hakeem left. She felt sad and empty. She had only known the large tribesman a short time, but he was kind and made her feel safe.

Almost immediately, Andreas came hurrying to warn her. Gyorgy was planning to sell her into slavery in the slave market at Eskisehir! It was good money, and Andreas couldn't protect her.

She panicked. Hakeem was gone, perhaps far ahead. Moira and Andreas covered for her, as she tried to run after him. She couldn't stop the tears. Her heart was hammering in fear. She was feeling desperate and alone.

Little did she know then that Hakeem and his horses weren't moving quickly at all! Hakeem could barely get Nadeer to walk along the road , and Farah was following listlessly.

From time to time the big horse would swing his neck to throw Hakeem an accusatory glance.

Hakeem himself had little heart to push on. He tried to remind himself he was doing the best thing for the little girl.

Then, in the distance behind him, he heard Jacinta's voice. She was crying and running.

"Hakeem! You bastard! Do you think you can dump me like a sack of barley? Do you know what they mean to do? They will sell me into slavery!" she screamed in a high-pitched voice. Finishing with, "You're just a coward and you're a liar."

Hakeem heard her throw in what sounded like a string of Gypsy curses, her small face red with anger. He spun his horse, a look of fury on his face.

* * *

He was angry! He was galloping back to her! He would beat her, and take her back!

Jacinta had nowhere to run. She had no one who could protect her against such a fearsome man. She waited, helpless, her head was down and her shoulders slumped. A solitary tear ran down her cheek, but as she tried to wipe it away, only more came.

As Hakeem drew near, he wrenched his horse and leapt from the saddle, but instead of hitting her he fell to his knees before her. He tipped her small face up, wiping quickly at her tears with his hand as if to dry them.

"Oh Jacinta," he cried in distress, and crushed her small form against his chest, tears welling in his own eyes. "I didn't know, please forgive me. I will *never* do that again. I promise, *never, ever* again."

He gathered her up in his strong arms and lifted her onto Nadeer. "Gyorgy!" he spat on the ground as he mounted.

It would be a lethal mistake to go back to the Gypsy camp. They quickly rode on, leaving Jacinta's paltry possessions and the money Hakeem had given behind.

Nadeer seemed happy now, and trotted along with a spring in his step.

Hakeem kept murmuring in distress, "I'm so sorry!" Jacinta sat in his arms, twisting the material of his vest in her hands. Her tears wet his shirt. From time to time she would hit him, on the chest or the shoulder, as hard as her tiny strength would allow.

Hakeem's obvious remorse repaired some the wound she felt, but she felt so *angry*, she had never wanted to be left there in the first place!

By the second day, the relationship started to thaw. On the first day, Hakeem had made no comment on her weak attempts to punch him. On the second day, every time she hit him he would say "Ow!" This would cause her to try to hit him again, with all her might.

So a 'Hakeem and Jacinta' game eventually emerged, from her attempts to hit him and his mock attempts to get sympathy, his complaints about her savagery, and his enquiries of whether she was ready to forgive him.

If he asked, "Can you forgive me?" she would give a sulky, "No!" This was followed by another punch. This usually elicited another apology.

Slowly, Jacinta began to relax back into the relationship. Hakeem was now decided. For better or worse, they were a family of two, and any of his future calculations included his young Gypsy ward.

The greatest characteristic of the Anatolē Gypsies was resilience, and soon enough Jacinta perked up. Hakeem continued Farah on a lead, Jacinta sometimes sat the smaller pack horse. It didn't have a proper saddle, but he rigged up some blankets till he could remedy the situation. Often, however, she would simply say, "I want to ride with you," and would climb onto Nadeer, to be enfolded in Hakeem's large arms.

She talked continually. So much that Hakeem sometimes lost track of her questions and comments, so he all he could do was make a noncommittal grunt or say 'Yes, Jacinta", having no idea what she was saying. This didn't seem to discourage her at all.

She was great company and, he noticed, very clever.

Chapter 11: Shopping For a Girl, and a Troublesome Young Slave

It was several days later that Hakeem and Jacinta arrived early at a large town. He needed to reprovision and buy some clothes for Jacinta, all she had left was what she was wearing!

Hakeem felt baffled as to how to buy clothes for a small girl, and heaved a sigh of relief to find a huge shed that sold a wide range of travelling provisions . They didn't have the sort of quality of horse tack that he required, but they had clothes! Practical travel clothes, hard wearing, and of course earthy, simple tones! This at least made one problem simple ... or so he thought.

"I won't wear these!" Jacinta shouted and pushed grumpily at the pile of clothing he was sorting for her. He looked at her, puzzled.

"I'm not a boy!" she screamed angrily at him. "Is that all you think of me? I can't wear plain white like that, that's for funerals. And all these others are so dull! That's all you wear! Why do I have to look like you?"

Hakeem looked helplessly at the clothes he had chosen. He felt crestfallen and confused. Then Jacinta bowed her head and started to cry.

Hakeem felt a surge of panic in front of the crying girl. She had been through so much already. He could hardly stand it!

"I'm sorry Jacinta. I'm no good at this. Do you think you could choose for yourself?" He coaxed the small girl, who looked at him coyly. "Then, you can have whatever you want!" he added, trying to entice her.

Jacinta let out a little squeal of excitement and hugged him, giving him a wonderful smile. It felt *so* good. He noticed her eyes and cheeks were surprisingly dry for one who had been crying, but her happiness was so delightful! Her excitement so infectious!

Jacinta insisted on choosing the shop and led him firmly outside.

She whispered, asking whether they could use the money he had taken from her family's killers.

"No," he whispered back. "That's yours. I have put it aside for you when you grow up. Till then, it won't be touched."

Her head jerked up. For once she was completely speechless.

Hakeem looked embarrassed. "I always meant it that way. I told Moira. I said I would give her more money, if you needed any, but not from that."

Jacinta was in shock.

She didn't know about the money negotiations. Hakeem certainly hadn't been trying to dump her with Moira and Moira and Andreas seemed nice. What went wrong wasn't their fault.

And she would have a sizeable dowry! Wow! She could hardly believe it. She had never had her own money, she never expected to.

She didn't know what to say. "Thank you, Hakeem," she managed in a small voice, as she gazed up at him. He bent down to give her a kiss, and suddenly she launched herself at him, arms around his neck. As he caught her, she tried her very best to hug him to death.

They stayed like this, hugging each other for some time. Jacinta drew her feet up as high as she could, and Hakeem gathered her feet up in his hands and gently rocked her back and forwards. She looked the happiest he had ever seen her.

Eventually she murmured. "How much can I spend?"

He shifted her to his hip. "Anything in reason, I suppose," Hakeem shrugged vaguely, gesturing with his hand.

"Hakeem, how much money *do* you have?" she whispered in his ear.

"Huh? I don't know. I've got enough … I guess." He pulled a heavy purse out of a pocket and passed it to her. It was so heavy that she almost dropped it in surprise!

Jacinta pulled the drawstring and peered inside in total disbelief. "Hakeem, it's *so* much! Don't you ever count it?"

"No. I got money quite a few times, I don't really spend a lot." He shrugged, screwing his face up as he tried to think how much money he might have now. Then he gave up the effort, he had no idea at all.

"Hakeem, you're hopeless!" she scolded, in shock and fond exasperation. Her head was shaking from side to side in utter amazement.

"You'd better leave the bargaining to me," she said very firmly.

"Alright," Hakeem agreed meekly.

In one respect, Hakeem was not a typical tribesman. His people made bargaining a national sport. It was customary to spend half an hour and more haggling.

For more expensive goods, the initial price was twice or more what was reasonable. The customer would then make a ridiculously low offer. This was accompanied with good-natured banter and dramatics. The shopkeeper would complain that he would be ruined. He had a large family to support! The customer, would alternatively cajole, scold, accuse and appeal to the shopkeeper's good nature.

If it got to the shopkeeper starting to put the goods back on the shelf, or the customer starting to walk out, each had reached their limit.

After this, there would be friendly smiles and the customer would be served small cups of sweet black tea while the goods were made ready.

In the monastery and in the army, most of Hakeem's needs were supplied. He never learned how to shop, and later he tried to avoid it. Most things he bought weren't expensive, and he felt sorry for small shopkeepers if he bargained too hard.

Rather than haggle, he usually asked "What's your best price?" If it seemed reasonable, he paid it. If not, he usually went elsewhere, even if they tried to call him back.

For bigger things, like personal battle kit, he took Elwan or he ended up paying too much.

Jacinta hopped down, all businesslike, as she took the problem in hand. "Now, follow me," she commanded and marched determinedly into the very middle of a confusing maze of stalls and shops.

Hours later ... after traipsing endlessly around ... Hakeem was going utterly insane!

"Why didn't you buy that one?" he asked, completely bewildered.

"I didn't like it," Jacinta said simply, as if explaining something to a small child.

"Then why did you spend so much time looking at it and bargaining?"

"I wanted to see what I could get it for," Jacinta patiently explained, a bit surprised Hakeem didn't know that.

"Why did you look at it, if you didn't like it?" Hakeem continued, baffled.

"I just wanted to see."

Then it struck Jacinta. She turned to the big man in disbelief. She was shocked by the very thought!

"You don't *like* shopping, do you?"

It was hardly credible.

Hakeem smiled weakly at her and gave a mighty yawn. Hakeem would have said he didn't tire easily, but a morning of shopping with Jacinta and he felt hungry and stiff and his mind felt foggy.

And they hadn't bought anything! Wasn't shopping about *buying* things? Now, how *could* he have gotten such an idea?

To women and girls, obviously shopping seemed to be a thing unto itself. Buying wasn't needed, not at all. They could spend hours and hours just looking examining and comparing prices and still feel satisfied. And they seemed to enjoy doing it.

It was incomprehensible to Hakeem.

Jacinta took the big man in hand, and shepherded him to a small outdoor restaurant. After food, Hakeem felt better. As he was sipping a second cup of tea, Jacinta was jigging up and down in her seat excitedly.

She suggested she go to a stall nearby while he rested for a bit more. Hakeem looked around cautiously. "Alright, but don't get out of sight and don't forget …"

"I know, for the tenth time ... it'll be cold and wet in the mountains." She tried to imitate his man's voice which set them both laughing. "Don't be silly," she smiled. "I've been here before and I've wandered around these sorts of places since I was born!"

Hakeem struggled to keep a straight face to hear her say this. He almost added "I know, and you have lived *such* a very long time, haven't you, you old woman, you?"

* * *

"Oh dear Goddess!" Jacinta thought to herself with a smile, as Hakeem appeared near her soon afterwards. He was supposed to be sipping his tea. All she had done was to look at some clothes around the corner of the store, where Hakeem couldn't see her. When she turned around, there he was, leaning against a post ever so casually scanning the surrounds. He acts like he's a bodyguard and I'm some sort of Royal Princess, Jacinta thought, not a Gypsy orphan girl.

It wasn't long after this, that Jacinta led her big companion down a twisting series of narrow lanes, to a huge clothing shop. "This is it," she announced, as she bustled in.

Soon the colourfully dressed shopkeeper, his wife, and two sons were talking to Jacinta rapidly in their own strange tongue, the Gypsy language. Gypsies called themselves and their language "Romani" from "roma" meaning "man".

The term 'Gypsy' came from a mainland Greek misconception that they came from Aígyptos. The elves and Shantawi knew they were Indo-Aryans from the land around the north of India that the Aryans tribes had conquered a thousand years before.

Gypsies persisted with their nomadic lifestyle, and this meant they were often persecuted by others who settled and claimed the land they travelled through.

They were many nomadic peoples but the Gypsies were the greatest of all, and they maintained a close-knit culture which transcended national boundaries. No wonder Jacinta expected a better price here. The owners obviously had extensive contacts, the quality and range looked incredible.

Jacinta perched on a stool and chattered away, while Hakeem sat glumly in another corner of the shop, bored and not understanding what was going on. They were the only customers, as it was close to midday.

Then Jacinta said something that drew *very* unfriendly looks towards Hakeem. One of their sons started to rise, but was restrained by his mother's hand. As Jacinta talked, the temperature in the big shop started to chill. The owner looked at Hakeem, as if he was a piece of dog filth.

Hakeem felt hurt, he wondered what she was saying to her fellow Gypsies behind his back. What did she secretly think of him? More so, he was becoming alarmed and loosened Mir in its sheath.

Then Jacinta and the family became serious and businesslike, bringing out a bewildering range of cloth and clothes. Hakeem remained ignored, on his stool in the corner. He saw a small pile of clothing that they could take straight away and a bigger pile of cloth and clothing that needed sewing or adjusting. There was a second blanket each.

Jacinta was looking at a very fine scarf, which looked like it came from Aígyptos. She kept picking it up and putting it down regretfully with a sigh. It was obvious to all that she liked it.

"Buy it, if you like it," Hakeem called out from his position on the stool, then added as a helpful afterthought, "if you can get a good price."

"No Hakeem, it's far too expensive," she replied in Greek. "Though it is nice ...," she added wistfully.

"I'm sure we can afford it. Go on, get it ... if you can get a good price," he called out loudly.

Bargaining *definitely* wasn't Hakeem's strong point!

Suddenly the owner and his wife looked at Hakeem in astonishment. They talked rapidly to Jacinta in the Gypsy tongue. The owner started to walk over to Hakeem, smiling broadly. Jacinta jerked up and almost fell off her stool. She scurried around and tried to push the man back. She seemed agitated, talking very excitedly and waving her free arm energetically.

He ignored her, and favoured Hakeem with a broad smile.

"So," he said as he approached, talking in that gorgeously accented Greek Jacinta used. "I know you are displeased with your slave here. My wife and I find the work in our shop rather heavy at times. Perhaps you would allow us to buy her from you. Though she is unworthy, we will give you a good price."

"BUY her! Slave!" Hakeem jumped up in shock and outrage, knocking over his stool. "What has she been telling you?"

"Only what a cruel and stingy master you were. You wanted her dressed well to show off your wealth, but would beat her if she didn't get a good price!" the owner replied, enjoying the tribesman's obvious confusion and Jacinta's agitation.

"JACINTA!" Hakeem roared, and started to march over to where Jacinta cringed back in a corner. The couple were shocked by his anger, and they hurried to grab him to keep him from reaching Jacinta. They may as well have tried their strength against an ox.

Hakeem ploughed slowly across the room, dragging the man and the woman behind him.

Jacinta flinched from him, frightened by his rage.

He towered over her. "How could you say such things? Do you know what people will think of me?" he asked incredulously.

As he bent closer, his voice was almost back to normal volume. Jacinta looked at the floor and said nothing. When it was obvious that Hakeem intended no more than to scold the girl, the shopkeeper relaxed.

"Well, it seems that things are not quite what we may have been led to believe," he said mildly.

Hakeem stared at him, stuck for words. He allowed himself to be led, completely stunned back to the stool. "She's my foster daughter," he managed.

The shopkeeper permitted himself a chuckle. These tribesmen were famous for their stiff-backed honour. The trick the young girl had played on her foster father was delicious.

He imagined them recounting the story over and over: You should have seen his face! I thought he was going to have apoplexy! Then he roared like some great bear; he was huge! None of us could stop him. We thought he would beat her. In the end, all he did was ask her why she did it.

In his imagination, he would go on about the girl. He'd heard all sorts of hard luck stories but she was very good. She had all of us believing it.

She's one to watch, that one! Jacinta had struck a very tight bargain, but it was worth it for the joke she played. He'd even give her a good price on the expensive cloth if the tribesman didn't withdraw his offer.

"Do I beat you, Jacinta?" Hakeem asked conversationally as he brought his stool over and placed it close to her.

"No, Hakeem," she replied sheepishly.

"Should I beat you, Jacinta?"

"No, Hakeem," Jacinta replied with a small smile.

"Do you want me to beat you, Jacinta?"

"No I don't, Hakeem," Jacinta smiled and couldn't help a little chuckle, as she recognised a Hakeem teasing game.

She couldn't quite believe there wouldn't be further repercussions. But Hakeem was obviously recovered from his shock.

Jacinta had been truly frightened. Her heart was still racing and her breath coming rapidly, as if she had run a race. Again she thought he would beat her, and the mildness of his eventual response surprised her.

"I need to pay them some money," she said eventually.

Not realising how strange it looked, he passed his complete purse to the small girl who was obviously in charge of the shopping. She competently counted out the money. "Don't forget the nice scarf you wanted," he reminded.

They would have to return tomorrow for the alterations and the garments that had to be made up. Then they would pay the remainder, but the shopkeeper simply *couldn't* let them leave!

Misunderstanding the situation, he hadn't offered the tribesman the usual hospitality. He couldn't in all honour allow them to leave now!

While Hakeem was offered tea and small cakes, the owner chatted to him. Hakeem was back smiling, and showed himself as a polite and respectful guest. The shopkeeper started to get a sense of his character, and couldn't help smiling to himself and chuckling as he recalled the trick Jacinta had played.

Jacinta had recovered, and took half the cakes when Hakeem offered them to her. She chatted away, in her own tongue, to the shopkeeper's wife. She seemed to enjoy the chance to talk to one of her own kind, so Hakeem gave her some time. At one point she grew sad, and the old lady put a hand on the girl's shoulder. Talking about her family, Hakeem knew.

Then she looked smiling across at Hakeem, with a look of pure adoration. He smiled in return. Then the old lady said something and laughed, Jacinta looked sheepish as she laughed back and flashed an embarrassed glance at Hakeem.

While he intended to give Jacinta time with the kindly lady, he found the old Gypsy man entertaining and knowledgeable, so he was enjoying the company. The old man insisted on measuring him and offering him a free shirt, but Hakeem politely declined.

"Well, for a Gaje, you are a good man," the old Gypsy eventually said as they were leaving. "You have a lovely and clever daughter. You *really* should leave any bargaining to her!"

Hakeem smiled ruefully, as he grabbed Jacinta and pulled her towards him affectionately. "As long as she doesn't land us both in jail, we should get some really good prices."

The old Gypsy roared with laughter.

As they were walking, Hakeem asked Jacinta. "What's a Gaje?"

"It's our term for outsiders. Used the way he did, it's an affectionate term."

"So, it's got another meaning?" Hakeem was curious.

"Er, peasant."

Hakeem laughed, "That's what you call outsiders?" He was beginning to realise there was much more to the Gypsy culture than he realised.

The next day Jacinta woke before dawn and lay drowsing. The clothes would not be ready before the mid-afternoon, but she couldn't contain her excitement. Over breakfast she jiggled up and down in her seat, chatting continually about clothing and cloth that she had seen. Hakeem had trouble remembering half the stalls, let alone pieces of cloth but he manfully tried to pretend interest. She went on and on, till he had to keep reminding her to eat her food.

To contain some of her impatience, he took her grocery shopping to the morning market. Jacinta insisted on changing back into her old clothes. "Jacinta," Hakeem said as she came back down. "This is not necessary. We have enough money."

She looked at him seriously. "When I was young, we often did not have enough money for food. It's something I'll never forget. Besides," she added with a bright smile, "this is fun!"

Hakeem, who had never found shopping fun, shrugged, and followed on.

Later he had to look for a third horse and a saddle for Farah … no, not a third horse just to carry Jacinta's new clothes! They needed to carry enough gear and food for the two of them on the journey. It may seem a luxury, but in truth it was a minimum. They couldn't carry enough on the two mounts. Farah was already laden with his 'kit'. Hakeem would only don his armour for the more dangerous stretches.

It would be unfair and impractical to ask their two horses to carry more. Never ask a horse to carry more than a third of its own weight. They would be travelling through arid lands in central Anatolē and again to reach the city of Karsh. Hakeem had the tribesman's good sense of direction, but also their deep respect for the desert and arid lands. They would not be going into the true desert or off the travelled roads, but he would take extra water and supplies as a matter of course.

Now, buying a horse was *one* area where he didn't need any help! He certainly knew horses and was a very shrewd judge of their worth. Possibly, there wasn't a Shantawi alive who could be cheated buying a horse.

* * *

The morning market was near the entrance to the town and consisted of several huge semi-permanent rectangular tents spread over a large open area, paved with stone. It was owned by the town and they rented space to the stall owners within.

Each large tent was roughly dedicated to multiple stalls of similar goods, varying from benches for handicrafts, to mats on the floor for fruit sellers, to crates or baskets, depending on what was being sold. The town provided guards against the inevitable pickpockets and thieves, and there was daily cleaning.

Only certain ingredients would keep, so the town's women shopped every day and bought just enough for that day. The time for the morning market was from an hour or so after dawn till midmorning. In summer this meant that things could be sold fresh, before the heat of the day.

As they entered, Hakeem was almost knocked over by the chaos. His senses were assaulted by the noise, sights, and smells of the market. There was limited time to shop and people were everywhere, all talking and shouting at once.

Sellers were calling their wares, servants or housewives were haggling, and workmen calling to each other. There were narrow laneways between stalls, but they were overwhelmed by the press of people. Barefoot children and street urchins were running back and forwards, women with large baskets and men delivering supplies.

There was a confusion of smells: pleasant smells in the sections for fruit, tea, incense and spices, appalling smells from the meat, paltry and fish markets.

Jacinta delved into Hakeem's purse and happily went ahead. She seemed in her element, Hakeem grimly trailed her into the chaos. He tried unsuccessfully to be unobtrusive as he could, in this world of women shoppers. He overheard Jacinta talk of her life as a 'slave', but no longer of ill treatment.

They bought salt fish and preserved meat and fruit but avoided the fresh meat market, which was a cruel place. They would get fresher meat from small villages on their journey. Hakeem could hear barking at the back of the meat section as they hurried past. He didn't even want to know what that was about.

The next stop was the fresh fruit section, concentrating on things that would keep, such as apples and oranges. Hakeem drifted up, "You don't have to buy those apples, they are small and wizened, we can afford better."

"They're for the horses, silly," Jacinta scolded him.

Hakeem subsided after this, and simply left it to her.

He insisted on carrying all the sacks to leave Jacinta's hands free. So the sacks and packages she kept passing to him got more and more awkward and heavier and heavier.

It earned him some very strange looks. Most men would get their women and girls to do the carrying, if they were in the food market at all.

A vendor offered him some rope, so he roped several sacks together and carried them, slung over the shoulder. Jacinta's donkey, that's what I am! He smiled wanly at the thought, but he had to admit, Jacinta was good at shopping. Being a female of an itinerant family, Jacinta knew exactly how to outfit them for the journey. Hakeem was an excellent leader of men. He could accurately work out what was needed to provision a group of any size for a journey ... as long as no one asked him to do the actual shopping.

Without help he would be totally lost. He imagined himself with several lists and preferably a large number of helpers. Even then he would stumble, double-checking his calculations, dropping his lists and wandering disoriented back and forwards looking for the next item in the crowded market, and always paying too much.

He was baffled by the young Gypsy girl's ability. Jacinta could do this in her sleep! She seemed to know exactly where to go, what to get, how much to pay, and in what order to shop. All Hakeem could do was follow in her wake, doing the heavy carrying.

Soon it was all accomplished.

They took their supplies back to the inn and then set out to get the spare horse.

The livestock market was held one day a week and was split in three sections: poultry one section, sheep and goats in another. The final section had cattle, mules, donkeys and horses to be auctioned in turn.

Donkeys were the cheapest and most popular, camels were too expensive and not used here, so far from the desert.

The cattle sales were on and the horse sales would follow so Hakeem had time to carefully inspect what was on offer. It was Jacinta's turn to be impressed. Hakeem's attitude to buying horses bore no similarity at all to his attitude towards any other form of shopping.

He only wanted a solid pack horse, but he fastidiously spent time examining each and every horse, murmuring quietly to Jacinta what she should look for.

She didn't know there was so much to horses.

He seemed pleased with the deal he got, on the third horse he bid for. It was a busy, exhausting day but eventually they were wandering back to the fabric shop.

The owner greeted them at the door, grinning broadly. "Here's the wealthy but cruel Gaje and his unsatisfactory Romani servant." Hakeem chuckled and Jacinta looked embarrassed for a moment. Then her excitement took over.

It would not be practical for either Jacinta or Hakeem to take too many spare clothes on the journey, but each of Jacinta's outfits didn't take up a lot of space. Clothes are very important for females, Hakeem had realised by now, and Jacinta was no different.

He had told her what he wanted her to get, some serviceable daily clothes, undergarments, two good outfits for herself, a cloak, sandals, boots and extra blankets.

Waiting was a small but beautiful collection of Gypsy clothes.

Romani dress is distinguished by a love of bright colours. Their travels give them access to a range of dyes and fabrics not widely available, and their strong connection with circuses and entertainment adds to their fondness for bright garments. Colours that would clash, if combined in the clothing of any other people, seem to work perfectly for Gypsies.

White was a funeral colour but is acceptable with coloured embroidery. Primary red (which signified blood) brought bad luck but crimson on the other hand, is very popular.

Jacinta had two full dresses and a few practical pants for riding and working, but even her pants were decorated with embroidery on the hems. There was a selection of undergarments for daily use and some with frills (no one would see her wearing them, but girls were girls).

There was an exquisite and warm fur coat and the softest of boots, a size too large, but Jacinta explained she could wear thick knitted socks and grow into them.

The owner's wife braided Jacinta's hair then she modelled her dresses, she was beaming with delight. Hakeem and the owners of the shop were enjoying watching her excitement and admiring how pretty she was. When she was in her best Gypsy dress, Hakeem reached into his coat and brought out a small cloth parcel. Jacinta opened it slowly then let out a delighted squeal and hugged the big tribesman.

Silver earrings, they were exquisite! Hakeem had noticed her ears were pierced but she had no ear rings and somehow, he had bought them while she was distracted.

"He's not bad for a mean and cruel master, I'd say!" the shopkeeper teased her as his wife helped her wear them.

It was a big and exciting day and it was good to relax in their room that evening.

Hakeem always made Jacinta take the bed, he preferred the floor. Jacinta always felt a little uncomfortable with this. He was older, he was some sort of officer and he was a male after all!

As Jacinta recovered from the trauma of her loss, it happened less, but Hakeem still sometimes woke in the morning with her asleep on his shoulder.

Sometimes he woke, suffocating and hot, to find her having pulled herself and all her blankets down on him till he was buried in layers upon layers.

The worst was when she would sleep on or near him and (though asleep) would kick and kick with her heels till he couldn't stand it anymore, and had to put her back in her own bed.

After the excitement of the shopping trip, Jacinta was sitting on the bed organizing his money into neat piles of coppers, silvers, gold eights, quarters and full gold coins.

He'd just finished explaining to her that he would definitely *not* be passing, to anyone else, the two debased gold coins she had found. She was shocked by his, "but someone gave them to you, Hakeem!"

If someone gave them to *him*, why on earth couldn't he give them to someone else?

No! They would go to the gold smith for salvage, even at a fraction of the face value ... and there would be none of her colourful stories.

Jacinta was humming to herself, as she happily counted the coins. Hakeem was thinking of how different it was to raise a little girl. As he watched her counting the money, it occurred to him he needed to start her education.

"Jacinta, I'm going to teach you to read and write and do calculations," he announced. He expected an instant argument, but she meekly nodded almost absently, "Yes, Hakeem."

Then Jacinta looked up from her counting, "Hakeem?"

"Hmm," he replied.

"Will you teach me how to fight?"

Hakeem's head jerked up in surprise, "Why?"

Whenever he was out of town, he would practice for half an hour and more before breaking his fast and Jacinta would usually perch on a rock or stump to watch. Perhaps it shouldn't have surprised him that she was interested.

"Well," Jacinta explained, "When my family was killed, you killed the men that did it. It would feel good if I was able to take revenge on them myself."

Hakeem sighed and shook his head, "No, I won't teach you."

Jacinta knew as soon as she said it, she had given the wrong answer.

"No, wait," she tried again, desperately. "Sometimes people need help, and they are not strong enough and I can also defend myself if I'm attacked."

"Good answer." He smiled. "We'll talk about revenge later. It wouldn't have done your family any good, and it wouldn't have taught those men any lessons. If you took pleasure in killing them, you would do very serious harm to yourself."

"Do you mean to say that people who do evil really hurt themselves?" Jacinta asked, puzzled.

How could that possibly work? she wondered. If they got away with it, weren't they happy?

"Yes, very good," Hakeem smiled and nodded. "That's exactly what I mean. They may cause pain and suffering to others, but the worst damage they do is to themselves, their souls. Remember this, it's very important: you can't kill people. People don't really die."

Jacinta looked puzzled, "Huh?" Then she realised what he meant, "Oh yeah, life after death. I'll believe THAT when I see it."

"Again, that's an excellent answer, little one!" Hakeem replied with enthusiasm. "You should *never* believe something, just because you're told it. It is important to experience these things for yourself."

Jacinta sighed, sometimes Hakeem got a bit weird on her around his religion, but this was *really* weird. "Like die you mean?"

"No, Jacinta," he laughed, and then became more serious. "When people die and are reborn, they often don't recall a lot about their past life, the greatest effect is on their soul. Let's leave this. Many things are best learned by experience."

A shiver passed through Jacinta. "Learn by experience?" She had learned to love and trust Hakeem. She knew he was strange at times, but she feared what he said. It was scary enough to think he was touched in the head, but if he was somehow speaking the truth, it was absolutely terrifying.

As if reading her mind, "Relax," he said. "It's not crazy and I promise, not scary. It's a simple and natural part of life. In fact it's reassuring, but we'll come to that later. There are some things you have to *do*, or *see*, to understand. You shouldn't take another's word for it.

"Everybody gets messages about life, but most ignore them and concentrate on things that are not important. All you have to do is be open to them, and meditate on the lessons you are given. It's really *is* that simple. All the answers you need are inside you.

"Let's get back to the training. First, you need to understand that it's only to be used for your defence, and that of others."

Jacinta nodded, though she wondered where the life of a mercenary could fit in.

"And," he continued, "always try to avoid a fight *at all costs,* if you can."

She gave another solemn nod.

"Finally, if I am your teacher, you must obey me completely in all matters related to your education or fighting or training. If we are ever in danger, you must do whatever I say immediately, without any question."

"Wow, do any teachers ever do the wrong thing?" she asked, considering.

"Yes, some do. You know me, would you trust me that much, Jacinta?"

"Of course I would! I mean, I agree." Jacinta nodded.

"Then I will teach you," Hakeem announced.

Jacinta gave a small whoop, and threw herself at Hakeem to hug him.

He smiled at her and pretended to be solemn, "Welcome, pupil. We need to buy a few other things for your training, but I know about these and it won't take long. Now, the first lesson will be tomorrow night. After that you must meet and communicate with my God," he said.

Jacinta felt scared, Hakeem had never shown any tendency to do magic, but a God?

"Why would he want to meet me?" she asked in a small voice.

Hakeem smiled, "I'll show you the morning after tomorrow. God knows you already. Remember, I promised you it won't be scary. You must trust me.

"It's a wonderful experience. Anyway, who said anything about 'he'?

"In the meantime, now I want you to get some sleep."

Chapter 12: Meeting God, and a Most Determined Pupil

Sleep?

He may as well have asked Jacinta to fly up into the air!

Her mind was racing. He was going to teach her how to fight like he did. But despite his reassurances, he scared her. Meeting with a God? She was bursting with questions.

It had to be a trick! He had said he wouldn't train her unless she 'talked' to a God, was that what he had said? Well that was easy … it wouldn't happen, and yet he seemed dead serious, and he already said she was his pupil.

She tossed and turned. Then tossed and turned and kicked the blankets. Then she tossed some more. Eventually Hakeem shouted at her to sleep.

The next day she woke late. Hakeem was already downstairs breaking his fast.

'Hakeem is always eating, or drinking tea!' Jacinta thought to herself in disgust. Couldn't they hurry things up today?

Anyway, now he will insist she eat something and drink boiled milk. Was he trying to make her fat? Almost daily when they stopped, he would carefully inspect the village cow. Then check that the milk was boiled long enough and then insist she drink at least one glass.

Greeks never drank milk; they thought it was barbaric, why should she have to?

Oh! she thought, frustrated, Hakeem could be *so* fussy at times!

Hakeem smiled when he noticed Jacinta was in a hurry to leave. As if leaving earlier would mean the evening would come sooner.

He insisted she eat. The effect on her of a better diet was already dramatic. She seemed to be growing in front of his eyes. He made a mental note to measure her.

For Jacinta, the morning dragged on and on. They had to backtrack to the shops. As promised, this did not take long, except for choosing a training bow for Jacinta. Hakeem seemed to spend almost as long time examining what was on offer, measuring her up and talking to the man who made them, as if he were buying another horse.

Jacinta had no idea what he was looking for, but he could be such a fusspot. And he complained about *my* shopping!

Then she smiled at herself for thinking this, and allowed herself to feel some excitement. This was for her, after all.

While Hakeem loaded the horses, Jacinta did what she could, and then kept pacing back and forwards as he very carefully packed everything. Hakeem watched her out of the corner of one eye and tried to hide his smile.

As they slowly ascended some wooded hill country on their mounts, Jacinta found herself drowsing, despite the excitement. Two nights of restless sleep were catching up with her. She woke with a start in her saddle to find that Hakeem was stopping early for the night.

They had moved back from the road to a small lookout. It was a beautiful spot near the top of the hill, looking over a broad valley with the coastal mountain ranges in the east.

The mountains were magnificent. The tallest all had snow despite it only being late summer and almost the start of autumn.

Hakeem drove Jacinta crazy by methodically setting up the camp in the usual way. She helped as much as she could, gathering wood, unsaddling and brushing the horses, unpacking the chicken, vegetables and spices. Why did he have to set rabbit snares for heaven sake? They had enough food! Didn't he say that he was sick of rabbit?

It was a dry camp, so he had brought extra water for the horses. He set some out, and then gave them some oats before allowing them to graze.

Couldn't he be quicker with the fire? Why dig a latrine pit, even a small one? He always did that! Then as he cooked, he hummed to himself.

Still no word! While she couldn't contain herself any longer, *he* was relaxing with the inevitable cup of tea after eating. "Haven't you forgotten something?"

"No little one. Let me finish my tea. I need to teach you how to breathe."

She pouted at him. Was he only going to tease her? "I know how to breathe, Hakeem."

"If you can't breathe, it's hard to meet God." Hakeem smiled at her.

What's he talking about? Jacinta thought. If she stopped breathing … that's when she would meet God. But he had finished his tea.

He folded a blanket and set it down for her, getting her to sit on it and checking that she was as comfortable as she could be. Then he sat facing her, cross-legged, which she quickly copied.

"Now I want you to take a slow deep breath," Hakeem started. "Not so deep it feels a strain. Try to relax completely … that's it!

"Now breathe out … very slowly.

"As you breathe in and out, I want you to concentrate on the point just below your nose, where you can feel the coolness of your breath as it comes in and out." Hakeem's voice had taken on a hypnotic quality, as he encouraged her. "Just concentrate on this and nothing else. If your mind wanders, just bring it gently back. Try to empty your mind and focus on your breath."

Hakeem would pause for a while, and then gently encourage her to maintain her concentration. It was very relaxing, but Jacinta's mind was racing here and there! She was thinking of shopping, of the clothes she had bought, of Hakeem teaching her fighting and talking to a God.

"Concentrate, Jacinta," Hakeem encouraged gently.

She tried to focus. Concentrate on what ... nothing?

Her breath.

Eventually she managed. It felt very calming and somehow different but after a while, she could feel herself falling asleep. This wouldn't do!

Then Hakeem was saying, "That's enough. You did very well. This step is very important. Much comes from it, both in our religion and our fighting. I must teach you both.

"You can practice again tomorrow, and I'll be there to help."

Jacinta could hardly stay awake. It seemed no sooner had she fallen asleep than Hakeem was waking her up again.

It couldn't be morning yet, could it? She opened one eye, and saw it was hardly first light. Hakeem had put more wood on the fire and this gave them enough light to see by.

Hakeem smiled down fondly. All he could see was a heap of blankets, showing some tousled curly black hair and one eye peering through the tangle looking blearily up at him.

He insisted Jacinta have a couple of wheat cakes and clean herself up a little. Jacinta thought she would be too nervous to eat, but then she realised how hungry she was. He also heated up some oat porridge, adding a generous dollop of honey and a pinch of salt

He made sure she was as comfortable as he could, before they started. Again he folded a blanket, for her. He sat on bare rock. Then he got her to sit facing the mountain range. He started her on the breathing meditation, warning her to never look directly at the sun.

They were on a rise, looking out over the dark valley below with the mountains only as shapes in the distance. Slowly the valley could be seen more and more clearly. A cock crowed and pigeons started to coo. Cows started to call and a dog barked on a farm below. Now Jacinta could see a river winding its way through the forest, fields, and the road headed east, deserted at this hour.

Jacinta loved sunrises, but wondered how this one would be different.

"Nature is preparing to give a special show," Hakeem warned her. "Meditate," he said. "Keep with the experience."

So Jacinta waited, ready.

They were to see something of breathtaking beauty. No one could really watch sunrise over the mountains and not be moved. Like any great show, this one relied on subtle unnoticed changes.

Like watching a stage magician, the observer's eye was drawn to a faint glow behind a dark outline in the distance. It was like the opening note of a symphony, but this was in vision, not sound.

At first faint, it grew stronger and stronger, growing in power and promise. Before the warmth of the day the clouds hung, layer upon layer, impenetrable and black ... now they were becoming dull grey and softer, more clearly seen.

Imperceptive at first, unnoticed, dawn's alchemy was being wrought. As they were watching, the mountains slowly took form. The fluffy clouds had become an exquisite pastel blue-grey! And then ... the still-hidden sun splashed the undersides of the clouds with its beautiful soft rose hue.

At last the climax came! The sun peaked over the mountains, and the sky caught fire! It was a perfect symphony, rising and rising in a glorious crescendo of colour.

After a while, Hakeem stopped. Jacinta sat for some time, eyes now closed, silent. She continued the breathing, her small face one of peace and rapture.

"Well, what do you think?" Hakeem asked when she finally relaxed back from the meditation pose.

She was in awe. "Oh Hakeem, that was *so* beautiful. I love sunsets and sunrises. They are best over the mountains, but I've *never* experienced anything like that."

"The meditation allows you to be fully open to the experience," Hakeem said gently.

"Thank you so much for showing me, Hakeem but you played a trick on me. You worship the sun God."

Hakeem smiled. "You're very close. We do use the sun as God's symbol, and most of us call our God Apollōn, the God of light and wisdom. You already know we do.

"God is in all things but in beauty we can see God more clearly. Sunrise over the mountains is one of the most beautiful things I can imagine. That's why I brought you to this spot."

"But you said God would talk to me. I didn't hear anything!" Jacinta complained.

"No, Jacinta. I didn't say *talk*! I've never heard God with my ears." Hakeem spoke carefully. "Think back ... did you feel anything?"

Jacinta looked thoughtful; she paused and then answered carefully. "Yes ... something that loved ... the sort of love that was so strong it ached!" She finished in amazement, humbled. She hadn't realised it, until she herself had said it.

Hakeem was very impressed by her reply. "Was there any message for you?"

"I think so ..." Jacinta said thoughtfully. "About how I should live my life. It'll take me ages to think it all through, though."

Hakeem laughed. He was a bit in awe of what Jacinta had just said to him.

"So, who is the teacher now, and who is the pupil? You got all that first time! It took me years and I was considered an excellent student."

"But you said I would meet God," she persisted. "I didn't see him. That wasn't God, it's what he made."

"No! Think, Jacinta!" Hakeem insisted. "God was there. You met God. Do you expect to experience God, as if God were a man? I've never 'seen' God. I don't know if that is even possible. Did you think God thinks in the language of men?

"Nonetheless, you really were in God's presence, receiving God's message. Many see God as like a man, or a woman, or a man with a bull's head. I can't say any of these are wrong, but this is not what I experience.

"Some of these men are, to me, very holy and close to God. You will feel God's presence as you meet them or enter their temple, but I believe we impose what *we* are on God and see God as being like us. I think that's our heads talking.

"Some believe God demands great temples, praying at altars, the sacrifice of chickens and goats, or complicated rituals. That's not the message I receive. I think that's for humans, not God.

"If it helps them to focus, then it is a good thing but it is the trappings of belief, and if we focus on the trappings too much we can lose the core. God does communicate with us, but in our hearts.

"We are on this earth for a good reason. We are shown so much, but much is *also* kept from us, I think, also for a reason. Perhaps if we know too much of what's beyond, we won't be able to do what we are here to do."

"Is this what your religion teaches in your temples, then?"

"No," Hakeem laughed. "Of course not. If we taught like this, we would not have one common follower left! People work hard six days a week, they don't want to think hard on the seventh. That's not a criticism.

"People come to the temple to relax, meet friends. They love festivals, rituals. The temple translates, tells them how to live a good life, it reassures when they are troubled and grieving. It adds joy to weddings and births. People need something familiar, something that is simple that they can understand. We give them the same message, but in a different way!"

"You tell lies? Shayvism tells lies?" Jacinta was scandalised. "How can that help?"

"Not lies! The temple shows the path, but for those who don't specialise in the mysteries, it teaches by allegory. Shayva said, '*It is not from knowledge that people grow.*' If it were, much wouldn't be hidden. It is from living, from life and searching to be better.

"Humans are curious by nature but in this, searching to know things we cannot know may lead to a trap. We expect to find answers, using our heads, not answers growing out of our hearts. We might miss completely the messages that we *are* given so freely.

"How we love, how we live our lives and how we handle our troubles, how we treat others. That's how we *really* grow. That's why we are here, the rest isn't important.

"The life of a monk is *not* superior to the life of a mother or a father. It's just a different path, to learn different lessons.

"Never look down on those that are humble. In the journey, they may be further along than you. They are living the humbler life for the lessons they need to learn. There can be great wisdom and goodness in humble people.

"Being a king or grand abbot, having power or prestige, is not always better. In truth, power often proves to be a terrible danger, to those that wield it.

"When I was younger, I wanted to be a monk and a celibate. I saw that as the only way to dedicate my life to God, but I was wrong. To dedicate one's life to being a monk is a wonderful thing, but not for me. That's what our Grand Abbot knew, and I didn't understand just then.

"No matter how wise I became in philosophy, being a monk was for me a retreat from life. I would have been avoiding what I had to *do*."

There was a lot to consider. But Hakeem gave her a sense of a God that was alien and distant from the world of men. "It seems lonely," she said. "If God is so different from us, we don't have the sort of God like a father."

"Jacinta," Hakeem said. "I'm not trying to convince you. I'm trying to help you see for yourself. Now, look into your heart, don't use your head.

"Does it feel that you are left alone like that? Don't you ever feel the hand of love and guidance? Don't you ever get the sense of a plan for you? Don't you at times sense something or someone watching over you? Don't you sense your family near? Haven't you felt that great love?"

"I have felt all those things, Hakeem, but you are giving me a headache!"

Hakeem was at once solicitous. Jacinta amazed him in what she could understand. The temptation was to go further and further. He couldn't believe this was only the first lesson but what was he doing, talking to an eleven-year-old girl like that? He stopped the lesson, and gave her some easy physical tasks to do.

They didn't go far that day; in fact they merely descended to the nearest water. Hakeem had more planned for the day. "I'm going to teach you how to fight." he said, once they had set up camp.

"Yes!" Jacinta thought bursting with excitement.

Hakeem laid the rabbits he had skinned earlier near the fire. Jacinta said she would cook them later. She insisted Hakeem couldn't cook rabbit. After he had tasted what Jacinta could do, he had to agree. She assembled some of the spices she had bought.

"Now, I plan to teach you unarmed combat," he announced gravely. "First I have to show you how to stand and how to walk."

Jacinta had seen him practicing stances and fluidly and rapidly moving from one stance to another. This will be great! she thought, if I don't end up killing him because of these dreadful jokes!

* * *

Training Jacinta and teaching her letters and numbers slowed the journey considerably. Jacinta felt anxious but Hakeem wouldn't brook any argument. If she were to be trained, there was only one way: she would be trained properly.

Whatever they could do verbally, they did as they rode along. A lot related to Shayvist philosophy, and Jacinta was getting used to Hakeem's habit of reflecting her questions back to her.

But if everyone was encouraged to find their *own* answers to everything, how could any of them be expected to agree on anything?

"Hakeem? Do we get rewarded if we treat animals well?"

"Reward is the wrong word, little one," he said with a gentle smile. "If one conducts oneself correctly, with love, it causes strength of spirit, lightness and joy. If we conduct ourselves in hate, it causes a sickness in our spirit or soul.

"Just compare it to training our bodies. To get a healthy body we must eat good food and exercise. That in itself is a pleasure and a joy. To get a healthy soul we do good deeds and have good thoughts. That again in itself is a pleasure and a joy.

"You asked if we should treat animals with love and kindness. Do I need to answer? What does your heart tell you to do? But we must live in the world too, and the world cannot be perfect, that is also part of the lesson. Sometimes we eat animals, but we must always be humane."

"Even rabbits?" Jacinta asked with a smile.

"Yes," Hakeem said, chuckling, "even rabbits. Some of the monks become vegetarian by choice, but if you are to train to be a fighter, you must eat meat. Remember, there is no such thing as death."

"What about wild animals?"

"Again, do I need to answer? Does your heart say you should treat animals cruelly? But if you are a farmer, you must protect your crop from animals and birds, or your chickens from a fox. Sometimes this is just how things are, but if you torture a fox or animal just because of its nature, or kill it for no reason, your heart must say that is wrong. Forget what your head or others might say."

Jacinta was amazed at what the tribesman knew, and Hakeem was stunned at how quickly the Gypsy girl picked things up. The Shayvists believed in a balance between training the mind and the body, this was how he would train Jacinta.

Once Jacinta had learned the fighting stances and how to move between them while maintaining her centre of balance low, he taught her standard punches and how to block. He started to teach her the use of the bow, and here he showed her how the meditation exercises helped the arrow to hit the target.

"How do you expect me to be 'one with the arrow'?" Jacinta complained, "or 'one with the target'? Do I look like an arrow, Hakeem? Or perhaps you think I look more like a target board?"

Hakeem laughed. Despite her playful comments, Jacinta was a determined student and was learning rapidly. He had taught boys of her age, but never girls. The boys he had taught now seemed slow and clumsy by comparison, and she was such a delight to have around.

Hakeem puzzled over the differences between males and females as he sat watching Jacinta practice archery. She was carefully and methodically aiming each arrow at the target he had set up. She was becoming an excellent shot for this level of training. Later he would teach her how to aim without sighting each shot.

Outside the monastery where Hakeem grew up girls and women were considered inferior. Even in the order, female monks were very rare. True, individual attitudes varied and there was usually a special bond between girls and their father, and boys and their mother.

As Hakeem was lost in thought, he saw Jacinta's bow arm wobble. The bowstring slapped her bare forearm! The shot went wild! Hakeem winced, he remembered Origenes. It must have hurt!

Her bow arm should have had her elbow pointed more to the side and her wrist cocked at 45 degrees with the bow not so much as gripped as rested against the ball of the thumb.

He had explained all this to Jacinta, and exactly what would happen if she didn't get each part right but for Jacinta he hadn't repeated the lesson many times, which he would do for a group of boys. He almost bit his tongue to stop himself calling out and reminding her.

Jacinta bent over rubbing to rub her arm and he frowned in sympathy, but waited to see what she would do next. She moved her bow-arm around, rubbed it and took a few breaths to steady herself. It must have really stung.

Then she sighed and brought her bow up and calmly put an arrow in the centre of the target.

"Great shot!" he called out loudly.

"You didn't see the last one, I hope." Jacinta called back.

"The one where you had your elbow pointed down, rather than more to the side? The one where you got your forearm hit really hard by the bow-string?" Hakeem enquired. "No I missed that one. I'm very proud of you, though; you didn't let it unsettle you."

Jacinta grinned sheepishly. "If it hits me like that every time I get it wrong, I'll learn that part quickly enough! You're right about controlling my anger though. Not getting angry with myself or the bow was the hardest part."

Hakeem watched her settle down again, and went back to thinking about men and women.

When he was young, one of his masters was a female monk from Cīna, but otherwise he had very little contact with women.

He liked women, he liked them very much, but he felt anxious and awkward around them. If he were truthful, he held them in some awe. He was more relaxed if they were married to a friend … he could talk easily to Myriani, Elwan's wife, or Nikoleta, Helios's Queen.

Until Jacinta, he simply had no contact whatsoever with little girls. He marvelled at how happy having the little girl around made him, and he couldn't wish for a brighter or harder working student.

He was at a loss to explain the general attitude to girls and women. Men and women are different, but in a way that complemented each other, not one better than the other. Men usually had stronger muscles and were taller, but women were superior to men in other ways.

Choosing clothes or shopping! he thought wryly.

He knew elves had a different attitude. Women were revered for their power of creation. The elves worshipped that most ancient of all deities, the Earth Mother Goddess, the great creator.

"Hakeem," Jacinta called, breaking his reverie. She had put the bow aside and was sweaty from doing a set move pattern. Jacinta was starting to appreciate bathing as much as Hakeem.

"When are you going to teach me how to use my knife?" she finished.

"Now, the best form of defence," he started to instruct her.

"I know." she said sitting down across from him, smiling at the oft repeated lesson. "Being prepared and avoiding a fight."

"Because of your size at the moment, range techniques are best for you," he continued. "You are getting stronger and building muscle, but because of your size and strength the bow is your best weapon.

"'I'm trying to teach you what will be useful at your age first, but until you're older, you need to avoid any serious fight. A knife alone is a poor offensive weapon. It works best with surprise, or as a last line of defence.

"I'm not even going to try to show you unarmed techniques against weapons. If you are unarmed or armed only with a knife, then fighting in those situations is more likely to get you killed than save your life, at least at present."

He stood up. "You've done enough today and we need to get going, but later I'll train you in some very special in-fighting techniques. Let me show you. This is the basic punch."

"That's too short! That's no good for me at all, Hakeem!" Jacinta protested, laughing in surprise.

Hakeem smiled, it was precisely the reaction he hoped for!

"This is a very deadly style called 'Wing Chun', from 'Cīna', the land at the end of our world. It was invented by a senior lady-monk called Nn Mui, a grand master of many styles. Wing Chun is named after Yim Wing Chun, the first student to learn it.

"Yim was her family name and Chun means spring. I was told different things about 'Wing'. It may mean 'glorious' or it may mean 'song'."

"Spring song! Such a beautiful name!" Jacinta smiled.

"And such a beautiful lady! I'll tell you her story some time," Hakeem said, getting down to business. "Now Wing Chun is all about using the minimum force, by deflecting your opponent and counter-attacking at the same time.

"Hence it can be applied against a more powerful opponent. You trap their arms and legs and grab them, to control their strength and prevent them from hitting you back. It's an ideal way for you to start to learn how a woman can overcome someone with a man's strength."

This was sounding better all the time, thought Jacinta.

"Alright," said Hakeem. "It's a shame we don't have someone your size for you to practice with. Throw a punch at my head but try to relax. I won't hurt you. Feel how you're blocked and I can strike multiple times."

Hakeem had to crouch low. He was so fast! Jacinta felt her arm gripped and jerked forward and down, then she was pulled forward with her arm was trapped against her body. Meanwhile, forehand and back hand punches snapped rapidly, only an inch from her face, throat and abdomen as he alternated the hand he used to control her and trap her limbs.

Great! He'll show me this, she thought.

"You are right about the range, and there are techniques for getting within range of your opponent if you want to specialise in Wing Chun. It's not my main style, I need more range. It's especially good for self-defence. I think it will be best for you."

By all the Gods! She thought, it's not his main style and he can move like that!

"I will teach you the fighting style of the beautiful but deadly lady," he said smiling, pleased. "I will have to teach you how to be strong, first. In any case, I think you're ready to start that."

Jacinta had trained hard at the stylised movements; already she felt her muscles growing and becoming firmer and her punches harder. What did he mean: he would teach her to be strong before he would teach her Wing Chun?

Was this another mind control exercise?

* * *

88 years! That was it! Jacinta had it worked out. It was 88 years plus a few moons or so!

In another 88 years and a few moons, Jacinta would be 100.

And *this* would be exactly how she would feel!!!

She had started on the strengthening exercises. Strengthening exercises? Every muscle in her body ached and she shuffled weakly along, as if bent with age. She was only eleven, yet it felt like she was an old woman a hundred years old.

Such a fine way to start the day!

No, I don't want to live to a hundred, she realised. Anyway, these damn exercises will kill me first. The other night she fell asleep before her evening meal.

The strengthening exercises she had to be able to do, *before* she even started to train in Wing Chun, were unbelievable. Later she was supposed to continue with the strengthening exercises each morning, *before* doing training in the fighting style itself. She wouldn't be able to do anything after these exercises.

Being slumped over a horse was bad enough.

"Strengthening exercises?" she grumbled to herself. She was too weak to fight an angry hen. Hakeem told her this would improve her health and happiness ... well, there was most definitely no sign of anything like that yet.

Hakeem broke into Jacinta's reverie: "For heaven sake, Jacinta, slow down! You're young, so your body can take it, but don't be in such a rush." Hakeem was doing one-arm push ups, as he talked.

Hakeem had given Jacinta a goal of strength to reach before starting Wing Chun. This was how he was taught. Jacinta was already strong and athletic for a girl her age, but she was determined to get there faster.

At first, this had exactly the reverse effect. The *more* she trained, the *less* she could do.

According to Hakeem, there were exercises to build speed, there were stretching exercises, there were exercises to build power, and there were exercises to build heart and lung fitness. There were warm-up exercises, and there were cool down exercises.

There were even exercises you could do while sitting or standing without moving, if you could believe something like that!

All exercises, he explained, had their benefits *and their dangers. Some* soreness in the muscles is beneficial, especially when you are young, but soreness in a joint or tendon could be serious; these are slow to heal and prone to permanent damage.

Some exercises were especially dangerous: speed training well beyond the limit of endurance can damage the heart or extreme straining can cause apoplexy even in young people. Lifting too much the wrong way can injure the back, jolting from punching and kicking can damage the neck and other joints, and this can accumulate over time.

Building far too much muscle could slow one down in a fight unless one also did speed training.

Jacinta was in a growth phase so she especially needed to warm up before training. He didn't want her to do too much speed training while she was growing, without eating *a whole lot* more or she could be stunted, he told her.

He watched what she ate like a hawk. Or maybe, she thought, a cross between a hawk and a grandmother!

Just now Jacinta was doing sit ups and she was getting close to the goal for push ups and sit ups. She was determined to get there, no matter what. She had struggled on determinedly, panting and bathed in sweat, her small face flushed with the effort. Hakeem watched her intently. He had already needed to force Jacinta to rest more than once before.

But Jacinta was completely determined.

She had begun to understand something. It had seemed to be fun and exciting at first, but this wasn't a game. He was completely serious. He really *was* training her to be a warrior.

Talking of a style of fighting invented by a woman brought this home. Hakeem said that when he was young, the other boys were always older. He was trained by a female monk who had come to study with the Shayvists. She showed him how to turn the older boys' strength against them.

It seemed silly now that Hakeem once had to learn how to fight someone bigger and stronger, but he assured her that there were still others out there who were stronger than him, whatever she might think.

Being female wasn't an insurmountable barrier.

She could deal with the differences of weight, height and strength. She knew, though, that if she was ever to become good enough to fight seriously as a girl, she had to be smarter and train harder than any male ever had to.

There were many other reasons she was so motivated: she loved to learn and Hakeem was so proud of her. He really knew how to teach. And, well, she adored him and wanted to be more like him.

And there was one special reason. It was something that would never leave her. Can you imagine what it was like to have your parents, your brother and your sister murdered in front of you? Can you imagine, as small child, having one of the murderers trying to run you down on horseback as he taunted you?

Yes, Jacinta without any doubt was Hakeem's most determined student ever. If she could, she never wanted to feel that way again. If she could, she would protect others from such an experience. Anyone who couldn't defend themselves.

Jacinta was on the path to becoming a warrior.

Just now however, Jacinta was trying to do one more sit up, and she couldn't. She got only halfway up and couldn't get any further.

She flopped back, her stomach muscles were on fire. She grunted and tried again and again but only got her head and shoulders off the ground before she had to drop back helplessly.

She lay back, gasping like a fish on the bank. Maybe I will just have to admit defeat, she thought. She tried again and couldn't even raise her head.

She sighed, nothing for it but to give in … and, then … she found … she couldn't get up at all!

She tried to twist and squirm, but her abused muscles had quit on her: they refused her orders.

I'm like a turtle stuck on its back! she realised.

Hakeem was looking down, grinning widely and mouthing, "I told you so." Curse the man!

She couldn't get up to chase him. Stuck on her back, she tried weakly to kick at him, but she couldn't do anything.

Suddenly it was funny.

As Jacinta started to laugh, so did Hakeem, as he carefully helped her up, lifting behind her back. Her stomach muscles hurt *so much* when she laughed.

Hakeem passed her a bundle of blanket wound tight for her to hug down on. Then he held her curled up in his arms to ease the pain of laughing, and they lay on their side, laughing together.

Chapter 13: Paladins, Lady's Choice, and a Visit to a Caravanserai

The learning didn't all go one way.

Not long after they had first greeted the morning sun, they were both riding Nadeer. Jacinta was enclosed by Hakeem's arms and resting comfortably back against his chest.

"Hakeem, I find watching sunrise even more beautiful, now. Thank you, so much. I suppose you watch it whenever you can."

"It had been a long time," Hakeem sighed.

"But why?" Jacinta sat up straight and twisted around to look at him. She wanted to do it often! They usually got up at first light and this made it really worthwhile.

Hakeem smiled sadly. "You seem to understand things so quickly, Jacinta. But I can be a foolish man."

He sounded so bitter. As they rode on, he told her about his flight from the monastery .

"But you say the abbot was right."

"Of course he was right! If I never left, I would never have met you, little one." He smiled as he gave her a fond hug. "And many others, I had a lot to learn about friendship, I'm still learning. It's a bit late to find that out, now. The old man has died."

For a while, they rode in silence and Jacinta let him be.

When they stopped for midday in the shade, Jacinta asked, "Do you still have the letters?"

"Aha," Hakeem nodded.

"I think you should read them," she said firmly.

Hakeem felt a touch of fear, but she was right, of course she was. He went to his saddlebag and removed the small parcel. He felt his hurt and shame surge through him afresh. He plonked himself down next to Jacinta and sighed.

He wasn't sure how long he sat there, but he felt a small hand on his arm. Jacinta was looking at him with a look of understanding and compassion.

She's only eleven.

But it helped somehow. He took a big breath.

"You may as well get it over with," Jacinta suggested.

As Hakeem read the first letter, he was overcome with grief. Tears began rolling freely down his cheeks. Jacinta moved closer till she was sitting in his lap with her arms around his neck and her head on his chest.

"He called me, 'my dear son'," Hakeem finally managed. "'My dear son, if I may call you that.' He forgave me, forgave me straight away. I didn't know."

Hakeem realised how much he loved the old man. Loss on loss: his unremembered parents and the woman who fostered him till he entered the monastery , the Grand Abbot and now Elwan.

All his lonely times, he had built a wall inside himself. He always held back. For him, to become a monk was to hide away. The wise old man had known it all along.

Something had been thawing in the heart of the tribesman, but now the dam had broken, feelings were flooding over him. He held Jacinta close, wetting her hair with his tears.

"I love you," Jacinta said softly, kissing him on the cheek and hugging him. He kissed her forehead and hugged her fiercely in return. "Thank you, Jacinta. Thank you for everything."

Finally he gave a shaky laugh. "Jacinta, I'm sorry. I don't know what you must think of me, now. I'm supposed to be big and tough."

Jacinta heart was filled with love for the big man. She had found he was not the monster he had at first seemed. Now she realised, with a touch of awe, that this strong fearsome warrior could need her, at times, almost as much as she needed him.

Jacinta hugged him again and looked up at him with a fond expression. "You want to know what I really think? I really think you should read the rest."

Hakeem rapidly scanned the rest of it. "I'll read it to you in a minute. But he understood! He said I'm to be a paladin. I was never expelled. I'm still part of the order!"

"What's a paladin?" she asked.

"I'm not really sure. It's some sort of religious knight," Hakeem said, but he had already opened the second letter.

"It's all here and in this book! It looks like I was already under consideration for it, without knowing it.

"This book is a copy, but the original must be very old and the dialect is a little unfamiliar.

"Let's see, I will have to prove myself worthy, but they say becoming a paladin is something pre-ordained by God. That could be another way of saying Karma, but I think they mean something else. There's only been very few. It fell out of use, I guess, but there's no shame at all in being a paladin."

Hakeem gave a smile of relief. He felt honoured and humbled.

"There's mention of oaths, of dedication to God, and protecting the weak," Hakeem continued.

"Sounds like you already!" Jacinta beamed, and then became serious. "Do you think I could become a paladin?"

Hakeem looked at her in surprise. She was so wise for her age, she tried so hard and she learned so quickly.

"You know, I think you could!" he answered slowly, thinking. "We'll see, I suppose."

"Can a paladin still marry?" she asked.

"Uh huh, depends on who I marry I guess." Hakeem was distracted by the book he had been given, and responded to what he thought was her concern. "Oh! You're not getting rid of me that easily. I told you that. On my oath as a candidate for paladin, *you* are my daughter!" He announced this so grandly with a flourish of his arms, that they both had to laugh.

"At times I'm can be such a fool."

"Can I remind you of that regularly?" Jacinta asked with a sweet smile.

Hakeem sprang up with a cry, pretending to grab at her. She was dodging around him, as he chased her. He kept threatening to tickle, and pretended he couldn't catch her. She was pretending to run. Soon they were laughing so hard, they had to fall down on the grass, helplessly laughing.

* * *

What was secretly playing on Jacinta's mind for some time now hadn't gone away. It came to a head one night, two weeks later.

Hakeem had complimented Jacinta on how well she cooked the rabbit, and how she made it tasty. He was at peace, quietly sipping his tea and reading a little from his book.

"I'll cook it just the way you want, when we're married," she said, giving him a serene smile.

Jacinta looked up in alarm. Hakeem was choking! He was starting to go red, then almost purple!

Perhaps some tea went down the wrong way.

As he was recovering he was staring at her incredulously and gasping and coughing, still unable to talk. She stared right back at him in stubborn defiance. "Yes...?" she enquired, one eyebrow raised.

Hakeem thought carefully how he should explain this to her. "Jacinta, you know I love you more than anyone alive," he said admitting it to himself.

"It's decided then," she said smugly.

"No, wait." He held up his hand. "You won't be able to marry till your 16, I'd planned 18 for you. No I didn't mean me!" he said to forestall her reaction. "Someone nice, I'll be too old."

"I'll decide who's nice!" she said firmly. "Even when I'm 18, you'll only be 28. Besides, Gypsy girls are sometimes married at 12."

"Not this Gypsy girl!" Hakeem said, shuddering at the thought.

"Jacinta ... Jacinta! You are so beautiful." He tried to ignore her talking over the top with, "I'm glad you think so."

"One day, you will meet someone and fall in love."

"I already have!" she declared triumphantly. "I know you love me. You say so."

"Alright," he said trying again. "I meant someone *younger* than me. You're my daughter and now a very special student."

"I'm not your blood daughter, and sometimes students marry teachers," Jacinta replied.

Hakeem was at a loss, then he realised it was only a crush after all.

"Jacinta, as far as I'm concerned you are my daughter, and I am your father, and that is not open to negotiation. I expect you at some stage to meet someone else, and I will be a very protective and proud father. Understood?"

Jacinta yawned settling down to sleep. "We'll see," she murmured sleepily, with a dreamy smile.

After Jacinta feel into an exhausted sleep Hakeem sat up for a while thinking.

He felt unsettled at the thought of eventually losing Jacinta. Marriage between them, for him, would always be impossible. She would always be his little Jacinta. He couldn't imagine thinking and dreaming about her in the same way he did Sara.

He had another shudder when he thought of how some men could touch a child in a bad way. Then he had an image of Jacinta as a happy young woman, carrying a baby.

Grandparent!

It wouldn't be another love lost, just change, adding rather than taking away. He hoped it would be so. He still felt a pang at the thought that fathers, one day, had to let go. He thought of her crush on him and chuckled. He'd have to be careful somehow.

* * *

Fortunately there were no signs of any change in Jacinta's behaviour towards him. She seemed to be happy with their relationship as it was. Jacinta knew things about men and women that even Hakeem didn't know, but it was likely that her concept of husband and wife was still a childish one.

Good enough, he thought: there was enough in life to carry on with without borrowing trouble.

He insisted she keep up her proficiency with each past lesson before he would teach her new techniques. He wanted her to be able to defend herself in normal situations, as soon as possible. He didn't know why he felt in a hurry, but he did.

He was suitably rewarded with a 'Jacinta groan' when he suggested he teach her how to fall down!

He couldn't teach her full overhead or shoulder throws. She really needed someone closer to her size and weight for that. A high throw was too risky anyway against a bigger opponent or someone skilled.

He taught her how to break her fall, what she could do if trapped on the ground, and a range of trips and counters to a lunge or rush. With only Hakeem to practice with, she was learning how to fight a powerful opponent; using an opponent's weight and strength against him.

In all the lessons, he went easy, but at first she couldn't upset his balance at all. It was asking a lot of her. Jacinta was absolutely determined. Eventually, if he ran at her with any speed, he would find himself on his back with Jacinta expertly punching down on him.

She was visibly putting on muscle for a girl her age, and was already fast. While they were using non-contact sparring, if she misjudged the distance, he was starting to feel her hits. On one occasion, while sparring, he was distracted trying to teach, and her kick was fast enough to score a solid hit to his groin.

She smiled as he bent over in discomfort, but when she saw he really was in pain, she ran over concernedly and helped him to a seat.

"Yes," he grunted between clenched teeth. "That's how to do it."

Jacinta was caught between sympathy and laughter.

They were now well within Anatolē's dry central plateau. Even though it was called a plateau, it was a land of rolling hills, mostly dry dusty grasslands, with scrubby bushes and stunted willow trees interspersed with river valleys.

It drained inward to the dry inland rather than to the sea, so there were salty lakes. It had limestone deep beneath, resulting in interesting caves and deep sinkholes dotted throughout the land.

Jacinta took one of his smaller scarves to make a headdress to match Hakeem's. Her first attempt unravelled after a few minutes of riding, but she got him to show her again, and she persisted till she was proudly wearing a smaller matching version of Hakeem's.

Though it was already autumn, it was still dry and unseasonably hot. They rested and slept in the hottest part of the day and rode in the morning and cool of the evening. Hakeem began to fuss over how much the horses were drinking and started to nag Jacinta.

"Am I a horse now?" Jacinta asked him with a laugh. "I can drink water on my own, Hakeem!"

This region was more dangerous, sparsely populated yet often travelled. It was known for bandits and occasional barbarian raiders. For safety, they joined with other travellers at every opportunity. Hakeem donned his breast plate and they both kept their bows strung in their saddle holsters and quivers handy.

Even their horses seemed more alert and watchful. Yet all they saw were nomads in the distance with their herds of Angora goats or sheep, and their horses.

Whenever they could, they stayed each night in way-houses or inns. At these places, they had a small room with nowhere to practice in private, so Hakeem showed Jacinta the slow smooth exercises the Chin used to build speed and strength.

He chuckled when Jacinta inevitably scoffed at the slowness of it, as he hoped she would. Their banter had become part of a game that had developed between them, but in this case, Jacinta really was astounded at how useful these particular exercises were.

They were only two or at the most three days from the westernmost chapterhouse of Hakeem's order, when they pushed on well into the evening to reach a great caravanserai.

Caravanserais were huge compared to the inns and way-houses. They were rest stops for caravans, and some could accommodate the men and animals of several small caravans at once. They provided baths, entertainment, cooked food, supplies, the services of prostitutes, and wine and beer. But the main attraction in isolated regions was guaranteed security for the night.

It was Jacinta's first chance to dress up, so she insisted they first stop at a small creek to bathe, brush her hair and don one of her Gypsy dresses and her special boots.

Hakeem unsuccessfully pointed out that all this could be done better, *after* they reached the caravanserai. He worried that a dress would be an impractical thing to wear for riding, but Gypsy dresses are loose, and Jacinta flounced into the saddle without a problem.

"Shouldn't you wear trousers underneath?" he asked with concern. "Won't you get chafed?"

Jacinta snorted and tossed her head. "Mind your own business!" she said loftily and spurred Farah, sitting up straight with her head held high with great dignity.

Hakeem was left with nothing but having to mount Nadeer and catch up.

He was amused by her fussing. Caravanserai had some very rough clients, but he felt Jacinta deserved a chance to dress up, if that was what she wanted.

The Caravanserai was only a dark outline against the inky sky by the time they reached it. It had been the fort of a minor robber baron. Servicing the caravans was more profitable than robbing them and they were much more likely to come back!

It still had the reassuring look of a medium sized fort. It was marked out by four solid looking walls; more than twenty feet (seven or more metres) high, with towers at each corner, and one near the gate.

Outlined against the darkening sky, they could just make out two sentries with bows, patrolling just inside the top of the walls. The one entrance was guarded by a sturdy bronze door which was open and cheerfully illuminated by two torches in sconces, on either side of the gate. There were also free standing torches in holders near a bench set up outside. There was the friendly glow from inside and they could hear the sounds of music and laughter beyond the entrance.

Jacinta and Hakeem had to surrender their weapons except knives as they entered. Hakeem wrapped Mir and its scabbard in a cloth and handed it over as well. It would be absolutely secure. The caravanserai lived by their reputations and anyone caught stealing or smuggling weapons inside would be facing frontier justice.

The inside courtyard was lit like a night market. The great pitch-torches in sconces, gave strong, if flickering, light to all the paths and service areas. As they strolled inside, the sound of music and laughter coming from the fort's own *kapeleion* (taverna) was loud and welcoming.

With people here taking a sleep during the midday heat, the taverna would be open till well into the middle watch.

Most men would sleep in the open, but sheltered quarters ran the length of one wall and Hakeem had paid for a small private niche for the two of them. They had already bathed in the stream and would take their main bath in the morning.

An underground stream supplied clean water to a well in the centre, and the latrine system was bucket based with a deep cess-pit just outside the walls.

At the far end of the fort were stables and a generous tip meant their three horses would be pampered.

Hakeem walked ahead, to check that their horses were well looked after and to supervise the porters with their luggage and the setting up of their beds. Jacinta was dawdling behind, trying to look everywhere at once, so she was well back when she passed a group of caravan guards drinking.

A drunken voice called out as Jacinta passed. "There goes one of those filthy tribesmen and his Gypsy whore. Can't he handle the older ones?"

Hakeem whipped around, his hand resting on his knife handle. He could ignore insults to himself, but Jacinta, now that was a completely different matter.

"No!" Jacinta called out firmly.

The last thing she wanted was Hakeem to start a fight in the Caravanserai. She would handle it alone better, hopefully by ignoring the man. There was a scuffle as the man's friends removed his knife, and tried to make him sit down.

He stood unsteadily. "No!" he mimicked, sneering. "So the little girl has to protect her cowardly boyfriend. Mind your own business, Gypsy slut."

Jacinta stopped, as he stood up to approach her. She looked at him calmly, but didn't take her eyes off him. Her face was expressionless.

This incensed the man. "And what are you looking at? I'll teach you some manners!" He started to move more determinedly towards her.

Jacinta made no reply. Hakeem saw Jacinta watching the man steadily. She didn't assume a stance, good. Don't show your opponent you are ready.

She didn't go for her knife, Hakeem noted with relief.

A huge guard was hurrying up, but Hakeem put his arm out to restrain him. Let's see if she can handle this.

The drunk wandered up to Jacinta and bent over as if to look at her, then he moved forward and swung his right hand at her to slap her hard. She calmly dodged under it. Moving closer, she trapped his arm after it missed her, pushing it against his body moving her leg closer to prevent a kick. Then she landed a very credible punch to his face, and danced back out of the way.

The man looked at her in shock, gingerly fingering his lip. He didn't expect to be hit back, and she hit so hard. She was only a girl but she didn't hit like one!

The man's friends came spilling out, but they were cheering Jacinta. Jacinta was still staring at the man intently, waiting. She still had not revealed any particular stance or style.

Thoroughly stung and starting to sober with the exertion, he lunged hard at her only to find himself stretched, face forward in the dirt. He had a bleeding chin and sore jaw to add to a swollen and bleeding lip.

Good girl! Hakeem cheered inwardly. She was avoiding anything too fancy where he might catch her. Now she merely moved a safe distance away, and waited, to see what the man tried next.

The music had stopped, and people spilled out of the taverna to watch. As the man was thrown face down in the dirt, the crowd went wild with cheers. Someone shouted excitedly, "that's it girl! You show him!"

There would be a riot if he hurt the girl.

Not yet time to break it up, thought Hakeem, though he was starting to feel anxious. He wanted Jacinta to learn, not get hurt.

He could step in rapidly, but it would be too late if Jacinta was hit by this powerful man. He looked like a trained fighter.

Her antagonist got up carefully, dusting himself off. He was bleeding from a number of scrapes. One of his group called out, "three silvers says you can't catch her in two hundred heart beats."

The man nodded his acceptance as he spread his arms and started to circle Jacinta who stayed almost motionless, watching him, just turning enough to keep facing him. The only problem for him was that he had spread his legs apart in a wrestler's crouch.

Hakeem started to smile with pride when Jacinta stepped forward with her left leg and really put her right hip into the kick. She used the rhythm of the swing to focus the maximum power at the point of impact.

The man was totally unprepared. There was a "thud," loud enough to be clearly heard by the crowd, as the toe of Jacinta kicked his testicles with as much force as she could manage.

The man let out a sound like "Ooot", as many of the watching men winced in sympathy.

He bent over in terrible agony, his face was crimson. Jacinta watched him carefully, keeping all expression from her face as one of his friends helped him to a seat.

She didn't need her caution, he could hardly walk!

The audience erupted in raucous laughter and wild cheering. Hakeem had to struggle to get to Jacinta and lift her up. Everyone was trying to congratulate her at once. She squealed as Hakeem tossed her in the air and caught her, to great cheering and clapping. Hakeem was so proud. He would deal with any overconfidence later.

"It really works, Hakeem!" Jacinta said, breathless with excitement. The "I wondered whether it would," earned him a playful slap over the back of his head, as she hugged him happily.

Suddenly there was a surprised murmur. Hakeem! So, that was who was training her!

That's Hakeem! People strained forward, to see the legendary tribesman. What's he doing with the clever Gypsy girl?

But the moment was Jacinta's.

Jacinta was talking rapidly in Romani to the Gypsy dancers and musicians who had come up to congratulate her. Hakeem made it *very* clear to the Gypsy man in charge that she was his daughter. He didn't believe Gypsies really kidnapped little girls to avoid having to pay a bride price ... they were unfairly accused of all sorts of things, but Hakeem decided he could not be too cautious where Jacinta's safety was concerned.

He needn't have worried. Jacinta would normally be completely safe anywhere in the caravanserai, and now that she was so popular, her safety was assured.

She had left him to go to the taverna. The man's daughters started to give her dance lessons. It must have been a familiar dance and the dance troupe soon had another young performer.

Almost everyone surged over to the taverna to watch. Jacinta looked so beautiful and was flushed with exercise and excitement when she joined with the two young women. The crowd was delighted and cheered and stomped and sang out encouragement. There was a shower of generous tips.

The leader of the caravan guards came up to speak to Hakeem. He spoke Galilean Aramaic, close to Hakeem's native dialect.

"My name is Šimʿôn (Simon). I owe you an apology for Yaʿkob (Jakob). He *was* a good man. We were friends from the same village, on the lake of Galilee. We had fought together for Troia."

Hakeem nodded, most people knew of Galilee. It was fertile land, crucial strategically and in trade, west of Hakeem's homeland. The great river, *Yar-dane* (Jordan, meaning "descender") fed the large fresh water lake sometimes called a sea, and then continued south to drain into a salt sea called the 'Dead Sea'.

"Since his young brother was killed in the battle for Kanakala Grove, he's ruined," Simon was saying. "I'm really finished with him after this. Always drinking, always spoiling for a fight, and souring everyone's mood.

"He hates anyone like you, who could have fought for the other side. He will be thrown out of here now and won't be joining us again. That's if the crowd or the guards don't kill him first!"

The caravanserai owner had placed Jakob in a holding cell behind iron bars, for his temporary protection. There were two huge guards with cudgels facing off a large and angry crowd.

The herders, camel drivers, and guards that travelled the great trading routes came from all races along the great routes and beyond: Chin, Mongols, Turks, Indoi, Badawiyyūn (Bedouins), Babylonians, Nubians, Scythians, Egyptians and Greeks ... there were too many to mention, but they had one thing in common: they made the best money travelling through some of the most difficult, harsh and dangerous country imaginable.

They were tough men and they had witnessed an unprovoked assault on a little girl by a stranger. By any code, this was unforgivable, and now this girl was very popular! They were calling for him to be brought out.

The plan of the caravanserai guards was simple: escort Jakob across the courtyard through the door, and take him out somewhere quiet. They would give him a thorough cudgelling, not quite enough to kill him; and then they would rely on the harsh environment to finish the job.

Jakob had no misconception of what fate held in store for him.

But if they tried to shift him now there would be a riot! It wouldn't stop at whatever people did to Jakob. Once something like this had been triggered, it would likely ignite everyone in the caravanserai into fighting. So they had to keep him till people lost interest. In the meantime, the owner and his guards eyed the crowd with increasing nervousness.

"I would like to talk to him," Hakeem said to Simon.

Simon smiled ruefully. "What, do you think you can talk some sense into him?" he said incredulously. "Lord knows I've tried. Isn't it a little late for that?"

Hakeem waited, impassively watching the Galilean.

Eventually Simon shrugged and led the large man to the cell. The guards looked nervously at Hakeem, but he gave his word that he wanted to talk to their prisoner, not offer violence.

He announced his intention to the crowd, and asked for silence. Then he and Simon were dutifully locked in with the prisoner and sat, one on each side. The audience waited, crowding forward to see what was going on.

Jakob sat miserably. He was dirty and unkempt, his face was bruised and puffy and his lip had been bleeding. Whatever intoxication he had had was completely cured. He sat waiting for the tirade from the big tribesman. Well, he deserved it, attacking a small girl like that!

"This is Hakeem, *the* Hakeem," Simon introduced the tribesman. "Did you have any idea who you were trying to pick a fight with?"

Jakob's humiliation was complete. A fight with Hakeem would be quickly over for him.

He waited for what Hakeem would say. He felt only contempt for himself. Well, there would not be much waiting left for him now. His parents only had had two sons and neither would be returning. If his father knew about him, he would never be welcome home again.

The tribesman sat in silence for a long time. Eventually all he said was, "I'm sorry for your loss."

Jakob looked up in surprise.

"Your brother was at Kanakala Grove?" Hakeem murmured.

Jakob nodded, it wasn't at all what he expected Hakeem to say.

"What was his name?" Hakeem asked gently.

Jakob to his great surprise, found himself talking about *Matityahu* (Mathew). The crowd outside started to drift away, the fun with the prisoner seemed to be over. The guards gave a sigh of relief, as an emergency drifted down towards an anticlimax.

Jacinta came up later, and Hakeem waved the guards to let her in. She sat curled up in Hakeem's lap, as Jakob and Hakeem continued their earnest conversation.

Mathew was three years younger and was born breechling, with a deformed foot. Their parents only had the two children, and Jakob became the protector of his little brother.

Mathew on the other hand, was always absolutely determined to do anything anyone else could do. It was hard for him to run far, but he gamely persisted despite what was sometimes great pain.

When Jakob left their home, to enrol as a mercenary with distant Troia, Mathew begged to be allowed to come. Jakob insisted he stay to look after their parents.

Later he heard that Mathew had managed to enlist. Not suitable for the forward army, Mathew was pressed into garrison service, in the fort at Kanakala grove. Well inside Troian territory, there was no expectation of the garrison seeing action.

When the Troian campaign against the weaker Aiol army unexpectedly collapsed, there was chaos. Once the tide turned, allies defected and Troia's old enemies joined the Aiol cause. There were many desperate attempts by the Troians to prevent the march on Troia.

The battle of Kanakala grove has passed into legend. So impressed were those who witnessed the courage of the defenders that even now, they are spoken of with great reverence by their former enemies.

All was lost. In fact this was the last major campaign of the war.

A garrison, a small lochos of not much more than a hundred men, stalled the march of a full *taxis* (legion), giving time for the remaining Troians to reorganise closer to their city.

Eventually the main Aiol army caught up with the besieging force.

Hakeem came there as Aide to Helios. He described the valiant defence to Jakob. He told how Helios, the Aiol king, offered honourable surrender again and again to the defenders but they refused. The Troians didn't know how vengeful the Aiols would be, and the Troians believed they were defending their homes and their families.

When the gates and obstructions were finally cleared to allow entry, Helios sent five full lochoi of elite heavy infantry in with orders to capture any defenders, if it was safe to do so. Only a dozen were saved, none surrendered.

As Hakeem related the story ,the eyes of Simon and Jakob shone with pride. "Now I ask you," Hakeem said. "If Mathew had the chance that day, would he have thrust his spear into my guts?"

"Yes, of course!" Jakob exclaimed, with a chuckle. He felt a pride, a pride he thought he'd lost.

"I ask you, what brother would you want ... a coward? Or do you want one of the heroes of Kanakala Grove! The very enemies of those defenders will always speak of them with awe. The leader of their enemies, King Helios, ordered a monument raised to pay respect to the courage of the defenders of Kanakala Grove!"

Jakob began to cry. He had never known the full story. He mourned again, freshly, his loss.

But this time he felt not only the loss; he felt great pride in his brother. He also felt a strong arm around him and the small hands of the Gypsy girl, taking one of his hands in both of hers.

Hakeem squeezed his shoulder. "Jakob! You felt you always had to protect your brother. Stop being angry with yourself! You loved your brother.

"He became a man, grieve him yes, but be proud!

"He was given the chance to surrender, but he chose to give his life for what he believed in. He and the others died as heroes. Can you be sorry he was a hero?

"You know your parents don't blame you. Go home, they love you, you're all they have left."

He drew Jakob up. Jakob looked into Hakeem's face, in wonder, tears streaming down his cheeks, and he hugged the tribesman fiercely.

"You must go home," whispered Hakeem softly patting his shoulder.

The crowd had all but dispersed. Hakeem motioned to the guards who opened the door but instead of leaving Jakob inside, he escorted him from the prison.

He announced loudly in Greek. "Let him through! He's suffered enough already."

Simon sent one his men scurrying for Jakob's possessions and some supplies, as the two escorted Jakob to the main gate, Jacinta trailing behind.

Just beyond the gate, Jakob gave Hakeem another fierce hug and looked into his face, puzzled by a wave of affection and respect he felt for a man he thought was his enemy.

It was Simon who softly quoted the old saying, in awe, "and it was said 'I looked into the face of my enemy and I found him to be my friend.'"

"Thank you, Hakeem. If I may call you by your name," Jakob finally said. "Tonight you saved my life, but I feel you somehow saved me, in a way I thought no longer possible. May the blessing of the Great God of my ancestors rain down upon you!"

Jakob turned to Jacinta. "Please accept my apologies, Jacinta. You certainly brought me to my senses. Though with the way you can kick, I pray I never need your sort of help again." He said with a chuckle.

He still was having difficulty walking.

Then he turned to his friend and countryman. "Farewell, Simon. I mean to make amends. Thank you, my friend, for standing by me longer than I deserved."

They left him with his small pile of supplies and possessions, as they and two of the guards walked back to the caravanserai.

Simon turned to Hakeem with a smile "Well, I don't know how you did it, but you did! You must be a magician! I really can't thank you enough! You must let me buy you a drink.

"Now, tell me, is it true you grew four feet taller during the battle for Pergamon?"

"Of course," Hakeem said, taking Simon in one arm and Jacinta in the other. "But things didn't get really interesting, till I grew wings and multiple arms, and flew around the battle field like some great beetle. That's when I started to breathe fire, I'm sure you heard about that."

The two were laughing like old friends as they walked back in.

* * *

It was a late start for Hakeem. Jacinta had fallen asleep beside him, as he stayed drinking and talking with Simon late into the night. Simon's wine was a vast improvement on the Greek distilled wine in every respect … except the hangover.

Jacinta was up early, and had spent time with the Gypsy musicians. They were disappointed that Jacinta couldn't stay to join their show that night.

When Jacinta came back from there, she was wearing one of her other good dresses. She had had her hair cut, styled and braided by the older Gypsy girls. She looked very pretty.

The caravanserai owner couldn't be more grateful. Not only was a disaster averted and an unsavoury episode settled without fuss, but also the reputation of the establishment was greatly enhanced.

It would be a great story to tell! When a refund was refused, he pressed a small silver chain on Jacinta, which complemented her earrings.

Chapter 14: The Western Chapterhouse and a Troubled Novice

This chapterhouse was not far from the city the Greeks now call Ikónion, after the legend of Medusa. The nearest mountain pass exiting Anatolē was still far to the east, so they would not pass this way on their return.

Jacinta was disappointed that she couldn't see the city, but Hakeem had never for a moment shown the slightest impatience with the delay her training was causing, so she limited herself to a token grumble.

They had just passed a fortified village not far from the chapterhouse and were talking as their horses ambled along.

"If they believed the purpose of life is to live and experience it , why do the Shayvists have so many monks?" Jacinta asked.

It might be simpler if he admitted he hadn't thought about it very deeply, but it was a good question and he would try to answer.

"Monks are needed to guide others. They show the way and to organise the sect. They are the heart, and the followers are the body."

"But most of them live away from others in communities meditating."

"That is the seed that supports the work the order does. The monasteries teach those who go on to teach others."

"But you said that gaining knowledge is not how one grows spiritually, one has to follow one's heart. Why do they do all that study?"

"They are turning their attention inward. It may seem simple but growing spiritually requires a struggle. It is like exercise for building muscle, that is what we mean by learning, not some special secret knowledge that no one else can have.

"We need learning that comes from outside us and inside us. That is why even those who ascend can only do so after many lifetimes. It is their Karma."

Jacinta had a way of asking questions that made Hakeem think.

"And for me, part of my Karma is to be plagued by a small Gypsy girl who asks me endless questions till I am hoarse with explanations. That is, when she's not talking my ears off."

Jacinta laughed and stuck out her tongue. She feinted at throwing a cherry seed at his face but when he ducked, she threw it in earnest with impressive accuracy.

"Why don't we all become monks, then?"

Hakeem checked that there were no more cherry seeds coming his way, and then continued. "That's the mistake I myself made. It is another path. It should be in line with a monk's Karma, what they need to learn. Not taking the easiest path as it would have been for me. Not all lessons can be learned by being a monk.

"For me being a monk would have been a retreat from my path. I wouldn't have met you."

"And that would be no good for you at all," Jacinta agreed. "But why do you worship Apollōn?"

"Shayva was a soldier and his experiences in a war made him become a priest of Apollōn. Apollōn is the God of wisdom and Shayva developed a mystic sect of Apollōn. Most of us call the God we experience 'Apollōn'. I think it is all the same God as others might call by other names, but I don't know that for sure. We are too limited to comprehend all but a very small part of God and different people may experience different aspects.

"I will quote Shayva to you: '*It is possible to experience and join with something wonderful that we call God. The purer our heart, the clearer our experience is, but full knowledge and experience of God is far beyond us, and is not needed. Accept what is shown. It is much already.*

"*By insisting to know what we cannot, we may miss what we can. A priest or priestess, even if great in their temple can lose sight of the path they should be treading. Even when studying the mysteries do not miss an important task you are given. That would just be study for study's sake.*"

"So don't become a monk," Jacinta concluded.

"In my case, no," Hakeem agreed.

They had topped a rise and could see the chapterhouse clearly now, and they both fell silent as they studied it. Hakeem was training Jacinta to scan her surroundings carefully, as warriors do.

This chapterhouse was part of a large farm and the buildings were a collection of rambling mud brick buildings on level land halfway down a hill. This region, so close to a major city, had been safe for a long time, yet everyone in the Anatolē Steppe took precautions and the chapterhouse was surrounded by a high stone wall as well as a reinforced gate. In the hills around they saw herds of Angora goats and sheep. In the dip of the valley there were wheat and fruit trees, so they obviously had access to water.

This was the smallest chapterhouse of the order, but still housed over thirty full-time monks, plus novices, temporary guests and staff. Almost all Shayvist monks were men and only few married, so there would be few women at a chapterhouse, and few children apart from the younger novices.

Some merchants would carry letters for a fee, and Hakeem had written to the abbot, so he and Jacinta were expected. As he identified himself to the brother guarding the door, the doorman struck a clear note on a brass chime. As he entered, Hakeem felt a pang of homesickness for the monastery at Karsh.

The monk led them immediately to see the Abbot, Omar. Omar was a big bear of a man. While his curly hair had gone grey with age, he moved with confidence and grace for a large man. He looked every bit the master of unarmed combat and the use of the quarter staff that he was.

He refused to allow Hakeem to bow. Instead he hurried forward and clasped him in a hug so powerful that Hakeem could feel his bones crack.

"Welcome, welcome! I have heard many good things about you! My good friend Samit is very impressed with you. No more than to be expected from a paladin candidate, of course. I hope you're not too tired from your travels?"

Hakeem smiled and shook his head. "No, 'Abbā (Father). We took three days from the Great Caravanserai, so have made an easy ride of it."

"Good," Omar said. "I have to travel to the Black Sea region to take over as abbot at the chapterhouse there. The post has been vacant since the old abbot died last winter. My replacement here has already set out but I have delayed my departure, to travel with you.

"I really hate to ask this of you, but would it be alright to leave in the morning? I don't know why but the whole region up there has become unsettled recently. Even the elven lands are no longer safe."

"Father, I'd be most pleased!" Hakeem said with delight. "Can I introduce Jacinta, whom I have taken as my pupil? If you would agree to teach her, it would be a great honour."

Omar bowed solemnly to Jacinta and smiled. "Jacinta, I'm pleased to make your acquaintance and I would like to see what you can do, having Hakeem as your master!

"Well, it's decided then, I will be taking one other. His name is *Dāniyyêl* (Daniel) and he can train with Jacinta. He is a half-blood elf and has to tolerate bullying so far from the elf heartland."

He rang a bell and Jacinta was escorted by a matronly old lady to the female and married quarters. Hakeem warned her he would not see her till the morning. He would be talking to the abbot till late.

The next morning, Jacinta stumbled out of bed and ate the breakfast they had left out for her. Why couldn't they stay longer? What sort of hospitality was this? On second thought, staying cloistered in this male-dominated place would be horrible. There were so many places she was not allowed to go. She hurried to join the others getting ready to depart.

Omar was taking two pack-donkeys and this caused the first problem. Hakeem had redistributed the load and had obtained another saddle, so Omar rode the third horse, but what about Daniel?

Jacinta saw a boy, about her age and size, with a pale face and freckles. His eyes were a startling green. The pointy ears of an elf were poking through his silky red hair that he had cut short. He looked around uncertainly.

"I don't want to ride with a girl!" he whinged.

"Well," Jacinta replied. "You don't have to! I most definitely don't want to ride with you if you take that attitude. As far as I'm concerned, you can walk!"

Hakeem and Omar said nothing. They waited impassively, astride their horses. Hakeem seemed to be struggling to keep a straight face.

Daniel gave up out of desperation, and apologised. He asked Jacinta if he could ride with her. Jacinta looked as if she would rather eat droppings from her horse than agree but she managed to mumble something grudgingly.

Hakeem transferred the two youngsters to Nadeer and for the sake of peace folded a small blanket between them. Jacinta was in front and had the reins. Daniel would be sitting behind, hanging on in whatever way he saw fit.

It would do, though not in a working canter, unless the two cooperated much more. At least they should be somewhat comfortable in the ride, if not the proximity to each other. It promised to be an interesting trip.

Daniel was crimson with embarrassment. "I still don't like it much."

"Well hop off then!" was Jacinta's angry retort.

After that, Daniel decided to keep his peace for a little while at least, but soon the sound of bitter arguments reached Hakeem and Omar. Hakeem looked speculatively at Omar who gave a tired grin.

When they stopped for the night Daniel was looking particularly stiff, because he had tried to hang on without touching 'the girl'.

That evening, Jacinta came up to Hakeem quietly. "How long am I supposed to put up with that arrogant pig before I drop him on his head? You or Omar just have to sort him out before I do."

Hakeem laughed heartily. "Sounds like it will happen very soon then. But have you forgotten all I taught you? What's the point of a moral lesson if you can only use it when things are easy? Would you like to be able to fight only when it is easy?"

Jacinta looked at him in horror. "You have got to be joking! Are you saying, I'm supposed to put up with him? That's *my* training, is it? What about *his* training!"

Hakeem spoke seriously and quietly to Jacinta. "I am not telling what you must or must not do. That is your decision. As to his training, that is Omar's problem. As to his attitude, that is Daniel's problem. Indeed, he has been the victim of bullying, and I suspect his response has not helped him much.

"Do you presume to judge him, perhaps? If you do, do you know what made him like he is?

"Or do you hope to change him? Well perhaps bullying will do the trick, it obviously has not been tried before. He seems the sort to take it in good humour, don't you think?

"Or is it all part of the problem? It is painful to hear we have faults. We can only really accept them if we feel we are still acceptable even with faults. Daniel is well beyond that, he just feels hurt and angry. Because he is hurt, angry and feeling bad about himself, he acts irritably and mistrustfully. This makes things so much worse.

"How he acts is not your problem. How you let it affect you *is*. You talk of wanting to be a paladin. There must be physical training, but other forms of training are necessary if you are to become more than just a fighter.

"I believe Daniel and his bad manners have been sent to you for you to practice something extremely important for a paladin. How else can you get stronger except with this sort of provocation?" he smiled. "You are very lucky to have Daniel! You should thank him!"

Jacinta looked suspiciously at Hakeem. He meant what he said (apart, of course, from the bit about thanking Daniel for being obnoxious).

"Tell me you are joking," Jacinta pleaded. "I'm grateful already, if that's what you mean and if he keeps it up, then I'll have to use him to help me train a whole lot of other skills, which are more physical!"

Hakeem laughed. "This really is important. A paladin must be able to rise above anger, greed, jealousy, pride, all those things. A paladin must gain compassion, even for those who seem to be enemies.

"Have you already forgotten about Jakob at the caravanserai? Did you learn nothing from that? I am giving you a task. It is to care for your reaction to his provocation. It's up to you how you respond to it. I won't interfere."

"Well thank you very much, your great teacher-ship-ness, sir! And thank you for being the wise Sensei you are!" Jacinta announced grandly. "I can see that this humble, unworthy student is so privileged to have you, and of course the worthy Daniel, to instruct me." Jacinta finished, finding it hard to keep straight face. Soon the two broke down laughing.

Hakeem wanted to add something, and began talking urgently. "This is a difficult task I have given you, Jacinta. No one has been able to help Daniel, many have tried. The problem is a deep one. I don't like to talk about other students, but I owe it to you. For Daniel's sake, please don't repeat it, though it's no great secret where he comes from.

"Daniel has been in training for a year and it is all but decided he is not suitable. Omar wanted to give him a last chance by taking him on this journey, and giving him personal attention. He is concerned about what will happen to Daniel if he is expelled.

"Knowing he may be 'released' has only made him worse. Daniel won't listen; he has just become very bitter. Omar was going to come down hard on Daniel for how he was behaving, but I have asked him not to intervene.

"I feel Omar is just about to give up on Daniel."

Jacinta had a grave, thoughtful, look on her face as she left. She planned a long period of personal meditation before dealing with Daniel again.

* * *

A great change had come over Jacinta. Omar looked at Hakeem and raised an eyebrow enquiringly. If he had known the Jacinta from before, he would be incredulous.

Jacinta was not the same Jacinta that Hakeem had first met. Her training and her experience of the God of Shayvism had wrought a change. If it was going to be a beautiful dawn, she never tired of greeting it, and dragged her 'lazy' big companion up to be with her.

The great love and calmness she experienced through this mediation formed her approach. Hakeem had shown Jacinta how to apply the lessons from meditation to fighting. Now she had to learn how to use it to deal with her reaction to Daniel's barbs.

This did not mean that she didn't see what Daniel was doing. This did not mean that she placated him, but rather that she responded serenely to his provocation. She just achieved a distance from it.

So when Daniel complained about travelling behind a girl, she merely acknowledged he was finding it difficult. You are sweaty and stink, was responded to with a calm, "yes, I will bathe when there is an opportunity." It was windy, cold, uncomfortable, the horses smelled and so on. She understood what he was saying, and wasn't completely unsympathetic. Unspoken of course, was acceptance that his reaction was his own.

Daniel regarded her responses with suspicion. He thought she must be secretly poking fun of him, or maybe she had been told to be nice. For Jacinta, at some point it did become funny, giving serene replies to his constant whinging, but she was careful not to laugh.

Daniel didn't really want her to be aggressive to him, but he expected it. When it didn't come, at first he became even more tense and irritable. Probably it was the tension of waiting for the explosion to happen. It was like he was testing her ability not to react.

But having the chance to be listened to, Daniel started to talk about himself and his past. Jacinta listened with an occasional brief comment. Jacinta started to understand Daniel and she was moved by what she heard.

He never knew his father, who was likely a full blood elf. Indeed Daniel looked more elf than human. He had an unmarried mother, who was in disgrace from her clan. She had been taken in by a distant relative, but had to face terrible prejudice. Daniel was seen as worse than a bastard. He was a half-elf bastard.

His mother had to work hard and was given little money for it. Daniel was the symbol of her shame, though she never let him feel this. He remembered her as always being tired and sad.

From small, his mother worked and he was raised by a woman who was not paid, an act of charity. She never spoke a harsh word to Daniel but gave him impersonal, somewhat disinterested care. The only time she would rouse herself was when Daniel was hurt, physically or emotionally. Then she would comfort him, as she did have a good heart. When he was very young, the only way he got any love was to cry or complain, Jacinta concluded.

Daniel hated the elves for what his father had done, but he looked too much like an elf to be accepted as a human. Being small, he was a target for bullies.

He was alone, unhappy and angry and became a whinger. A technique he had learned before he could reason no longer worked; it only worsened things. Then he became like a dog that was so used to being kicked that it snarled at strangers.

It was worse if anyone got close to him. He longed to be accepted but this longing made him open to hurt. As he became dependant on someone's friendship, he became more and more fearful (and irritable) that they would turn on him.

He would misinterpret small actions. In the end it seemed as if he eventually attacked anyone who tried to befriend him.

With the repeated rejections, he felt bad to the core. Criticism made it worse. As he felt worse about himself, he became more miserable and unable to relate. In the end it was easier to be angry.

Or so it seemed to Jacinta.

And then his mother, knowing he was unhappy but bright, brought him to the chapterhouse in the hope it would be better for him. In a way, it was another rejection.

He had been there a year and was facing expulsion.

He was trapped. Whose responsibility was it to change this? It was Daniel's. This was his Karma. He needed the experience of struggling out of this suffering, changing his reactions. He could either choose to be strengthened or worsened by it.

But did this then mean nothing for Jacinta? No, it was her Kama to encounter someone like Daniel and her task (she knew without being told) to see if something could be done. So being angry with him, agreeing with him, or removing him from responsibility would not help!

Others had tried to 'talk' to him, or reason with him, or tell him he was being bad and difficult. It was beyond him to trust them. It was hopeless, or so others had concluded.

It had been, until now.

Slowly Daniel started to thaw. The journey wasn't all bad. He started to make friendly comments. He wasn't yet likeable, but he was no longer so unpleasant. He began to hope he might become accepted by his three companions, it was something he so desperately needed.

Omar marvelled at the change. He and Hakeem followed closely Jacinta's lead. Hakeem felt intensely proud of his young student, but scrupulously avoided showing favouritism to her over Daniel.

Daniel had been a slow learner in fighting. He was better suited to clerical duties. He was not big and he was timid. It was there the crisis finally struck.

Jacinta easily beat him in strength and speed. She was well ahead of him in unarmed combat. Whenever Daniel had a problem, it always strangely seemed that Omar and Hakeem were elsewhere, doing training on their own. So Jacinta had to be patient, show him, and look after his ego ... all at once.

He was too timid to try the falls and throws. He had been bullied, had lost confidence, and had little chance to regain it. So Jacinta would look for some soft ground to practice on. She let him throw her. He became worried he would hurt her (she was worried too, but made sure she didn't tense up).

They had to learn to trust each other and work together.

Slowly he started to idealise her. And slowly, she and the others noticed, he was no longer unpleasant and it was increasingly possible to like him. Of course, jealousy, anger and the need to show off would surface at intervals. What went wrong was perhaps a mixture of all this.

Jacinta hadn't started on weapons apart from the bow. The quarter staff was the next step. Jacinta was now having the privilege of being trained by Omar, an acknowledged grand-master.

Daniel had been learning for a year under Omar, and Jacinta could not match him. Omar had left them to practice after giving a demonstration of what he wanted them to do.

Hakeem noticed something in what Daniel was doing that got him to pause and start to walk, then run, back to where the children were. Daniel was showing off, he was attacking Jacinta with a series of movements that she was hard put to block. This was above her ability and dangerous. They were not even in protective padding! He had no business 'demonstrating' this to her!

She had helped him with unarmed techniques, but he was ready for these. She was a beginner with the quarter staff and this was not supposed to be what they were doing. What on earth had gotten into him? Omar noticed the same thing and stared puzzled for a moment, and then he started to move to stop it. There was no time to shout a warning.

Daniel tried a more advanced move and grinned, but Jacinta had no chance to block. Whack! The quarter staff of heavy wood hit hard across the cheek.

Jacinta dropped her staff and bent over in agony. She dropped to her knees, clutching her face in both hands. Tears squeezed from her eyes. Hakeem ran up and bent over the distraught girl and comforted her. When he could, he checked her eye on that side, there was no double vision. So the eye and the bony cavity it sat in weren't affected. He gently probed around the wound.

"I don't think it's too bad. The cheek bone isn't fractured. You'll have a big bruise, though," he announced.

Daniel was standing there frozen. His face was white like chalk. He looked like he was going to cry. "Daniel, can you fetch some water?" Hakeem asked gently, as if nothing major was wrong.

Daniel went to get some water quickly and Hakeem took some of it on a cloth, and asked him to boil the rest.

Jacinta was curled up in pain, struggling not to cry. The skin was split and bleeding; she would need some stitches. Omar studied it gravely.

He eventually three neat tiny stitches in, and black ointment to prevent infection. Having the stiches inserted stung and Hakeem held Jacinta in his arms while she faced it bravely.

"This should not be too bad, it's along the lines in the skin and not too deep." Omar concluded as he studied it carefully. "Also she's young and growing. I think it will be a small scar. Shame it's on the face, though. Do you get thick scars Jacinta?"

Jacinta shook her head.

"So, unlikely any permanent damage done," he concluded. Jacinta was red eyed and in pain, but sufficiently recovered to push them away.

Omar looked very grim. He took a big breath and started to gather himself. Hakeem laid his hand *very* firmly on his friends shoulder and gripped down hard. When Omar looked at him, Hakeem firmly shook his head.

Daniel was pale and shaking. He flinched every time someone looked at him, or passed near him. They kept him busy so he could not collapse into tears or misery. Then Hakeem and Omar sat down and Hakeem gestured to Daniel to come to talk to him.

"You never liked me, anyway, did you?" Daniel said accusingly, as he came closer reluctantly.

"So," Hakeem considered, "I caused this."

"I slipped on the wet grass," Daniel claimed.

"Is that what happened?" Hakeem enquired mildly, and looked steadily at Daniel.

"Jacinta should have blocked that. I had told her how," Daniel added.

"So it was Jacinta's fault. Perhaps she is unsuitable for this training. Perhaps I should send her away."

"No, you know it was me. I don't know why I did it!" Daniel shouted, angry and upset.

"Daniel, do you have cause to be angry with us?" Hakeem enquired. "Concentrate, this is important. Tell me what was inside you before you did this."

"I felt nervous and angry, not at Jacinta. Then I could do something better than her, it made me feel powerful. You're going to send me away, anyway."

Hakeem spoke calmly and seriously. "This isn't about us, Daniel. You say you didn't want this to happen. You must understand how it happened if you are going to do anything about it.

"Fear and anger makes you attack people who are trying to help you or be your friend. You can see how dangerous that is, but hating yourself won't help. It is caused by a deep wound. Hating yourself just pokes the wound and makes things worse.

"If you let us, we can help you. We would still like to but you have to trust us, not fight us. You can give in to this and let it take control, or you can try to take control of it. Those are your choices."

Hakeem paused looking intently at Daniel. "Daniel, what is the answer?"

Daniel was in anguish. "How can you not hate me? How can I not hate myself? I must leave!"

After a year of training, he should have better control than this, Hakeem knew. Daniel was in danger of withdrawing into self-pity and tears, and then no one could talk to him.

"If there is so much to dislike about yourself, is it not time to do something to be proud of?

"This is your chance. Don't you see? God has given you an important and difficult task. Isn't it clear you have a task? Are you going to turn away from it? It is not an easy one, but if you listen to us, we will help you. We are not your enemies and never were.

"You said you want to leave. Does this mean that you don't have the courage to face your hurt and anger and defeat it? If you do not wish to control this thing, you may leave. But you will carry this thing with you, wherever you go.

"If you agree to stay, there will be consequences. You are not allowed to train in fighting until Omar says you are ready. You may never be allowed again, this is not punishment.

"We had hoped the training and discipline would help you. It is too dangerous for you to have this anger and also be able to fight. You could do harm to others and hence yourself.

"If you stay, we will concentrate on one thing and one thing only: allowing you to control your fear and anger. You will be on probation and you know what that means."

Tears began streaming down Daniel's face. "Please .... please help me," he said in a small voice. Hakeem took him up in to his strong arms and held him until the tears stopped. Daniel looked up with gratitude at the two men.

"Jacinta will hate me!" he said sadly.

"Perhaps she will," Hakeem said. "If she does, it is your task to control your reaction to how she treats you now. How she acts now is her responsibility. How you react to her is your own. Sinking into self-pity and hating yourself or others is not the way out of this.

"You need faith that a path will be shown to you, even when things seem most black. This was how it was for me, and this is how it was for Jacinta. Our tasks were first shown to us when things seemed most bleak and hopeless."

Daniel's head jerked up in shock and hope, he had assumed life must have always been magically easy for these two.

Hakeem nodded to confirm the truth of what he said. "Yes, when we were at the bottom of despair, we started on our tasks, not realising we were doing so at the time.

"Now, you said you were instructing Jacinta. Something has gone wrong. What are you going to do now?"

"I can't talk to her."

Hakeem merely nodded his acceptance.

Almost immediately Daniel stood up, and reluctantly walked over to Jacinta.

Daniel looked pale and frightened, on the point of tears. "Why did you hurt me?" Jacinta asked. She looked at him through a tangle of black hair, her cheek bruised and puffy with its stitches.

"I was angry, but not at you."

"Ouch, Daniel" Jacinta said and stretched out her hand to him. He grabbed it and held it for a long time like something very precious, kissing it.

"This has to change, Daniel," was all Jacinta said.

* * *

Fortunately Jacinta had no serious damage, and would likely only have a faint scar. Not too bad for one who was destined to be a fighter. Daniel had hit her hard, but not with his full power. Poor Jacinta!

Jacinta forgave him almost immediately, not to say he wasn't on probation with her. But she knew he would never hurt her again like that.

She was left with a large bruise that went through a very interesting pattern of colour changes over several weeks. She wasn't permitted certain types of training until it healed, maybe the bone was bruised.

Her cheek really ached if she did anything strenuous at first, or bumped it, or smiled…or laughed.

Omar was prepared for backsliding or minor glitches, but this was a new Daniel. Daniel was shocked about what happened and there was no chance to pretend it wasn't his fault or to be angry at others.

They remained friendly to him. He was forgiven. This stunned him more than he could ever say. Jacinta, Omar and Hakeem gave him something he had never experienced: acceptance. Even when he had faults, he was given a way to work on his problems. He marvelled at them.

He was not permitted to practice fighting, but the reason was obvious and this wasn't because they hated him. Daniel had meditation and Omar's quiet voice giving him instruction. He had no other tasks around the camp.

The days were shortening but it was a time of beautiful sunrises and the four travellers greeted each dawn together. Omar and Hakeem sat together, and Jacinta and Daniel sat meditating, side by side.

Daniel was deeply affected by what happened. At first he was very quiet. Then he started to relax around the other three. He started to look happier and happier.

He had hit his rock bottom when he hurt Jacinta. She was his only friend, and he hurt her for no reason to do with her. Even then, these people cared for him. He would never go back. If they thought he was worth another chance, he was going to show everyone, especially himself that he was worth it! He had been given a precious gift and would never be the same.

A smile would appear on his face. He became increasingly pleasant and helpful. He started to laugh.

* * *

Daniel and Jacinta had ridden a little ahead and were chatting happily away. "I think your student is going to work out now," Hakeem murmured to Omar.

Omar nodded. "He is so determined and has been able to go very deep with his meditation practice. I think it's something to do with his elf heritage. You know there are very few who are mixed elf and human so it is hard to know what that will mean. The other day, I became scared and had to check he was breathing! I marvel at what you two have done. I couldn't help him. I marvel at Jacinta!" Omar said. "Jacinta has only started training and is already so advanced. She learns so quickly, she works so hard.

"Don't lose this one, Hakeem, we need her in the order. She is the best I've seen for a long while. She may become the best I've ever seen. Yet I never saw you when you were young."

Hakeem laughed "She wants to be a student paladin. I had little doubt before, now I have none. I love her dearly. I want her to be my daughter and sometimes I feel so proud I could burst. Am I biased? Yes I am, but I don't think I'm wrong in this case

"She will never match me physically in my prime. But she will become a powerful female warrior if she keeps this up, perhaps the best of her time. As to wisdom, I am already her student and she is my teacher."

"No, you are right about her," Omar responded, laughing. "I will gladly add my recommendation for her to become a student of a paladin, and I am second only to the Grand Abbot. And while we are onto this, I have seen and heard enough. A paladin is not really elected, they are recognised. There can be no doubt at all about you Hakeem, you are a paladin.

"The Grand Abbot has the word of many, including his predecessor. Unofficially, I think he has decided and my word will simply confirm his opinion. You are a paladin, and a student has been sent to you in the form of your daughter, though why this is so, we don't yet know."

"I think the Grand Abbot's plan to reawaken the ancient practice of appointing Religious Knights was a good one," Hakeem said.

"Why do you believe the practice was stopped?" Omar asked quietly.

Hakeem laughed. "Next you will say there has been no one worthy, since the last paladin. Why that's almost three hundred years!" He paused and began chuckling again as he thought about it.

"Well," Omar was a bit nonplussed. "I don't think worthy is the word. More ... er, suitable ... or suited to. But anyway as for the adoption of your daughter, you have my word. It has to be confirmed by the Grand Abbot, but that won't be a problem."

"Thank you, my friend," was all Hakeem said, his mind was far away, thinking of his daughter.

* * *

Daniel was continuing to become a better person. He continued to make amazing progress in deep meditation. Only towards the end of the journey was it thought that he could slowly re-enter physical training. He would never be a great warrior, but he had accepted this.

While Omar was intensively occupied with Daniel, Hakeem was back training Jacinta.

"I first couldn't see how anyone could help Daniel, but all I had to do was not get angry with him," Jacinta said in wonder. "Then I could begin to understand the problem."

"I'm really proud of you!" Hakeem replied seriously to his student. "Many people had tried. Even Omar gave up in the end. Daniel was headed down a dark path. I was deeply concerned for Daniel the grown man, but it was his Karma to be given chances. It was up to him to take them or not."

"I don't fully understand about Karma," Jacinta said.

"Nor do I, not fully," Hakeem laughed. "Nor does anyone I know."

It was a new Daniel that kissed and hugged Hakeem and Jacinta as the friends parted. Daniel and Omar went on to the local chapterhouse and Jacinta and Hakeem would meet them there later. But first, they would visit Myriani, Elwan's widow and Kassandra, their daughter.

Chapter 15: A Tribesman's Daughter

Hakeem had hoped to reach Myriani's farm before mid-winter solstice, which was a very special celebration amongst the elves, but by his estimate, it had occurred soon after they parted with Daniel and Omar.

Not too long before they reached Myriani's farmhouse, something happened to make Hakeem frightened for his young ward. It was mid-day and Jacinta was doing some set moves and Hakeem was helping her. Hakeem bumped against her chest and Jacinta let out an 'Ow!'

She had a tender lump on her chest! No, Daniel hadn't hit her there, Jacinta had just noticed it. She turned her back on him and eventually reported she had a very painful lump under her left nipple. Hakeem felt a chill of fear. Could this be an abscess? It was so near to her heart.

Hakeem was good with sick animals, he could look after soldiers and do field dressings but he felt lost in his ignorance of small girls. He didn't want to look at Jacinta's breast. Jacinta had another look and said no, there was no redness. No, she didn't feel sick or feverish. No, there were no swollen glands under her arm on that side.

And, NO! She *most definitely* didn't want her father to look!

Hakeem felt a wave of relief when Jacinta indignantly refused showing her breast to him. It didn't sound critical, and they were only two days from their destination. The elves would know what to do. Yet, if things got worse, he didn't want to delay treatment.

If it needed lancing, would it affect her ability to breast feed on that side, or her ability to use a bow, he wondered.

He strained to remember the details of a cow he saw treated for milk fever, but he was too young. It was all too hazy.

He took to asking if things were changing until Jacinta was thoroughly sick of his fussiness. She promised to let him know, if he only stopped asking her! Even then, she kept catching him watching her, frowning in his concern. When she caught these looks she would sniff and toss her head or simply irritably say, "No change!"

Hakeem expected her to have difficulty with riding or training. He eased off on her training and was very cautious not to bump her again. He tried to stop her doing her chores or cooking until Jacinta yelled angrily at him.

"For the hundredth time, I'm fine. Now just let me be, Hakeem!"

The big man took on an expression like a scolded puppy, which made Jacinta feel guilty, but she had to make him stop somehow. He was being so irritating!

It had been ten days already that they had been travelling through the Black Sea region. They wouldn't be crossing the coastal mountains and forests to the sea itself but (short of that) there cannot be many places in the world as beautiful.

At first they had travelled through an alpine region that was untamed and wild, with towering craggy peaks and deep narrow gorges, where tall waterfalls seemed to fall forever down to wildly rushing mountain streams. Hakeem said it was far prettier in the spring and summer with the alpine grasses.

While the leaves were long gone from the oak, beech and the other trees of the lowlands, everything was lush and green.

Rain, mist and snow often rolled in to shroud the far mountains. The slopes high up were covered with dense pine forest and snow.

The paths were treacherous and narrow, so at first, they had to lead the horses most of the way. Many times Jacinta felt dizzy with fear from the heights and the slippery trail, but she never let Hakeem know. She was leading Farah, who was smaller but very sure-footed.

As Hakeem had warned Jacinta, it was very cold and they were camping out, but they were well provisioned and the weather had been otherwise kind.

They hardly saw another soul. The few elves they met would smile and greet them politely enough. They would answer questions if asked, but didn't seem interested in stopping to talk. It was the way of elves, Hakeem explained, especially male elves. They would study things for hours but never say much.

Gradually the wild rugged mountain trails gave way to more settled lands. At first Jacinta could only glimpse houses and villages built high up on the slopes, with patches of mountainous meadows here and there.

As she saw yet another one so high above her, she wondered how the elves got up there. There was no direct connection with the narrow path they were leading the horses along. Were they just born up there and never came down? If the road to the village followed the last side-path she had seen, it was so far back. Maybe they never came the way Hakeem was leading her and the horses.

The slope was so high and steep, she imagined one of their children or even one of their houses, slipping and just tumbling over and over, all the way down the mountain.

Sometimes she saw where the elves had strung ropeways across narrow gorges, but she didn't find out how they worked and didn't want to.

Once, looking down to a loudly churning white water river far below, she saw a boat by the bank, just before where the gorge narrowed. She wondered how anyone would dare brave such a river; it seemed like something you would do only once. What would it be like when the snow started to melt? And yet, a boat was there!

Now, as they were closer to Myriani's farm, they were reaching better farming country with more open, rolling hills interspersed with forest. They passed meadows with goats, beehives wrapped in black canvas to protect them from the cold, orchards and apple groves (bare in the winter).

The houses didn't seem so precarious, and she could finally get close enough to admire the gaily painted wooden huts with the thatched roofs the elves used. Elves didn't clear as much around their homes and farms as was the human custom, nor did they cluster their villages as closely. It must be the elvish love of trees.

There seemed to be any manner of fruit trees: sweet chestnuts, walnuts, hazelnuts, pears and cherries to name a few.

They still met few elves, though Hakeem said they were being watched. The elves would be more in evidence once their presence was accepted.

As they drew closer to Myriani's farm, Hakeem was becoming quieter. He seemed pre-occupied about something and Jacinta wondered what it could be. It wasn't her lump, there had been no change since they had first discovered it.

It was something Hakeem had long put from his mind. If Myriani and Kassandra disapproved of him and Jacinta, it would be almost too hard to take. They were the closest thing he had to family.

* * *

There was no way to warn Myriani of their arrival, so it was a surprise. It was early afternoon and Myriani looked up to see three horses ambling up to the large farmhouse. When she recognised Hakeem, she came running swiftly up the slope from the bottom meadow, calling out joyfully, to her daughter, Kassandra.

Hakeem dismounted and hugged the two elves for a long time. He hadn't fully realised just how much he had missed them.

Kassandra had grown into a lovely young woman and he held her back for a moment in his arms, to admire how she had grown.

"Hakeem," was all Myriani could say as he hugged her, and then she started to cry.

Jacinta had stayed on Farah, feeling shy and uncertain. Hakeem turned back for her, so she slid down into his arms and he hoisted her onto his hip. He turned to face Myriani, with a somewhat fixed smile on his face and Jacinta on one hip.

"This is Jacinta," he said, a little guardedly. "I rescued her when her family was killed. She's travelling with me," Hakeem explained.

Jacinta looked at Hakeem in surprise; was he ashamed of her? No, that wasn't it, yet he was clutching her so possessively.

Did he feel frightened of what they would think of her? Yet that didn't make sense, they had no reason to dislike her.

Then it hit her. He was afraid of what they would think of him, a single man and a soldier, adopting a little girl. Elves could be harsh in their judgement, it was said. The only experience she had had was with her friend, Daniel, and he was certainly difficult at first.

Myriani and Kassandra looked at Hakeem. They could see he was tense but they didn't understand. He said Jacinta was travelling with him, well they could see that easily enough. What was wrong with him? He would be taking her to family presumably, what was the problem with the little girl?

Jacinta whispered desperately to Hakeem. "Let me down, Hakeem!" She started to wriggle to get free so she could meet Hakeem's elf friends.

Hakeem looked at Jacinta blankly and then let her slip down to her feet, but still stood, clutching her tightly.

Seeing the big man so defensive and protective, a sudden understanding hit Kassandra. They weren't simply travelling together.

She gave a shriek of pure delight.

"Hakeem! She's your foster daughter! Oh Hakeem that's so wonderful and she's *so* pretty!"

Myriani called excitedly. "Hakeem! That's wonderful!" Her eyes teared again as she admired the pair standing together.

Hakeem let out a ragged breath as Myriani held her arms out to Jacinta. Jacinta thought she might have to kick Hakeem in the shins to make him let go, but with a struggle she managed to disentangle herself.

Hakeem had a good heart Myriani knew, but he was so shy and kept his distance from others. To see him so protective of the small Gypsy girl warmed her heart. He seemed changed. Was it this small girl who had changed him?

Hakeem gave a shaky chuckle, Jacinta was accepted.

* * *

It was not long after they arrived that Hakeem explained the fear he had for Jacinta. She had developed a painful lump under one of her nipples, and Hakeem was almost beside himself with worry.

Myriani, to his relief, seemed to take it as a fairly simple problem and steered Jacinta into her bedroom and closed the door. They were in there for what seemed a long time, and Hakeem waited anxiously outside, trying not to pace. Kassandra was preparing food in the kitchen, so Hakeem explained his concerns as she worked.

Kassandra looked at the anxious face of the big tribesman. She nodded gravely, as he talked about what he could remember of the treatment of a cow with milk fever.

She agreed this really could be serious.

She turned her head to cough (which allowed her to free the smile she was desperately trying to supress).

When she turned back, she was able to manage a serious and concerned face again and master the urge to giggle. The big tribesman trying to raise a small girl, it was so cute!

Hakeem couldn't understand what was taking Myriani and Jacinta so long. Then he began to hear the sound of occasional laughter, the clear pleasant notes of elf woman's laughter and Jacinta's own musical laughter. Eventually Myriani and Jacinta came out arm in arm. Myriani smiled at Hakeem's anxious expression.

"We've decided to put you out of your misery." Myriani started. "Jacinta and I have to have a series of talks."

Myriani took a deep breath and tried to work out how to explain it to the big man.

"Hakeem, you're a male and … Jacinta *is, well* … a female!" She announced grandly.

Hakeem looked puzzled and then relief and understanding passed across his face. "You mean this is normal?" he enquired, amazed.

The two were acting as if they were part of some special secret society. Kassandra was snickering nearby. Jacinta looked particularly smug.

"Over the next three years Jacinta will be developing breasts. Now you do know about those?" Myriani teased.

This was delicious! Hakeem's ignorance of the ways of females was almost complete.

Hakeem was blushing furiously, but he ploughed on gamely. "Is there anything I need to … er …. er …. er will it hurt? Do I need to do anything?"

"No," said Myriani. The three women were thoroughly enjoying his reaction.

Myriani wondered what he thought he could do. A regular inspection perhaps … as if Jacinta would allow that!

Why was Hakeem so much fun to tease? He was so naïve and shy around women, in contrast to how he was in most other things. His embarrassment made him so loveable … fierce warrior indeed!

"There's nothing *you* need to do. Nature has got on fairly well without you all these years. It shouldn't be painful like this, by that stage." Myriani finished.

Hakeem felt so relieved he collapsed into a chair. He had to chuckle at Myriani's teasing. So a tender lump under the nipple in a young girl may the first sign of the normal change into being a woman.

The three 'girls' fussed around, offering him a small pot of tea and some small cakes to show they loved him dearly, even though he was a *male*. Then Jacinta and Myriani withdrew for a solid half hour of talking.

Hakeem sat sipping his tea and contemplating the idea of Jacinta becoming a woman. How would this impact on her training? How would this impact on the easy physical closeness they shared? He couldn't imagine. He knew he never wanted anything to cause an emotional distance between them. Then he thought of another man coming to love his daughter. A small tear came to his eye. He felt worry, sadness, happiness and pride all together.

His little girl was starting to grow up.

Perhaps Jacinta felt it too. When she came out of the bedroom, she silently climbed into his lap for a long hug before she joined Myriani and Kassandra with their chores.

* * *

Jacinta loved her talks with the older woman. She loved being Hakeem's foster daughter but missed having another female, especially an older woman around.

Myriani was so wise in the ways of the world, and it was the sort of frank discussion that only females can have together.

Myriani was touching on topics about men and women that Jacinta would not have to worry for years, but she preferred Jacinta to be prepared. It was information her foster father would hardly be able to give her!

It was on the afternoon of their fourth day that it happened. Perhaps to impress, perhaps daydreaming, Jacinta seemingly casually remarked. "Of course, you know Hakeem and I are lovers."

She didn't notice the temperature in the room rapidly plummeting. Myriani had become very icy, "Really?"

"Yes, he really knows how to satisfy a girl," Jacinta continued, smiling to herself and completely missing the horrible danger she was in.

"Then you know about the birthmark?" Myriani enquired innocently.

"Oh yes, that." Jacinta replied, "You couldn't miss that."

"Was it on the left or the right buttock?" Myriani enquired.

"On the left," Jacinta promptly supplied.

"How do you manage with his injury?" Myriani continued.

Injury? Jacinta started to panic. "Oh, we work around it."

"Now you listen to me," Myriani said coldly. "You're nothing but a silly little girl!"

Jacinta was completely mortified. She wished the ground would swallow her up. She had wanted to impress the older woman. All she had done was to earn her scorn.

She had accused Hakeem of what was a loathsome crime. How on earth could this have seemed like a good idea?

That evening Hakeem noticed an abrupt change in Jacinta. She had been so happy, now she was so downcast she hardly ate before she went to her room early. Was she sick? Had someone said something nasty to her? He didn't think it was possible; Myriani's family and friends loved his foster child almost as much as he did.

He noticed concerned looks from Myriani's daughter, but was surprised that Myriani herself seemed oblivious. She was carrying on as if nothing was amiss. As soon as he could go, without causing a fuss, he went to the room Jacinta shared with Kassandra, but she seemed to be asleep already.

He didn't get to talk to Jacinta the next morning but noticed she went off to the sheds with Myriani's daughter. He hoped the older girl could help her with whatever was bothering her.

* * *

"You said what?" Kassandra asked incredulously.

"I know!" said Jacinta miserably.

"That's serious! Before the Great Earth Mother what came over you? You know what Hakeem's like."

"I don't know. Really if there was anything in my life, I could take back, I'd take that back."

"Did you apologize to mum? That would have helped."

"I was too scared of her, she really cut me down. I deserved it. Do you think she'll tell Hakeem?" Jacinta asked plaintively.

"Do you think she won't?" countered Kassie.

"How long have I got?"

"Not long *meli* (honey), if I know Mum. She practically raised me on her own. Dad was away so much."

"He'll be so hurt!"

It looked like Jacinta had gone too far this time. She doubted Hakeem would have anything like his often mild reactions. "I hope he beats me. I'll feel better and then he'll forgive me faster. I hope he forgives me."

Kassie waited with the young Gypsy girl, to give her support. Jacinta sat morosely. It was a most unhappy wait, but not a long one.

At the same time as they waited, Myriani and Hakeem were sitting on the veranda drinking tea. "I've wanted to talk to you on your own, Myriani. You know if you or Kassandra need anything you only have to let me know," Hakeem started.

"Thanks," Myriani replied. "But we are doing well here. The land is good to us."

"But the work is hard and Kassie will be getting married soon, and will leave."

"Don't worry about me," she said. "Ian and Kassie are coming back to help me work the farm, and don't forget the money you brought, Elwan's share of the plunder. I still think you added to it, no matter what you say. Anyway, I've got some ideas of what to do, once I have more help.

"This is my home and I'll always have a place here."

"I was thinking, Jacinta likes you and I think she could do with a woman around. I like you, I find you an attractive woman," he finished, blushing.

"Hakeem, No!" She laughed incredulously. "I'm almost twice your age! No! Absolutely no! ... but thanks!" she laughed.

Hakeem was blushing furiously. "You know I really like you, Myriani."

"Well, I thank you. You've given my self-esteem a big boost, I must say, but the answer is no!"

"I don't think I'm seen as marriageable material," Hakeem smiled ruefully. "That's the second refusal I've had this trip."

"Perhaps you need to try offering something else." Myriani smiled mischievously.

"Uugh," Hakeem was too embarrassed to talk for a moment.

"I want to talk to you about Jacinta," Myriani started. "There's never been anything, you know, between you and her has there?"

"No!" Hakeem replied loudly, horrified at the thought, but he was not really angry he was asked. He had always been able to have an honest conversation with Myriani. "How could you think that of me?"

"I didn't, I just needed to check," she answered. "You know, I wondered about you and Elwan. You were so close, but Elwan said 'no'."

Hakeem laughed. "I'm not a lover of men, at least not in that way.

"I was to be a monk and celibate. It seems like I will continue that way. But not for any of those reasons," he added quickly. "I didn't realise, I was, well, scared of women. Would they like me? Could I make a partner er, satisfied? You know."

Myriani couldn't stop herself from laughing at the idea women wouldn't find Hakeem attractive.

Her laughter helped him relax; she was good to talk to about these things.

"I *know* it was silly." He was blushing, shaking his head. "But that's how I felt. I didn't need to be so scared." He responded to her raised eyebrow with a laugh. "No, nothing happened. It was in the early part of the journey, but I admit to some regrets."

Myriani just shook her head with a smile. "You're a strange one at times, Hakeem."

That Hakeem was intensely shy around women had been so obvious to everyone, except, apparently, Hakeem. It was good to hear that was the only problem.

Her mind strayed briefly to candidates for match-making, but for the moment there was something much more important to discuss.

"Have you thought of what you are going to do with Jacinta? She's going to have a strange childhood."

"Myriani, I've thought of nothing else since I rescued her." Hakeem shook his head at the irony of her question. "But it's all decided, I haven't told her yet, but as soon as I receive permission, she will be Jacinta *bint* Hakeem."

"You know you don't have to do that. You saved her life. She can stay as your ward. There may be complications, if you want to marry."

"No, this feels right. If I'm forced to choose, I will choose Jacinta as my daughter." Hakeem looked intently at Myriani. "There's something you really need to understand. I saved Jacinta, but in a way she saved me. Inside me there was a wall against my feelings, deep down a part of me was dead.

"You won't understand this, because it refers to the Shayvist belief about paladins, but Father Omar believes Jacinta has been sent to me for a reason."

Myriani nodded. "elves believe in fate too, Hakeem," she chided him gently.

She understood what he was saying, she had always felt a deep pain in Hakeem before, a hardness.

"I love Jacinta. I'll be proud to call her my daughter," he finished.

"Well, you're going to have a handful with that one as she grows up."

"Don't I know it?" Hakeem laughed. "Did you know, she said she plans to marry me when she is older?"

He snorted in amusement and took a large swig of tea. Just then Myriani told him.

Tea sprayed over the lawn and Hakeem turned an alarming colour.

"She ..." he croaked, struggling for breath. "Jacinta ... Jacinta ... JACINTA!" he bellowed. The first call came out sounding like someone was being strangled, the last "Jacinta" thundered clear down to the valley.

He seemed to be choking again, but managed to say to Myriani between coughing, "Can you leave me to have time with my daughter? I think we need to have a talk." He finished with a grim look.

Myriani was frightened by his temper. She considered the wisdom of allowing the eleven-year-old to face him alone, but she decided not to provoke him further, so she reluctantly moved inside.

* * *

"JACINTA!"

At a pat on the shoulder from Kassie, Jacinta started to walk reluctantly up the hill towards the house, but as she got halfway there, her courage collapsed.

A swirl of thoughts made her panic. She had accused Hakeem of what he would see as a loathsome crime. What was the punishment for her doing that? Would he send her away? Would he stop loving her?

Suddenly she was running. She could hardly see for tears.

She threw herself at Hakeem's feet grabbing tightly at his legs. Hakeem stared down at Jacinta's untidy mass of black curls; the young Gypsy girl had dissolved completely into sobbing and tears.

Hakeem was prepared to talk *very* sternly to his ward. He saw this as a serious matter, Jacinta really needed to understand that.

He knew it was a prank of course, after all, there was no real harm done. But he had no chance to say anything.

All he could understand was "S-s-sorry" and "F-f-forgive m-me." He'd never seen her so remorseful.

He was a bit at a loss as to what to do. He pulled Jacinta (with some difficulty) off his legs and put her crosswise on his lap. Where had Jacinta got such strength, he wondered?

There was a sobbing "N-never" after which she gave up talking. She clung to him and tried to burrow her face deep into his chest while he cuddled her and rocked her. He saw Kassie walking up the hill.

Just then the door slammed and Myriani came charging out, in a complete rage.

"How could you! You brute! She just a little child, for the Mother's sake!" Myriani rounded on him angrily. "What have you done to her?"

Hakeem just looked helplessly at her, lost for words. Jacinta attempted to say something but was incoherent. Myriani angrily tried to jerk Jacinta out of his arms. Hakeem didn't resist, but Jacinta did and all Myriani managed to do was nearly topple them both off the chair.

"I'll have you know, this is my house, and I won't tolerate any barbaric behaviour," Myriani continued angrily.

"Did he beat you?" Jacinta gave a small shake of her head.

"Well, did he threaten you?" Jacinta gave her head another shake, as she buried her face deeper into Hakeem's shirt.

"Well what did he do?" cried Myriani in confusion.

"Mother!" Kassandra cried, hurrying up. "Hakeem did nothing. He didn't even growl at her, a severe case of guilty conscience, I'd say. You've made a fool of yourself, mother."

Myriani went pale. Hakeem had only ever shown her and her family kindness. She would have said she didn't hold any of the famous elvish disdain for the race of humans, but there it was. She was quick to see Hakeem as a heartless barbarian. She knew him better than that!

It felt like she was hit with a bucket of ice water, as she saw in shock what was deep inside herself. She was appalled. Her legs felt weak.

"Oh Hakeem," she said, tears welling in her eyes as she sank to the bench next to him. "Please forgive me. How could I? I'm a fool."

She clutched at his shoulder. He put his free arm around her and pulled her firmly to him.

Kassie looked down on the tribesman with each arm around the two crying women and a look of confusion on his face. "Would you like a cup of tea?" she asked brightly.

He looked back at her blankly.

"You probably couldn't manage it at the moment anyway, with both your arms busy," Kassie continued. "Do you always have this sort of effect on women?"

"I don't know what effect I have on women," Hakeem returned ruefully. "But no one wants to marry me."

"Don't you say *that* in front of some of my friends." Kassie looked at him appraisingly. "One look at you and we'd have a riot on our hands."

When Myriani had recovered somewhat, she left the two, after hugging Hakeem and kissing him fiercely on the cheek. She received a fond smile in return.

Jacinta had quietened but not yet emerged from burying her face in his shirt. Hakeem spoke to her gently. "Well, I hope you've learned your lesson."

Jacinta sat up and looked at him nodding, vigorously. She looked a wreck. Her hair was all over the place, her eyes red and face tear-stained.

"No more of those lies, please, young one," he finished gently.

"I promise, never ever again. No more nasty lies about you."

It sounded a bit like a *limited* guarantee, but it would do.

"Now I'm not sure what you thought I was going to do, but I think you've learned your lesson. Have you?"

She nodded vigorously. She couldn't believe it. "I thought at least you would have punished me."

"Well, I think you've punished yourself. Do you think I should beat you?"

Jacinta nodded her head sadly.

"Well, you leave me no choice!" Hakeem yelled suddenly.

Jacinta shrieked in shock as she found herself spun upside down and thrown over his knee. He only gave her a playful tap on her bottom, and then spun her back upright and gently shook her, "Is that enough?"

"I don't think so," she sighed.

Instantly she found herself being spun again for a repeat. She squealed and managed a small smile. He's hopeless!

"Do I beat you Jacinta?"

"No!"

"Should I beat you, Jacinta?"

"Yes!"

He then held her firmly face down on his lap and repetitively tapped her lightly on the bottom, demanding she surrender. Jacinta struggled helplessly to get free and then … she grabbed his knee with both hands and bit it.

Hakeem jumped up with a "yeow!" only just managing not to drop Jacinta, he jerked her up laughing and started to tickle her. Myriani came out with a cup of tea for Hakeem to find the pair playing a wrestling/tickling game with great hilarity.

She shook her head smiling. Hakeem would make Jacinta a thorough tomboy given half a chance!

Though maybe not, Jacinta was so definitely female. She would be a real handful as she grew.

* * *

It was hard leaving Myriani and her family, especially with Kassie's wedding to Ian in a few weeks. But Hakeem was becoming increasingly concerned about how long he would be away from Aiolía.

As far as he knew, things were quiet and he wasn't urgently needed, but he still fretted.

He would receive any mail at the northern chapterhouse, especially an answer to his adoption request.

They made good time to the chapterhouse and Omar and Daniel, were waiting to greet them. Hakeem saw Daniel greeting Jacinta shyly, blushing furiously. After an early meal, Jacinta took command of Daniel and demanded a tour. Not too much time later their excited voices could be heard from the courtyard.

Hakeem settled down to talk to the abbot and read a letter that had arrived for him.

"Well," Hakeem said. "At least I'm not missed. Things are very quiet. Samit plans to retire his active commission on my return, but will stay on as King's Adviser. He won't be out in the field much anymore, but we will have the benefit of his experience. Samit reassures me he's still in good health; he just getting older and wants to take it easy.

"I guess that confirms my new command at the head the Shantawi Cavalry. I find it all a little daunting."

"I can think of none better," Omar said, looking at Hakeem seriously.

Hakeem sighed, "Well I was taught by the very best. I just hope I have Samit and King Helios close enough to give me advice when I need it. I wonder who Helios will promote to overall command with Samit retiring."

"I've got good news for you," Omar smiled, changing the topic.

"Did you get an answer?" Hakeem asked, obviously excited.

Omar nodded. "You have permission to adopt Jacinta!"

Hakeem gave out a small whoop. He asked him to keep it a secret. He hoped to surprise her.

"It sounds like the Grand Abbot plans to confirm you as a paladin in a ceremony when you arrive in Karsh, so I need to warn you about that," Omar continued. "He needs to meet you himself of course. He's heard a lot about you from Samit, King Helios and me. It's a big decision, though, and he will need to talk to the Sheikhs of the ten tribes."

"As I understand things," Hakeem replied. "This is almost a formality. I was hoping you could confirm me here in a simple ceremony, and why did I have to ask the Grand Abbot permission to adopt Jacinta?"

Omar studied Hakeem for a few moments. "You don't know do you? You've got no idea, do you?"

"About what? I'm to become a paladin, but what difference does that make? Wasn't it the old Grand Abbot's idea of renewing the practice of religious knights? He was right, it is a good idea, though I really think there should be more of us, not just one or two at a time.

"I am proud to be chosen, and I hope I will be worthy. I even have my first pupil. But why all this incredible fuss?"

"Sit down," Omar said gravely. "I'll call for some tea."

Omar continued after the tea arrived. "It's a little complicated," he said. "We haven't had many paladins, so most don't know about them.

"A paladin is a cross between one of our religious and a knight. To be a paladin, you need to be seen as pure of heart." He waved aside Hakeem's objections. "That's for the Grand Abbot to judge, not you. Only the Grand Abbot can 'recognise' a paladin."

Hakeem waved this aside. "I think everyone is making far too much of this and why ask the Sheikhs of the ten tribes, for the sake of all that's holy? Just so I can work as a mercenary and still be linked to the religious."

Omar paused. "I know you believed the practice of appointing paladins was discontinued."

Hakeem nodded. "It's being re-instituted, it's a good idea."

Omar looked at his friend very seriously. "It was never stopped."

Hakeem looked puzzled. "But..." Then he felt a lurch inside.

Omar continued gravely. "None have been sent to us, Hakeem. You are the first in such a long, long, time. And we may already have a second."

Now Hakeem was looking very sobered.

Omar knew he was placing a burden on his young friend which would change him forever. "You will be a paladin and the *emīr* (commander) of all our mercenaries, which makes you the most senior warrior of all the tribes. Do you know of the *Ra'al* (Warlord) of our tribes?"

"Warlord?" Hakeem echoed.

"The Warlord," Omar repeated. "The Warlord is appointed by the Grand Abbot, on advice from the ten tribes. Usually the Abbot doesn't have a candidate.

"The Warlord takes command of all our warriors and soldiers, when we or any allies are threatened. He has the power to make treaties. He can mobilise all armed and civilian forces and direct defences.

"Growing up in the monastery, you may not have heard of the Warlord. We haven't needed one to take control for over a hundred years."

Hakeem was starting to feel as if he was in a waking dream. He felt a floating feeling, as if he could see himself and the abbot from afar. He had such a strong feeling he had had this conversation in this place and at this time before. He didn't know what this feeling could mean. Something was occurring at this point which would change his life forever.

He knew what came next. "Who is the current warlord?" he asked, knowing the answer.

"Samit, and..."

"He's retiring" Hakeem finished for him. That made Hakeem the most senior in rank, despite his youth, but so what? They hadn't needed a warlord for a hundred years.

"Don't you see?" Omar asked. "You are to be the Warlord and a paladin. We believe paladins are sent by our God. They are sent only rarely, one at a time, and they are sent each with a task.

"No one knows what task or even tasks, you will be given. For one it was setting up the military training of the monks; the others were leaders in a time of trouble"

"Trouble?" echoed Hakeem. "You are starting to scare me, Omar. Am I to be given no choice in my life? I am committed to King Helios and I am a father. Where will this paladin thing take me?"

"For this," Omar continued, pouring tea for both of them, "you need to have faith. It is likely you are exactly where you need to be, doing what you need to do."

"Trouble!" whispered Hakeem with a shudder. The hairs on the back of his arms and neck were standing up. He glanced out the window. The afternoon was starting to fail behind a bank of clouds. He shuddered as the scene darkened.

Omar continued quietly. "The elves have a prophecy, unimaginably ancient. It is about a time of great testing. They believe that time is upon us, and now we are given you. You are our paladin and you will be our warlord. We can read the signs. Yours will not to be an individual quest.

"You are here to lead the mobilisation of all of the tribes. Hakeem, you have been sent to lead us to war."

Hakeem could hardly breathe; he stared sightlessly out the window. "And I am tied to Helios of Aiolía and Helios is tied to Troia and Troia is tied to Lydia," he whispered.

It involves them all!

Omar nodded. "I am sorry, Hakeem."

Hakeem was appalled, what dread thing could threaten the Shantawi, the elves and all of Anatolē.

He knew, but didn't know how, that something was coming to threaten the safety of everyone he loved. He thought of them all: Jacinta, Myriani, King Helios … everyone.

He felt very sobered indeed. Suddenly nothing was frivolous. It was all closing in. It would rest on him. Grimly, he drew himself up.

He whispered, not to Omar, but to his God, "I will not refuse."

He would give his life and all he had, if need be, to protect those he loved.

"I'm sorry my son," Omar repeated.

"Thank you, Father," Hakeem said softly. "Would you do me the honour of leading me in prayer? I need to pray, I think we will all need to pray before this is over."

After a period of prayer, and a slow walk around the chapterhouse, Hakeem felt a little better. He came back to the room Jacinta was allocated, not far from Daniel.

Jacinta was resting in bed, still looking flushed from exercise. "What happened to you?" she asked. "You look so serious!"

"Yes, I was talking to Father Omar about some serious things," Hakeem said. Then he brightened up. "But I have some good news. I'd like to change your name," he announced.

"Hakeem!" Jacinta looked puzzled. "I like Jacinta! I don't want to change it."

"I agree, Jacinta's a lovely name. I think you should keep it. But I still want to change your name."

Jacinta was used to Hakeem's sense of humour. She simply pouted, sat up with her arms crossed and waited for him to tell her. She was caught between frowning and half smiling. He really liked to tease, especially when offering her some treat. She had no idea what was about to come.

"How would Jacinta bint Hakeem sound? I've got permission to formally adopt you, if you'll have me," he finished.

"If I'll have you? If!" Jacinta squealed and launched herself across the bed at Hakeem, who scooped her up in a hug. Jacinta was crying; she was laughing and crying and clutching at him.

Hakeem felt wonderful. He marvelled at Jacinta's power to lighten his heart.

"The ceremony will happen the day after tomorrow. There are other things planned for tomorrow," Hakeem said.

"Yeh, there's some important guest. Everyone's abuzz with the news. Do you know anything about it?"

"Yes I do, Jacinta. I'm the important guest."

"Hakeem!" she laughed at his teasing. "Can you ever stop joking?"

"I am serious," Hakeem replied, looking away for a moment.

"But you're just a ...." Jacinta stopped. Hakeem had never told her what rank he was. "I thought you were ..." Suddenly it hit her.

Nadeer wasn't the horse of a normal soldier. Hakeem was well off ... his special sword and fine armour.

"Hakeem, I mean Dad, you aren't a minor officer are you?"

Hakeem shook his head. "I'm a little more than that. I'm sorry I've never told you till now. I *was* a cavalry captain ... well better than that, I suppose, as I was the leader of King Helios's personal bodyguard and his special aide during the war. Then I was the military advisor to our delegation to Troia.

"But when I return to Aiolía, I will become a Cavalry Taxiarchos. I will be the Commander of the Shantawi mercenaries."

A full commander! Gods! Her new father would be a full commander! He was only twenty two, how was that even possible? I must be dreaming! But wait on.....

"Also, I did a few small things in the recent war and I have a little bit of a reputation."

People had been talking in awe of the special visitor. Jacinta had seen Hakeem fighting and training. Wherever his name was mentioned, his reputation seemed to be known, but for some reason she had never thought deeply about that, until now.

She had no doubt that he did considerably more than 'a few small things'.

She was shocked by the scope of the revelation. Curse Hakeem, he should have told her!

Jacinta's head was starting to spin. What else could there be? But Hakeem was continuing. "My becoming a paladin, you already know. What I didn't know until just now is that it's a little more important than I thought."

There were way too many "littles" in this talk!

Jacinta was starting to panic.

"It looks like if war threatens my people, I will be nominated as the one to take command, and I will get the title of Warlord."

Jacinta's mouths dropped open, "What, of the tribesmen? Warlord of *all* the tribesmen! In peace, what is your title?"

"Er, Warlord."

"I thought you were a mercenary."

"Well I am. It is the way of our people. I'm still expected to earn my keep," Hakeem replied.

"Hakeem, I'm not sure I *know* you," Jacinta was shocked. "I feel lost all of a sudden."

"Jacinta, you know me, better than anyone." He gripped her shoulders and stared anxiously at her face. "You know the *real* me. Please Jacinta, you know I love you so much."

"I don't feel good enough. I'm a peasant Gypsy girl. I just don't belong as an important man's daughter."

"Well, I say you're more than good enough!" Hakeem said, "If I ever had to choose between all this and being your father, I'd choose you."

"Thank you," Jacinta said in a small voice. "I suppose I always knew you weren't ordinary. But I never thought it could be anything so big. You don't say much about yourself."

She kept her next thought to herself ... and you fight and teach so well, you're freakish!

"I think you will be very special too, in the end. I've never met a student like you."

Great, Jacinta thought, I can become a freak too.

All she said was, "If there is anything else, please tell me now."

"I don't want to scare you," started Hakeem

"What! Are you joking?" Jacinta almost shouted. "Now you say you don't want to scare me. Tell me, tell me now!"

Her voice was rising, and then he told her the rest.

"Trouble ..." Jacinta reflected, thinking.

Gypsies are unquestioning in supporting their family in trouble. It sounded big, but Jacinta wasn't as worried by this 'trouble' as much as by the fact that her new father was so important.

His status was simply unimaginable to a Gypsy girl, growing up in poverty, but as far as 'trouble' was concerned she had a child's faith in the abilities of her new father.

Hakeem was right, she decided! She did know him. He was gentle, quiet, and humble. He was wonderful, and she loved him. Gypsies are if nothing else, adaptable. She would take things as they came.

They talked some more and Hakeem stayed to tuck Jacinta in. "Good night, Jacinta."

"Good night, father, er, Sir."

"Don't 'Sir' me!" Hakeem replied in mock outrage, shaking her shoulders a little and tickling her through the blanket. She laughed back in glee. As he hugged her and kissed her goodnight on the forehead, he felt capable of facing anything, anything at all.

* * *

The next day was taken up with martial arts demonstrations and contests. In the morning some of the novice monks had a chance to demonstrate their techniques and get a lesson from the 'famous' Hakeem.

Before lunch, Hakeem did a demonstration of his uncanny speed and accuracy with a horse-bow, guiding Nadeer with his knees. Most of the audience were used to smaller horses and were stunned by Nadeer's thunderous power and speed, with the horse and rider moving as one.

It was a familiar drill to Hakeem, and he managed to hit all the targets dead centre, whilst galloping around the obstacles in a stunning display of power, speed and control. Nadeer obviously loved showing off and enjoyed it as much as the audience.

The adoption ceremony the day after was a quiet one. It involved Hakeem, Daniel, Jacinta, Omar and an official witness. Hakeem gave Jacinta a lovely silver ankle-bracelet to match what she already had. She was delighted. Then the four friends hugged each other and shared a final meal and some gossip.

During the meal it began to be obvious that Jacinta seemed to be working 'father' into almost all her conversation, with a slight dreamy smile.

They were speaking Greek, not Aramaic, and Omar started a word game to try to work *patéras* (father) into whatever he said, with a small pause beforehand.

In the end, the two children were giggling uncontrollably every time they heard, or anticipated, Hakeem and *Father* Omar using the words.

Hakeem decided to make it an early night, and as they were walking back, Jacinta called "father!" again, but when he replied, "Yes, Jacinta?" Jacinta had to admit, "I'm sorry Hakeem, I can't think of anything to ask you. I just like the sound of calling you father."

Hakeem stopped and lifted her gently up till she was sitting on his hip and looking into his face. "You know what?" Hakeem said smiling at his daughter, "I really like the way you say it. It sounds really good to me too."

Jacinta put her arms around his neck and hugged him as hard as she could. Then Hakeem began to walk with her draped over his shoulder bouncing up and down in an exaggerated way with each step. "Father," he said and tickled her gently. "Father," he repeated with another tickle. Soon the pair were laughing and cuddling excitedly.

Neither Jacinta nor Hakeem could get to sleep immediately, both were lying back and smiling. It was good they were in separate rooms, Hakeem realised. He probably couldn't have stopped Jacinta talking all night.

Jacinta could hardly contain herself. Hakeem her father. She had a family again. She no longer thought of marriage to Hakeem, but she loved the idea of Hakeem as her father.

* * *

Mindful of the passage of time, Hakeem was keen to leave early the next day.

He decided to take a shortcut as the snowfall had been light this winter. This would allow him to stay one night at Myriani's, to drop off a wedding gift: two gold bangles for Kassandra. The route was rugged and little travelled but it cut across elf land, so should be safe.

They set out early and made good time. Omar knew the route and gave them directions to a cave were travellers often spent the night. They rose early on the second day, hoping to make it to Myriani's that day or early the next. It was a long ride but Hakeem really wanted to do it in one day.

Chapter 16: Assassins, Prophecy, and an Elf Princess in Danger

Djorn looked gravely at the wounded man as Elana and one of his maids tended his wounds. The escort sent for Elana had been ambushed and only this man survived. Someone was hunting the Princess and someone in Elgard had betrayed them.

They couldn't wait for a second escort. Her conception had taken far too long. Time was running short now and Elana had to get home.

He could not guarantee her safety here. He did not have a fort. All his fighters were only local farmers, militia men. Till she reached her home, she was in terrible danger and brought danger to everyone around her.

Such was the reputation of the Western Elves that they hadn't had to do any serious fighting here for some time, and most of his veterans were starting to age. Well, it would have to do. They'd done it once, they would do it again.

He had four strong sons, experienced in woods-craft and had sent his servants to summon whatever force would come. Other men, he had sent out to hire mercenaries and guides in secret.

He would meet them on the road. He had to leave here quickly: this place was known. They would be safer in the woods.

* * *

The men of the house were quiet and grim as they readied themselves and their horses. They tried to reassure the women folk, but the women could see their men were frightened. Elana and the other women were pale and subdued. Their enemies could come to this house.

Eugenia would go to her cousins with the other women until the house could be secured. The men would take Elana to the safety of the woods. There they would meet with the rest of the men at a secret place.

Elana found herself hugging Eugenia for the last time. "Thank you, madam. You have been kind to me. I'll never forget you and your family. I would like to call you friends, all of you. Bringing trouble to your home is the last thing I would have wished."

"Elana, we are proud if you name us friends. You have been a pleasure to have. You will make a brave and gracious queen for all our people, Western Elves as well. The Great Mother has chosen well."

For an instant, Elana's control slipped and she clung to Eugenia, crying. She only wished she could have had a mother like Eugenia, and a family like her family. With a profuse apology she put on a brave face and thanked and hugged each of the others including the maidservants.

Then Elana turned to smile tentatively at her maid, Iona.

"Don't even think it, my Lady, you're not getting rid of me, I'm coming!" Iona stated firmly and loudly. "You have always been kind to me, my Lady," she finished softly.

Elana didn't expect it and her tears came again, so she could only nod and smile. She felt a renewed surge of fear to think of the danger she was taking everyone into.

There was no time, they had to go.

* * *

It was night and they could hear the men searching for them. All the others were dead.

Elana whispered to Iona "Better you didn't come."

Iona whispered back, "My lady, I am privileged to stay with you now. I'm not smart, but you have always treated me well."

Elana felt tears of gratitude. "I'm lucky to have you. Maybe there might be maids who are smarter. I don't think I could find any who was a better friend."

They both giggled a little and squeezed each other's hand, then they crept on together, their hearts racing in fear.

* * *

Shortly after setting out on the second day, Hakeem motioned Jacinta for silence. The two travellers unpacked their bows and notched an arrow each. As Hakeem was scouring the forest and ridges, he realised what it was that alerted him.

It was too quiet.

They left their horses and crept up a hillock that gave them a view over the trail ahead. Where the trail separated into two, there were signs that a large number of horses had passed in a hurry.

Hakeem didn't know for sure if it was trouble, but he wouldn't have stayed alive this long by ignoring his hunches. He had a very bad feeling, and Jacinta was with him!

He had to fight an impulse to simply turn back. This was too close to Myriani's place. If there was any danger here, he needed to know about it.

Then he saw something through the trees. It was an elf, sitting with his back to a tree, slumped as if tiredness had caused him to fall sleep and the bow to drop from his hands. He had three arrows sticking from his chest; a crimson stain had fallen to the snow beneath.

Hakeem and Jacinta stayed still for a good time, listening, Jacinta looking very frightened.

Hakeem feared the horses would make noise, but they were well trained.

There seemed no one around. This made sense: it was simple to hide the evidence in this forest, so whoever had done this was in too much of a hurry.

Unless, it was a trap, but a trap for whom?

While Jacinta kept guard, Hakeem donned his breast plate, shin guards and the rest of his armour. He hissed instructions to Jacinta. If anything happened to him, she was to go straight to the chapterhouse. No heroics, a message *must* be sent out. Jacinta nodded, looking pale beneath her dark complexion.

He carried his bow behind his shield with his quiver over his shoulder and went down to investigate the dead elf. He moved very cautiously, keeping to cover and scanning the surrounding bush and ridges. Shortly before he reached the body, he relaxed and stood up, motioning Jacinta to join him, though his eyes continued to scan.

As Jacinta came up, he whispered for her to read what she saw.

"Well," Jacinta said softly, unsettled by the dead body, but not as much as one would expect. "He still wears his gold ring. Unless the killers were afraid of magic, which is not at all likely amongst such, they were in too much of a hurry. This is not robbery, it's murder. They went on to chase others. I suspect they'll come back, but I don't think they are nearby now.

"Look at the quality of his clothes, and the design on the ring," she continued. "He wasn't poor or ordinary."

"Very good," Hakeem said. "But did the unlucky elf manage to give an account of himself?"

Jacinta bent down curiously. "His quiver's not full. He may have used some arrows hunting, but I don't think so, this is a war-bow. I think horses were tethered over there." She pointed. "The snow's trampled by horses, so it's hard to tell. There's blood on the ground over there and signs of at least one body being dragged." She pointed again, puzzled. "They hid the bodies of their own men despite their hurry, but not their victim."

"I think at least three bodies were dragged." Hakeem nodded with approval. "But who could sneak up on an elf in the bush?"

"Yes, who could?" Jacinta agreed thoughtfully. "He must have been part of a group that were expecting others, so they didn't hide. Elves, if they wish it, are hard to find. They were unlucky or betrayed. But this one didn't even try to take cover! He sacrificed himself for the others, but he's a senior elf Lord! He must have been protecting someone who was even more important."

"Excellent!" Hakeem was astounded she could read so much. "Likely the light was bad, as the murderers did a poor job of covering their tracks. With the state of the body, this makes it last night. Now lead me to the other bodies and we'll know why it was so important to hide them!"

Hakeem took the ring and put it in a pouch, it would do for later identification.

It was not hard to find three bodies hastily dumped under some tree branches. Hakeem recognised them as Sumerian, the original inhabitants of Mesopotamia. They were unmistakable: dark complexions, broad noses, dark curly hair and beards.

But Jacinta saw something else "Hashshahsin!" she hissed, pointing out the distinctive dagger. It was a small religious sect and contained a number of Sumerians. Their name meant followers of "Hassin".

They were universally despised and hated. Relatively small in numbers, they lacked military strength to protect their religious communities. Instead they took to assassination.

Experts in stealth and penetrating security, their famous daggers became a symbol of terror. A dagger left on a pillow, would serve as a convincing warning.

That any would-be conqueror would lose his life deterred many until they were finally overwhelmed in a revenge attack, after an attempt on a nearby ruler's life.

Those left could be hired for money, a great deal of money. To hire so many must have cost a fortune. Someone was very serious about killing whomever these men hunted.

After they brought their horses closer, Hakeem pointed out further tracks to Jacinta, some of people in boots running desperately, pursued by horses. They soon came upon two more dead elves and an impressive number of dead assassins. Though heavily outnumbered, the elves had made this a battle the assassins would have little taste for. The assassins had their own bowmen but it was no surprise that they were a poor match for elvish archers in the dark.

The horsemen had been forced to dismount and lead their horses. Further on, Hakeem and Jacinta found the last two dead elves. It was hard to track further on the rocky ground but Hakeem thought he could detect tracks of two who had escaped, women in dresses he thought. He hoped they knew the countryside well.

The horsemen had obviously tried to encircle the remaining escapees but had since gone on. So they hadn't found them yet. Where were the ones who escaped? Where were the rest of the assassins and why were all the dead elves dressed like nobles?

They moved forward cautiously, keeping to the cover.

Suddenly a high pitched scream of agony startled the two, it was shockingly close. A woman was dying! They could hear excited men's voices and then a sharp male yell.

* * *

The man had stabbed at Elana but Iona pushed the princess hard to the side and spun in time to take the sword thrust herself. As Iona staggered back, Elana drew her knife and flung herself at the man, in a fury, but she only managed to wound him in the shoulder (that wasn't covered by his leather armour).

He cursed and cuffed her so hard she saw a flash of light. Stunned and half-conscious, she felt herself being roughly stripped naked by the men, and she could hear them hammering stakes into the ground. They dragged her across the ground, naked and bleeding.

For stabbing their chief, Elana would die slowly but first she would be violated by all these men.

She felt consumed by anger and despair as they staked her out. So many good people had died for her and for what? Hers was to be a short and bitter life. It would end in this lonely place, in pain and failure.

The Prophecy and the last hope of the elves had come to nothing.

She shut her eyes hard against the tears. Her captors seeing this, laughed at her, pointing excitedly. No, she decided. She would show them courage till the end.

* * *

A magic far-seeing glass was being used to watch Elana from a far place. Watching was a group of elves including a great elf lord and a shadowy barbarian, a guest from the east.

The vision darkened and was gone. "We have lost sight of the bitch!" The elf lord cursed. "It will be some ancient magic, there are many ruins buried in that land. Now I will miss my show." He spat, disgusted.

"Do not worry, my lord," one of his men said. "We won't see Elana again."

* * *

Hakeem and Jacinta tied the horses and crept to the top of a nearby ridge. They could see the murderers had caught the last of their quarry.

One elvish maiden was leaning against a rock bent over clutching at her stomach. There was a stain spreading rapidly across her dress. As they watched, she toppled forward and lay still, face down in the dirt. One of the assassins had removed his armour and was having a wound on his shoulder bound.

Two assassins were holding a half conscious fair haired elvish girl, maybe 17 or 18. They were cutting and tearing all the clothes from her.

Hakeem noted a youth minding a large group of horses, and a single lookout, on a small rise. Hakeem counted ten in all, four of them bowmen. The assassins had paid a high price to capture this elf.

Hakeem couldn't understand what they were saying, but their intention was plain.

The fair-haired young girl could only be one person. She had to be Princess Elana of the Eastern Elves! Only she would be important enough for the other elf nobles to sacrifice their lives.

It was astounding, what would she be doing in this wilderness?

Trying to find a way back across the mountains to her home, but where were her guards? All there had been was a handful of elf nobles and a maid.

He motioned to Jacinta and they moved back from the ridge, to talk quietly. Jacinta knew what was coming and looked pale and frightened.

"I want you to go back to the cave," he said quietly.

Jacinta started to shake her head in horror, mouthing a silent "no." She was shivering violently with tears rolling down her cheeks.

"Please, no, they'll kill you Hakeem! There's too many!"

"Now listen to me," Hakeem murmured urgently. "If anything happens to me, news of this has to get out. If I don't join you in one turn of the glass, I want you to head for the monastery and raise the alarm.

"Myriani will care and love you for my sake." He passed her all his remaining money.

"I can't lose you too!" Jacinta clutched desperately at him.

"I'm sorry Jacinta, this is what I am. Even if it kills me, I will try to help that girl.

"Now, you gave a promise to obey me if there was danger and I need you to do so. Remember, I love you more than my life itself."

Jacinta and Hakeem kissed each other and hugged fiercely, reluctant to let go. Jacinta knew it was useless to try to talk him out of this.

Hakeem walked with her back to their horses. He would need Nadeer and a lot of luck for what he planned. The assassins were staking the girl out and would rape her before killing her.

It would be an intensely pleasurable scene, or so Hakeem hoped. But he was not thinking of pleasure for himself. How could anyone keep a proper watch, with such a show going on?

The Hashshahsin wouldn't expect to be disturbed. They may be fearsome killers by stealth, but they were ill suited to the woods.

He needed all the luck he could get but, when he peered down on the scene again, he smiled. Apart from the lookout, the bows, shields, weapons and armour, even clothes were being laid down in preparation for their fun. He calculated a good vantage point for himself and thought through what he would have to do. He took out four arrows, three he passed to the left hand that held the bow and one he fitted to the bowstring.

A great cheer arose as the leader was taking off his pants. He bowed to the audience with a big smile on his face, gestured to his erection and stepped towards the girl who struggled desperately, tied spread-eagled on the ground. Hakeem was too busy to spare more than a glance at her naked body.

He stood up and quickly fired two arrows in succession. The guard and the youth minding the horses were hit square in the chest. Thank Apollōn, they made little noise. But something alerted the leader who spun round, to receive the next arrow sent with lethal aim.

There was time for one more shot, as pandemonium broke loose. Men were scrambling to get their weapons; one of the bowmen was his next running target. That left three bowmen.

Hakeem could have picked them off in a game of hide and seek in this wilderness. He really was that good, but they would kill the princess, so he had to act quickly.

He didn't waste his time on the men with shields who were clustering together, trying to crouch behind their shields. There were three bowmen to eliminate. One was aiming at the helpless princess but Hakeem's superior speed put an arrow in his chest, while one of his friends sent a panicked shot whistling past Hakeem's ear. The other remaining bowman's aim was even worse, and he died with Hakeem's next arrow. The last remaining bowman tried to run for better cover. Hakeem quickly fired, taking him in the back.

Moving with great speed, Hakeem dropped his bow rather than take the precious seconds to secure it. He needed to be amongst the assassins below, and quickly. He leaped up on Nadeer, drawing Mir and loosening his shield at the same time.

And then it happened.

He had missed a second lookout hiding behind a rise. He felt a sensation like being punched hard as his right thigh and was pinned to the saddle by an arrow.

He couldn't do anything. He couldn't get off to recover his bow. He had Nadeer pointed the wrong way and partly downhill, it would be difficult to turn. He couldn't reach the bowman on horseback who was sheltering behind the nearby trees.

He brought his shield around to guard his back and slipped Mir down to lever his leg free, while desperately trying to bring Nadeer's head around.

Nadeer was trying, but he was pointed down the slope and his hooves were slipping on ice and loose rocks. He would lose balance if he tried to turn.

There was nothing for it. He would have to complete the charge down the slope with his back exposed to the archer. He wondered how far he would get. The man seeing this grinned and ran up closer for a sure shot. While Hakeem struggled to help Nadeer regain balance, the assassin stopped and started to draw his bow.

He'd probably aim at Nadeer, which would leave Hakeem helpless trapped under a dying horse or thrown by his panicked mount.

Hakeem tried to fruitlessly guard both himself and his horse with his shield. With Hakeem twisted around, Nadeer wouldn't move forward. Hakeem was in no position to guide the horse with his knees, and his hands were full.

Just then there was a loud 'thunk'. The man grunted and looked up in surprise. The arrow fell from his fingers and he coughed weakly. As the man slumped forward, the arrow sticking out of his back could be clearly seen. Jacinta was rapidly running through the bush.

"Jacinta!" Hakeem yelled in relief and delight.

He waved his sword and turned to let Nadeer have his head. As he did so, the breath caught in his throat, his heart almost stopped. From this higher view, the full dangerousness of the slope was revealed.

Nadeer obeyed his command, but the big horse was far too heavy, the slope would never bear his weight.

It was slippery with ice, rocks and mud. Three quarters down there was an overhang. The horse would have to negotiate the treacherous surface, give a jump and then somehow pull up very sharp at the bottom, so as not to blunder into the swordsmen, or the trees and rocks beyond.

Hakeem felt a surge of fear and guilt for his loyal horse, but Nadeer did not refuse. He was magnificently strong and fast, his hindquarters slipped on the loose pebbles till he almost sat on his rear before surging forward and crashing through the scrub that lined the slope. If so much as one hoof caught, it would be over.

Somehow he did it, and Hakeem was amongst the remaining assassins. He had managed to free his leg from being pinned to the saddle but it was taking further damage by the jostling. He forced his mind to block out the searing pain. He couldn't afford to feel faint or be distracted.

The remainder were swordsmen, ill-trained in formation fighting. They had used the time to start to advance on the helpless princess. Hakeem savagely barged them from his left, using his shield and horse to good effect. He was able to cut two down quickly and the remaining two did not take long.

Jacinta came running up but he barked at her, "Keep guard for me, Meli!" He was pleased that she looked alert and competent.

He half slid, half fell, off Nadeer, who was thankfully unscathed. He gave the horse a fierce hug, wanting to stay there hugging Nadeer for a long time.

Instead, he grabbed his water bottle and his cape and limped over to the princess who was … without any doubt … the most beautiful woman he had ever seen in his entire life.

For an instant he could do nothing, but stare down at her beautiful face and her body. He was struck dumb.

She had golden shiny silky hair, cut short, almost boyish. Her features were fine in the way of the elves with blond lashes and startling green eyes. The pointed elf-ears peeking through her hair looked so incredibly appealing. Her blush under a dusting of freckles and her pale skin was perfect. He tried unsuccessfully to avert his gaze, but she was so wonderful.

She was tall and slender, slightly built. She had a young girl's small breasts but they were filling out and the nipples were reddened due to a pregnancy. The small bump in her abdomen suggested it was early. Somehow, this made her even more desirable.

Her beauty was not diminished by scratches and bruises and dirt. Only an instant had passed, but Hakeem was completely captivated and stunned by her beauty.

"So!" she screamed at him at the top of her voice, showing none of the usual musical cadence of an elf. Her face was distorted with rage. "You fight for the pleasure of having me! Now you gloat, as if I'm a prize. Get on with it, pig. No woman can get over her revulsion of you. No one will get into your bed, no matter how much you pay. A woman tied up is all you can have!"

Hakeem realised he was staring down at her. He burned with shame and clumsily covered her nakedness.

"Great Lady, please forgive me," he said, as he sat next to her, clumsy with the pain from his wounded leg. "You are so beautiful," he whispered softly.

"DON'T MOCK ME!" she screamed. She was on the verge of angry tears, face red with the effort as she struggled against her bonds. Her eyes widened, as she saw him take out his knife, and she threw herself back and forward in desperation. Hakeem was appalled. Would she think he had taken all this trouble just to cut her throat?

Why of course! The assassins tied her facing away from their camp, so she couldn't see. They wanted to make it even more terrifying. They wanted to play with her, to see her break! Taken aback by her agitation, he shouted, "TRUCE!" loudly. There was no mistaking the Elvish word, a formal offer of friendship and mutual aid.

Elana slumped back, no longer struggling. She looked at him, eyes wide in shock, as if he had suddenly grown a second head. Then she nodded her agreement jerkily, with a look of confusion on her face.

He continued in Elvish, as he cut the leather binding her hands. "Princess, I came to rescue you. Forgive my crude behaviour. I shouldn't have stared I know. I speak true, I was overcome by your beauty." He reached out to massage her wrists but she jerked back. Then he passed his water across to her as he worked to free her legs.

A lunatic, she thought, accepting the water. I've been rescued by a barbarian lunatic. I'm ugly and fat with child, dirty, smelly, covered in bruises and scratches, dragged through the dirt and he finds me beautiful!

Hakeem asked her if she was seriously hurt. Her ribs were giving her sharp pain, one was likely cracked, but when he offered to examine them she angrily shrugged him off.

"What, haven't you seen enough, barbarian?

"You speak our tongue like a dog growls, but it's impressive enough, I guess. Few know our tongue."

Hakeem felt ashamed. He had looked, however briefly, at her naked body. He took advantage of her, and she was a princess. He felt mortified but had trouble banishing the image from his mind, and felt fullness in his groin.

At the same token he was starting to feel weak from blood loss. He quickly fashioned a tourniquet from leftover leather bindings.

"This one's alive," Jacinta warned, from higher up, "and also the young man up with the horses."

Hakeem painfully pulled himself upright using his sword and limped to the dying assassin. "Who paid you?" he asked. The man spat weakly. Hakeem nodded and rested his weight on his sword as he leaned over him.

"You fought well," he told the assassin.

"You fought like a daimôn," the dying man acknowledged.

"Death almost touched me, I missed the other lookout." Hakeem said.

"Yes, we almost had you, but for your little girl. Who would have thought it? She's a treasure. What are your names, so I may know?"

"She's my daughter, Jacinta, and my name is Hakeem," Hakeem replied.

"The Hakeem? … Ah, then there is no shame."

"No shame," Hakeem agreed.

Elana had crept up to join them, wrapped in Hakeem's cloak against her nakedness. She looked at the barbarian talking to the dying assassin with a profound sense of unreality. It was as if they were talking over a pot of tea, talking of old battles, or some game just played.

It was bizarre and what did it mean that the assassin knew the barbarian's name?

"Are you ready?" Hakeem asked formally. The injured man smiled his thanks, and nodded, closing his eyes. Hakeem brought his sword up, and with a huge convulsive movement, pushed Mir deep into the man's heart. Elana gasped at the abrupt brutality of it. Then it came to her, the blow was struck in kindness.

Hakeem then painfully limped up to the boy, barely 16. "I don't want to die!" the boy gasped.

There was an arrow in his lung and red blood bubbles were coming from the wound, blood trickled from his mouth when he coughed. He was pale and starting to pant. He was going dusky blue on the lips and extremities.

What are you doing here? Hakeem wondered as he looked at him. Why was someone so young involved with assassins? Hakeem sat down next to him, held his hand and wiped his pale and sweaty face.

"No one dies. It's just a crossing over," he reassured the boy.

Elana's sense of unreality was growing. This barbarian spoke Elvish! Minutes before, these men were killing each other. The assassins were less than human. They deserved nothing but hatred and disgust. Yet this barbarian offered one of their wounded respect and kindness. And now in the middle of this wilderness he was giving spiritual comfort to another.

She also had a bewildering glimpse at one of the enemy. Why he was barely older than a child, and he was so frightened.

Hakeem held the boy until he went, talking to him about survival beyond death, calming him and helping to face death bravely. He felt a surge of anger at whoever got the boy involved in this business. After the boy had gone, Hakeem pulled out the boy's dagger to stare sightlessly at it for a while.

The exertion had restarted Hakeem's leg bleeding. He was starting to feel cold and dizzy and couldn't stand, he dragged himself against a rock.

The elf princess had found her horse, and had quickly dressed. She brought something to attend to his leg. "Where are your men?" she asked, looking around.

"Aiolía," Hakeem whispered, feeling faint.

"No," she said as she sat and expertly unrolled tools and small packets from a leather pouch as she got ready to attend to him. "The men that helped you rescue me, where have they gone?" She spoke slowly and carefully, as if to a simpleton.

Hakeem shook his head wearily and shrugged, "Just us."

"You don't expect me to believe."

Suddenly it struck her! Eleven trained assassins and only one man!

As if reading her mind, Hakeem said "Jacinta killed one. It's their training: they are not as dangerous out in the open."

Since last night, Elana had been in the middle of a waking nightmare. She hadn't slept, she hadn't eaten, and she'd had nothing to drink before this barbarian arrived. She could hardly think clearly. She felt at the point of physical and emotional collapse. Now this experience was becoming increasingly surreal. Had she passed beyond the real world into a region populated by the insane?

Her companions were outnumbered six to one. They were all dead. This barbarian human rode in and fought eleven men, and he was trying to explain that it was easier than normal.

Oh, of course, he had help from a little girl, that explained everything!

It occurred to her she was lucky to have this madman. A sane man wouldn't attempt to rescue her against such odds. She gave up trying to understand this madness and, with a mental shrug, concentrated on examining his leg.

The most popular arrows were of the Bodkin type, the ones with a sharp fine point. They were cheaper, flew better, were more penetrating of armour and wouldn't tangle in the quiver.

The broad-tipped arrows do more damage. They had a larger head and were harder to pull out of a wound. Hakeem was unfortunate to be hit by one of these.

It had gone through his thigh but during the battle the head had sunk back into the wound. She tried moving it gently but it was firmly stuck.

She would have to push it through to break the head off. After checking for splinters she would pull it back the other way.

If she tried to simply pull it straight out, the head was designed to come off inside the wound. Then it would have to be dug out

The Gypsy girl, Jacinta, was using the assassins' fire to boil water, good, the girl was smart.

Hakeem watched as she widened the cuts in his trousers at the front and back to examine the wound. He saw she worked competently. Elves are known for their knowledge of remedies.

"I've got nothing for pain," she said. "I'm afraid, this will hurt."

"Can I watch you, then? My Lady, you are just so beautiful. I can hardly look anywhere else." He sounded like a small boy asking a favour.

Elana nodded, curtly, to the request. Sure, go ahead, if it makes you feel better!

He had just saved her life and almost got himself killed in the process. It felt strange to be watched by this man, but if that was the worst he demanded, well and good. She could put up with that. But the sight of her would help with the pain?

Almost nothing you say should surprise me now, Elana thought. She was starting to wonder if she was imagining all this. Am I delirious, perhaps?

She wasn't prepared though, for how intimate it felt. She felt heat in her face, and it was hard to concentrate. Should she have agreed so readily? But it had seemed a small thing. What was the matter with her?

She shook herself mentally, and asked if he was ready. Then she lent all her weight on the arrow shaft and heaved. Nothing happened.

She felt the arrow caught and cautiously, very carefully pulled it back, twisting it back and forwards slightly to free it. Hakeem sucked a sharp breath in and gritted his teeth. It must have been hot agony. His face showed a flicker of the torment he must have felt. How could he show such little reaction?

Who or what are you? she wondered.

The head was no longer caught. She nodded, satisfied, prepared to try again. Jacinta came up behind to lend her weight and Hakeem grabbed the shaft with his right hand. Elana counted in Greek and they all gave a great heave. They did it.

Hakeem hissed with pain and then he snapped the head off himself.

She smoothed it of splinters and then carefully pulled it out and threw it away. Hakeem was panting and looked almost grey. He was losing too much blood.

She had to stop the bleeding and quickly!

She undid his belt and urgently grabbed his pants to pull them down and ... he resisted, catching his pants with one hand.

What next, she wondered?

"Hakeem, neither you nor I have time for this!" she said urgently. "You've seen me naked and I have to stop the bleeding, now, or you will die!" Hakeem nodded and let go, and he leaned back tiredly.

Jacinta fetched a cloth to cover his groin and then hovered nearby, her face full of concern. Elana was focused on the wound, but she caught a brief glimpse of his manhood concealed behind his hand. Well, he's got no cause for embarrassment there, was her irreverent thought.

She expected to be repelled by physical closeness to this barbarian, instead her body was reacting very differently. No, she couldn't possibly be feeling that way towards him! Buzzing around her head was the repeated thought, "he thinks I'm pretty."

She really must be losing her grip on sanity.

She forced herself to focus on the wound ... oozing, let's see ... a stitch there. Now, release the tourniquet ...Very good, no spurting blood with the pulse, it missed the main artery ... Three deep stitches joining that piece of torn muscle ... Good, dust with powder... close, now.

Hakeem had propped himself up to watch. He was obviously intrigued by the internal stitches and the powder, so she explained as she worked. "The stitches are specially made. I use gut for quick dissolving, that's for inside a wound. Sometimes I use sinew; it's stronger but is chancy with infection.

"I prefer specially treated silk to stitch up skin," she continued as she worked. "Try to remove the outside stitches in a week or they work into the scar. The powder will help prevent infection and speed healing. It's very good. I was taught by my uncle and I learn every chance I get."

"Thank you, Princess Elana," he said gravely.

Again she got the impression of a small child as the big warrior stared into her face.

She felt a flush in her face, her heart was racing, and she was breathing fast. Splendid timing, Elana thought, I'm feeling like a giddy house girl with her first boy. Very sensible, too! I'm the princess and he is a what? A soldier, sweaty and dirty and bloody, straight from a battle.

A hired killer!

Some queen I'll make!

Hakeem asked help to sit propped up and some water to drink. He looked tired, but better.

Jacinta crept up and being careful of his wound, curled up on his shoulder. The warrior must have adopted the Gypsy girl, Elana realised.

As she watched the love between them, she felt a powerful surge of envy. She longed for her own father to love her like the tribesman loved the girl.

"Are you alright?" Hakeem asked Jacinta and felt her small head nod against his chest. "I'm so proud of you, you know that?" He got another nod into his shoulder.

"It must have been awful," he continued. "I'm sorry I haven't been able to give you any time. I'm so sorry you had to see all this and I'm sorry to frighten you so much. Yet you kept your head and saved my life. You killed a man. Are you alright about that?"

Jacinta lifted her head to look at Hakeem in the face and then put her head back on his shoulder and nodded.

They sat there for some time. "Jacinta," Hakeem started. Jacinta lifted her head and looked into Hakeem's face. "Whatever, you do Jacinta, next time if I give you a direct order like that, please ignore it."

She knew he was joking, but he was rewarded by a contented smile and Jacinta snuggled deeper into his shoulder, her arms around his neck. Jacinta didn't feel like talking much, but simply murmured, "Gypsy women stick with their men."

He patted her shoulder, "I'm glad they do."

There were plenty of supplies at the camp and Elana began preparing barley broth and adding some of the preserved meat. She added dried herbs in a bowl ready for Hakeem and had bowls separate for her and the girl. She noticed with surprise her hands were shaking as she measured the herbs.

"Princess," Hakeem called to her, "you've had a horrible experience, much more than us. I had to attack when they were most distracted. That was the worst moment for you, but the only way I could fight so many. I'm very sorry you had to go through such a horror. Are *you* alright?"

A single tear ran down her cheek.

This man was gentle and considerate of others, and he was right. She saw her companions give their lives to protect her. All the violence, the death and her sense of guilt, the strong sense that she was unworthy of those giving their lives for her.

The worst part was the stark terror of being caught, frantically searching for a way to escape and the final despair and end of all hope.

She had expected to die in torment.

When fighting broke out, she couldn't see what was happening. She thought the assassins were fighting to be the first to rape and humiliate her. Then this brutish, terrifying, stranger appeared, bending over her. She never dreamed she would be rescued.

She felt completely drained. She felt numb and cold, through to her very bones. She had trouble focusing her mind. She kept getting flashes of those that died: Djorn, the last time he looked at her, before he rushed to stall the assassins, Iona, throwing herself in front of a sword thrust and the dead boy of the assassins, whose body she and Jacinta had only just dragged away.

She was near the end of her strength, but had been taught not to show weakness. Her hands seemed to be trembling even more. She mutely bowed her head.

No, she definitely was not alright!

Elana, to distract herself, asked Hakeem who had sent him to find her.

It was only a chance encounter! Thinking the Elf Lands safe, he had taken a shortcut. What were the chances that they would meet in this isolated wilderness? She should be dead.

Hakeem explained to her how they had guessed who she was, and yes, he was a mercenary.

"I have to get home," Elana said urgently. "It's very important. I will give you a reward for rescuing me, and if you help me get home, you will become rich beyond your wildest dreams."

Hakeem nodded. "My lady, I thank you for the offer of payment but it is not necessary. I will escort you home and you are now under my protection."

"What?" Elana couldn't believe what she was hearing. "Did you not hear what I said? I *said* I can make you fabulously wealthy. Are you mad? You can't refuse payment!"

Hakeem smiled to be described as mad. He didn't expect this elf, from the royal court, to understand humans.

"Princess Elana, you are an elf princess. I am a Shantawi and I am sworn to King Helios. Firstly, as I am already employed, I cannot let you engage me.

"Secondly, it would be a very black day indeed when an elf princess in need has to pay a Shantawi, or one in service of King Helios, for help.

"Lastly, you are in trouble and danger. Even if it were only your maid, I would help all I can. If I would give help to your maid, how could you *not* expect me to help you?"

He paused and chuckled, "Don't worry, with these horses and what we can get from the assassins, Jacinta and I will be rich anyway. Even after we return what is owned by the elves."

Elana felt a flash of irritation. So he would compare her to her maid. And a few horses, the human had no idea of real wealth. Then she felt ashamed and confused: Iona hadn't hesitated to give her life for her.

To add to the sense of disorientation, she was sitting on the field of a battle with this desert barbarian, but he was nothing like she expected. He was refusing a reward for risking his life. He had rescued her and would continue to help her, for what?

Honour, she realised with shock.

She had heard of the Shantawi tribesmen, and their obsession with honour, but had never known what it meant. Her stepmother had taught her to look down on servants and humans. But her stepmother and the foolish, foppish nobles she surrounded herself with would know nothing of honour.

Children when very small don't question what adults tell them. Some of these beliefs become buried deep down and held into adulthood with the strength of natural law. They are never questioned.

Now Elana found something about humans that she thought was a core truth was so obviously false.

She had suddenly awoken to a world where water flowed uphill, and fish could swim in the air. She had been the one who had been crazy all this time, and now she was having difficulty believing what was in front of her eyes.

"You don't understand," she went on, "I have a lot of money with me, more than you could dream of. I must get home as soon as possible. Take me through the northern mountain pass."

"Great Lady!" Hakeem almost wanted to shake her in alarm. "*Never, ever* mention your money like that again. You are safe with Jacinta and me, but you are travelling in some very dangerous parts.

"As for going north, can you *not* see? You *can't* go that way. You haven't told me what's going on but whatever it is, it's exceptional. There is a very powerful group trying to kill you.

They are wealthy and so well-informed that they could find you even in this wilderness.

"There is only one way to pass through the mountains with winter coming on. They know where we would have to go. We'd be easy to track in the snow. We'd never make it.

"We cannot go north, and we need to leave this region quickly. We *must* head in the direction they least expect. First, I will take you to some friends who will help. Then I will take you south, to the city of my childhood.

"On my honour, and on the honour of my people, once we are in Karsh we can arrange help without limit. Even if we have to raise the desert tribes to help you, it will be done."

"So far away?" she asked in shock. "Are you a coward?" she sneered.

It was out before she knew. What a stupid thing to say. She was appalled at herself, but couldn't take it back.

Jacinta rounded on her, her faced screwed up as she almost spat at her in outrage. "How dare you! He nearly died to save you! You fancy elves think you're better than us. You haven't even thanked him. Well I'll tell you, there's no finer person than Hakeem. You think you're better, but you're wrong."

Hakeem gently hushed his daughter. "Jacinta! She's been through a lot."

"Oh!" Jacinta countered, "And what about me? I thought I'd lose you!" Jacinta, who had been so strong, collapsed sobbing. Hakeem clutched at his daughter and held her. She was so young and had been through so much.

Elana's self-loathing was intense. She sat frozen and two further tears ran down her cheeks. What's wrong with me?

"I thought I would die," she said, her voice was hollow. "I thought I would die horribly."

She had always been taught to despise humans as brutish. This fighter was certainly fearsome, but he was so gentle with the Gypsy girl, and in his treatment of her. He behaved nothing like she expected.

"I meant to thank you. I just can't find the words that could possibly say what you have done for me. I'm sorry, I couldn't believe anything would rescue me. I still don't believe it."

Hakeem replied gently. "You are in shock, and you are very tired. No apology is necessary for a small discourtesy. You are safe now." He sat hugging his distraught daughter.

"Please, you must help me! I have to get home soon," Elana begged him, sick to the heart. Getting home was all she could think of.

"Elana, look at us," Hakeem said gently. "I'm wounded. You are not a fighter and you're pregnant besides. I never wanted to bring my child into danger.

"These are professional killers. We only succeeded this time through luck and surprise. As I said, whoever is after you is powerful and is well informed. We must go into hiding and I must take you to people I can trust, and don't say we can hire men with the money you have.

"That's how your party got caught, was it not? You were waiting for friends to join you, and assassins came instead."

How did he know this? Elana had been trained to underestimate humans: their courage, their intelligence, their honour, she felt dazed. She kept slipping back into her prejudice and Hakeem and Jacinta kept jerking her out of it.

Hakeem nodded as her reaction confirmed it. "There was an escort from your home city as well wasn't there?" he guessed shrewdly. "I think it didn't wait with you here, so was sent from Elgard to fetch you back, but it was ambushed before it got here. Then your friends decided to take you themselves with whatever force they could raise.

"Princess, do you have any idea of the scale of what you are facing?

"Your enemies have been three steps ahead of you at all times. I think you had better tell us what's really going on," he finished grimly.

Elana hesitated, what would he do if he knew?

"Princess Elana," Hakeem added gently. "Think! If you don't trust us now, you never will. You have my word, whatever secret you have, is safe with me. I suggest it's not a secret to your enemies."

Elana bowed her head and nodded. "You're right. I don't even know who my enemies are," she said, fear and exhaustion in her voice.

She told him what she knew. Hakeem looked thoughtful. Jacinta peered out through a tangle of black hair, but listened intelligently. The Gypsy girl was being rapidly caught up in great events but she retained her Gypsy pragmatism. She took things as they came.

After Elana had finished, Hakeem gravely rubbed his beard. "Well if you and your daughter are to re-establish some empire of the elves, the list of enemies you have is a very long one. Even if they don't believe the Prophecy, you would be a rallying point for the elves. The death of you and your child would demoralise the elves seriously. What are you to do, now that Djorn Grey has been killed?"

"I don't know," Elana said miserably. "I don't think it was supposed to happen, it's all wrong. I was supposed to be long pregnant before this. I am supposed to deliver in a few moons. I've got to get home."

"Can you tell me what the Prophecy says? It's easy to see if the Prophecy is either wrong or it's been misread," Hakeem concluded.

Elana was shocked that he would say such a thing. But Hakeem exuded practical competence. She found herself trusting the big tribesman. Djorn was a good man, but he was obviously out of his depth when Elana's escort failed to arrive.

"I don't know the part of it that gives the dates, that's very obscure. I can quote from the main part which is like a summary," she said. Then she started to tell the words in ancient Elvish followed line by line with the translation into Greek.

"Wait, "Hakeem stopped her. "I once met men who came from a land far to the north and west. They had the hair and eyes of elves, but they weren't elves. They were human, big men, strong but fair in their features and had beards, dressed in furs. Their tongue sounded something like your old tongue."

Elana nodded. Elves did not like to admit to these people, as it confirmed the connection between elves and humans, as if there could be any real doubt. "Yes, that's where the elves originated. Not many humans know this."

Hakeem encouraged her to go on with the Elvish Prophecy:

"Age came unnoticed. Must that which has been so splendid, finally pass from the world?

The young are not ready, the old are fading.

Only through weakness can it again be strong. The magic lost, the great fallen, the mighty humbled, the eternal heart stilled. Dust choking our cities and wild dogs walking our streets.

After an age they will come.

The mark is on her, Dragon Queen, greatest and last of her line, born into the time of testing. The third comet comes at her birth.

Stranger yet is her daughter, brave little warrior. So wise and yet so young; her blood flows not from the land of the great tombs. The blind will not see, the deaf will not hear, wise fools will not understand. Her wisdom will awaken magic new and old. The family will bear witness to her becoming.

When hope fails, he comes; father and lover, the greatest among great warriors. The dark man in whom shines the great light. Dead blood of the dolphin flows still within him. His sword is like no other, bearing ancient runes of power.

When that which was so strong is weakest, then it might last. As the enduring ends, then it might endure. That which can never be must come to pass. The dolphin must fly and eagle swim. Love must unite the old and young.

Give your trust to the great betrayer. Seek help from the man who has died. Seek the strength of heart of the two women who love them beyond death itself.

Look for the mirror that reflects not, in the last; then the book that must never be read, in the eldest. Enter the locked room that is in no place and take its key.

The Eldest and the Youngest must unite to awaken the glory. Only then can you stand and not be washed away by the great tide. Only then can the greatness begin again.

When the final time comes God's warrior must journey into the deepest, that terrible place, to find the weapons and armour that are made for the man who never was, nor ever will be and awaken that which lies within.

Only death will end the one of ancient evil but he will never be killed. He is the one that no one daimôn, no one living, no one dead, no one made or no one not made and no one of the races of men can possibly defeat."

When she had finished Hakeem looked dazed. " It is so long, and it could mean anything! … A dead man? How can he help?"

"The only dead men I've ever known aren't very active at all," Jacinta piped in, earning a glare from the elf. "And I don't know how much I would want to trust the great betrayer."

The girl was making a mockery of the Holy Prophecies!

"And entering a room that is nowhere with its key locked inside," Hakeem added shaking his head. "Why do they make it so obscure?"

Elana was shocked. "So the wrong people don't understand it."

"What about the right people being able to understand it?" Jacinta retorted.

"I admit that I don't understand it all, but I am no sage," Elana sniffed. "The wisest of the elves have long pondered these words."

Again the elvish arrogance, Hakeem thought. If one were hired to be a wise man, it wouldn't do to say you didn't understand something.

He spoke slowly and earnestly. "Elana, a really wise person would admit he didn't understand those words, they are deliberately obscure.

"You tell me you are the one destined to be the last Queen of your house. How do you know that?"

Elana stood up, "I'm the living heir to the dragon line, when my father or stepmother dies, I will be the Queen." As she said the words, she felt the weight of her destiny. She was no longer the girl that began the journey.

She realised the quality of the people who gave their lives so she could live. She had faced death. Meeting Hakeem and Jacinta forced her to discard much of what she had been taught in the cloister of the Elvish Court.

Her father didn't love her, but it didn't matter.

She would be Queen, the Queen of a people facing a time of great testing. She turned and showed him a small birthmark on her upper thigh. Even Hakeem had to admit, it looked like a tiny dragon taking flight.

He felt dizzy and flushed when the elf princess turned and lifted her dress to show him her beautiful thigh. It must be the loss of blood, he thought, his mouth hanging open in admiration and surprise.

Jacinta caught his look and scowled angrily at him.

Elana explained a different calendar was used back then, which she didn't understand, but she was born in the magical time between astrological ages, which is called "the end of days." A comet was in the sky at her birth.

In ancient Elvish, a child wasn't talked about as a daughter or son until they had taken their first few strong breaths and lived a day. Then they can be officially presented to family and friends. This occasion was called the 'becoming'. The time of her daughter's 'becoming' was specifically set by Elana's date of birth and wasn't in doubt.

"Well then, the time is right. You're the Mother," Hakeem continued, not trying to work out the complexity of royal elf succession. Though only one of them ruled, they could have a king and queen who were father and daughter or very rarely two kings and no Queen or even two Queens.

"How did they find out Djorn Grey had to be the father?"

"Who else could it be? He was the living heir to the Western Elves. He had direct lineage to the Kings of Old. Their symbol was the dolphin.

"The Western Elves were the greatest of our people and he was the greatest amongst their descendants. He had dark hair which is unusual amongst us Eastern Elves. So our union was to produce a daughter who would unite the Eagle and the Dolphin branches of my people."

Hakeem shook his head. "But you're talking of a lineage thousands of years old. Surely there could be others. Tell me about the rest of the Prophecy."

The last and greatest wizard of the elves, not finding a worthy pupil and becoming infirm, hid several items of powerful magic. It was at a time of fading of elvish magic.

There was more happening to the elves; she would not discuss this with humans. The elves were failing, and now were not far different from humans. The Prophecy promised a restoration, no one knew what "awaken the glory" meant, but all the elves hoped to get back some of what they had lost.

"What caused the loss of magic?" Jacinta asked.

"I don't know," Elana admitted glumly. "Not all is lost but it's hardly a secret. We think it might be caused by the heavens. You won't know this, but the stars move in the heavens in cycles great and small."

Changes in the heavens and astrological ages. Jacinta couldn't imagine it. No wonder the Prophecy was important to the elves. No wonder Elana was so desperate.

Djorn was dead and Elana's pregnancy came far too late. Her baby couldn't be born at the time for her 'becoming' in front of her family and still survive. If she went to the desert city, she would be travelling at the time predicted for the 'becoming' of her daughter.

But none of it made sense. There were simply not enough elves left to restore their old empire.

"It sounds like hiding the most powerful items may have weakened the elves. If he foresaw this, why did he do it?" Hakeem asked.

"He had no choice," Elana replied "He explains it. He was getting old and he had no successor."

"That's not it," Jacinta interjected. "He wasn't talking about himself at all."

"Foolish chi…" Elana started but stopped.

It was as if she had been struck across the face.

She felt a cold feeling inside. Could it have been the elves that had become unworthy? Did Ælward intend the elves to fall? It was a ghastly thought; all that suffering.

She thought back on elf history. At first generous and wise, the Elder race came to fear the humans, and the elves were not as they were.

She thought back to the words again, what if the 'eldest' was all the elves, not just the remnants of the Western Elves? What if 'the youngest' was not Eastern Elves, but humans? Her father had always been strong in his support of humans.

It was almost too much to take in, and why had no one else thought of it till now? Becoming Queen, she always thought she would continue with what her people and the ones who had gone before her were doing already, but the elves could not continue as they had.

The great union the Prophecy spoke of, might it be a union of humans and elves, but not as servant and master? It was a sobering thought. But as she thought of Hakeem and she thought of the elves, she knew it was the truth.

She had to challenge thousands of years of ingrained thought and habit. Elana had been through too much, had too many shocks. She couldn't think it all through. How could the small Gypsy girl see something like that so easily?

"You have given me something very deep to think on Jacinta, thank you, but now we have work to do."

Elana wouldn't allow Hakeem to move. She gave Hakeem and Jacinta more broth and helped Jacinta tidy the camp. Then the two girls attended to the horses and started to organise the supplies.

Out of habit, Elana started to give Jacinta a list of jobs. The young Gypsy curtly told her to do them herself!

It was obvious that the young Gypsy girl was far from impressed with her, and Elana felt ashamed.

"Jacinta, please forgive me. Can we start again? Without you and Hakeem, I would have died in terrible torment. I owe you both so much."

Jacinta didn't like Elana, but what could she say to that?

She relaxed a little. "Hakeem's right. You have been through so much, you are still in shock and who can blame you? ... But I thought I would lose him!" For a moment Jacinta became distressed again, thinking back and tears came to her eyes.

"Maybe a royal elf like you wouldn't understand, but my whole family was killed and Hakeem is all I have left." She told the story of her own rescue, and the recent adoption.

Elana's heart went out to the young Gypsy girl, and she was filled with admiration for Hakeem. "He's wonderful. You must love him so much, " she whispered, captivated.

Then she realised she was just standing there, watching Jacinta work and shook herself mentally and asked Jacinta what she wanted her to do.

She found it hard going, and she was awkward at first, but even though she felt weary after all she had been through, it felt good doing the physical work of watering the horses, removing their tack and letting them run free. Jacinta said they would have to come back for most of them later. There *were* an awful lot of horses, Elana realised.

Jacinta still felt furious with the selfish ingratitude and arrogance of this elf princess. She was shocked Hakeem seemed attracted to her, another good reason to hate her. But now she found Elana meekly following orders and being a pleasant companion. It seemed she was used to helping around, something Jacinta would never have expected of an elvish princess.

Jacinta gritted her teeth. She would much rather hate this stupid elf.

She assumed Elana, an elf princess, would view her and Hakeem with true elvish disdain. But Elana couldn't stop chatting about Hakeem, with a dreamy look on her face. He was so strong! He spoke Elvish! He was so brave! He seemed so kind! He knows so much!

Jacinta was becoming alarmed.

Elana seemed just as taken with Hakeem as he was with her. It was Hakeem this, and Hakeem that.

"Keep away, keep well away, you nasty … elf, you," Jacinta thought grimly. She felt like growling at her, "Hakeem's mine!"

Elana found Jacinta a smart and delightful companion. Working with her and chatting together was soothing, after her awful experience. It never occurred to Elana that Jacinta felt jealous of her, she was too distracted by thoughts of someone else, someone who lay nearby.

She was amazed to hear the details of her rescue. He charged down the slope AFTER he was shot by an arrow and pinned to his saddle. Elana was speechless.

He had covered her nakedness, and offered her water. When she thought back on it, he was *so* embarrassed that she was naked. He was so sweet. He was so honourable.

She felt like running to Hakeem and kissing him in gratitude. This was definitely *not* a good idea, even *if* he weren't so badly wounded. Her mood around Hakeem just then was far too dangerous. She may not be able to control what she did after that!

She giggled, it was not what he would do to her, it was what she might do to him.

"You know he will want to take the first watch," Jacinta murmured. Elana nodded and smiled in understanding.

The two kept their bows and quivers to hand as they re-joined Hakeem. He was resting with his bow on his lap. He had had more broth and water and was looking better. Everything was as ready as they were going to get it.

It would be an early night. Elana gave her patient something to drink which he humbly took without questions. After a little while, Hakeem announced he was sufficiently rested and would take the first watch.

Jacinta simply smiled at him. She had her coat wrapped around her and had lifted up her bow and quiver. As she started to move to the shadows she said, "I'm taking the first watch, father."

Hakeem noticed he was feeling sleepy. He suspected some sort of conspiracy between the two 'women'.

He looked at Elana who smiled at him sweetly, her head slightly tilted as if enquiring what he was about to ask. All he could think was how lovely she looked, and how much he loved her smile. He couldn't help but smile back. The last thing he remembered was smiling at Elana and her smiling back.

* * *

By the morning, Hakeem was amazed at how good his leg felt. He was in a lot of pain and it was stiff and weak but he should have been in agony.

There had been a lot of tissue damage, due to the type of arrow and the abuse he had subjected his leg to. Infection should have started, which could lead to a loss of the leg or even death. At best it should be a slow recovery, if it didn't finish him as a fighter. This was one area of elf magic that apparently hadn't been lost.

Elana cautioned him to be very gentle with his leg for many moons, until it was fully knit. In truth it was a surprise to her as well. She insisted on bandaging it before he put his trousers on, much to Hakeem's obvious embarrassment and her amusement.

This day, they faced the melancholy task of removing the personal effects from the dead elves, for return to their families. They removed the remaining money, jewellery and weapons from the dead assassins. It made an impressive haul. Hakeem and Jacinta would have an enviable collection of the rare assassin's knives.

Hakeem was amazed at Djorn's ring and spent some time examining it before putting it away again. Elwan had one that was identical which Hakeem had left with Myriani.

Elwan said he was related to elf nobility, was Djorn a cousin?

Elana was morose the whole day. She looked sadly at the faces of those who had died for her. They had loved and valued her and what did it bring them?

Hakeem and Jacinta were worried about her mood. Would all she had been through affect her pregnancy? Hakeem wished he didn't have to rely on her and Jacinta to do his work.

It was beyond the three of them to give the elves a decent burial. Using two saplings, tent cloth and rope Hakeem rigged a 'travois' (sled) behind one of the smaller horses which allowed the girls to drag the dead into the shelter of large rock. Then they piled stones and branches over them.

After abusing his leg in the fight, Hakeem was not foolish enough to strain it further. He helped as much as he could, limping around very gingerly, using a stick for support.

He would have liked to do something for the assassins but one look at Elana's face silenced him. Now, looking at an exhausted girl and the pregnant woman, he realised how foolish he was, thinking of giving them more work to do.

They redistributed the load between the horses they would take, the rest they would have to send for. No one was keen to spend another night at the scene of the attack, so they made their way back to the cave. After there, Hakeem would make for the chapterhouse, but Elana hadn't given up on going through the pass.

"I can't see how there can be any more trouble now these men are dead. We could get through the pass before the snow gets heavy," she started.

"Let me get this right," Hakeem said patiently. "You say you didn't expect trouble until the escort sent by your father was slaughtered with only one survivor, a group of thirty elves well-armed, well trained and ready for trouble.

"You move on with a group of forest elves, who are surprised and cut down in their very own forest. Whatever force they had gathered was ambushed and never arrived to join them. That means there is at least one other *very* large and lethal group of armed men out there but more likely several.

"You are betrayed by a group who must be elves. Someone seems to know your every move and you say you don't expect further trouble." Hakeem paused, "Look at us, Elana: a seriously wounded warrior, a small girl and a young pregnant woman unused to hardship. You want to travel a lonely and dangerous pass with winter coming on, against a force or forces that have wiped out three armed and wary groups of elves already.

"Can't you trust me? I know about these things, it is what I do. If you want to live and deliver that child, you have to run away, not gallop towards danger. Believe me when I say that you won't get through that pass alive, even with a large force.

"I'll get you home. It might not be before the birth but at least you and your child will be alive. It is better to arrive late than never arriving at all."

Elana looked at him in horror, "Late? You can't mean that! You don't understand, the Prophecy cannot fail. Better I were dead, than to return a failure."

Hakeem simply restated, "Elana, please trust me, I really do know what I'm doing."

But Elana was terrified to arrive late. If she left it later, she would be heavy with child and completely at the mercy of these humans.

Then there was the problem with the dates. The recognition of her daughter by her family was already scheduled for a certain date. The baby wouldn't be near ready to be born before then. Now she would still be travelling and not near home.

What did it mean?

Had the Prophecy already failed? Had so many died for nothing? Was hope gone already? She felt sick to the depth of her heart. She only wanted to get home.

Her head and heart said she could trust these two with her life. But they didn't understand. Why wouldn't Hakeem agree to take money, curse him! She would feel more in control. Jacinta warned her not to offer payment again, that would be seen as very rude to a Shantawi.

What sort of crazy mercenary had she fallen in with? One who it was offensive to offer money to, that was the type.

Elana wanted to cling to this strong and competent pair. The thought of going on alone was terrifying, but she needed to be brave. She was an elf princess!

* * *

They were travelling slowly and the trip from the cave would now take more than a day but when Hakeem woke the next morning he realised he hadn't had a normal sleep. He woke up with a strange languid feeling and the sun was already up.

Jacinta was making breakfast. She looked half asleep, her hair and clothes rumpled. "She's gone," she said simply. "She must have put something in the broth last night. She took one of the bows, two horses and supplies. Stupid arrogant elf!"

"She is very foolish," Hakeem agreed mildly. He was using *that* tone again.

Jacinta stared at the fire. "She's terrified her stupid Prophecy is going to fail. The stupid cursed thing, it doesn't make any sense at all," she said glumly.

"It must be hard to have all your friends killed and to be driven mad thinking you have failed your whole race," Hakeem replied.

Jacinta sighed deeply. "She is stupid and arrogant, but leaving us was one of the bravest things ever. Someone has to go after her, Hakeem."

Hakeem nodded, but he wasn't up to riding a horse into the mountains. The first thing he would do was press on to the chapterhouse.

Chapter 17: Desperation, and a Dying Elf

Hakeem and Jacinta hadn't gone far, when they came across a dozen monks riding, fully kitted for battle. The monks had heard a large party of well-armed Eastern Elves had been massacred on their way to visit Djorn the Grey.

They took news of the death of Djorn, his sons and all those elves very badly. It was bad news indeed for the chapter house and the nearby elvish settlements.

Not only was it a terrible loss, but there were enemies on the loose capable of killing large groups of armed and wary elves.

Hakeem told them about an elf noblewoman who had escaped from the assassins and was heading for the winter path to Elgard. There was no mention of 'princess' Jacinta noticed.

The monks fetched a wagon for Hakeem, to rest his leg, and helped him back to the chapterhouse. The healer there was astounded at how good Hakeem's leg was doing after all the abuse it had suffered. He re-bandaged it, but warned against further riding for a moon and half at least.

Omar was very grave, when he heard all the news, including the mention of the Princess.

Hakeem was surprised he included Jacinta in the meeting.

"Djorn the Grey, " Omar said, "his sons, and all the others. It will take a long time for this region to recover from such a loss. The princess, I have heard, is an empty-headed fool. This is how she throws away what good people have died for."

Hakeem felt he had to defend her. "She's not nearly as bad as they say. She worked just the same as us getting ready to leave and she did an expert job with getting the arrow out and sewing up my leg. She's saved my leg, if not my life.

"She's been to hell and back and she didn't fall apart. She's been driven half-crazy by the Prophecy. I think she feels it has failed with Djorn's death."

Omar knew about the Prophecy. He was very interested in Jacinta's idea that the Prophecy predicted a union of elves and humans. It was no surprise that the elves wouldn't think of this.

But then he said something that almost made Hakeem's heart stop.

"They are looking for her, Hakeem. They are looking for her all over. Elana and the baby she carries have many enemies, humans and some powerful elves. Who they are exactly, I don't know yet but there are several parties out there searching for her."

Hakeem was very slowly limping back and forward. He stopped. "Can I use one of the wagons?"

"I'll send three of my monks with you as well, any more would only attract attention. If you find her, bring her to Myriani's village, I'll meet you there with Daniel and Jacinta.

"In the meantime I'll arrange for the bodies and personal effects to be returned to the elves so their families can arrange a proper burial.

"I won't use your name. We don't know who to trust. I don't see how any of the monks could be involved, but the less they know about this, the less they can give anything away." He paused. "I will hide most of the knives, they are too obvious. We will sell the other horses and weapons far away, to set up a false trail. Leave a part of your money and valuables with the order. We'll look after them for you and Jacinta till you need it."

He turned to the Gypsy girl, "Jacinta, you are already a Shayvist. With your permission, I'd like to confirm you as a student of our order. We don't have many female monks, but I know you will be worthy. You will continue to train with Hakeem, but if anything happens to him, you must come to the nearest chapterhouse. If you have any doubts about what it's like, you can ask Daniel."

Jacinta looked stricken. As far as a commitment to the Shayvist order, Jacinta had no doubts. She wanted to join, but she was being asked to make preparations for her father's death.

She looked to Hakeem for guidance but he had turned slightly away, his face was expressionless.

She nodded slowly. "Thank you, Father. I'd like that very much."

Hakeem exhaled softly, he had been holding his breath.

"I'll take your vows tomorrow," Omar continued, " Hakeem will have left by then but I'll record Hakeem's sponsorship and will formally accept it so there can be no question of you, a girl, joining the order. It's not a long ceremony, but there is a celebration attached.

"Welcome to our family, Jacinta."

"Thank you, Father Abbot," Jacinta replied politely, looking a little happier.

"I'll leave at first light, so I'll say my goodbyes now," Hakeem announced.

He turned to Jacinta, "As for you, congratulations. You don't know how glad it makes me feel. The order is my family, and now it is yours. I am very proud of you. I'll take father's privilege and come and tuck you in, young lady! I won't be long, off you go."

Jacinta kissed him on the cheek and left.

When Jacinta had gone, Hakeem turned to his friend. "You mentioned Daniel," he said simply.

"Yes, if you'll have both of us," the abbot replied. "I want to continue training Daniel and Jacinta together, they are a good match. I have a pressing need now to take him to Karsh, so we'll travel together."

"I'm glad to have you with us, but is it wise?" Hakeem looked apprehensive. "I'm going mad with the worry of taking Jacinta into danger. She's already seen things she shouldn't have. She's still short of twelve, and was forced to kill a man.

"I have given my oath not to leave her, but should we be risking a second child?"

"You, no we, have a remarkable daughter there. She seems to have gotten over whatever horror she's faced. She's very brave in sending you off almost immediately. I expected her to say something against it. I haven't explained this to anyone else yet but Daniel's talent is truly remarkable. It is why I need to get him to Karsh as soon as possible."

Hakeem was astonished. "That good?"

Omar nodded slowly and seriously. "Yes Daniel is that good. I need to ask the Grand Abbot Maluch to see him. I tried Daniel in the water and the sand ran out."

Hakeem head jerked up in surprise. Some deep meditation masters, in a trance like state, can endure being submerged in water. The sand in the timer is set for safety, at eight minutes.

"It was me who stopped the immersion, I became alarmed." Omar continued. "He wasn't even breathless. He didn't seem to know how long he had been there and for the moment, I haven't told him. The contact with you and Jacinta helped him fight the darkness within himself, but it also seems to have unlocked something outstanding.

"I think he is destined to become an important member of our religious. Such a talent! But why has it come at this time? It seems everything is happening at the same time.

"Just get her back, Hakeem. Whoever is after the Princess can easily deal with an armed party. We would need something the size of an army to really keep her safe and we don't have that, not until we can get to Karsh. We will take her in a small party, disguised as a family. It's the only way.

"And as far as danger to Daniel, I've talked to him. It's my responsibility but sometimes the young can't be protected. I think whatever is coming, will come for all of us."

He turned to face Hakeem. "The time will come when nowhere will be safe, and no one will be safe."

Hakeem felt a shiver. He knew what was frightening his friend. So many dead already, and it hadn't even started.

His meeting with Elana, which seemed a wild chance, was no accident. Whatever was coming would also come for the elves.

Somehow the beautiful elf princess and he were at the centre of a gathering storm. They would bring danger to all who were around them. What was it, and how did it involve the ancient Elvish Prophecy?

He needed to find Elana and get her to Karsh. He could have tried for Aiolía or Troia but whoever was looking for her would expect something like that.

He wondered, would he see Aiolía or Troia again?

The two men sat in silence, and then Hakeem went to spend time with his daughter. He wanted to make any time he had with her count. He found her waiting for him, sitting on her bed.

"Are you alright, Jacinta?" he asked.

The Gypsy girl nodded, looking solemn.

"I thought you wouldn't want me to go," Hakeem said.

Jacinta smiled sadly. "Father, when you adopted me, I knew you were a warrior and a paladin. Of course, I don't want you to go, especially wounded like you are, but that's no good. It is what you are.

"I love you and am proud of you. Don't *you* worry about me, I'm safe here and amongst friends. I have the faith you have taught me. I am the daughter of a paladin. I know how to be brave, father."

She smiled a bit, "At least you're not easy to kill. Anyone who thinks you are is in for a nasty surprise." A single tear ran down her cheek at that and she hugged him as tight as she could. "Just come back for me, father," she whispered.

Jacinta couldn't hide how frightened she was. Would it always be this way for her when her father put himself in danger? Hakeem felt a great surge of love for her. This wasn't what he expected, from the young girl. Especially after all she had been through and she wasn't even twelve yet.

"I am blessed to have a daughter like you, Jacinta. You know I love you very much. I won't say there won't be danger, but it should be less. If her enemies have found the Princess, she is dead already and there will be four of us this time.

"As you say, I'm not easy to kill. If they want me to, I'll show them that for you. I'll meet you at Myriani's farm." Jacinta nodded.

"If we can find the Princess, Daniel and Father Omar will journey with us to Karsh. We will travel disguised as a family and smuggle the Elf Princess away with us."

"*Her*? You're going to bring *her* with us?" Jacinta almost spat in disgust. "Haven't you done enough for that elf?"

Jacinta's face was screwed up in outrage.

"She is so arrogant and she's *stupid!* You rescue her and what does she do? Why she heads straight back into danger like a moth to a flame.

"She has cost so many lives already. Why should we keep rescuing her? Get her to travel with someone else. She's a royal elf, she can get someone else to take her!"

Hakeem felt a little amused. Despite her age and peasant background, he knew that Jacinta would be more than a match for the royal elf, if needed.

Jacinta versus the royal elf could make this a memorable trip indeed but had Jacinta forgotten the lesson she learned with Daniel? Perhaps fate decreed that Jacinta would now get a chance to deal with another haughty elf.

Hakeem really doubted Elana was as haughty as she first appeared. The life of the elf princess had not been as wonderful as most thought, he suspected.

Instead he softly said, "Her escort of Eastern Elves was slaughtered. I don't even know if the Eastern Elves know to send another escort. Djorn the Grey's group of elves has been decimated. Perhaps we should let her travel by herself."

Jacinta's opened her mouth in shock at his suggestion. She closed it with a snap. That would be a death sentence.

Her shoulders slumped, but she still glared at her father and then she sighed.

"You're in love with her, aren't you, father?" she said softly.

Ho! So that is it! Hakeem thought.

"Jacinta, she is an elf princess, for the sake of the hundred Gods." He chuckled a little. "She has to marry a descendant of the Western Elf royal family. The two of us have no future together, none *whatsoever.*"

Jacinta gave in with ill grace. Hakeem hadn't denied being in love with the elf, but at least Jacinta wouldn't have the 'elvish stepmother from Hell'.

Hakeem and Jacinta sat talking a little while longer. Jacinta gave him a fierce hug just before he left. He was about to stand up but realised Jacinta was still hanging on. He waited, and then she let him go. He kissed her good night and tucked her in.

Jacinta lay for some time. She was unable to sleep, thinking of Elana. She hated the idea of having to travel with the elf, and she hated seeing the attraction between her and Hakeem. He said it wouldn't come to anything, well it better not! She clenched her jaw at the thought.

Then she thought how difficult Daniel was at first and how Hakeem said Elwan wasn't easy when he first met him. What did people see that was so great with these elves? Then she thought of Myriani and Kassandra. There was a certain something that was very special about elves. She wasn't sure what it was. How they moved, how they talked, how they lived so close to the natural world, their music and their wonderful singing.

They said the elves of old were even more wonderful. The elves had lost their magic, what happened to them? Was it continuing?

No wonder the Elvish Prophecy was so important to them.

Jacinta also knew she wasn't being fair to Elana. She was a skilled healer, that had to be unusual in a royal elf. And when they were working on the horses, she wasn't at all unpleasant, and she did apologize and seemed to mean it. The elf could hardly be expected to be at her best after what she went through.

She really hadn't tried to endanger Hakeem going off on her own. That was an incredibly brave, if foolish thing to do. It was that stupid Prophecy driving the poor woman mad.

She most definitely didn't want Elana to die. If she didn't like her, why did she feel so terribly frightened for her?

She sighed, was she destined to be continually plagued by these pesky elves? That thought made her giggle a little. Why me?

After that she managed some sleep.

* * *

Mikha'el (Michael) came out of the tavern and walked over to where Hakeem and the other two monks waited. They had left the wagon hidden and were wearing local clothing. Michael talked softly so only the other three could hear, his breath steaming in the chill air. As far as they could tell, they were alone and no one was watching them.

"Well, good news and bad news, I'm afraid." Michael said. "The good news is that she was here, and left only two days ago. So we aren't too far behind. She was making it obvious she carried a lot of money, probably not even aware she was doing it. She hired a group of small time thieves, fortunately not the worst group, nor one of the others asking around for her.

"Whatever's happened has happened already. There's a very good chance they have simply taken her out into the wilderness and left her there. Most locals would be superstitious of killing an important elf, outright. The question was where?

"The band she left with hasn't shown up. I'm hoping they've gone to ground somewhere. There are some very nasty customers who are asking after them now."

There was nothing for it. Michael and Hakeem went together in the worst and most likely direction. The two others split up to check out the other two likely ways.

* * *

One of the items of elf magic that had been found in secret, in 'the last' (the last great elf city, Elgard). It was the mirror of far seeing.

Elana's every move was being watched from afar and it had helped trap her. Now something happened again to darken the vision.

"It's happened again!" the young elf lord said to his companions. "I've lost sight of her. Last time, I thought she would die. This time the bitch is dying, I'm sure of it!"

* * *

Elana had lost the feeling in her feet some time ago. She had lost a lot of blood but was starting to feel warm and sleepy, and that was a bad sign.

They had taken everything, even her coat but hadn't otherwise touched her. They were, if anything, apologetic. They were sorry, it was just too much money and they could have all of it without taking the risk of trying to get her to Elgard.

Of course, it meant she had to die, and soon she would be dead.

She had sucked on some snow for her parched throat but it robbed the last of her warmth. She had huddled in a small cave last night and then she decided to walk out. No one knew where she was, and there was no one to search for her.

She saw two men, walking along the trail. Their eyes were cast down. Was it the robbers coming back? She didn't have anything more to take.

One looked to be a big man. He seemed vaguely familiar, but her mind wasn't working well. He was limping.

Suddenly he was running awkwardly in the snow towards her. She felt herself swept up like a small child in his strong arms.

"Oh, Hakeem," she cried out in despair. "I lost the baby."

* * *

Hakeem sat with Elana while Michael brought the wagon. One of the other monks had already found Elana's thieves, all of them dead. There was no sign of the money.

Hakeem's small party were caught between worry about being found, and worry about Elana who was gravely ill. They were careful to disguise their tracks for a good distance, at least wagons in this country, at this time, weren't unusual.

Hakeem warmed the elf with blankets and holding her close to him but she had lost a lot of blood from her miscarriage, and was feverish. Her chest made rattly noises as she breathed.

He could hardly make her drink! Desperately he prayed that someone at Myriani's would know what to do.

But she was already starting to fade. She hadn't said anything coherent, except about losing the baby and now she had lapsed into unconsciousness. She was alternately burning and drenched in sweat.

She had given up on her will to live, her mission had failed.

By the time they got to Myriani's place, her breathing was irregular and she was starting to look bluish on the lips. There was a blur of faces as he carried her inside. An old lady from the village came, but took a cursory look and left, shaking her head and muttering.

Hakeem was hardly aware of who came and went, as he tried to nurse the dying elf. He looked up through his tears to see Omar and Jacinta standing in the doorway of the small room. All he could smell was the stink of dying.

"I don't know what to do!" he said through his tears. "She's dying. Somebody help me!"

"You are a paladin," Omar told him. "You have the power of Apollōn, the God of healing."

"But I don't know how to use it! How can I?" Hakeem was desperate, and sobbing.

Jacinta was moved with pity as she looked down on the dying elf. "Listen to me, Father." She said intently, trying to get through to him. "If anyone can, you can. Don't use your head to talk to God, use your heart."

Of course! Hakeem realised Jacinta was right. How could he forget? If God would grant this, it didn't require a complicated ritual.

They closed the door and ensured they wouldn't be disturbed, no one else must know what was going on. They prayed briefly, Elana was all but gone, there was very little time. Hakeem sat on the end of the bed, he drew his great sword and rested it on the floor, bowed his head and concentrated.

* * *

In the far distance, there was a faint voice calling her. It was too faint and too far away.

I have to leave, Elana thought, I have failed.

Then she felt something of awesome power and love surrounding her, a great light at the end of a long tunnel.

With all her heart she wanted to go there but something was gently pressing her back. It wasn't her time.

Then she sensed Hakeem, or was he there all the time? For an instant they merged and she was awed by what she saw.

But what had she come across at first, and what was Hakeem doing here?

* * *

Hakeem felt himself spiralling down and down. There! There was infection and fluid in the lungs: the after-birth had not come away cleanly and there was infection in her womb. The infection was streaming into her blood, and her body was losing the fight. He patiently worked, concentrating intently.

He moved from the womb to the lungs and slowly the disease cleared. Deep in his trance state, Hakeem felt like laughing for joy. He could do it! Without him knowing, his eyes were streaming with tears.

But as he possessed and cleansed her body, his heart lay open to her. She didn't know how, but she saw he was in love with her.

Eventually Hakeem paused, and gazed down into the beautiful elf's face. Before he realised what was happening, she opened her eyes, reached up to grab his neck and kiss him on the lips. He didn't want to break away. He had thought he'd lost her.

Elana said, "Someone or something sent me back. I dreamed of you Hakeem! It was wonderful." Eventually he lowered her arms for her and kissed each of her hands.

"Well," said Omar.

He was even more than surprised by what came *after* the healing.

"That worked out rather well!" he said mildly. "Now, none of us can say anything about this, we have more than enough problems as it is. We will have to say we simply prayed to God and he answered our prayers."

Elana's astounding recovery couldn't be kept a secret from Myriani and Kassandra, but they agreed to not ask too many questions or say anything.

They suspected Omar of something miraculous. They variously tried to subtly pump Jacinta, Hakeem and even Elana for information. For Elana it was easiest, she didn't know what happened. All she knew was that Hakeem loved her!

Chapter 18: Hakeem's Lady and Her Reluctant Ally

Elana was very weak and needed to sleep most of the time. She felt no urgency about returning to Elgard. In fact the prospect of facing the Royal Court filled her with dread. She only wished her father had not confirmed her as the future Queen.

At first she was left feeling morose, but slowly she was able to emerge from her dark mood. The new friendship with Jacinta helped, and she began to get caught up in the excitement of Kassie's wedding.

No one was allowed to know who she was, so there was no-one to treat her differently, no one to address her as "Princess." They called her Martha, Aramaic for 'lady'. No elves had Aramaic names. Whose stupid idea would that be?

Hakeem's of course!

She was surprised at how much she liked being just another elf maiden, she liked it a lot.

Myriani mothered the frail elf. Elana would have loved to have a mother like Myriani. She saw the easy, loving relationship of Myriani and Kassie. It was a form of richness that she had never had.

She started to enjoy the relaxed gossiping and fun, as the women fussed about their chores. She would have liked to help, but even staying awake was a struggle. Jacinta didn't have a lot of chores and the others were busy getting ready for the wedding, so Jacinta was the one who kept a vigil by the elf's side.

Jacinta had a good heart and she couldn't but feel sorry for the elf princess, hardly more than a girl herself. Jacinta saw her almost die. Her mission had failed and she had lost her baby, she was so weak and so sad.

Jacinta could hardly recognise her as the cold and haughty elf princess she first met. It was as if all Elana's defences had crumbled and been swept away.

The young elf seemed so vulnerable, emotionally and physically. Small kindnesses would reduce her to tears.

She was so weak and seemed almost pathetically keen to be liked by Jacinta, Myriani and Kassie. She didn't push herself forward, was content to just sit with the other women and listen. If asked, she would shyly make suggestions but was a gold mine of wonderful suggestions for elf parties.

What Elana didn't know was that Jacinta's head was in a whorl of confusion. To ask the eleven year old Gypsy girl (despite whatever training she had) to be fair to someone who had come out of nowhere to compete for her father's love was asking too much.

At first Jacinta was shocked, jealous and disgusted. The father she idealised was making a complete fool of himself. What had got into the man? Couldn't he see what she was like?

Now she realised it was her, not Hakeem, who had made a mistake about Elana. Jacinta found she couldn't help but like Elana, but why couldn't Elana forget about Hakeem for the sake of the Gods? That would be much simpler.

She kept going on and on about how wonderful Hakeem was, without seeming to be aware she was doing so. Jacinta no longer thought about marrying Hakeem, but he was still hers. Would he have time for her if he fell in love?

Myriani and Kassie had been delighted that Hakeem had found such a lovely lady. They had been ready to match-make if they had to. They knew 'Martha' wasn't all she seemed, and suspected from her manners she was high born, but she didn't act at all superior. If they knew who she really was, they would have apoplexy.

She was so obviously in love with Hakeem, from her behaviour and shy comments. But what was wrong with Hakeem now? He seemed to be going out of his way to avoid her.

Eventually Myriani and Kassandra decided to bring Jacinta into a ladies' conspiracy, to find out why he was acting so strangely.

Elana was sitting propped up with pillows. Jacinta was forced to grudgingly admit just how beautiful Elana looked, with her fair skin and her silky blond hair. She was improving and was able to walk a few paces, but she still got *so* tired. Elves are pale at the best of times but her illness and recovering from anaemia certainly didn't help.

Myriani was now explaining the situation to Jacinta, as if she couldn't see for herself.

"So we want you to see what the problem is, and why Hakeem is staying away."

"Oh, could you, Jacinta?" Elana's eyes were moist with gratitude. "You have been so kind to me."

Jacinta felt like snarling at her. Instead she replied, as if uncertain, "It feels a little like spying." She said, considering. "I would never, ever, want to do anything at all underhanded to my father."

Elana looked crestfallen. "Of course not, I understand." But tears started to run freely down her cheeks and she bowed her head.

Jacinta felt her arm suddenly clamped by a wood vice!

Now it was as if someone was turning the handle, making it tighter and tighter. She turned her head to see Kassandra smiling dangerously at her. Kassandra, a farm girl had an amazingly strong grip. Jacinta was sure her arm would be injured!

"Could you excuse us a little while?" Kassandra announced casually to the others. She was acting as if nothing was happening, as she meaningfully increased the pressure on Jacinta's arm. "I want Jacinta's help with something for a moment."

Jacinta was sure she would be left with finger shaped bruises.

Kassandra kept a firm grip on her as she marched her into the kitchen and out the back door. Then she spun her around, gripping her by the shoulders and standing over her, looking very angry.

"Are you still going on about wanting to marry your father?" she growled, her eyes flashing dangerously.

"No, of course not!" Jacinta countered flushed. She felt panicky under the elf's angry glare.

"Don't you love your father?" Kassandra asked coldly.

What sort of question was that?

"Of course I do!" Jacinta retorted, feeling distressed.

"So why don't you want to see him happy? You know he loves Martha or whatever her name is and she obviously loves him. Stand there and tell me she's not nice."

Jacinta bowed her head in shame, Elana was *too* nice. That was making it all harder.

"Perhaps you are too selfish, to share your father's love," Kassandra continued. "That would mean he never finds himself a woman while he has you. Is that what you want, Jacinta?"

It felt like a dagger was being plunged into Jacinta's heart.

"I'm sorry," she said, starting to cry helplessly. "Hakeem is all I've got. I couldn't bear to lose him."

She felt Kassandra gathering her up in her arms. "Of course, *meli* (honey), don't you think I don't understand that?" She said gently, stroking Jacinta's hair. "You must trust the Goddess. If you share love, it grows. If you don't it dies. I've had time to get to know Martha. I think you can share your love with her.

"Anyway, you don't want the big oaf wandering around like a useless lump for the rest of his life, now do you? Who takes charge of him if you get married? These sorts of things are too important to be left in the hands of men."

Jacinta had to laugh at the description of her father. She nodded and dried her tears. After washing her face, she went in search of her father. She felt very determined now.

The Hakeem she found was immersed in his own shame. He had taken advantage of the elf princess, when she was weak and vulnerable. He loved that kiss, but that was probably a side effect of the healing. He blushed furiously, explaining this to Jacinta, eyes downcast, playing with something in the dirt.

Jacinta tried to make reassuring comments, but Hakeem *knew* she was just trying to make him feel better. She was too young, she wouldn't understand.

And now Elana felt she loved him. He was just trading on her gratitude. She was a princess, by all the Gods, and he was what? An orphan and a mercenary. What a mess he had made of things.

Yes, he did love her, how dare he?

What an idiot Hakeem could be. Jacinta found she could do nothing to convince him.

It was not often that Jacinta was at a loss for words. How on earth could these two make something that was *so* straightforward, so complicated? She felt like hitting her father over the head with a rock. Completely defeated, she retreated to Elana's room to report on the problem, minus the 'princess' comment.

Elana let out a big sigh and settled back contentedly with a dreamy look on her face. A frown she was starting to bear disappeared. Hakeem loved her!

"He said what?" demanded Kassie in complete outrage. "What an idiot. Does he think women are so weak-willed that they don't know their own minds? I have half a mind to march out there and tell him off, right now." She looked around for support, but Elana was hugging herself and whispering softly. "Hakeem loves me. He really does!" with a dreamy look on her face while her mother and Jacinta were looking amused.

Kassandra felt like smashing something, these two lovers were hopeless!

But Myriani had more experience with these things than her daughter. "All we have to do is to give Martha time undisturbed with Hakeem. Do you think you can take it from there?" She asked Elana. Elana nodded excitedly, chemistry would do the rest. Hakeem tended to go all mushy around 'Martha'. He wouldn't stand a chance.

The next morning Hakeem was sitting on a bench outside the front of the house. He was looking forward with pride to being the one to present Kassie. For the moment, he was passing some pleasant time observing the female of the species and trying to see if he could understand them.

A small girl, a little over three was twirling around in delight in her new dress. Women liked to be pretty, admired and loved, and they liked clothes, he realised.

For boys it's more about being strong and brave and getting ready to be a man.

That nine-year-old girl really enjoyed minding the younger children, that made sense. She would be a mother one day. There's Jacinta jiggling with excitement talking to the older girls. Boys do something very similar around grown men.

Then there's that sixteen-year-old flirting with the two older boys, she's really enjoying the attention (girls like to be attractive, and they like boys). She's playing one against the other. Is she really interested in either? Then it struck him, she's enjoying practicing. It was a game she would soon have to play in earnest. Just as young men practice their own games.

Good luck to her, he smiled fondly to himself.

That young mother was talking to a friend about her new baby, that grandmother bragging about her grandchildren; old men brag about their families too. Women hold the family and home together, they are smarter about that somehow. Most men need to get old to gain that sort of wisdom.

A group of women passed, busy with their tasks and chatting. Why did women chat so much? Well it would hardly do for men to chat when they were on a hunt, or walking through enemy territory.

He smiled at a thought of a group of soldiers chatting like women. Hang on, sometimes they do.

And women are so beautiful! When they are happy, women and children get that special 'glow' about them. It made men feel good just to see them happy. He loved watching women. Such delightful creatures!

Suddenly he felt a surge of fierce love for these folk, these common folk: women, children, men and boys all. He solemnly renewed his promise to himself. No matter what was coming, no matter what it would take: if he had to move heaven and earth itself, he would protect these people he loved. He would succeed. Anything else was unthinkable.

"Hello!" Hakeem was so absorbed in his thoughts that the sound of Elana's voice made him almost jump three feet into the air.

"Sorry, I didn't know I was so scary," Elana smiled.

"Oh no, my Princess!"

Well, maybe just a little scary!

"Maybe you don't like me. If you want, I can go away," Elana suggested.

Hakeem was thrown into a confusion of denials. It wasn't true! If he tried to hide his pleasure at seeing her, he would hurt her. He was mortified at the thought of hurting her. He looked around but no one was close enough to help.

"Please sit down. I would enjoy your company, really, " he admitted, his resistance crumbling. "How are you feeling?"

"If you hadn't stopped visiting me, you would know how I'm feeling. Am I so horrible you have been avoiding me?" Elana said. "But you wouldn't visit me, so I had to come in search of you. Well, I feel weak and dizzy, if you must know. Can I lean on your shoulder, please?

"Thanks, that's better. It would feel more comfortable if you put your arm around me, yes, that feels nice. I was starting to think that it was *you* that would need to be tied up, before I could catch up with you."

How could she joke about that awful experience? He thought. Well maybe that was a good thing, she was getting over it. Hold on, what was she saying about him? His mind was a swirl of confusion.

It felt so wonderful to lie there with her snuggled in his arms. Without even knowing he was doing it, he looked down and kissed her lovely face. She wrapped her arms around his neck and kissed him on the lips.

She felt him tense a little, and said between gritted teeth "Hakeem don't you *dare* try to get up and go somewhere else."

He gave her a sheepish smile and relaxed back again. He couldn't help but gently stroke her lovely silky hair. Hakeem looked around for someone nearby. No one was around. He didn't for a minute dream all the women were going the *long way around*, via the back door of the house.

Elana really was exhausted from struggling out to the veranda. She fell asleep in his strong arms. For Hakeem it was a wonderful feeling, and he sat cuddling the young elf but he looked at her face with concern. She was thin before, but now she looked sunken around the eyes.

Trying not to limp, he lifted her up and carried her gently back to her bed inside. As he lowered her down onto her bed, his face was inches from hers. He noticed she had woken and was looking up at him. She locked her arms around his neck.

"You're not going anywhere," she said firmly.

He obediently remained bent half over, and then sat on the edge of the bed with his neck still trapped within her arms. He couldn't take his eyes off her lovely face.

"I need to get these clothes off you," she said pushing his shirt open. "Oh my!" she exclaimed in appreciation as she saw the hair and muscles of his chest.

Hakeem shrieked loudly! "Elana! Your hands are freezing!"

Elana was giggling and shushing him, as she worked on his trousers. "Shush, that's not my name, remember? Here I'll warm them on this!" She lunged.

She could hardly contain herself as he gave an "Argh" through his gritted teeth and jumped up. He tried to stop his own helpless laughter. She looked so thoroughly desirable and full of mischief.

He started to pull at her dress. When he had it (and her underclothes) off, there was no mistaking his look of admiration, or his feelings.

"How are my breasts?" she asked him, anxiously.

"They're lovely, all of you. You look so perfect." Hakeem smiled, shaking his head in wonderment. He felt dizzy, drinking in the sight of her.

"Are they too small?" she hissed urgently. "They were worse before."

What was she asking, wondered Hakeem? Elana was tall and lanky, just like her elf forbears. He sat on the bed and looked down on her with a rapt smile on his face

"You are so beautiful the sight of you takes my breath away." And she was: pale golden hair, so fine and silky, startling green eyes, and perfect milky skin with the faintest dusting of freckles.

Her body was simply that of a thin young woman, she was perfect. He loved everything about her and couldn't imagine her any other way, well maybe a bit more muscle, even a strong elf doesn't show a lot of muscle.

He bent his head and stretched to kiss her on the lips. Then he started to make love to her very slowly, taking his time. As his lips snuggled her ear, she felt his beard tickle. As he kissed the base of her neck, she felt her body start to tingle and her shoulders want to shrug up.

She reached up to grip his shoulders. He moved his lips along her collarbone, working his way slowly, kissing and teasing with his beard. His kisses slowly awakened her, she found herself yearning for the next touch of his lips. His hand started to move, first massaging and gently rubbing her right shoulder as he moved his mouth to her left shoulder, tickling with his beard again. She gasped as his hand on one side and his lips on the other simultaneously found her nipples.

"Hmmm," he said, smiling and resting his head on her chest, with her nipple in his mouth and working his tongue and lips to suckle. His hand was gently massaging her other breast and nipple and moving up and down her abdomen. Elana's nipples had become fully erect and she was tingling all over.

"I like them just fine!" he murmured, smiling. She giggled and gave him a playful tap on the back of his head.

He laughed and pushed her back, but he was gentle, so very gentle. He was considerate of her weakness, and also her pleasure. As he continued so very slowly, moving his hand lower and lower, teasing back and forward, she felt her body arching back. She couldn't contain the sensation. She felt she would explode.

Oh! She couldn't hang on much longer! And then Hakeem moved his body to cover her, there was a sharp pain and then a wonderful feeling of him inside …

* * *

Hakeem just lay there smiling, and looking into her face.

Elana felt absolutely wonderful. She felt so good about her body. He loves it, and he loves me. He finds me beautiful.

She felt like wrapping her legs around him to keep him inside forever, but she also felt sleepy and fulfilled. She could not remember ever feeling so happy.

Strange, here she wasn't a princess, and she had lost everything she believed in. She had almost died twice and yet in this village of peasants, she had found true friends. In the arms of this mercenary, what did Myriani say his rank was?

Captain, that was it. Her father commanded several legions in the field and she would too, one day .

In the arms of this wonderful man, she corrected herself; in the company of these wonderful people, she had found love. "What are we going to do?" Hakeem asked, thinking the same thing. She shushed him and started to kiss him on the chest. Don't think about the future she told herself, don't spoil this.

Soon their passion was reignited. Then they let their bodies react and the love and pleasure took over once more.

When the two emerged, the party was about to start. It was one week before the wedding itself, and this was to 'introduce' Kassandra to the groom's family. In truth, they had known her since she was born.

Hakeem thoroughly enjoyed his part in presenting the beaming Kassandra, to joyous applause. He cut a dignified figure. Most of the night, however, he had trouble looking anywhere else but at his elf lady.

Now Kassandra was formally promised to Ian, the ritual fire was started so she could burn the three objects from her childhood, a small rope doll, one of her childhood outfits , and a wooden toy. This was more formal than the coming celebration. The four parents and Ian and Kassie having to act out prescribed parts and there were lots of the wonderful elf hymns.

Hakeem, his part done, spent a large part of the party leaning back with Elana's head (she fell asleep again) on his shoulder. Everyone realised how ill Elana had been, so no one minded.

The elves who knew Hakeem and the story, kept stealing delighted glances at the couple. It was so romantic! He was seriously wounded and yet he went in search of her. She had almost died, but here they were and they were so in love.

Later Hakeem motioned to Jacinta, who was starting to look sleepy. He ended, propped against an embankment cuddling his two 'girls'. Elana woke briefly and fussed with the blanket, to make sure it covered the sleeping Gypsy girl, and then settled back with a contented sigh.

Hakeem wanted to fix this happiness in his mind. Nothing could feel better than this. He thought fondly of the old Grand Abbot. You wise old man, how could you see so much?

Chapter 19: The Wedding of Kassandra

For Elana, the next few days were the happiest of her life. It seemed that the further away from being a princess she was, the happier she found herself.

Jacinta had some lingering uncertainty about Elana. She seemed so nice, but could it be an act? Just two days before the wedding Jacinta accidentally came up behind Hakeem and Elana in the garden.

"You don't understand!" Elana was saying, tearfully. "I would really like to give her something for the wedding. But I've got nothing. I've even had to borrow clothes. They've been so nice to me, no you bought that. I wish I could give something from me. I've never felt like this, if I could have kept one of my necklaces, but they left me nothing."

They had rescued very little of her possessions. They had some weapons she left behind when she 'fled' from Hakeem and Jacinta. It was true, she had nothing of value.

Jacinta heard Hakeem murmur something, then a squeal from the elf. "Oh Hakeem, that's beautiful. It's perfect. Please don't be angry, but I have to pay you back when I can. Where on earth did you get it?"

Jacinta thought she knew what it was. If it was that gold ring, Elana was right, it was perfect. She melted back into the shadows. Well, well, a certain stuck-up princess more concerned about a peasant than herself. This elf was definitely earning a second chance from Jacinta.

When Elana showed Kassie the ring later, the reaction was all anyone could wish for. Kassie cried and this set Elana off. The two were laughing, crying and hugging each other. Elana let it be known she had borrowed from Hakeem, but would pay him back.

Then Myriani and some of the other women came into the house, they started to cry and make "Oh" and "Ah" noises.

Oh, no! Jacinta thought in disgust. This is infectious! She went in search of Daniel and Omar, hoping for some vigorous quarter staff practice. She realised now why most of the men were keeping out of the women's way.

* * *

On the afternoon of the wedding day, Kassandra had her wedding bath and a massage with sweet-smelling oils supervised by the women of her village. Ian would have his special bath at his home.

Elana did a wonderful job of organising Kassandra's fine golden hair, so it was a mass of tresses, braids, ribbons and tiny flowers. Elana looked tired but happy, propped up on cushions to watch.

Elves don't mind cold weather. The second half of winter was the common time for elvish weddings and they were always held at night.

Kassandra was dressed in a wool chiton, sewn and pinned from a single large rectangle of material. It was red, the festival or marriage colour. The garment was loose, and draping it and folding it simply, but elegantly, was an art. It was tied with a cord of woven yellow silk. Over this, she had a lovely fur coat and fine sheepskin boots. All this was for warmth because underneath she had to be naked.

Perhaps Kassandra was to be a farmer's wife, but she was an elf. She looked inhumanly beautiful and fair.

Hakeem was smartly dressed in white pants and top. He wore his medal from the King Helios around his neck and his crescents of Shayvist Mastery, now all gold, on his waistband. Over this he wore a fine cloak. Jacinta had chosen one of her Gypsy dresses, her boots and her coat.

The preparations were finished, all of the bride's party were now ready, and they waited in anticipation, their breath steaming in the cold air. Just on dusk, singing could be heard and the smoking torches of the groom's party could be seen coming in the distance. Kassandra dropped a veil, to conceal her face.

Hakeem cried out in a load voice, "Who goes there?"

To which Ian replied, "It is I, who have come for that which was promised me!" He was leading a great horse (that looked suspiciously like Nadeer) decorated with ribbons and flowers.

Hakeem called out in a mighty voice, "Come forth, you are judged worthy. Please accept this daughter, whom we love, cherish her as we have.

"I, as her father, call on the Great Earth Mother to bless your marriage with children, happiness and prosperity. Please accept these small gifts as symbols of our love for you both."

There would gifts to the groom from the bride's side, but these were really for the bride, from her family and friends but given to the groom. Traditionally these were things like gold bangles that the bride could sell in extreme circumstances, livestock was not uncommon. Unless the bride was wealthy in her own right, this was her dowry.

Though Ian was now responsible for supporting his wife, this allowed the bride's family to help the married couple. If the bride's family were poor, the cost of gifts could result in hardship.

This moment was going to be a little awkward. The dowry contained the gift of the beautiful ring, courtesy of Elana. Since Hakeem's recent visit, Myriani was wealthy by village standards. So the dowry was generous. Myriani could have given more, but Ian's family was proud and there was a danger of offence.

Kassandra brought the dowry forward and bowed her head as she passed it to Ian. Ian's party froze.

Hakeem's great voice range out. "The dowry is a generous one. But I have seen Ian, and tested his quality. Proud must be his parents and proud too am I that such a man would come to claim my daughter. Now do you accept?"

Ian's party relaxed. This was not an insult, it was a compliment. There were smiles and nodding all around. "I accept this dowry on behalf of my son, Ian, and my new daughter, Kassandra," said Ian's father.

"I thank you," Hakeem added. "You do me and my family a great honour, to see our daughter in union with such a fine man!" Ian's family, feeling honoured, was looking relaxed and happy. "Sad though we are to see our beloved daughter leaving, proud are we of the family she joins."

The truth was that Kassandra's mum, Myriani and Ian's parents were quite 'modern'. The marriage had been decided by the children with the enthusiastic approval of the neighbouring parents. This ceremony was a formality that bore little relationship to the reality of a love made in heaven.

Ian offered Kassandra an apple he had carried from his home, to symbolise his promise to feed and look after her. She seemed to thoroughly enjoy it under the cover of her veil, finishing it all, even the core! There was some laughter and murmured comments over this.

Ian then lifted Kassandra up onto Nadeer, and mounted behind her. Nadeer, loving an audience, neighed and pranced and then he bowed his head and moved off at a dignified pace to Kassandra's new home. The wedding party followed, singing and beating tambourines (traditionally to frighten harmful wood sprites), and the women sprinkled flowers from baskets. Fortunately for them, it wasn't too far.

Then Ian helped his new bride down, lifted her veil, and kissed her to great applause. He swept her up, smiling, and proudly carried her into the house. The wedding party stayed outside drinking and partying till Ian opened the door a crack and waved a white sheet with a small blood stain (to prove Kassandra's virginity, by tradition). Just in case , Kassandra's dress had a dolphin medallion fixed with a pin.

Ian and Kassandra were allowed to join the party at this point, but before this could happen, a hand was seen to grab Ian by the arm and pull him firmly back inside. The door slammed shut, to raucous applause. There was no sense now waiting for them to emerge.

The crowd moved over to where the party would be held. Hakeem had bundled Elana in enough blankets to almost crush her under the weight and brought her up, via a cart. Jacinta, Myriani and many others were more than happy to look after Elana, who had become a much loved, if somewhat shy companion.

Hakeem had permission from both Jacinta and Elana to join the drinking party.

No doubt he would regret it the next day, no doubt at all.

They had placed the pitch torches at intervals, and further light came from a small bonfire. There was little breeze, so the windows of the house had their wooden shutters pushed wide open and lots of fat beeswax candles could be seen glowing inside.

The surrounding trees were hung with small paper lanterns. The paper delicately painted with figures and scenes, and then made translucent with small quantities of coloured oils. It was glued to a wicker frame with a candle placed at the bottom.

Several women launched brightly coloured paper hot-air balloons to obtain good luck for the couple. They were gossamer light and floated gracefully up to the tree tops in the still air. (They would be harmless to the forest in winter).

Being an elf party, there were small packets of salts and powders which when added to the fire or sprinkled onto a torch gave brilliant glows of orange, green, and blue. There would be a flash, and for moments, the whole scene would light up in one of the bright colours.

Seating was mostly stumps and logs, but the neighbours had also pooled any available chairs.

A massive log split down its length, and placed on trestles formed a table. It contained a wonderful spread of roasted meats, fish, pies, cakes, stews, breads, preserves, and more.

How did they keep some of those fruits fresh? Hakeem wondered. Apparently they made clever use of snow off the mountain. There were elf-sweets and biscuits. Elves loved anything sweet.

On a small fire, an elvish man was roasting skewers of meat.

The younger children had already eaten, after which they each received a small packet with toffee and fudge. There were also pretty hair ribbons for the older girls and small dolls for the younger ones. The boys had been given carved whistles, so there were children running backwards and forwards and constant piping in the air.

For the later, several drums and flutes, plus a harp were brought. No human can hear the lady elves sing one of their beautiful haunting hymns to the Goddess, or one of their songs of love, and not be enchanted.

There is a certain magical beauty in elf celebrations. To an elf, to worship the Mother Goddess is always to walk in beauty.

Jacinta taught some of the women the Gypsy dance steps to a popular Greek song. Men and women usually danced in large mixed groups often in a circle, all moving in step to the music. Some dances were for men or women only, some were for both.

The dances for elf women were very graceful. Later there was the exquisite, almost mystical dancing to a slow Elvish song. Jacinta stood to watch it, her hand held to her mouth, entranced by its beauty.

By this stage, Ian and Kassandra had made an appearance. Overhead, there was a garland of flowers made of dyed silk. They first had to stop and kiss under this before they could join the party.

It was a very long kiss.

Hakeem spent some time examining the elf powders. Especially the tight paper cylinders the elves had sealed with clay at one end and had a small hole at the other. They contained a black powder and if one lit the end with a hole, they sometimes gave a loud bang and sometimes a fierce jet of red flame. It was great fun if a little dangerous.

He opened one and examined its construction carefully. Perhaps the powder could be wound in a thin paper tube and pushed into the cylinder to make a safer way of lighting. He wondered what effect these may have on horses in a battle but he had no time to ask.

Some men had retired to one side to chat and drink together. Hakeem joined them, and he and Omar began matching each other drink for drink. It was very good wine. Omar wasn't visibly affected, while Hakeem looked increasingly drunk.

The last thing Hakeem remembered was walking arm and arm with Ian's father, singing off key. What they discussed seemed to be of such enormous importance. It was a shame he couldn't remember any of it the next morning.

He missed the hundred and one things Elana and Jacinta told him about the party, when they were discussing it the next day. The food was delicious, he remembered that, and he woke with a headache, he most definitely remembered that.

The next day the elves insisted on celebrated Jacinta's twelfth birthday.

Humans did not celebrate children's birthdays like the elves did, and Jacinta had no idea when her birth was, only that it was late in winter. Most humans were illiterate and hard pressed to tell their age, let alone their birth date.

Even if Jacinta knew the date, human calendars were so difficult compared to the Elvish Solar calendars that it probably wouldn't help much.

They used a lunar calendar, which helped with the moon's cycles but they had to repeat a 'moon' every three years to catch up with the seasons and the solar cycle.

When this month is added and when feast days are celebrated can vary from city to city.

Knowing the year is made more difficult by the human habit of calling the year after the reign of the monarch (or the equivalent). A year would be called the fifteenth year of the reign of *Basileús* (King) Amyntas II in one kingdom and something completely different in another.

It might be tolerable if you spent your life living in the one city and kept track using feast days, but a wandering Gypsy family had no hope of keeping track at all.

They had a quiet ceremony with the family, and a small feast. Elana and Hakeem gave Jacinta a heavy hunting bow as her present, relatively plain for an elf-bow, but beautifully made. Myriani gave her an exquisite silver dolphin broach.

Kassandra and Ian visited the next day. Kassandra fairly glowed, and Ian looked so proud.

It was good to see them, as Hakeem and Omar planned to leave the next day. It was judged that Elana had gained enough strength to travel.

Hakeem sent a coded letter to Samit, Helios and the Grand Abbot. He wanted to let them know what was happening and warn them. It would take much longer to get to Karsh and he didn't know when he would be able to return to Pergamon.

* * *

The leave-taking the next day was particularly hard for Elana, who hugged Myriani and Kassandra tearfully, reluctant to let them go. She promised to return if she could.

Myriani took Hakeem aside. "Look after that one. She's been through a lot and seen a lot. I suspect something's not right about her past, but she's a very special lady. You're lucky to have her."

Hakeem didn't know when he could visit Myriani again but it did his heart good to see her and her family settled, and they approved of Elana and Jacinta.! Myriani and Kassandra was the only other family he had outside of the order.

Chapter 20: Flight, and Anything You Can Do an Elf Can Do Better!

A few days south of the Black Sea region, they pulled over and got ready to travel as Gypsies. Omar had obtained a black dye for Elana's hair, which certainly changed her appearance, though Hakeem thought she was just as beautiful.

For their complexions, Omar had a very light brown stain that resisted water as long as they were careful. Omar and Hakeem didn't need it, not all Gypsies were as dark as Jacinta. Elena ended looking fair for a Gypsy, but at least not nearly as pale as a sickly elf! They would say Elana had mixed blood. Daniel would become Hakeem and Elana's child.

They were a family: a husband, wife and son, and a niece (Jacinta was too dark to be Elana's child). Omar was Hakeem's father and was grandfather to the two children.

Omar had a comprehensive collection of Gypsy clothes hidden in the wagon, even embroidered undergarments for the girls. How the old bachelor knew what to get, Hakeem couldn't imagine.

Elana, as a *romni* (married Gypsy woman), wore an embroidered and beaded bodice over a plain blouse, her skirt was multi-layered and she had a woollen shawl. She wore a *diklo* (Gypsy hat or bandana, in this case a bandana) in scarlet, which concealed her pointed ears.

Jacinta kept most of her simpler garments and her good boots, which added to the picture by being somewhat mismatched to the rest of her clothes.

The men and Daniel wore baggy shirts with leather jerkins, coats, and baggy trousers with sashes around their waists. They all had serviceable boots and sandals. Over the top they wore cloaks.

One thing missing were the usual Gypsy bangles and jewellery, one of the ways the Gypsies stored what little wealth they had. They would pick up some on their journey.

For weapons, they bristled with daggers and the men had their Shantawi swords. They all kept their bows handy and five quarter staves were stored in the wagon. Hakeem and Omar could hardly be passed off as artisans or entertainers, so they would be mercenaries, returning home with their family, which explained why they were better off.

It also allowed Hakeem and Omar to carry their 'kit' (armour).

They had a wagon, covered with six wooden arches over which hemp canvas was stretched. It was drawn by two horses and they had three other horses to allow the others to ride. Nadeer could hardly be owned by a travelling Gypsy and he would have to go to Karsh separately, with some of their finer things

Elana asked if they would stay in the usual traveller's stops, but Hakeem told her they would be staying in the villages. She simply said, "Yes, Hakeem," and smiled adoringly at him. They would use Elana's infirmity as an excuse for lodging in villages.

They would be safer than camping out, and no one in their right mind would consider looking for an elf princess in a human peasant village.

* * *

At first, Hakeem rode in the wagon with Elana, but as his leg improved so he could sit a horse, Jacinta displaced him. Elana and Jacinta became inseparable; there really is something special about the friendships women form with each other.

Jacinta reminded Elana of Seléne; she loved to chat with the bubbly Gypsy girl. Jacinta wished her small family of two could become a family of three, with Elana.

Hakeem wondered what the two of them found to talk about the whole time!

He heard comments like, "You said what?"… "What did he say?" This would be followed by the pair laughing hilariously. He guessed, correctly, that he was a common topic of conversation.

That the two 'girls' he loved got on so well warmed his heart. He was initially worried Jacinta might be jealous, and was relieved she wasn't. One day he asked her about it. He was driving the wagon and she was ambling along with her horse nearby, while Elana was sleeping inside.

"Of course not, silly!" Jacinta replied with a smug look. "After all you're allowed three wives!" she spurred her horse and trotted off.

Hakeem was speechless. She was joking, Jacinta was joking! He desperately prayed that she was joking!

It was a time of physical, emotional and spiritual healing for Elana. At first she needed to sleep a lot, bundled in blankets against the bitter cold. Gone was the elf tolerance of cold weather. She slowly gained strength and regained her weight. Mainly, she felt loved and she loved back in return.

Hakeem cherished and fussed over her. He especially didn't want her to become pregnant. He wouldn't allow her to use any of the herbs for that while she was so run down, so while they slept together each night, they had to restrain themselves except certain times of her moon. Or at least Hakeem had to restrain himself. More than once he had to warn Elana off her teasing mischief, starting things they couldn't finish.

Each of the travellers made it a point of honour to speak Romani to each other, with Jacinta correcting their accents. She also taught them about Romani customs, beliefs, songs, and legends, anything she could think of. All four were good at learning, but Elana seemed the best.

Hopefully it would be enough.

Hakeem's thigh healed enough for him to begin strengthening exercises and he only limped towards the end of the day. That he would make a full recovery was remarkable after the abuse he subjected it to. Perhaps some of his ability to heal others also applied to himself, or perhaps it was related to the elvish treatments.

Jacinta and Daniel practiced quarter staff and unarmed combat regularly, under the vigilant eye of Omar.

Elana was slow to regain her strength, but regain it she did. Slowly Hakeem taught her strengthening exercises, and then he decided to show her the use of the bow. He set up a target, showing her how to aim and draw with a thumb ring.

Then Elana turned her back and started to walk away, putting the thumb ring in her pocket and pulling out a three-fingered leather glove, she switched the arrow from the outside to the inside of the bow, the way used for a three-fingered grip.

"Alright, use the elf draw, but where are you going?" Hakeem called to Elana.

"The target's too close from there," she called back as she turned around and nocked the arrow. "You're quite safe, but may wish to move."

That's too far, Hakeem thought, scurrying out of her way. She wants to prove a point, it seems, but she can't hit anything from there. Elana pulled the bow back effortlessly and put a perfect shot near the centre of the target.

Then she did it again, and again.

Without a word, Elana and Hakeem walked to the target to collect her arrows. Jacinta appeared and came up to stand next to Elana. They both folded their arms and looked at him with matching smirks on their faces. "How did the archery lesson go?" Jacinta asked Hakeem, with seeming innocence. The pair collapsed helpless with laughter, hugging each other for support.

Hakeem smiled, shaking his head ruefully. It would be a long time before he heard the end of this.

It was very ancient history now, but it was a disastrous encounter with the elves that originally tamed the Shantawi. Before that, they had been feared raiders.

The wealth of the Eastern Elves was legendary. So an ambitious warlord amassed a large army from all the tribes and, with promises of rich plunder, they set forth on the long journey north to Elgard.

As he entered the homelands of the elves, his force was lured deeper and deeper into the forest by the elves. The tribesmen were fearless, but they found themselves strung out in narrow pathways, surrounded by trees. They couldn't gallop or fight with their horses, as they did on the open plains. They couldn't join together. An elf could be hiding anywhere in the forest.

Eventually it started. Arrows seemed to fly from the trees themselves. They were being systematically slaughtered, as they tried to retreat. Still they refused offer after offer of surrender, till the warlord overruled his men and put a stop to their dying. They gained the grudging respect of the elves for their courage.

The warlord gave a binding oath that they would not be the aggressor to their neighbours ever again. It is a matter of pride that the Shantawi have kept their promise through the centuries. The elves are not the only ones with long memories. Honour above all else became the Shantawi's greatest source of pride. On occasion a neighbour misunderstood their "peaceful" ways, much to their cost. They are implacable foes, and what they take, they keep.

So he should have expected it, Elana was every inch an elf once she had a bow in her hand.

Hakeem asked if he could study Elana's bow. Elves traditionally used long bows. There is nothing quite like a full-sized bow for accuracy and power, but shorter bows were easier to carry and store and some elves had started copying the shorter 'Scythian' bows. They were perfect for horseback, better in difficult terrain or for swiftly moving targets.

Hakeem's bow formed a flattened and rounded "M" with the ends curved up (recurved), a bit like the bow 'Cupid' is supposed to shoot lovers with. It formed a "U" on full draw.

The noise a short bow makes as it releases an arrow is slightly louder than a long bow as the string hits the bow on release. Not loud, but enough for an experienced archer to recognise the difference.

It was made in layers, to make it powerful for its size. Hard wood, like maple, is chosen for the centre. The belly (on the same side as the string), has a strong layer of animal horn which compresses and springs back and the outside is tendon which stretches when the bow is drawn. All the layers are glued and bound tightly. His arrows had bodkin (fine) points.

Up to that point, Elana's gear was similar but that was where the comparison ended. It was rather plain for an elvish weapon but everything about it was a work of art.

Elana looked very smug as she watched Hakeem examine it, and Jacinta looked amused.

Her gorytos had green and red stitching and beautiful tanned leather. Hakeem still had the one Origenes had given him. It was serviceable but was starting to look decidedly shabby.

Her bow-string was made from silk thread and seemed remarkably strong, far better than his waxed hemp. Hemp was notorious for taking up water and rotting so it had to be kept waxed to protect it.

Her arrows were sharper, the nock fitted more snuggly and the shaft of each arrow had a separate section of harder wood near the tip to prevent the arrow breaking.

The bow itself was simply decorated for an elf royal. It was bound with silk soaked in glue and the tips and grip were re-enforced with bone. It had a protective coating of lacquer, to prevent excessive sun or rain. The colours were natural but inlaid with tiny fragments of shell to shine like rainbows in the light.

Hakeem glanced up at Elana. All he could do was shake his head in amazement. "You must be joking!" was all he could say. It didn't have to be this perfect!

He drew it a few times experimentally. You can't draw something as powerful as a battle-bow with two fingers. Elves used a glove and three-fingered grip which means the arrow sits on the inside of the bow. The rest of their party used the thumb ring which meant the arrow lies on the outside of the bow.

Hakeem had been taught that coordinating a three-finger release was more strain and less accurate, but it didn't seem to hamper the elves!

Hakeem's bow generated a force about equal to Elana's normal body weight, heavy for a horse bow. Elana's bow was probably just under Jacinta's body weight. He nonetheless smiled and nodded when he felt it at full draw. It was impressive for a woman. Elana and Jacinta were looking at him closely while he examined Elana's equipment.

"What do you think?" Elana asked, for a moment serious.

Hakeem shook his head and grinned apologetically. "Elana, your bow is not only beautiful but beautifully made. You elves have taken something we humans have made for more than a thousand years and have shown us how it *should* have been made all this time.

"As far as your archery, you are more accurate than me over distance, though I am faster and stronger. I would be grateful to get lessons from another elf, if you will agree to teach such as me."

Elana blushed and grinned back, her eyes tearing a little: Hakeem was proud of her!

So Elana became the one in charge of teaching archery, including to Hakeem. She had formidable accuracy over distance, but she was not yet fit enough to be even nearly battle ready.

Hakeem wanted Elana to start learning the quarter staff and unarmed combat under Omar. The quarter stave was one of the favourite practice weapons of the religious monks. They are cheap and effective and could be used to disable, rather than kill.

Spears with a shield for formation fighting are relatively easy to learn and good for building an infantry. Staves in individual combat are an entirely different matter. They can be used to bash or poke and there is a complicated range of blocks, thrusts, strikes, sweeps and coordinated movements, even short leaps.

When Omar offered Hakeem a lesson, he didn't scoff. The stave was not Hakeem's weapon of choice, and he could never have stood against Omar in his prime but Elana, Jacinta and Daniel were privileged to be about to witness two grand masters practicing the art.

The two kitted up with padded protection and started slowly. Hakeem was surprised at the speed and fitness of the old man.

Then they got faster. The bout became a blur of rapid feints, lunges and strikes as they battled back and forward. The crack-crack of the sticks echoed loudly across the valley.

The small audience watched in terror as the speed and savagery of the fight increased. Surely one would be injured or even killed; for once it looked like it might be Hakeem.

They attacked each other with deadly force as they feinted and thrust, circled, moved back and forth and swept and struck. But neither would try such a thing except against an extremely skilled opponent, or damage would surely ensue, they needed trust that the other would not miss in defence.

While the others watched, aghast, Hakeem and Omar were testing each other, not really trying to kill or maim one another.

It seemed to last forever and it was Hakeem who broke it off. Both were dripping with sweat and panting. Hakeem's leg was obviously giving him pain.

"We need to do this more often. I have to get back into regular training," Hakeem gasped.

"Not bad, though I hoped for better," panted Omar. "I still don't think you can beat me."

Hakeem smiled broadly and bowed formally, the quarter staff in one hand. "May the day never come, Master!"

Omar smiled in his turn. "Still, you are good, very good."

So a routine started. The pupils were Hakeem, Elana, Jacinta and Daniel. Omar taught the stave and unarmed combat, sometimes with help from Hakeem. Hakeem would also at times give lessons in Wing Chun to Jacinta and Daniel. Elana taught the bow, tracking and woods-craft.

Hakeem took the lion's share of the camp work, to allow the others to continue their training, while he slowly regained the strength in his leg.

* * *

Hakeem was surprised to find Elana was so competitive!

Anything a human could do, an elf could do better. There was some male-female rivalry as well and Hakeem, being Hakeem, couldn't resist setting up a teasing, competitive atmosphere.

He pretended to be jealous and competitive, while in reality he was fiercely proud of Elana. Jacinta always sided with Elana, Daniel and Omar were more of an amused audience.

It was such a delicious game!

One day, Elana and Hakeem were arguing about horse training. Hakeem was taking a view he would never support except to keep the argument going. According to Elana, you don't train horses; you develop a bond where they wish to please you. Hakeem was taking the view that they were dumb animals (no tribesman would think that for a moment) and they just needed expert training.

Hakeem and Elana went to separate ends of the small field and both called to Jacinta's horse, Farah. The horse tossed its head and nickered. She hesitated, looking backwards and forwards between the two of them as they both called her as temptingly as they could. Finally, she decided, and trotted quickly to Elana.

What a traitor, Hakeem thought, stamping his foot in frustration, he owned Farah first!

Both the girls were crowing, Elana showed the hidden apple Farah knew she would be carrying, and made a big production of giving it to her, while stroking and praising her.

"Hakeem," Elana yelled triumphantly as she trotted back with the horse. "Anything you can do, I can do better!"

"I know something I can do that you will never be able to do." Hakeem teased as he walked back.

"And what's that, human?" Elana challenged, with her hands on her hips, pretending to be stern.

"I'll show you later, if your time is right. There's one elf at least, who thinks I'm good at it." Hakeem was rewarded with Elana smiling and blushing. What could she say?

Chapter 21: Peasants, a Great Lady, a Pig, and Fighting a Post

It was late winter and the nights were cold.

The five 'Gypsies' were heading mainly south and a little east across the dry steppe of central Anatolē, famous for its horses, sheep and goats.

Karsh, the oasis city was beyond Anatolē, in the northernmost part of the great desert which was to the south. It was on a couple of alternate rather than primary trade routes, but the land was kept peaceful and the taxes were minimal and so Karsh prospered.

To get there, they go through the Kilisian pass to the eastern Mediterranean coast before heading south- east into the desert.

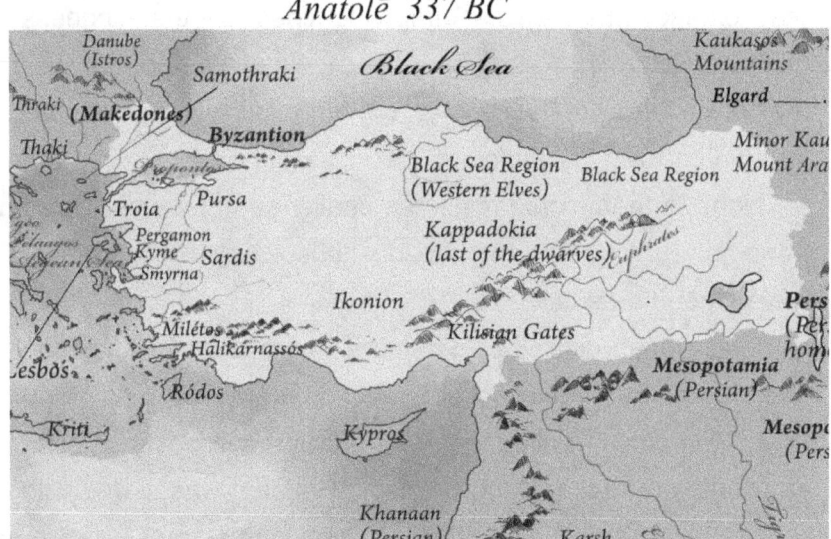

Anatolē 337 BC

The hunt for Elana would be concentrated in the north. They would assume she was headed east over the north mountain pass to Elgard.

Staying at the human villages was an education for the elf princess. At first, there was always initial wariness upon encountering a family of Gypsies; it relaxed when Hakeem explained that he wanted to *pay* for food and lodging and showed his money.

When they heard that his wife was still weak from the chest fever, it all changed! Soon the women were bundling Elana inside, while Hakeem would be enduring a stern dressing down by some old grandma for travelling too soon in the season with a sick wife.

Elana learned a lot about the local herbs, and was fed enough of the ginger chicken-broth remedy for weak chests to last her a lifetime.

The travellers never failed to charm their hosts, especially the shy elf lady. Elana was deeply touched by the kindness of simple peasants. Even after she regained her normal weight, being an elf, she looked far too thin for any self-respecting human peasant grandma!

None of them could resist the challenge to fuss over her and feed her up. Once started, the local hospitality was legendary for a very good reason.

It was often difficult to get the villagers to accept payment in the end, and the travellers soon found other ways to pay for their keep. Elana was skilled in the elf arts of healing, which became 'ancient knowledge of the Romani'. Hakeem was skilled with all to do with animals. Jacinta trained the group to be fair entertainers, and Omar was a skilled builder, blacksmith and craftsman.

Elana was hopeless in the kitchen, but was excused due to her weakness, but she did help in any way she could. Jacinta and Daniel were very used to chores. Hakeem and Omar would pitch in with their strong backs. It was usually possible to find ways to repay their hosts.

They also stopped at markets and purchased their jewellery and lots of small gifts for children and adults that they would meet. Human peasants unlike elves had large families and there was never a shortage of children: cute and endlessly curious.

Elana was having the best time of her life. Her world had been turned upside down. Those who were supposed to be most despised, she loved best. She had travelled from the Royal Elvish Court, to the home of petty nobles, then elvish peasants and now human peasants. The further they got away from the Elvish Court, the happier she was. She found the fussy human grandmothers adorable. They reminded her of a happy period of her childhood, being loved by her nursemaid Ailya.

She never wanted to return to the palace. She wished she weren't who she was. She would be happy being a wife to this wonderful man and a mother or sister to Jacinta.

But staying in such villages was not without shocks for an elf princess. Elana remembered whispering to the others, 'I can't believe I'm walking on a floor made of dung and will be sleeping on it tonight!' (It was the usual mud and cow-dung mix; the action of something in the cow's stomach on grass produces something with waterproofing qualities)

"Yes, comfortable, isn't it" rumbled the pleasant bass voice of Omar as he brought a load of their bedding inside.

At times, the toilet facilities were surprising and even unpleasant. Lucky it wasn't summer. She had to avoid public bathing for obvious reasons, but could usually skirt around this; she didn't have to pretend shyness.

Her favourite story, which would bring Jacinta into hysterics, was describing a toilet in a farm yard. "I couldn't see how it could work. It was a hole that one squatted over. It was on one of those houses built on a slope against a mound of earth, so there was a floor below. Below the hole there was a ramp made from treated mud, it was surprisingly clean. It seems that they dumped all sorts of scraps down there.

Being a Lady...," (Jacinta always started to giggle at the description of the clean ramp, and the Great Lady seated over the hole above.)

Elana strengthened her aristocratic accent, "....and used to servants, you know, I didn't think further, since they obviously kept it clean.

"Just as I started to relax, I heard some disturbance below, a snuffling noise. So I looked down and it looked up! It was staring at my bottom in anticipation. I just couldn't continue."

"And such a fat looking pig!" they would cry in unison, rolling around laughing.

After this, Elana lost some of her elvish love of pork. Would a pig really eat such things? She didn't even want to ask.

When they could get away with it and if they were offered pork (as a rare treat), the two would make snuffling noises at each other and collapse with laughter. When Elana realised *one* of the sources of manure for those wondrously big vegetables the peasants grew, she was beyond surprise.

Elana was getting an experience that a royal, especially a royal elf, rarely had. She was mixing unnoticed with humble people, and found she loved them as much as she hated those at court. She learned about cooking and women's tasks, local herbs and watched the men building, repairing roofs, building fences from saplings to keep cattle in, innumerable small tasks. It was sometimes hard work, but the land was good for the soul, something an elf would never forget.

She feared to return to her home and one day she was talking to Jacinta about this.

"I really don't want to be Queen. I wanted to give it all up and never return, but they wouldn't let me. I would love nothing better than to marry Hakeem, but it would never be allowed for me to marry a mercenary captain."

Jacinta coughed a little in embarrassment. "Well Hakeem needs to tell you about what he actually does. He's a bit shy about it, I think."

"Well, he shouldn't be!" said Elana, with fierce pride in her man. "He's so young and wasn't noble born. To become a captain at his age, he deserves to be proud. Why he may even become a full commander before he retires."

All Jacinta would say was: "That he will be a commander before he finishes, I have no doubt. He needs to explain this, not me."

Elana nodded her understanding, she knew about male egos.

She could make him a commander in her own army, but she wouldn't want to do this to him. As a human, he would be despised as sleeping with the Queen to get a command. 'Queen's consort' and a human, it would be a shameful thing to do to him at the elf Court. She sighed, what was to become of them?

It was near the end of their journey through Anatolē. By this time, they were became accustomed to thinking of themselves as Gypsies, if somewhat unusual ones. Once in the desert, they should be able to dispense with their disguises.

The three 'students' and Omar were practicing the push-pull and hand-trapping techniques of Wing Chun. The response to the opponent's moves needed to become instinctive and fast.

Hakeem was polishing a thick post and hammering four stout wooden handles in… at different angles. He was trimming them, checking the strength and humming away to himself. "What on earth?" asked Jacinta, as she and Daniel crowded around.

It was a thick post, taller than Jacinta. Near the top, at different heights, were two handles poking out at slightly different angles. "Those two aren't the same height, you have made a mistake," Jacinta pointed out.

"They're not supposed to be," said Hakeem, who was looking very pleased with himself. "Those up there are two arms when I shorten them, and this one down here is another arm, and the one below a leg."

"Well," said Jacinta. "I'm not as impressed with your work as you seem to be. It doesn't look much like a person on a post, and it's got three arms and one leg!"

"Nonetheless, this post will be your Wing Chun opponent," Hakeem smiled,

"Or at least will be when I trim it, a little. When I sink it into the ground, you'll find it a very tough opponent, and a punishing one. Few can fight it for very long." He shadow boxed to demonstrate.

"It is for a special exercise to practice your angles in fighting, and toughen your arms up."

Oh great, Jacinta moaned, more toughening up. She and Daniel had just got over bashing both sides of their forearms back and forward together for what seemed hours till they were purple with bruises. They had bruises on their bruises!

* * *

The journey south was considerably slowed. Hakeem briefly thought about whether he was justified continuing this way. Should he just make a desperate dash to safety? The sort of wagon they had, the type most often used by the Gypsies, was not built for speed. Any attempt at speed over uneven ground would only result in breakage and roadside repairs.

Only lately was Elana well enough to travel far in one day.

A dash for safety would also lead them to the main highways and involve camping out and staying at inns, exactly what their pursuers would expect.

The slow progress through less travelled roads and staying in poor rural villages should hopefully make them invisible. They also hoped the main search was the roads to the north and east rather than south.

How about spending time on training? Should they dispense with that in in the interest of speed? Hakeem had a view which allowed him little room to compromise. This was a long journey and only in Karsh itself would they be safe. Then he had to leave with Jacinta and Elana on a journey to the elvish city. At that stage, they would then be travelling with a large escort, but their opponents had enough manpower to attack them en-route.

Whoever attacked an escort under Hakeem's command would find they had made a dreadful mistake. But it was precisely due to his mania over preparation and discipline.

Hakeem was used to danger and had gained an admirable reputation of losing very few of his men in some lethal situations. Patience, planning and skill all played their part, but his most important rule was that all those who go into danger need to be supremely well trained, in peak fitness, and ready to fight.

Elana was in great danger, Jacinta had chosen a life with Hakeem and he could not shield her forever. Even Daniel, he suspected, would one day have to fight for his life and the lives of those he loved. The sooner they learned to be able to defend themselves, the better Hakeem would feel.

So were they able to defend themselves at the start of the journey?

Elana started tired, weak and thin. Now she was in better physical condition than ever in her life and starting to show muscle despite being an elf. She had the elvish ability with a bow but now was battle ready with it. She was thoroughly grounded in the basics of the quarter staff and was ready to learn the sword.

Hakeem himself was only now ready for active service.

Then they had two children, admittedly in training. Omar, Hakeem reflected with a wry smile, the old man, was the only one of all of them that started the journey in any condition to fight.

Let's see: an old man, an injured warrior, a princess unused to fighting, and two children. Could they really expect to fight a band of hired killers? So they relied on stealth, not speed. But

Hakeem would not sacrifice their being able to defend themselves for only a little extra speed.

Had he made a mistake? He was about to find out.

Chapter 22: Gypsies, and a Desperate Battle

Jacinta froze, three Gypsies were riding up. Their disguises would never fool real Gypsies!

Elana and Daniel hung well back, picking up their bows. Hakeem was wearing Mir, and Omar seemed to be casually carrying a pole, which he rested against the wagon. They hoped Jacinta could do most of the talking.

"*Droboy tume Romale,*" Hakeem called out. (It is good to see you, Rom).

"*Nais tuke* (thank you)," their leader, who they later found out was named Garran, called.

Hakeem gave a short bow, with his palms together and smiled, "I bow to that within you."

"It is with God, that we have found you!" the young swarthy leader smiled in return.

"May God be with you! Niece, bring our guests refreshments. Have you eaten?" Fortunately they had. They introduced themselves, while they sipped some local wine. As they chatted to Hakeem, Jacinta kept looking at their leader with a puzzled expression as if she was wondering if she knew him.

These Gypsies were part of a caravan that was headed for Karsh. They would be appointing a new warlord, had you heard? They should make a lot of money with all the crowds descending.

What tribe are you from? That's wonderful, you are our kin. You must come to our camp. Oh … the fever? The visitors casually moved back.

"Well I'm sorry" said Garran. Then the smile fell from his face. "*Gaje Gajensa, Rom Romensa* (stick with your own kind*)!*"

He spat at Hakeem's feet, his hand on the hilt of his sword. He followed it with a blistering curse.

He changed to Greek. "You are wise not to come to our camp, as you would not be allowed to leave. Your accents are good, but you didn't really believe you could fool Romani did you?

"Whoever you are, you are clever to have your weapons close. Know this, you are not welcome in this region. If my grandfather and the rest of my tribe catch you, it will not be pleasant for you.

"Leave while you may. And I pray you recover from your case of 'fever.'" He smiled almost pleasantly as he backed up to where his men waited with the horses.

Jacinta ran up and caught his sleeve, talking rapidly in an unfamiliar dialect. He replied in kind, then pointing over behind a nearby hill, the direction of his camp. They talked on for a few minutes.

"So," he concluded eventually, "I find you are travelling with my cousin. She brings great shame on her tribe, but for her sake we will not return with more men to kill you.

"But I warn you, you are in great danger and not just from us. People are searching for you. They know who you are, where you are and what you look like." then he switched to Romani. "When the fox hunts, the rabbit runs!"

With that, he leapt on his horse, and the three rode off.

They didn't need a second warning. The Gypsies were part of Jacinta's clan, what terrible luck. But at least he was able to give them warning. Deliberately or by accident, they had been betrayed.

Hunters would be racing to stop them from reaching the Kilisian Gates, the narrow mountain pass to the coast. Quickly, the travellers packed their wagon and started to move. Hakeem and Omar knew they would have to change their disguises, hide the wagon and abandon it. They stopped near a rise. Jacinta hurried up a slight hill to look over to the Gypsy camp while the others were readying their gear. Hakeem joined her in looking over the Gypsies, to check they would not be chased.

Not far up a small valley, by a stream, the Gypsies had made their encampment: wagons, tents and smoke from their campfires and horses, goats and sheep. They could hear the noise of dogs barking.

Jacinta sighed longingly, "It's going to be a gathering, and they are waiting for the rest to join them," she murmured.

Hakeem touched her arm and pointed to a spot back from the camp.

Jacinta gasped.

There were thirty or more armed men on foot, just behind a group of trees and they were getting ready for battle. They were on foot and poorly dressed … bandits rather than a raiding party.

They had to be desperate to attack a Gypsy caravan, but they had the numbers and would catch them unprepared.

"We must help them," Jacinta said desperately, looking pale.

Hakeem nodded. "We'll have to hurry."

Jacinta outpaced Hakeem on the way back, calling out urgently to the rest.

Omar started scrambling for his and Hakeem's kit. Elana passed Jacinta her gorytos and then snatched at her own bow and quiver. Daniel was out in front of them, running for the hill.

As Daniel started down the hill, Jacinta had just reached the crest. She moaned in anguish. The bandits had already started to move forward.

With tears in her eyes and her heart hammering, Jacinta ran for all she was worth, gaining on Daniel. Elana passed them both, running as only an elf can run. Jacinta reached inside herself for something deep down and tried to catch up with her.

Elana paused and muttered an Elvish prayer as she shot an arrow high into the air. It was an impossible shot, immediately she was back running. Jacinta heard the sound of horses galloping behind her. Would they be in time to sound a warning?

Just then, Elana's arrow hit one of the bandits and he let out a great cry. The Gypsy camp erupted into frenzy. Women were screaming and running after their children and men were grabbing for whatever weapons they could, but the Gypsies were in serious trouble, Jacinta knew.

Her chest was on fire as she reached the floor of the valley. Elana was well in front.

Omar galloped past. "Don't get too close and try not to hit us," he called out unnecessarily.

Hakeem thundered past. "Don't worry about how it looks, there's not too many of them," he shouted to Elana and Jacinta.

Elana paused and quickly searched for her second target. "Oh!" she was muttering loudly through clenched teeth. "Nothing to worry about, there are only thirty of them and we have *two* children this time. That should make it easy!"

She chose her third target and began to swear monotonously in Elvish as she fired as quickly as she could.

Jacinta caught up, gasping helplessly. Great, I made it, but I'm useless! She snatched at an arrow and tried to hold her breath as she aimed; the world seemed to darken for a minute as she released. She took her next arrow slowly, trying to control her heaving lungs. Her legs felt so weak they felt like they would give way.

The charge of Omar and Hakeem scattered the raiders. A few of the wagons were clustered defensively and the Gypsies were all sheltered there, but there were not enough of them.

Hakeem could hear horses galloping down the road from the other direction, a dozen young Gypsy men rounded the corner, riding hard to join the fight. Without them, more of the Gypsies would have been lost. The bandits were now caught between Gypsies and their rescuers. Harried by the mounted warriors, and being decimated by the wickedly accurate archery of the elvish trained, they were being rapidly cut down.

* * *

The battle was over and Elana had lost sight of Jacinta. She was now running around, frantically searching for her amongst the confusion. She had lost her diklo (head scarf) somewhere.

She found Jacinta kneeling beside Garran, tears streaming down her face. He had a bandit arrow protruding from the right side of his chest and was looking very pale.

He tried to smile. "Well, cousin. Did you know we thought you were dead? It's good to see you again after all. For me, the meeting will be a short, I'm afraid. Where did you learn to shoot like that, and is she an elf?"

"Quickly," Elana screamed. "There's time! Get him into that tent; I have to get that arrow out!"

"Elana!" said Hakeem dismounting. "There's nothing you can do for him. He is dying. Let his family spend some time with him. If you move that arrow he will only bleed to death."

"No, Hakeem," said Elana. "There's a small chance. For Jacinta, I must try."

Jacinta swung to face Hakeem and shouted at him in Aramaic. "You're right, father! *Elana* can't do it!"

Jacinta's meaning was clear.

* * *

Garran had collapsed and now Hakeem and Omar were in a desperate race to get him into the tent. Jacinta was jabbering rapidly. Hot water was brought. A horseman galloped for Elana's tools and supplies.

Jacinta was relaying instruction from Elana on broth and potions as she was working desperately. They prayed they would be needed.

The vast bulk of Omar stood between the gathering crowd of Gypsies and the tent entrance. "No one is permitted to see this!"

In the background, the rest of the second group of Gypsies was arriving in a confusion of loud shouting, barking dogs and the jingle and creak of wagons. The Gypsies clustered near the tent whispered hopefully about elf magic: "She's an elf!" "Why is she dressed like a Romni?" "How do they speak our tongue?"

Elana was badly frightened. She had got the arrow out, but Garran's body was heaving for air. The wound was bleeding from deep within and alternatively bubbling and sucking air. All she could do now was seal the outside wound and apply pressure. She didn't think it would be enough. She had to try.

She was hardly aware of Hakeem behind her, as he drew Mir and placed its point on the floor. Hakeem bowed his head and said a short prayer and then he concentrated ...

* * *

Praise the Mother! This was impossible, it was a wonder!

Garran was awake and in pain. He was pale, his breathing shallow and rapid, his pulse was rapid, but he was alive. He should be dead.

Elana couldn't understand.

The internal bleeding had slowed and then it stopped and when she closed the wound, the leakage of air and blood ceased. She looked at the wound. Her heart was bursting and her vision blurred with tears as she bound the wound. She used now a simple dressing instead of a pressure bandage, so she could watch it for any change.

Now to herbs! Nothing to make him sleep but something for pain (but not too strong)! Something to strengthen his breathing, something for the blood and something for strength and recovery. She dashed out to find their wagon that had been brought down.

"We have done what we can," Hakeem told Garran after Elana had hurried out. "You may have some weakness in your lung, but it didn't go badly."

Garran looked at him in wonder. "Didn't go badly? I was dead or at least dying and you were there with me. Who are you, wizard?"

Hakeem laughed. "I merely prayed to my God. Pay no attention to that fever dream. It was my elf lady who took out the arrow. Please tell no one of this, she travels in great danger, please help us."

"Help you?" Garran grunted, looking unconvinced by Hakeem's explanation that it was all a fever dream. "After bringing me back from the dead? You can ask anything, Lord."

There was a loud commotion outside. "Grandfather!" Garran whispered in alarm.

Hakeem poked his nose out to see an elderly Gypsy in fine clothes shouting angrily.

"You helped us, for that I am grateful, but don't you know who I am? My name is Djordji, the King of the Gypsies. I give the orders here! Let us see Garran before he dies and why are you dressed as Gypsies, anyway?"

Djordji was the most important and influential of all Anatolian Gypsies, the head of the greatest and largest clan. Of course, there was no such thing as a Gypsy King.

Romani don't tell *dinlo* (stupid) Gaje their clan secrets, and they love to fool them. They *most definitely* would never call themselves 'Gypsies', a symbol of the ignorance with which they were treated. So Hakeem understood exactly who Djordji was and what his true position was.

"Your grandson rests. You and his mother can visit him now, sir," Hakeem said, with utmost respect, and bowed. He finished with, "er…Your Majesty."

The Gypsy leader flashed a suspicious look at Hakeem. Then he and a plump middle-aged woman barged into the tent. From that moment on, Djordji became called 'the Gypsy King' by all who knew him. Only the Romani and a few others understood the joke.

Garran's mother screamed and ran to her son. Hakeem only barely grabbed her before she threw herself on his chest.

"You live!" she said, kissing him over and over. "But how can that be? I saw the wound." She ran outside in her excitement. "Praise the elf! She saved my son's life!" Great shouts broke out, a confusion of hope and disbelief. Then Djordji limped out. "It's true, he lives!"

At this point, Elana came back with some potion and broth, looking very weary. Someone immediately took the broth and potion from her. People were spontaneously grabbing her and hugging her and kissing her. Everyone was joyously showering her with blessings.

Elana smiled back shyly. "He is better than I thought possible. I think his chance is good, as long as there is no further bleeding or infection. I myself can't believe it."

The Gypsies knew she wouldn't admit to doing elf magic. That's why they weren't allowed to see. They knew there would be no bleeding or infection, and the recovery would be miraculous.

Djordji barged through the crowd to embrace and kiss the elf. "I will not forget what you have done for us, Lady. We have other healers that will help your work now.

"When you can, I'd like you to come and speak to me. There is a serious matter we must discuss despite all we owe you. I need to know why you are here, dressed as Romani and travelling with Jacinta whom we thought dead!"

* * *

"Jacinta is my half-sister's daughter's daughter," the Gypsy King explained as Hakeem and Elana respectfully bowed before him. "I call her my niece. Now that her family is dead, I am her guardian."

Hakeem smiled uncertainly, "She is now called Jacinta bint Hakeem. I have adopted her, according to my custom."

"Ah, but of course, you cannot!" said the King of the Gypsies. "Did you ask permission? Did you ask any Romani for advice?"

"But I tried to get a Romani family for her!" Hakeem cried in distress. "She wants me, just ask her. I love her more than anything!"

"If you tried to get her a Romani family, and for some reason it didn't work, that's a favourable point," the King admitted. "As to what she wants, she is young. It is my decision to make and I must consider the matter. If we had known, we would certainly not have permitted it.

"Also we have a matter of Gaje masquerading as Romani, that's very serious. I will forgive brother Omar and his pupil, as he has done us a great service in the past. They will have honour and welcome in our camp.

"You may have brought danger to our people doing this, though the help you have given will count favourably. You need to be bound by our laws, do you agree?"

Jacinta was nodding furiously. "Yes," Hakeem said uncertainly. It felt like his world was coming to an end. "Please..."

Chapter 23: A Gypsy Family, an Angry Princess, and the Shocking Truth

Elana and Hakeem sat clutching each other's hands and waiting miserably. The King had moved a little away with Jacinta, and a council of elders had formed. Jacinta was jabbering away rapidly. Damn, Jacinta hadn't taught them her tribal dialect!

Jacinta seemed to be doing most of the talking at first, and the others were asking questions. Then for a long time they seemed to be arguing back and forward. Jacinta was obviously trying to sway the council to her thinking, against much resistance. Eventually the members of the council and the King returned, with Jacinta looking very uncertain.

"Well then," the King started, "if you need to bargain, leave it to the young one. She tells me you are a poor man. Is that true?"

Hakeem shook his head.

"Very well, I didn't believe it anyway," the King replied. "I understand you rescued this girl and avenged her family. You acted properly in trying to return her to the Romani. What happened there will be attended to. Under those circumstances, the adoption is judged honourable.

"Since then, you have loved her and cared for her as your own. She obviously loves you and made certain threats..." He smiled. "There is also the matter of you masquerading as Romani. The law is clear on both points. Will you abide by my judgement?"

Hakeem and Elana nodded, dejected.

"Unless you are Romani I cannot let you adopt our niece." At a gasp, he held up his hand. "However, we Romani do not forget what we owe. We are willing to confer on you honorary status amongst us. I will adopt you into my family and you must give me your oaths. You will be required to honour our ways and submit to our law, whenever in our camp."

Hakeem broke out in an astonished grin. This was to be a rare honour indeed! To be named friend of the Gypsies.

"And then you can adopt me!" Jacinta finished.

"In the matter of impersonating Romani," the King continued. "I fine you one silver Mina each. This is lenient." Hakeem passed a handful of coins across.

Lenient? A hundred and twenty shekels or two hundred Greek drachmas?

Hakeem hoped not to be the recipient of too much more of this King's 'leniency!'

"And now, the bride price!" the King continued. Jacinta started talking rapidly again. There were expressions of astonishment and a lot of smiling and nodding. "Well, you have provided a dowry, I understand it is generous. You are forgiven a bride price."

"The last problem is more difficult. A single man cannot adopt a girl."

At that, Elana stood. Her voice rang out clearly, "I will adopt Jacinta with Hakeem. I love her. I will be proud to be her mother, if she will have me!"

Jacinta yelled, "Yes! Yes!" delightedly and she ran to hug Elana, both were crying as Elana picked her up and they hugged fiercely.

The King at last smiled. "So, it is settled. Tomorrow I will take your oath and confirm Jacinta as your daughter! Tomorrow we will celebrate. You will see! We Romani know how to celebrate!"

Elana was a princess, and Jacinta only a Gypsy orphan. Hakeem was so stunned by Elana's offer he hardly noticed being hugged then kissed by the Gypsy King ... on both cheeks! He turned to his beautiful lady, feeling choked with emotion.

"You would do that for Jacinta?"

"Of course I would, silly!" Elana smiled.

"Elana, do you think you could ever marry such as I?" he asked in a hoarse voice, overcome.

"Hakeem," she looked at him incredulously, putting Jacinta down. "Are you asking me to marry you?"

"Well, er, I know who you are. I'm nothing like that. But I love you so much. I must say so! Yes, yes. Of course I want to marry you."

"And," she demanded, looking stern. "Do you think that's how it's done?"

She looked so wonderful, standing there facing him with her hands on her hips. She was so beautiful, tall and proud, like the Queen she would become. Hakeem couldn't help himself, he dropped to his knees. He took one of Elana's hands in both of his, and kissed it. He looked up at her with adoration.

"My Lady, I loved you since I first met you. When I thought you would die, my heart almost stopped. You are the most beautiful lady I have ever seen. I know I can't offer much. I should not ask for more than what you have given me already.

"Married or no, you will always have my heart. I have no right to ask for such an honour but, will you marry me?"

Hakeem was appalled, he must be mad to ask such a thing. He had shamed her, she had to refuse.

But Elana let out a loud "whoop" and pulled him up into a hug. "Yes! Yes! I will marry you … in front of all these witnesses. I don't care what the elf court says, you will be my husband and I want to have your babies!"

Jacinta squealed and ran to give Elana a hug. Omar surged forward. The Gypsies let out loud cheers. What a celebration, three adoptions and a wedding.

One of the Gypsy women came forward to offer to loan her a proper dress. What a ragtag princess I am to become, Elana thought. I am now to be married in a Gypsy ceremony, as a Gypsy, in a borrowed dress whilst on the run from my enemies. And she was the happiest elf princess in the whole world!

The Gypsies were hurrying to make the preparations for the feast tomorrow. Elana gave her fiancé a long lingering kiss and smiled into his face.

"Hakeem, you have made me the happiest girl in the world. So, I am to be wife of a Captain!"

Hakeem coughed. Jacinta reminded Hakeem loudly it was time to explain his status to Elana. Elana looked back at her fiancé, confused.

Hakeem looked deeply embarrassed. He *was* a captain that was true. No, when he returned he didn't need to beg for his old job back. He was to be promoted to a full commander.

"A full commander, that's wonderful!" Elana was absolutely thrilled "You know when I first met you, I thought you were a troop leader. You haven't told me anything. Then Myriani told me you had made captain. At your age and an orphan, I was so proud of you.

"But a full commander! You need feel no shame in my court! Can you get us good seats when this new warlord is presented for the first time?"

Hakeem coughed, colouring. "I don't think he's so interesting, really it's all overdone."

Elana looked at Hakeem as if she was seeing him for the first time. Hakeem, jealous?

She had heard so much on her travels about the great and powerful new leader of the desert tribes. Much of his reputation, but not his identity, was widely known. She would be Queen one day. She just had to meet him.

Jacinta was having trouble keeping a straight face. "I'm sure you wouldn't think very much of the Warlord at the moment. Besides, you have already met him."

Omar and Daniel looked like they had both swallowed something the wrong way.

"What do you mean?" replied Elana, considering. "I'm sure the only desert tribesman I have met is Hak … HAKEEM!" She screamed, angrily.

"Oh Lord!" At that precise moment, Hakeem remembered something desperately urgent he had to attend to, at the other end of the Gypsy camp!

What Hakeem hoped to achieve by running was unclear. He was in a total panic. He felt terrified by just how much trouble he was suddenly in.

He was still not in full condition, but Elana was, and few can outrun an elf. Elana felt like calling for her bow, but this seemed just an overreaction. But only just.

"YOU LYING DOG!"

The Gypsies could not contain their amusement. Proposal only just accepted, and she already had started. This new 'sister' was certainly a spitfire! Look at him run and he's such a big one.

Hakeem desperately cried out to a crowd of Gypsy men, "Help me, brothers!" as he dodged past.

They couldn't contain their laughter. Not only did they *not* block Elana's passage but they opened up for her and cheered her on. Soon Hakeem was bailed up against a wagon, facing five foot eleven of furious elf!

"Elana, I never lied to you," he said, trying to back up, but prevented by the Gypsy wagon. "I just d-didn't get around to telling you!"

"It's the same thing!" Elana was furious. "You let me agree to marry you and you haven't told me anything!"

By this stage, Jacinta had caught up, panting. "Tell her the rest!"

Elana looked at Jacinta then rounded angrily on Hakeem, she couldn't look more furious. "Yes, tell her the rest!"

Hakeem looked puzzled. "There isn't any more, is there?"

"Oh," Jacinta countered. "What about being a paladin?"

"Oh that!" Hakeem said, watching Elana anxiously.

"Yes just that!" Elana stamped her foot. "What's a paladin?"

"It's a bit complicated," Hakeem said hurriedly, completely flustered. "You know how I love you, please don't be angry.

"Jacinta help me, I'm not very good at talking about myself."

Elana turned to Jacinta. "Well, you're right about one thing, anyway. I'm not impressed at all by the stupid warlord! Next he'll tell me he has a title and lands!" She laughed but stopped, seeing Hakeem's reaction.

He was turning a deep crimson with embarrassment and was trying to avoid meeting her gaze, his mouth was opening and closing but no words were coming out.

"Oh that silly thing," he managed hoarsely.

He didn't have a chance to say more. Elana linked arms with Jacinta, turned her back on him and stalked off, her nose in the air. Hakeem stood there, a picture of misery. He had just set the record for broken betrothals. As the pair walked back, with Hakeem miserably trailing behind, the Gypsy King motioned them over.

"It seems we have some serious matters to consider before we go ahead with the arrangements."

Members of his 'court' were filtering back in.

"I heard the names that were used. If you give false names, we don't question. But by law you must reveal your true identity if it has a bearing on the running of this camp. In this, I judge you in breech." Hakeem and Elana looked very chastened.

"But first," he continued "I overheard you. Hakeem lied to you, his betrothed, about his circumstances." He looked at Elana. "Is this true?"

Elana was still very angry. "It most certainly is!"

"So," the King considered. "He overstated his rank or financial circumstances. This is a serious matter."

"No!" Elana said, wondering how to explain this, "Nothing like that."

The King looked shocked. "He is married!" he shot a look of pure disgust, at the miserable figure of the tribesman.

"No, no!" Elana cried. "I agreed to marry him thinking he had a minor rank. He commands a force almost as big as my own! I agreed to marry him thinking I was part of a great destiny and he was a simple man, well not a simple man but, you know. I find his own people believe he has been sent by their God to lead in the terrible times coming.

"I agreed to marry him thinking he was a pauper. He is richer than I am in my own name."

"Darling, I did say I had money…"

"Shut up, Hakeem." Elana said out of the corner of her mouth.

"Yes shut up, Hakeem," the King agreed.

He pondered the facts for a few minutes more. "I was happily married for forty blessed years until my dearest passed away last winter. From this experience, I know exactly what must be done. What a fool! Why he must apologise immediately, and make it up to you!"

Elana looked smug.

"Do you still want to marry this man?"

"Of course!" Elana looked shocked. "For a start, I haven't nearly finished with him over this, and you couldn't trust such as him by himself, could you? Besides, I love him more than anything."

"We'll my Lady, he's a lucky man," the King sighed and shook his head, as if in disbelief at Hakeem's undeserved fortune.

Hakeem himself was looking like he had just had a reprieve from the death sentence. Silly, Elana thought, of course I was going to forgive him.

"And," the King continued, "it's obvious to me that the great Warlord of the desert tribes needs someone to keep him out of trouble."

For a man, he really does seem to understand, Elana thought.

The prime source of Hakeem's troubles since he first laid eyes on his lovely lady didn't occur to Elana, just at that moment.

"Now for the other matter," the King continued. "Our guests are not as they seem, which of course is not unusual or even unexpected." There was laughing amongst the Gypsies, but the travellers were looking tense. What was going to happen?

"Firstly Hakeem, it comes as no great surprise. News has already reached us of his great love for his Romani daughter and now we have seen it is so.

"You are a fine man, and we are pleased to have you as a father of our niece. You are great amongst your people. We cannot demand you submit to our tribe to have honour here. I release you from your promise to join our tribe, as an honorary member."

"No, King, if you will still have me," Hakeem insisted loudly. "I love Jacinta. You have offered me a great honour. I would be proud to join with her family." The King and the other Gypsies smiled, and many murmured in appreciation. They were very pleased.

"And to you, Great Lady, you will be a queen of the elves. Through your love of this Romani girl you are prepared to humble yourself. You are judged worthy, as if there could be doubt. You are also released from your promise."

Elana stepped forward also, and her voice rang out in Romani, every inch the queen she would become. "No, King of the Gypsies. I will be queen, and can't give any oath that counts against this duty. But I hereby give my pledge, I will do all I can to prevent persecution of the Romani. I would be proud to be seen as a member of your tribe. Tomorrow I do two things that I wish more than anything else, and I plan to do this under Romani law. One is to marry this foolish man I love so much.

"The second is to proclaim, as loudly as I can, my love for this girl. Long she has been my daughter in my heart. Now I have your permission, tomorrow I declare and demand that both elf and Romani recognise her as my beloved daughter!"

A mighty shout and cheering went up and people gathered around to congratulate them and give them their best wishes.

Elana saw Jacinta freeze as if in pain. She took the Gypsy girl in her arms and kissed her, why she was pale and shaking!

"Don't worry, *meli* (honey), it's me, Elana! I love you."

But something was seriously wrong with Jacinta, and the celebrations were starting to die down in confusion. Jacinta was staring into the distance. "Do you know who I am? It's tomorrow, you will adopt me. Do you know what I am?"

Elana looked at Hakeem in alarm, the girl looked so strange. "Why darling, don't worry, we love you. It doesn't matter what your life was before. Hakeem and I will never let anyone hurt you. You won't be involved in politics. You won't be my heir, except for the small holdings my mother left.

"Jacinta! Don't look so frightened!"

"And so," Jacinta continued just as strange. "I'm not to be frightened. Well, I am. You say I won't be involved in anything. Can't you see it? It's tomorrow, don't you see?"

"I ...Oh, Great mother!" Elana simply collapsed. One minute she was standing, holding Jacinta's hand, the next moment she had fainted. She was being helped on the ground by a Gypsy woman.

Confusion broke out. The King was starting to doubt the sanity of these strange travellers. Omar threw his head back to stare up to the heavens, plucking hard at his beard with both hands. He gave a great cry. "Oh Great God! By Lord Apollōn, it cannot be!"

Hakeem and Daniel looked at their companions in confusion.

"Can someone tell me what's going on?" the King and Hakeem cried, in unison.

Elana propped herself up, she was looking down but as she started to say the words, the hairs on Hakeem's body rose. He felt an awful sense of forebode, he motioned to Jacinta who crept up.

He lifted her into his arms and held her tight, as if to protect her from what was to come. She was trembling and her heart was racing.

It was the words of the ancient Prophecy!

"Stranger yet is her daughter, brave little warrior. So wise and yet so young; her blood flows not from the land of the great tombs. The blind will not see, the deaf will not hear, wise fools will not understand. Her wisdom will awaken magic new and old. The family will bear witness to her becoming."

"Hakeem, she is wise! Her blood does not flow from the land of great tombs … can't you see? She's not from Aígyptos! Her family will bear witness … the date is tomorrow!"

"I will present my daughter to my family and the world tomorrow!"

Tears were streaming down Elana's cheeks, as she climbed up to hug Jacinta.

"Do you still wish to do this, knowing what you do?" Jacinta asked her.

"In my heart you are already my daughter, no matter what happens. But I think it is I who should ask *you* Jacinta. Will you go through with this now, knowing what it means?"

Jacinta felt dizzy. "Elana my mother and Hakeem my father, to be your daughter I have no doubts. Think on all I am, a poor Romani girl and an orphan. Two wonderful parents, as you, this is more than I deserve.

"But then who you two really are, I lose the meaning again and again, excuse me. I just see you as yourself. I can't see you as great, no, that's not true, you are great, I know that. But great leaders and part of a great destiny, it's too much for my imagination.

"You are born for greatness, but not me! I am a simple Gypsy girl and I'm scared! This cannot mean me!

"With all my heart I wish to be a paladin, did you not know? I knew my father had a great task. I never thought for a minute … How could something like that come to me?

"Yet, already it has come! So soon, and what a task I am given! Too help save the elves and their magic!

"We three, our coming together is no accident. We are caught up in a fate set out in ancient times. I will face my fate with whatever courage I can! I will do whatever I am asked if it is within my small strength to do, but I'm still so small and so young."

Hakeem and Elana joined in hugging and kissing their daughter with pride. Jacinta was not the only one feeling confused and overwhelmed.

"But, Hakeem's not part of it!" Elana said, distressed. "He doesn't have any ancient royal elf blood flowing in him." She looked at Hakeem, who shook his head.

"Does he not?" Jacinta countered. "Did you note Hakeem's role at the wedding? Myriani is the widow of Hakeem's blood brother. Myriani told me her husband's full name: Elwan the Grey. When Djorn and his sons were killed, the ancient line failed."

"You are a surviving blood brother to the dead royal line of the Western Royal Elves?" Elana gasped and looked at Hakeem incredulously. "Do you intend to tell me nothing?"

She softly uttered the ancient words. "*When hope fails, he comes; father and lover, the greatest among great warriors. The dark man in whom shines the great light. Dead blood of the dolphin flows still within him. His sword is like no other, bearing ancient runes of power.*"

"It's him! He was right in front of me all this time!" She kissed and hugged Hakeem fiercely, tears running down her cheeks.

Hakeem who thought he would be in trouble, looked pleased but confused.

Elana thought about those who had died and was surprised her thoughts included the young assassin boy. "All those people … all those people who died, was it all for nothing?"

"Why that had to be, I cannot say. It is Karma," Jacinta said firmly.

Omar saw everyone automatically looking to Jacinta to answer the riddle, unanswered for a thousand years. That would be her role, he realised.

The Gypsies waited patiently to find out what was happening. Again Jacinta took on the role. It took a long time to tell it all.

At the end, Djordji addressed his important guests. "Well I can see we are witness to great events. To host your wedding in our humble surrounds, or to humble our great guests by adopting them into a Romani tribe, would only be an affront, you must wait for better surrounds," he concluded firmly.

Hakeem and Elana both cried out, "No!" in desperate protest.

Again Jacinta explained to all, "Don't you see? Our being here is no accident. There are certain things that have to happen in this very way and it has to happen here!

"My adoption has to be witnessed by my family. It is you, my people, who are appointed to witness the union. I quote the ancient words: *'The Eldest and the Youngest must unite to awaken the glory. Only then can you stand and not be washed away by the great tide. Only then can the greatness begin again.'*

"This isn't about re-establishing the Elvish Empire. Here Hakeem, show them your sword." There was a gasp as he drew Mir and passed it to the King.

"Hakeem and Elana would never be allowed to marry otherwise. You have given permission, they don't see being joined to my family of Romani as humbling. They see it as an honour.

"This is the start of something new. The elves call themselves eldest but they tried to remain masters. I think humans are referred to as the children of the elves, only the ancients know the truth or not of that.

"So we are to unite. The elves are eldest and wisest in some ways but not all. They no longer have the strength to face whatever is coming alone. Only in a true union with humans will they become great again.

"The future Queen of the elves offers, for a short period, to be your subject. What better gesture? My King! My people! We are offered an alliance with the elves!" She raised her voice loudly.

"Not as servants, but as equals. Each contributing what they have. Now, what do you say?"

A great cheer rang out and all present crowded forward to hug, kiss and congratulate the three. The King smiled when the uproar settled somewhat. "Just what I said before, leave any bargaining to the young one!" They all laughed.

* * *

It was evening and Elana had gone off somewhere. Hakeem wouldn't see her before the wedding. He was negotiating the cost of the celebrations, and the King was absolutely determined to refuse any money. It was a most unusual way for a Gypsy leader to treat outsiders.

The King was also insisting Hakeem join the Gypsy caravan. The search was for five travellers. Omar and Daniel could safely move on separately: two monks in a steady stream of pilgrims would not be noticed. Hakeem would be back to being a tribesman, allowed to join the travellers as an extra sword. Jacinta would blend in immediately.

Then it would be easy to hide Elana!

Hakeem didn't want to bring trouble on to the Gypsies. The King smiled. "Trouble? Now *you* will see what it is like to have Romani as family. Besides, you will not take these two girls, who are also mine, into such danger. You will obey me!"

Hakeem gave up and nodded in acceptance, smiling broadly. Then he looked deep into Djordji's eyes. "Never I pledge, ever, will I forget your kindness, my King of the Gypsies."

Omar came up to Jacinta with a few questions, before she left to help with Elana's preparations. "Well, you three are certainly destined to be an odd family, three extraordinary people," he said smiling. "But what about seeking the eldest, the deepest, and the last, and then there is that key?"

"I think that will be part of my task," Jacinta said. "Other parts will be given to those who follow after us. The elves lost the most powerful items of their magic. Their own prophet planned for them to fail, they had lost wisdom in arrogance; and yes fear of humans.

"It couldn't last and I think a fall later would be more terrible. I don't know what the full consequences would have been then. I suspect there would be no chance of union and recovery.

"We also have to find out what is happening to the elves. Why they are fading, before it is too late. I think that is my task too. The elves haven't found the answer, despite searching for two thousand years, so I think a human must find it for them. It all seems impossible, but I have to trust a way will be shown.

"I have decided not to worry about it tonight. There will be time and more for worrying soon enough, I'm sure.

"To unite with the humans, the elves have to lose their arrogance, which will be my mother's job, which is why she has been through the experiences she has.

"Humans were not ready to take over when the Empire of the Western Elves fell. We are ready now, but only if we unite with the elves. That was the plan, only together will we be strong enough to face whatever is to come.

"Hakeem's job is obvious. " She smiled. "I think he will be good at it!

"And we do not know yet what we are to face. Everything tells me that it will threaten to overwhelm us all."

Omar marvelled at the Gypsy girl. So young, new to the order, yet he had no doubt he was looking at the next Paladin.

He needed to talk to the Grand Abbot, formalising her role as an apprentice. She was being trained by the best.

Just now she was a young girl excitedly waiting for a wedding, a homecoming and joining with her family.

As Jacinta was walking away, she saw Daniel waiting to one side in the darkness. As she went up to him, he greeted her shyly. "Congratulations, you are to be famous. I don't think I'm ever destined for anything."

Daniel idealised Jacinta, who had overtaken him in almost everything. Soon the journey would end: His three friends were destined for greatness. Omar was a senior abbot and may become the Grand Abbot ... and Daniel?

Jacinta could not see his face clearly in the darkness. "I don't know what destiny will bring you it's true, but you know something?"

"What?" Daniel asked.

Jacinta moved closer, grabbed him gently and gave him a lingering kiss on the lips. "You will always be a very special friend to me." She kept her face close, so he could see her smile.

His heart felt like a bird taking flight!

"You know," she whispered. "If you like, some of the new wedding dances involve man and woman, boy and girl. I have had offers," she said vaguely. "But if you're willing we can agree to dance most together."

"I will dance with you," Daniel said, feeling absolutely elated. "Let no one else try, or they will answer to me!"

"I would like to dance with you, Daniel," Jacinta said softly, smiling at him. She gave him a light kiss on the forehead and was gone. At that moment, Daniel would have thrown himself off a cliff for Jacinta.

Chapter 24: An Impossible Dream, and a Gypsy Wedding

It was a dream, a wonderful, impossible dream and soon he must wake.

Elana hadn't said she would marry him. He wasn't waiting with Daniel, Omar and his new Gypsy friends for her to come. He felt weak and dizzy with anxiety. His heart was thumping.

Jacinta came first. It jerked Hakeem back into reality, and he almost fainted. She walked slowly, shyly but with great pride, carrying a small posy of flowers. She looked so pretty in her bright crimson and yellow Gypsy dress, her braided hair and blue ribbons.

And then, behind her, there was the most beautiful girl in the world! Elana, Princess of the Eastern elves couldn't be marrying him. He could hardly breathe, he couldn't see through a sheen of tears.

She came and stood next to him and took his hand, his hand was sweaty and trembling. He let go, for a minute, to wipe his palm on his trousers. Then they knelt together before Djordji.

"Relax, I'm not that horrible to marry, am I?" Elana whispered.

Horrible? He was the luckiest man on earth.

Djordji called out in a mighty voice. "Today, we celebrate a wedding and three adoptions. This in itself is a great cause for celebration but here we make history. Here on this happy occasion, great events unfold." At each pause a mighty cheer erupted.

"Before me kneels Elana, a beautiful lady soon to be the Queen of the Eastern Elves and Hakeem, a great warrior, soon to be the Warlord of the desert tribes. Not only that, they make up the two of the three foretold in ancient Prophecy, and the other one is our daughter, Jacinta!

"Common people curse us, accuse us and sneer at us but here the greatest people in all Anatolē and beyond have come amongst us, they join us, they humble themselves.

"I, Djordji offer to adopt these great people into my tribe, does anyone object?"

Pandemonium broke out! There was clapping and cheering, and some started to shout, dance, and play drums and other musical instruments.

At best, Gypsy celebrations were unruly affairs, and getting his tribe to hold themselves back from the celebrations for a formal part was like trying to hold back wild horses. Gypsy celebrations were unforgettable, but not because of any formality.

Djordji re-established sufficient order amongst most of them to proceed with the second part, the marriage. Gypsies held marriage and family almost above all else; it was a duty to one's tribe. One did not truly come of age until married. There were usually complex negotiations and celebrations beforehand and then frenzied celebration after.

But the formal ceremony in itself was simple; a declaration itself was all that was required. Elana pricked her thumb and put a drop of her blood on a small square of bread; still kneeling she placed some salt in her lap. Hakeem took the bread and some of her salt and ate the bread. Then it was Elana's turn as Hakeem took a square of bread and pricked his thumb...

Then Omar stepped up.

He called on Djordji to present Elana as he was her father. He used both words from the service to Apollōn and also to the Great Earth Mother. Then he asked Hakeem whether he was willing to take Elana as his wife, to love her, to support her and to honour her.

Hakeem took a shaky breath and opened his mouth ... and croaked! He tried again ... and managed to croak again! The guests roared with laughter.

Eventually he managed, "Of course I will," in strangled tones with tears streaming down his cheeks. This was followed by Elana in clear, beautiful Romani, "I will!"

Then there was supposed to be a symbolic kiss. But Hakeem clung to his beautiful bride, he couldn't let go. It felt like if he let go, she would be taken from him.

He enfolded her in his arms and kissed her on the mouth, the cheek and then her hair, he laid his head on her shoulder crying. He kept saying, "I just can't believe it, I love you so much." Elana held on for a few moments, and then she too, dissolved in happy tears and clutched at her tribesman. They were oblivious to all around them.

Omar and Jacinta were trying to separate them to finish the ceremony, without success, and Djordji was trying to attract everyone's attention, without any luck at all.

Soon Romani men and women with their keen sense of fun were pretending to try to separate them, sometimes in teams of two or three.

"I'm a strong man and I can't pull them apart!" ... "We all can't do it!"

The music had started again and people were starting to sing wedding songs and some were getting up to dance.

Omar gave up. He quickly tied the cord between Elana's right wrist and Hakeem's left before the pair could disappear under a small but noisy pack of Gypsies. Elana and Hakeem were still clinging to each other, with tears running down their cheeks. Omar sprung to his feet and nodded to Djordji who joined him in saying, "In the presence of these witnesses, under authority granted by Apollōn and the Great Earth Mother and according to Romani law, we now pronounce you man and wife."

"As if there could be any doubt," yelled Jacinta from the grass. Whether she was tripped over by the crowd or fell down laughing wasn't clear.

Then, there was no holding back the Romani!

Jacinta's adoption would be held after an hour's unplanned intermission. In hindsight, this was inevitable.

No food or drink would be allowed yet, but this didn't stop the Gypsies from partying. Music, dancing and singing was like food or oxygen to these people.

Most brides would be mortified if her wedding degenerated into such chaos. Elana knew exactly how the Romani married, and she loved it. She was running for her life, she didn't need a church service.

To Elana, she was already married; she loved this wonderful, foolish man. She wanted them each to have a chance to make a binding commitment, but more she needed something legal. She had to prevent her father's royal court from trying to forcibly separate them.

Her marriage to this wonderful man, the adoption of their gorgeous Romani daughter was, she now realised, foretold millennia ago and now it was formally recognised by these wonderful new friends.

No, it was recognised by her wonderful new family!

She was loved! Her heart was bursting.

If the Gypsies didn't make a fuss over a simple piece of formality, they were about to make a fuss unlike anything Elana had ever seen. From the youngest to the eldest, they would all join in.

She didn't miss the beautiful solemnity of a royal elf wedding, but if she did, she could have no complaints about what followed; the celebrations ran for three days.

There are no other people on this earth, absolutely none at all, that can party like the Gypsies!

* * *

Elana was taking a break in the often frenzied celebrations. At first she had to lead Hakeem around by the hand, he was in such a complete daze. Slowly he came back to himself, but at first he couldn't stop grinning like a fool.

Now, he was becoming more relaxed and confident. He followed her lead, but was looking very proud as they moved amongst the guests. He was starting to enjoy the party, though he was hardly drinking, he didn't want to be drunk on his first wedding night.

This was difficult to avoid, everyone wanted to toast the couple. Hakeem and Elana carried a wineskin of watered wine each and pretended to drink. Otherwise they would have both been unconscious by now.

The Gypsies, apart from Djordji, were poor, but they always gave what they could at weddings. Hakeem would expect them all to be his guests, so he must pay! Djordji was the father of the bride so he wished to pay!

Was Hakeem marrying his sister? Anyway, the "bride price" curiously amounted to exactly every coin that Hakeem was carrying. How did Djordji find that out? Hakeem himself had no idea, after he left money with the Shayvists, Jacinta shouldn't know ... but someone did.

The generous cash gifts that Djordji now organised with his tribe seemed to return Hakeem's money, less a face-saving compromise, which allowed both of them to contribute.

Elana was in a colourful pleated pink and blue dress. It was intricately embroidered and sewed with silver coins. As a top, she had a yellow blouse with puffed sleeves and a large crimson shawl. She wore a gilt pendant (on loan to her) which signified engagement. On her feet she wore sandals decorated with beads. Being married as a Gypsy, she wore no face paint.

Traditionally she would have long bushy hair tied up, which she would unbraid prior to being allowed to wearing a married woman's diklo. This couldn't possibly work at all with Elana's hair, but no one seemed to notice.

The cord linking them was long and allowed them to dance. Hakeem looked suspiciously like he was going through one of his training exercises. As he couldn't dance at all, this would not be surprising, but no one seemed to mind.

The feast was huge! There was plenty of wine and filtered bread-mash beer. They had a large open fire over which whole pigs were roasted, as well as lambs, chickens and a goose. There were huge wooden platters of every Romani dish imaginable with lots of breads, wild cabbage, goat cheese, nuts, fruit, and of garlic, onions and spices, honey-cakes and the usual pastries and Gypsy sweets.

But the most memorable part of the celebrations were the Gypsies themselves. Most of them could do other work, but almost all were accomplished entertainers and those who weren't should have been.

They had travelled the breadth of the land and learned from other travellers and entertainers. So they knew the songs and dances of many places, as well as being great musicians, jugglers, acrobats, tricksters, fortune tellers and so on.

Whenever they met like this, they were at play. The party was a chaos of Gypsies everywhere, spontaneously combining to have fun in numerous ways. There were men trying the exciting dancing of the far northern steppes. Some women copied the breathless female dancing of Iberia, stomping their feet and clicking their fingers as they circled.

A few women tried to copy the seductive female dancing of Babylon (without disrobing) but then a group of older men joined them with great hilarity. The old men were mimicking seductive women and would rush out to kiss any other man that wandered by!

A musician would start; others would join him, and then dancers, or the other way round.

Often they were inventing something on the spot, or simply showing each other how to do something … or practicing, but also there were clear favourites, where everyone throughout the camp would quickly rush over and join in a huge riotous group dance.

The Gypsies had their own music and songs. They could make one laugh, make one weep or make one uncontrollably want to dance. They played a few of their sad soulful melodies, but they were just so beautiful that they weren't out of place even in this celebration. It is true that the Romani, in the midst of their greatest joy, remember how life can be so difficult for them. For the older Romani, this gives their joy its greatest depth.

Gypsies, like elves, celebrated *life* itself, but very differently. Theirs was an earthy, strong sweaty lust for life!

Chapter 25: The Hunt for Elana, the Bādiyah, and Wādī Karsh

Joining with the Gypsy caravan slowed them to a walking pace. It took them five days to travel the ancient coastal mountain pass (the Kilisian gates) to Tarsos, the heavily fortified city on the coastal lowlands of Kilikia, the last major outpost of Anatolē they would pass.

The Kilisian gates are narrow and famous for bandits and ambush, but the travellers were very secure now, travelling in a large group of three hundred Gypsies.

It was just as well, as there was little choice of their route now and the search for Elana has moved south. Without the Gypsies, Elana and her four companions would be caught and killed.

After the fertile coastal region of Kilikia, there was a pass through the Amanos, the last mountain range they had to cross. It led them into a region of rolling hills, wheat and barley just south of Anatolē. The leader of the fourth large band of armed men had just made what he thought was a clever arrangement with Djordji when the Gypsy King rode back to where Hakeem waited.

"It seems there is a Greek man somewhere north of here that wants to meet my newest daughter," Djordji chuckled. "It is good to know at least one of us is popular."

"Do you know how much they are offering?" Hakeem's expression was grim. He hoped one day to meet this man.

"He insults us!" Djordji said in mock outrage. "A trifle, a single heavy Gold Babylonas Talanton, I was hoping to get ten times that much before I betray you both."

Gods in the holy mountain!

What was being offered was 60 kg in gold! Equal to two light gold talents (in the shape of a duck) or twenty talents of silver. Each silver talent was enough to employ a skilled man for more than a decade.

A heavy gold talent (in the shape of a lion) was enough to make every man, woman and child in the Romani camp fabulously wealthy. All they had to do was murder Elana.

She was surrounded by a group that is often seen as nothing more than a group of thieves and liars. Djordji joked of being offered ten times as much, but it wouldn't matter. The roads could be paved with gold for all the good it would do. The sun would stand still in the heavens, before any of the Romani would betray Elana, accidently or deliberately, from the smallest child up.

Those who thought such a thing was possible didn't understand the Romani. They are fiercely loyal and used to persecution and keeping secrets. Elana was now one of them and they were fiercely proud of her. Elana would not, could not, be as safe in the middle of a great army.

Djordji nodded to the crowds on the road. "I have never seen so many headed for Karsh. We would have been in great danger on the desert road with the normal sparse traffic. You can thank your abbot when you see him for me. Now we will be only part of a great flood of people."

Hakeem had wondered why the Abbot would do such an extraordinary thing as announcing Hakeem's election *before* he had even arrived in Karsh.

Now it seemed obvious. The Abbot knew they would be running for their lives. Without the announcement, there would be no Gypsy caravans and too few other travellers to hide amongst. They would have been dead.

The Abbot had absolute trust in their God, as of course did Hakeem. Nonetheless, Hakeem couldn't help but think that he had really better not fail whatever tests they had for him.

If he did, there would be large crowds of seriously vengeful people with his name on their lips.

* * *

Leaving the upper Mesopotamia (land of the great rivers) behind, they were travelling due south, through the land of *Kna'n* (Canaan), parallel to and just east of the coastal mountains.

It was the main trading route south to Aígyptos and they were passing some of the most beautiful and ancient cities in the world. The main Gypsy caravan didn't enter them, but there were groups constantly splitting off and re-joining the slower moving caravan as the Gypsies went in search of trade or money.

In the shelter of the coastal mountains, the land was dry outside any regions not irrigated by rivers or oases. Summer had passed during their long journey. The middle of each day was still hot but the evenings were mild.

Until they passed the city of Hamath and left the busy southern route, it was hard to prevent strangers passing close to where they were hiding Elana, so she spent a lot of time imprisoned in her wagon.

Driving a Gypsy wagon over the desert roads isn't too bad when you get used to it. The strong metal brackets under the wooden driver's seat are designed to act like a spring, and the driver sits on leather or woven padding. He or she can look ahead, and can brace themselves against the rocking of the wagon by pushing their legs against the kick-board.

Riding in the back is an entirely different matter.

The rear has no suspension. The wagon sits on great heavy wooden wheels reinforced and shod with iron, all riding on an iron axle. Elana, sitting in semi darkness, could not see what was coming on the road ahead. She couldn't brace herself.

All she had in her corner were some pillows, six dusty sacks of grain and a bed-roll. The wagon seem to find every rut or bump or boulder or would shake like a man with blood fever as it picked up speed downhill. It was enough to rattle every single bone in her body and her teeth for good measure!

Sometimes those outside would hear a muffled squeal, a whispered Elvish curse or a soft thump, sometimes all three, as the wagon lurched in and out of some ditch. Her wagon was completely enclosed so there was no breeze in the midday heat.

Anyone who had any choice was walking besides the wagon or mounted on a horse, but Elana never complained. She knew she brought danger to all who travelled with her. Even so, she would usually emerge at the end of each day looking stiff and exhausted.

As far as they could, the Gypsies travelled in a tight group and kept any strangers well away. They excused their bad manners by saying (truthfully) they had suffered one attack already. They said they had heard a rumour that some bandits had taken to infiltrating caravans before attacking them.

Whenever it was safe to do so, Elana, still in disguise, would join with Hakeem and Jacinta, walking besides the wagons in a large group of women and children and a few men.

It mostly had to wait until they had passed Hamath and had taken the side route going south and east deeper into the desert.

Elana was pleased that Hakeem and Jacinta decided to join her walking on what promised to be her first full day of freedom. She noticed Hakeem's eyes were constantly scanning their surrounds, especially every gully and hill. She looked at Jacinta on the other side to find her daughter was doing the same. They were probably no longer aware they did that.

Then Elana realised she was doing it too!

She'd been around these two too long.

"Isn't desert supposed to be yellow sand dunes?" Elana asked, trying to distract herself.

"We have that too, *matok* (sweet)," Hakeem agreed, "but you are talking about the deep desert where no one lives, we call that Ṣaḥrāʾ. This land we call Bādiyah, the desert where people can live. The people that live in *this* desert we call *Badawiyyūn* (Bedouins). My Shantawi are Badawiyyūn, which means desert dwellers."

Jacinta looked where her father was staring. Apart from dry gullies and hills, there was little to see, endless stretches of greyish-yellow soil, scattered coarse grasses and a few short tough shrubs. In the distance on the hillsides she could see some sheep herders and their flock. It was all so depressing and dull.

She wondered what the sheep found to eat.

"I hope Karsh looks better than this, *aba'le* (daddy)," Jacinta laughed. "Don't bother worrying about any invasion. No one would possibly want this terrible dreary home of yours."

Hakeem laughed back. "If you don't like this, think what it was like earlier in the main heat of summer. Even this land is beautiful, once you understand it but if you wish to see something truly beautiful, wait till you see Karsh!

We will be staying in the *Qaṣba* (citadel). It was the King's palace till the last King of Karsh thought he could take something from the desert tribes. We must have seemed peaceful at the time. Now we own the Wādī and the people of Karsh are our people."

"Karsh!" he said softly, almost to himself, with a distant look. "I haven't realised how much I have missed it."

Elana and Jacinta exchanged a meaningful glance.

"Haven't you?" Jacinta asked in an incredulous tone. "Well mother and I certainly realise it. It's all you ever talk about lately. It's all 'Karsh this and Karsh that!'"

Hakeem snorted, it made sense to tell them about the city he was taking them to, didn't it? Well, perhaps he *was* proud of his city, all who came from it were.

"You are joining the Shantawi now, so I'll tell you more about water in the desert."

Elana and Jacinta groaned softly and exchanged a tortured expression. Hakeem had been going on and on about the desert, almost as bad as Karsh, except he always mentioned the desert with grim seriousness, and he tended to lecture about it. Admittedly, Jacinta was his student, but did this include her being lectured about deserts?

"Water in the Bādiyah, is our greatest secret. Remember never share with outsiders what I am about to tell you. We know every small spring or well or seepage point. Each has a name and its nature is known." Hakeem began the lecture, oblivious of the reaction of his audience.

"We do not get much rain, but where we can, we collect it. In the better part, you might see ditches that collect all the runoff from a whole hillside draining to a small area or even a single tree. We also guard plants from the harsh sun.

"In rocky outcrops, if you know how to look, you will see carved channels disguised as natural weathering, they lead to deep hidden cisterns. We also hide small clay pipes to bring water many miles in secret. We have had thousands of years to learn how to hide this from those who would know our secrets and use them to conquer us." He smiled and paused. "Even our rivers are secrets; someone who doesn't know our secrets will say that no rivers flow here except when it rains."

"Father!" Jacinta protested, laughing. "How can your endlessly clever Shantawi hide a river? There are no running rivers near Karsh!"

"They can hide them easily, our endlessly clever daughter," Elana laughed, replying for her husband. "They are underground."

"Limestone!" Jacinta guessed her eyes alight with wonder. She had peered into the deep sinkholes in central Anatolē.

"Limestone," Hakeem agreed. "There is much limestone deep beneath our deserts. Water dissolves limestone, but unimaginably slowly. So the limestone under the desert has many channels and water can seep through it very slowly. Underground rivers can also flow from the mountains. More than a day's ride from Karsh is the ruins of an ancient city. The ground swallowed it up like a great sink hole. When I have time, I will show the hidden way nearby that you can climb down to find an underground lake and a small beach."

"If that is how you get your water, what about the oases?" Jacinta asked.

"Most of the large oases that we just passed so far are fed by rivers from the mountains but not near Karsh. Ours are springs. There are pools and even lakes where underground water comes to the surface or sometimes we dig wells. If you see a lake deep in the desert, it will have springs in its bed to feed it.

"Our *wādīs* (valleys) only run when it rains, here or on the mountains. Only a fool camps in a dry wādī. If it is raining in the far mountains and you don't know. The dry river can go from nothing to a full flood before you have time to wake and move. No one unfamiliar with the desert should travel without a guide and lots of preparation."

By now, Hakeem had thoroughly convinced Jacinta and Elana that the desert held many lethal dangers. They were about to encounter one more of them.

* * *

It was on the third morning after leaving Hamath and Elana woke with a fright. It was cool in the evening, and she and Hakeem were snuggled together, but where was he now?

The wind had picked up alarmingly during the night.

Outside, she heard men shouting urgently, people running and horses screaming. Were they being attacked? Everything was very dark, was something on fire? Her elvish senses couldn't detect smoke but should she get ready to flee?

She tried to poke her head out of the wagon but the flap was tied tight against the wind.

Just as she got her head out a little, she was abruptly shoved back by a Gypsy woman, yelling something at her in their dialect. No need to push so hard, I can take a hint!

She felt the wagon move around and then come to a stop. Then above the wind she heard Hakeem. He was shouting something about the horses as he jogged past.

If they were being attacked, the time for stealth was past and Hakeem would have warned her.

Then Hakeem was outside their wagon, tying extra sheets around it. Now she really was in darkness! Even he was having difficulty, battling hard against the wind which was now blowing a gale. She could hear a sheet was flapping furiously and making loud cracking noises as it flayed back and forwards in the wind.

Hakeem was trying to shout above the din, but what was he saying?

Habub? What on earth was that? Habub? Elana sat puzzling.

She was an elf from the mountains. Then it hit her! Habub, "powerful wind" in Aramaic. Of course, a dust storm; it must be a big one.

Hakeem untied something and pushed his head into the wagon. He let in a shower of choking dust, causing Elana to cough and rub her eyes. It was impossible to see outside. He was wearing his *keffiyeh* (head-scarf) tied across his mouth and nose. Only his eyes showed. He quickly pushed in some dry rations, goat skins of water, and a bucket toilet.

"Sorry meli, I won't be long. Everyone's safe, I've told them not to move about .You can't see anything out there!" with that he was gone. She thought he said, "horses…" as he left.

The great desert windstorms start like powerful thunderstorms full of energy, carrying hot air very high up. As it chills high up, the storm collapses. The little moisture they contain evaporates in the dry air, chilling it more.

So there is only a mighty blast of dry chilled air downwards from high up with no rain. Dust is much finer than sand. The wind sand-blasts across the dry land, charging the fine dust particles with static adding to the cloud of dust streaming into the air.

Dust storms can blow up within a hundred heart beats till you can see nothing around you and they can last days. To wander about in one was simply fatal. You could miss a path by a few feet and never find it. For those unprepared with spare water, or the foolish, they are another of the many lethal tricks the desert plays.

With another shower of dust and a rocking and creaking from the wagon, Hakeem climbed back inside. He carefully packed his dusty robes in a corner and crawled over to give Elana a long passionate kiss. "I think we are about to find out a lot about each other over the next day or two, my love, I hope you will still like me after it's finished," he chuckled.

At last! Elana thought. She had more than one or two questions for her new husband.

But then something else occurred to Hakeem that they might do (other than talking) while they waited. They *were* newlyweds after all.

* * *

They were only four days from Karsh, when something frightening happened.

They had been up before first light, eager to camp at a small oasis near the main road. The road was becoming crowded and their progress had slowed behind a long line of pilgrims and other travellers, most on foot, some on carts loaded with people or goods, all making for Karsh.

Everyone had to pull to the side while a large group of Shantawi horsemen thundered past moving north and kicking up dust as they went. They looked very grim and it took time for them all to pass. There must have been close to a thousand of them.

Hakeem was riding close to the van and Jacinta moved her horse closer to her father. She had strung her bow and was slinging her quiver over her shoulder. "What's happening, father?"

"I don't know meli, but stay very close. They have raised the tribes!"

He glanced anxiously to the covered wagon where Elana was hidden. Whatever caused them to raise the tribes would be very serious. Something like this hadn't happened for over a hundred years.

Should he offer his help? He didn't want to leave Jacinta and Elana and their new friends on the road in danger.

Half a turn of the glass later, they came upon a group of well-armed militia, fifty or so resting by the side of the road. Despite seeming at ease, they were watching everyone with intensity and their hands didn't stray far from their weapons. Hakeem dismounted and led his horse over to talk to them. Jacinta hung back with her cousin Garran and two other young Gypsy men.

Hakeem didn't use his real name but showed he was an officer. The sergeant and his men stood and saluted. As they were chatting, the sergeant was fingering a ram's horn he used for signalling. Then they burst into loud laughter together. Hakeem thanked his new friend and mounted to ride back, his face was split in a wide grin and his eyes twinkling.

"Don't worry," he said as he came closer. "Do you remember those armed groups that were searching for a certain elf princess and the new warlord? Well, someone found out about it here.

"The reaction was just as violent as you can imagine. They have declared a Ǧihād against them!"

Jacinta felt a thrill of fear. 'Ǧihād', means a struggle, to fulfil a holy duty to one's God. It is not necessarily always violent, but often it is.

The Shantawi were certainly not a forgiving race. Someone was hunting their paladin and a royal elf in his care. Their reaction was swift and brutal. They would be hunted down and killed, no matter how long it took now.

"I think Elana can ride with us now," Hakeem said confidently.

If he was disturbed by the fate of the men who had been trying to kill his wife, he hid it well.

* * *

On their last day of travelling, they were now moving very slowly along the converging route, but they still expected to reach Karsh before midday. Elana was now able to ride and had joined Hakeem and Jacinta just behind Garran and a large group of younger men who were in the vanguard.

"Jacinta, are you growing in front of my eyes?" Elana asked, studying her daughter closely.

Jacinta shrugged, *and why do parents love to embarrass their children?* she wondered.

Hakeem studied Jacinta in her Gypsy dresses and boots. Elana was right! It was over a year now. He had really meant to measure her!

"You will make me poor feeding you and clothing you, daughter of mine," Hakeem chuckled, his eyes twinkling with pride.

And if you two keep this up, I will leave you and join my cousin in front!

Just then, one of the men in front topped a rise and yelled out, "Wādī Karsh!"

Jacinta urged her horse forward to join her cousin. Elana followed after her, eager to catch her first glimpse of the city where Hakeem spent his childhood. As Hakeem's horse caught up, Elana flashed him a smile of appreciation.

"Hakeem, it's so beautiful but I have never seen so much date palm!"

Hakeem smiled back with pride.

It was if they were on a high plateau, looking down over the broad meandering wādī below. Elana found it impossible to imagine how the dry river could cut so deeply into this land and how long it would take.

It was easy to see how much was irrigated: it was covered by a wide flood of date palm, startlingly rich and green against the barren dirty yellow that surrounded it.

In the far distance, to the north, her keen eyes could just make out the great walls of Karsh itself.

The Gypsy caravan started to descend to the floor of the oasis. Halfway down the slope was a ridge, and they passed a walled mud village made of rammed earth and mud brick.

Hakeem had told Elana and Jacinta about them, the walled villages called *aghrem* (or *ksor*). The house walls were shared between houses, making it look like a maze inside.

Hakeem warned his 'women' they were, indeed, mazes and not to wander in without a guide. He said they are very good in both the heat and cold of the desert. The people, many of their animals, and all their stores were inside the houses. The outer wall, more than the height of two men, provided defence.

"These people haven't faced serious danger lately, have they?" Elana asked.

"It came very close, but no," Hakeem agreed as their horses followed the winding road down to the village.

Jacinta looked, to puzzle over what her mother could see. She hadn't thought about it at first glance but now she saw there was not even a watchtower and there were no true fortifications.

The defensive wall seemed to be simply the outer wall of the houses, reinforced with mud and straw but not very high. Perhaps the villagers would flee to Karsh if anything serious came this way.

From where they were, they could make out goats, camels, cows and sheep down on the oasis floor and hear the proud crowing of roosters.

The date season had finished, but several villagers were taking advantage of the passing crowds, selling their dates and handicraft and refreshments. One old woman selling dates saw that Elana was interested and offered some to taste.

"Go on," Hakeem encouraged. "You don't have to buy."

The purplish dates were delicious!

"They are very sweet, a thousand blessings from your God upon you," Elana called out in passable Aramaic, much to the woman's delight. Hakeem passed a few coppers and got a small basket woven from palm leaves and filled with dates for all to share.

"Nothings is wasted here," Elana said when she saw it.

Hakeem laughed. "We make rope, crates, roofs, posts, doors, fences, and furniture ... almost anything, from date palm. We don't have a lot of wood so we can't waste whatever we have.

"We call dates 'the fruit of the light'," he explained. "The palm can stand drought but they love hot sun on their heads and water at their feet.

"Our summer sun would bake the soil, so we use date palm or fruit trees to filter the light and plant vegetables underneath. That is why the oasis seems to be all date palm from a distance.

"This is no place for an elf in full summer, I'm afraid."

Elana nodded. She had found it hot enough even this late in the season.

A hen called excitedly for her small fuzzy chickens to see what she had scratched from under some leaves. Elana smiled as she watched the mother.

"It is a very ancient tree," she said, thinking of the date palm.

Elves have great knowledge of living things, especially trees.

"A good palm is greatly prized. We only plant suckers sprouting from a proven tree. We don't plant from seeds," Hakeem said, also watching the hen. "Ownership of date palms or animals are the measure of wealth amongst my people."

As they came closer to the Karsh, Jacinta was able to appreciate the great city and its huge walls that dominated all around, rising 12 meters (40 feet) high. The walls were made of mud brick and rammed earth.

To get rammed earth, a long wooden frame made from two long planks is reinforced with stakes and rope so it cannot be pushed apart. Heavy clay mixed with straw or dried brush is rammed hard inside and then the frame is removed. It is quicker and more solid if you wanted the base for a wall and often topped with mud brick.

The tops of the great walls were crenulated, to give cover for archers on its battlements, and were well endowed with towers, arrow holes, catapults and fortified gates.

Just upstream from Karsh, Jacinta could see where the wādī ran steeply downhill, and the great dam that Hakeem had told her about. It had been built hundreds of years ago, resulting in an artificial lake above Karsh. The dam controlled flooding and provided water pressure, allowing the people of Karsh to make their city so beautiful. There were four huge aqueducts carrying water to the city and its surrounding lands.

Throughout the city (Hakeem had told them) there were fountains, ponds, ornamental trees and gardens. Important esplanades were shaded and cooled in summer by artificial streams burbling on either side. Important citizens had running water inside their homes for bathing, drinking, washing, gardens, decoration and cooling in summer. Jacinta felt she had been inside already from all Hakeem had told her.

Karsh, Hakeem had said, was famous for its bathhouses. So that's why Hakeem loved to bathe so much! Some of these were extremely luxurious with tiles, statues, fountains, luxurious fittings, gardens and even gilt on their taps. If the desert nights were cold, fires were stoked under the floors and under the water channels to give warmth and hot running water.

If it was hot, they were cooled by running water and shade. For a fee, one could literally have almost any service, including hot or warm steamy baths, massages, oil treatments, food, wine, music, a private room, a party for friends or hire a companion for the night.

They were still an hour's journey from the city when the pace slowed to a tedious crawl, sometimes hardly moving at all.

Hakeem glanced idly up at the beautiful and strong city of his childhood, half bored with the delay. Then he paused, suddenly alert, and frowning.

He looked backwards and forwards, quickly scanning the city, the walls, the dam and the crowds. The smile dropped from his face, to be replaced by a puzzled look and finally a look of dawning horror.

His eyes returned, frantic now, looking back and forward to the walls, the aqueducts and the milling crowds. He was muttering under his breath. He shook his head in opened-mouthed disbelief.

He had to be wrong!

"Please say you don't see what I see, Elana. Please tell me my eyes deceive me," he whispered in pain.

"Oh, lover of my heart is it only now you see?" said Elana, distressed. "How is the storage?"

'With all this?" Hakeem said, gesturing helplessly to the crowds thronging the gates. "Not enough. I didn't know there could be so many people in the world, but even if we only get a fifth of this, it is far too many people. Perhaps we can build more storage."

"Look further," Elana replied gloomily. "Even if you pulled the city down and built it again, it's all wrong."

Hakeem nodded, grimly.

"What's the matter?" Jacinta asked, puzzled. "It's all so beautiful."

"Yes it is!" Hakeem replied bleakly. He kicked his horse and pushed his way rudely ahead, careless of others in his way.

"What's wrong with Hakeem?" Jacinta asked. She had never seen Hakeem moody before, and he had been so excited to go home.

"Give him a little time, Jacinta," Elana said. "It's a bit of a shock that's all. Yes Karsh is very beautiful and I'm sure we'll love it. That's the problem. If we face anything serious, we will lose Karsh.

"Hakeem thought of Karsh as a great desert stronghold. That it most definitely is not. Its walls are little more than for decoration."

Jacinta looked back to the city that looked so beautiful, proud and strong, and shuddered.

"Mother, tell me." she whispered in mounting fear.

"Poor Hakeem! He has seen real forts and castles," Elana said in angst. "He will have to explain this to his war council. It will be agony for all who love this place. Karsh has long been protected by the desert and the Shantawi. It has become a victim of its own success.

"Those mud and earth walls are designed to protect against tribesmen with ladders and scaling hooks. Modern siege equipment will flatten them within hours, but even if you could rebuild the walls and properly fortify the approaches to the city, see the lake above the city? What do you think will happen to the city if an enemy destroys the dam, especially if they build something to catch the water around the city? The city will be flooded and will lose all of its clean water, and what will happen to mud walls with water lapping several feet up?

"There must be a thousand ways to breech these defences, but even that is not necessary. There are too many people. Karsh can build great wells and have enough water. Besieged cities always have a flood of refugees first. Even with great stores of food Karsh won't be able to feed them all."

Elana paused, "If a great army makes it through the desert and the horsemen can't stop them, Karsh is best to not even bother closing its gates. Offer no resistance, and let them take what they want. Hope they will be merciful, which is likely. To defend it against a stronger force will only bring death to its defenders and all its citizens."

Jacinta looked back at the great city, this time, shivering with fear. For a moment, it seemed to blur and the sun darken. She had a premonition. Disaster was coming to this strong-looking city of her father.

Karsh was doomed.

It felt frightening even to ride inside knowing this. The happy crowd surrounding them already seemed to be fading, like ghosts of a happy time that had already passed.

"Don't worry," Elana smiled, reading the expression on her face. "Don't forget your father!"

Jacinta let out her breath with a whoosh. She smiled shakily. "We ask a lot of him, don't we?"

A little while later, Hakeem joined them again. He had regained much of his good humour.

He smiled confidently at the two women he loved. "We are a strong race, used to hardship. As it has always been and always will be, anyone who attacks us is in for a nasty surprise, a very nasty surprise!" He smiled grimly.

He would enjoy doing the surprising.

Chapter 26: A Memorable Entrance

Shamir, the *Rav Turai* (Corporal) of the south gate, had just had the worst two weeks of his entire life, and there was no sign of letup. He had hardly slept and hadn't seen his family in ten days.

The election of a Shantawi *Ra'al* (Warlord) only occurred every two decades or more, and it was a greater occasion than anything else in Karsh, even the election of a Grand Abbot (which in truth was a rather sombre affair).

Some who don't understand the Shantawi are baffled by the reverence they have for their warlord. Once he is elected, his title is hardly ever used. It confers unquestioned and absolute powers that many a monarch would envy, yet he rarely exercises any of them.

Despite this, the idea of a warlord is tied to the soul of the Shantawi as a warrior people. It is a sacred promise that, should there be any threat to their people, the Shantawi will rise as one man.

They will be led by the very best, they will fight with cunning and bravery, and they will give their lives, every one of them, if that is what is needed.

Even Shamir, born in the city and not amongst the desert tribes was not immune to the mystique of the Shantawi warlord.

Normally, Shamir would expect a great throng of the Shantawi, well-wishers, the simply curious and those looking for profit: entertainers, sellers, pickpockets and others, all descending on the city.

This was different. Everyone knew this election was a formality. The new Shantawi warlord would be a Shayvist paladin.

Most did not understand what a paladin was, but they knew there had only ever been very few in the history of the Shantawi and the Warlord had never been a paladin.

To add to the excitement, everyone had heard of Hakeem, but no one seemed to know what he looked like. Anyone who might have known was not telling. He was said to be travelling to the city in secret and was hunted by his enemies.

To make it worse for Shamir, some of his men had been taken away to increase the patrols along the roads and of course, Lazars, his sergeant, refused to help him.

He would have loved to see some of the shows, let alone the main ceremony, but it looked like he would see nothing but the south gate.

He had been forced to close the gate for the second time this morning, so that the jam of people beyond the entrance could clear. Everyone was hot and dusty and grumpy, and now there was some tribesman *demanding* to see him. It was probably a *Badawī* (Bedouin) mercenary officer. They always thought they were better than mere guardsmen. Well he would have to wait his turn, just like everyone else.

* * *

The city was full to overcapacity. The guard at the gate was shouting till he was hoarse!

"It doesn't matter who you are or who you think you are. You can't bring your horses or packs into the city. You have to camp outside and well back from the walls. Then you can proceed on foot. Unless you want trouble and to miss the ceremony, follow the direction of the city guards."

Everyone else grumbled loudly, yet turned aside ... everyone, except for Hakeem, that is.

The four travellers Hakeem, Elana, Jacinta and Djordji, the Gypsy King, were waiting under the watchful eye of the guards. It had all started earlier that day, with an argument between Hakeem and his two female companions.

"Look, Hakeem, you are deliberately travelling without any identification. You yourself have said that you lived exclusively in the monastery. No one in the town guard will recognise you." Elana tried.

"Please, father, it's not important." Jacinta added soothingly. "We've come all this way in disguise. Let's not look for trouble; all we have to do is leave our possessions with our Gypsy friends. We can walk in and go to the monastery and find someone that recognises you. We are almost there; all we have to do is keep this up a little further."

"It's ridiculous!" Hakeem shouted angrily. Then he lowered his voice, "it's ridiculous."

Hakeem would rather fight in battle than take part in this public ceremony. He felt irritable and tense, and besides he was so proud of his new wife and she had gone through so much.

She deserved to have a proper entrance to the city of his childhood, and now he found that no one recognised him. Well, we'll see about that!

"Look," he said, "All this fuss is about me, it's a humiliation to have to sneak into the city like a criminal. I will talk to the head guard of the gate and we will ride in, in style."

"Hakeem," said Elana. "I would never have expected you to care about such things. If you want, I can tell you all you will ever need to know about humiliation, but if it's important to you, we'll do it."

Hakeem smiled at her fondly. "It's not just for me, my love! You deserve an entrance that you will *never* forget."

And so, against the girls' better judgement, Hakeem pushed on till he was faced by the harried looking corporal of the gate.

There were so many other people claiming to be Hakeem's good friend, or a relative. There were even a number of unlikely characters claiming to be Hakeem himself.

When Shamir met yet another tribesman who claimed to be Hakeem, he confided that he, Shamir, was secretly the Queen of a well-known mythical land.

At that Elana and Jacinta desperately tried to pull Hakeem away, but he was determined.

It was when Shamir asked him the name of his companions that Hakeem realised all was lost. Elana hissed urgently to Hakeem that he would get them locked up.

He introduced Jacinta. Her name was already known in Karsh to be the name of Hakeem's Gypsy daughter. Shamir eyed the young girl in travel-stained Gypsy clothes and mismatched boots. Hakeem introduced the colourfully dressed King of the Gypsies, Shamir was sure there was no such thing as a 'King of Gypsies'.

Then Hakeem finally and bravely pressed on, and trying not to show any hesitation as he announced Elana, the Princess and heir to the fabulously wealthy Eastern Elves.

Elana took off her Gypsy scarf to show her pixie ears and smiled and nodded hopefully. Hakeem smiled at her fondly, thinking just how beautiful his lady looked and beautiful she was, even in her old Gypsy dress, with her silky hair dyed black and her skin stained.

Unfortunately, the one thing she looked nothing like was an elf princess. At best she could be quarter elf, and most definitely not a princess.

The corporal looked at the big tribesman in concern. Perhaps too much of the desert sun? It could be very dangerous in the heat. Or was he a madman perhaps?

Hakeem flinched. He was ready for a scathing, angry comment or even an order for arrest. Then the corporal looked at him another time, this time with joyous recognition. Hakeem was puzzled. He assumed he must have been recognized somehow.

Shamir shouted excitedly to his men, his friends, workers at nearby stalls and all those stuck in the queue to come and meet the important visitors.

He was thrilled! It was nothing like Hakeem expected. What was happening?

He looked at Djordji who seemed quietly amused. Jacinta and Elana could hardly contain their laughter.

"Hakeem doesn't understand!" Elana managed to choke out, causing her and Jacinta to almost collapse laughing again, hugging on to one another for support.

Hakeem was puzzled, what could be wrong? The corporal was neither angry nor scathing. He seemed delighted.

Hakeem looked blankly at the crowd rapidly gathering not comprehending what Elana meant.

The corporal faced the gathering crowd importantly and spoke in a loud clear loud voice. He seemed to be good at public announcements.

"Citizens of Karsh! Friends and guests, who have travelled to join us on this joyous occasion, I bring to you today a great honour! It is my greatest pleasure to inform you that some important dignitaries have generously agreed to pause on their journey into the city, to give the poor people at the south gate a moment of their busy time."

There was great applause. Shamir is very good! Elana thought.

"I think he's missed his calling," Jacinta whispered, echoing her mother's thought. "At least we're not being arrested. Has Hakeem caught on yet? He'll have a fit when he does."

Hakeem was totally perplexed, perhaps Shamir thought they were here to give some encouragement to the workers, not what he meant to convey, but he didn't mind.

That explains the misunderstanding.

Shamir dramatically paused and his gaze slowly swept his audience. Many started to laugh in anticipation. Like a master of ceremony, he introduced them one at a time: Djordji the King of the Gypsies, who bowed and flashed a toothy smile at the crowd. Jacinta and Elana curtsied and smiled prettily.

At the mention of Jacinta, the famous companion of Hakeem, the audience broke out in cheers and some started to bash their applause on empty wooden crates and hollow palm logs. When he mentioned Elana, Princess of the Eastern Elves the audience erupted in tumult! There was shouting and cheers with lots of 'welcome my Lady!'

Shamir waited for the audience to subside, holding his hand up meaningfully. He tried a couple of times to proceed, but was overcome by his own laughter. "And last, but by no means least we have the greatest warrior of our times. Our great leader ... our one and only , apart of course from a fair number of imitations ... our own, Hakeem!"

Hakeem smiled and waved uncertainly at the audience, but still looked bewildered. Did the corporal believe him, and if so what was happening? If he didn't believe him, what under the sun, did he think they were? He seemed to be very friendly towards them. He didn't seem to be poking fun at them. What was happening?

He looked back on his three colourful 'Gypsy' companions. Jacinta and Elana could see the moment when realisation struck. Oh, no! He was totally appalled! This was not happening! Not this ... Anything but this!

He looked at Shamir in horror! Shamir merely smiled back at Hakeem and nodded encouragingly. It can't be this, Hakeem thought helplessly.

Shamir, since he was small, loved circuses and visiting entertainers and here was the greatest celebration of his life. His lazy sergeant, Lazar, was enjoying himself but Shamir was stuck at the gate. He wouldn't see any of the shows.

Now he couldn't believe his luck! A group of three Gypsy entertainers, one with some elf blood had teamed up with some great wandering fool, and was prepared to put on a show for him and his friends.

He could have wept with gratitude. He was determined to help them as much as he could.

"But you don't understand," Hakeem tried frantically. "I am Hakeem. I *am* the one who is expected!"

"But of course, my Lord!" Shamir replied in mock astonishment and gravity. The audience was really enjoying this farce. The clown pretending to be Hakeem was very good!

Shamir started. "But, Lord Hakeem, where is your famous horse? I hear he is huge and has red eyes and eats flesh!"

Hakeem had an image of Nadeer gently accepting an apple from the children and taking them for rides. "My horse, Nadeer had to go on ahead of me," Hakeem explained.

"Of, course!" Shamir held his hand up, trying to control his own laughter. "Of course! It's not at all unusual for horse and rider to travel separately these days. I hear he's such a smart horse, he probably leads his own war band!"

The din from the audience was incredible. Even Hakeem had to laugh. This corporal was a born showman.

"My lord! You are a big man surely! But I heard the real Hakeem is eight feet tall!"

"Well, I wish he wouldn't eat like the real Hakeem!" Jacinta yelled loudly. "He eats all our profits!"

Hakeem glared at her, Jacinta wasn't helping at all!

Jacinta smiled back and swept her skirt back and forwards gaily, smiling for the crowd. She was a Gypsy and loved an audience.

It went on and on. Many people had fallen to the ground, barely able to move from too much laughing. Each and every one of them were wiping tears of laughter from their eyes.

Elana didn't look like an elf princess! ... Oh, I see she is in disguise, running from her enemies .... so, what is she disguised as? A Gypsy pretending to be an elf princess! That should confuse her enemies, it's certainly got us confused!

Oh, Hakeem didn't travel with his war-band because he has these two girls to protect him. (Elana and Jacinta tried to look like fierce warriors in their multi layered Gypsy dresses).

And your Jacinta is far too pretty, the real one was said to look like a troll. Was it true that she defended a caravanserai from a band of raiders, single-handed?

What was the one about Hakeem wrestling a lion with his bare hands? Yes, tell us that one! Jacinta and Elana begged.

And why did Hakeem seem so ill informed? He said he didn't recognise so many who gave their oaths they knew him well.

Jacinta and Elana went round collecting the coppers and even one or two silvers from the grateful audience. Shamir was encouraging his friends to be generous.

Would they all stop that? Hakeem thought. This was embarrassing, but he found he couldn't be angry. Shamir was a delightful fellow and easily the greatest entertainer any of them had met.

"Well, thank you my friend," Hakeem finished, after the final bow and the audience was reluctantly dispersing. "I don't seem to have convinced you, but I can't remember when I laughed so much. Clearly I was due for another lesson in humility."

Jacinta and Elana were drifting back up after farewelling everyone. They were counting their coins. Hakeem frowned at them. He *really* wished they would stop doing that!

"Well," Elana said, still laughing. "You almost had us thrown into jail, Hakeem, but you promised us an entrance into the city that we would never forget. I'll really never forget this one. I don't know when I've had so much fun! I'll be sorry now I have to get back to being a princess."

Shamir looked a little puzzled, why were they still talking like this? Didn't they know they could stop acting, now?

"Am I really supposed to look like a troll?" enquired Jacinta of no one in particular. "Thank you, Shamir, you were great! I must declare my face is sore from so much laughing."

"No," replied Shamir. "Thank you! You have really made my day. I'm on duty all the time and was missing out on all the excitement inside."

"That's not fair!" Jacinta said sympathetically. "Don't you have a single day off?" Shamir shook his head sadly.

Elana turned to her husband. "Well, you and your family will be our guests!" she announced grandly. Hakeem nodded enthusiastically.

"Are you going to put on many more shows?" Shamir asked.

"Just one," Elana said taking her husband's hand, "and just Hakeem, but it will be a very big one."

"Well, I'll be sorry to miss it, but good luck."

"Ha! Am I still not believed?" Hakeem announced tragically. "I said you would see it! ... Or have you forgotten who I am?"

"Well, we'll see, I guess. Stranger things have happened, I suppose," Shamir laughed. "Just make sure you keep away from the true Hakeem! I hear he's a mean bastard!

"Oh, and Hakeem?"

Hakeem turned.

"I'm sorry. You *still* can't take your horse that way."

Chapter 27: The New Warlord

Shamir was frightened.

This was serious! He was summoned to what was still called the Royal Pavilion. The main ceremony was about to start. Lazar said it was something about insulting some important guests.

He was escorted by two tall monks, was he under arrest? They were very polite but perhaps monks were polite to prisoners.

He wasn't being taken straight to prison. Perhaps he would be denounced first. He went pale with fright, his heart was hammering. He thought desperately about what was to become of his wife and children if he were in jail.

He was being led towards the area reserved for the Grand Abbot's party. The Grand Abbot was the most important man in the city, bar no one.

Had he given offence to one of his guests? He desperately searched his memory but couldn't think of anything. Who could he have offended badly? Who was so important?

"Daddy!" He heard the cry of his small daughter, and his wife shushing her. He couldn't locate them in the sea of faces. He heard a girl's voice cry out clearly, "that's him there!"

The guards were leading him higher, to some important seats. Then he saw Jacinta, waving from some of the best seats, with his second youngest, Chozai on her lap. Chozai was more interested in smearing honey cake everywhere than on saying hello to his father. Jacinta was expertly wiping his face and hands with a damp cloth.

Elana was holding their youngest *Tabatha* (Aramaic for 'gazelle') and chatting pleasantly with his wife Miriam who had their oldest boy on her lap.

Elana had the most exquisite soft loose gown on, it was an elf dress!

"Over here!" Jacinta encouraged. "Can we get you something to eat or drink?"

The two monks bowed politely, and left him to make his own way to his seat. He passed Djordji and a woman who had to be his daughter, who smiled and waved.

It was luxurious seating, with ample large cushions over the wide marble steps. There would have been room to recline, if it weren't for the children.

"Hello Shamir, I'm glad you made it," said Elana, with a smile, as he sat down.

"How?" asked Shamir almost dizzy with relief. He was feeling disorientated to find his entertainer friends amongst the official party. "How did you arrange for me to be relieved, and get these seats?"

"It was quite easy. Hakeem was expected to have more guests so he had seats reserved. No one had to be moved to make room," Elana explained.

"I thought I was in trouble." Shamir said. "Where is Hakeem?"

"Well, really," Jacinta countered. "The ceremony is about to start, silly, where would you expect him to be? Up here with us, do you think? And why think yourself in trouble, we said we would invite you and your family, didn't we?"

"Shamir was wonderful to us when we came to the gate, we'll never forget it," Elana chuckled as she explained it to Miriam.

Many of the nearby guests who had heard the tale laughed loudly, it was priceless! Shamir went crimson. He felt himself shrinking into the ground. He felt dizzy from shame.

"Oh!" was all he could manage.

"We loved it, honestly. We've all been through much worse but that was completely memorable! We love you for it," Elana reassured him, giving Tabatha a hug.

Shamir smiled in shaky relief. He *still* couldn't believe who Elana really was.

"Why don't you introduce me to this Great Lady and her adopted daughter?" Miriam asked her husband, "They only told me they are Jacinta and Elana".

"Yes," said Elana. "Why don't you introduce us? This may help." Elana very carefully moved her loose gown slightly, to reveal a small patch of inhumanly white skin under her arm, to the left of her breast. Under the dye she was pale! Then she showed him the roots of her lovely blond hair growing back, ever so slowly. "I can't remove the dye, I'll try again later."

"Yes introduce us," Jacinta encouraged with a smile, "You should know who we are by now. I'm glad you think I don't look like a troll!"

Shamir stared in shock at the pair, as they smiled innocently back at him. He thought of Hakeem, that he made so much fun of, and groaned in misery.

He had trouble believing he wasn't facing execution, but he seemed to have made some new friends instead. Then he realised what it meant.

He was the first citizen of Karsh who could say he met the great Hakeem, the elf Princess Elana, and their famous daughter Jacinta.

And here he was, with his family, sitting as their honoured guests in the best seats available to watch the event of a lifetime, while Lazar was doing his work for him. A great thrill passed through him.

More than time enough to worry about any possible beheading tomorrow. Hakeem wasn't anything like the legends growing up around him. He didn't seem the type to take offence over a small mistake, or so Shamir hoped.

* * *

They had tested Hakeem over three days. No longer could there be doubt, Hakeem was a paladin. Jacinta was questioned over several hours. The order and the Tribal Sheiks officially endorsed her as a student paladin.

Now the people were waiting in the Great Theatre of Karsh. It was built in the Greek fashion, a huge semi-circle of stone seats, built high into the side of a hill. At the bottom of the theatre was the circular performing-space called the *orchêstra* (from the word meaning 'to dance') it was designed for the Greek chorus to dance and sing and interact with the main players on the stage.

Behind this was the stage itself, with a small front entrance to the theatre at the side of it. The stage was backed by a stone wall where painted cloth could be hung to indicate scenes. It had an alcove where actors could change and any murders could be conducted out of sight of the audience. It was decorated by intricate columns, statues and carvings.

As in all Greek theatres, by some wonder, the acoustics were perfect. Even those high up in the top seats could hear perfectly.

Despite its great size, it was not nearly enough. Those who could get no entrance congregated in thousands on the steep hill behind or clustered as close to the front entrance as they were allowed.

Seats had been arranged on the stage and when Shamir had arrived, a young lady climbed the stairs to the stage and begun playing a *kithara* (a lyre, ancestor of the guitar). What followed was her reciting a beautiful poem to Apollōn in Aramaic accompanied by the exquisitely clear notes of the kithara .

After she left there was a pause, while the Grand Abbot (Abbā Maluch), Abbā Omar, the current *Vichira* (Mayor) of Karsh and other dignitaries filed in and climbed the stairs onto the stage.

Maluch stood and in a loud voice reminded the audience why they were all here. Then he led them in prayer.

Following this, there was a hush of anticipation.

A horn sounded and the Sheikhs of the Ten Tribes trotted their horses one by one into the orchêstra. They were dressed in immaculate white flowing robes and on their heads they wore their tribal kefiyyāt (*plural for head scarves*), held by dyed and woven rope circlets. On their necks and at their waists were badges and chains indicating their clan and status. The audience stood applauding as they turned to sit motionless, in a wide half-circle facing the stage, waiting.

Then there was silence. The audience, the whole city, held its breath.

Hakeem sitting astride Nadeer walked his horse till he could be seen, waiting just outside the entrance. Nadeer pranced slightly, and then stopped. Hakeem was also in white but had a thick purple waistband. He wore his sword and the four small gold sickles of Shayvist mastery, three in fighting, and one for knowledge.

A great gong rang to alert the city. The Sheikhs called as one, "Who goes there?"

Hakeem lent back in his saddle and answered in a mighty voice, "It is I, who would lead you! Do you accept my right?"

In answer the Sheikhs joined in the 'Zaghareet' (loud ululation from the back of throat) the audience surged to their feet and joined in. The noise was deafening.

All the visitors in the audience felt a great thrill pass through them, caught up in pride and emotion. These were the proud fighting people of the desert.

Hakeem drew his sword and nudged Nadeer forward to the centre of the orchéstra. He waited for silence and then Nadeer with his head turned to the side gracefully pranced, turning very slowly as Hakeem solemnly saluted the audience and each of the Sheikhs with his sword.

The hush continued as Nadeer continued to turn slowly till the man and the horse faced the Grand Abbot. Then Hakeem sheathed his sword. Nadeer pranced for an instant as if with impatience, and was still.

A child was heard to cry, "That's him, daddy!"

The Grand Abbot's voice boomed out his challenge, "Who dares come here, to ask for my blessing?"

Hakeem answered in a strong voice, "It is I, the one who has been sent! Do you recognise me and say I'm worthy?"

The Grand Abbot and Omar chanted in unison. "You have been sent to lead us. May Apollōn bless you and all who ride with you!" Omar held up a heavy gold chain and a badge.

Hakeem lightly jumped off Nadeer, and ran up the steps to the stage and then waited head bowed on the last step.

Normally Samit would bestow the chain himself. Omar read loudly the old warlord's proclamation, accepting his replacement.

Don't disappear, old friend, Hakeem thought, just don't disappear.

Father Maluch stepped forward and motioned Hakeem to join him. Then Maluch took a great breath and addressed the audience.

"Great Leaders! Shantawi and people of Karsh! Today we appoint our new warlord. Today also, all Shayvists recognise a new paladin has come amongst us, the first for centuries."

From the stadium, from outside and from up on the slope there was a riot of cheering and celebration.

Then Hakeem bowed and Maluch and Omar fixed the badge of the Paladin on his belt and the gold chain of the Warlord over his head. Over the cheering, the great gong of the city sounded ten times.

There were so many letters wishing Hakeem well that only the main ones were read: from King Helios of Aiol, King Leandros of Troia, and leaders of the other Greek cities, and finally from a certain Elana, princess of the Eastern Elves.

"That's you!" the same little girl in the audience shouted excitedly to the lady who was holding her. "Yes it is!" Hakeem called loudly back, which caused a ripple of laughter.

Then Hakeem was hugged and congratulated by the various leaders and dignitaries. He trotted down and lightly sprung back on Nadeer and then turned to face the audience and held up his hand, waiting for silence.

"Friends, great people of Karsh, Sheikhs and people of the ten tribes. Today, by God's grace I have been given a great honour, to serve you the Shantawi and people of Karsh as your

Ra'al and the 'Emīr of our mercenaries . I am also called by our God to serve as his paladin."

He paused and his voice became grim.

"We have not had a paladin for hundreds of years, not since the early days of our faith." Hakeem paused and scanned the audience slowly, so it seemed he talked to all.

"Each paladin is set a great task. My task will involve you as well, my people, because you are the chosen of Apollōn.

"Our task will be the greatest challenge that has been ever faced in the history of Karsh, in the history of our faith and in the history of the Shantawi." The audience was hushed for a moment and a then a murmur started and began growing.

Hakeem held up his hand and waited for quiet.

"Not today, but a great war is coming to us!"

He took a deep breath and raised his voice to a shout.

"It is then, my people, we will be asked to praise our God; not in his temples with our prayers, but in the defence of all we hold sacred with the strength of our arms, our horses, and our bows!"

Any other audience would be in turmoil but there was only a buzz, most simply waited silently to hear what was said.

"But," Hakeem continued, "we will not be without friends. Many in Anatolē will join with us. From the Greek cities of Anatolē to the West to Sardeis, I will be concluding alliances where I may.

"I have concluded a treaty with the Romani. Long have we been on good terms with our wandering friends. Now we will aid them where they suffer persecution and they will aid us in our trouble." Djordji and his family stood and took a bow, to great applause.

"I also announce an alliance between the Shantawi and the Eastern Elves."

There was loud murmuring at this. This was a great alliance! The elves and the Shantawi were on good terms, but the elves never made alliances with humans.

But if there was an alliance that would involve the Shantawi, all Anatolē and the elves, what were they going to face?

Hakeem had to raise his hand for silence.

"Princess Elana of the Eastern Eves and I have travelled here in disguise, a disguise she still bears. Many have been trying to kill her to stop us combining our strengths. As we speak, those men are being taught what it means to act against the Shantawi and the people of Karsh." There was loud laughter and mighty cheering at this.

"Princess Elana has done me the honour of becoming my wife."

Elana stood and the audience erupted in wild shouting and cheering. The elf princess, the future Queen of the Elves, marrying a Shantawi. They were the fighting desert people; a coming war didn't frighten them if they had such great friends.

"This will start now!" Hakeem shouted. "I am your Ra'al . I will invoke my powers this very day!" People were talking in fear and excitement; women were gathering their children closer to them. Hakeem had to wait, his hand raised.

"I call on you now to build your strength!

"In the time we have, let us grow our crops and multiply our herds. Look to your neighbours! By my sacred charge I do not ask this of you. I *demand* you, all of you, to put all arguments aside! Let not *one* widow or one orphan or anyone in poverty go hungry or suffer. Let not the old, the crippled the blind or the frail go in want. Find them reasonable tasks within their strength, as is our law.

"The time will come when individual strength will not be enough. We must stand together or we will fall. We will need even that little strength that the weak can give us. In what is to come, we will endure because ever we stand as one.

"From this time forward I name each and every one of you, from the greatest to the least, my warriors. In this time of preparation those who mill grain, sew cloth, tend fields will be my warriors, as much as any who practice with the bow and horse.

"Look now to your families; they are our wealth, greater than any gold. The mothers of our children are a strength greater than our strongest walls."

Hakeem took a deep breath and his voice echoed over the theatre and the hills.

"No matter how dark things may seem, maintain your faith. No matter how it seems, I will not fail you. When the time comes we will, as always, prove to be a strong and valiant people. In the end, we *will* prevail."

A mighty cheer went up that went on and on. People were standing and stomping and clapping. Such a speech may quell another audience, but these were the fighting people of the desert.

Hakeem sat his horse, his eyes glistening with pride and love. "Thank you, my people."

He turned Nadeer with quiet dignity and led the Sheikhs from the theatre.

For the moment, it was enough.

The audience was buzzing with excitement and restless energy. Fortunately, what followed were prayers and hymns to soothe and calm the audience after such a grim speech.

Chapter 28: An Elf in a Hurry

It was only a fortnight after the inauguration when Elana heard that her Uncle Hector was in the Palace.

She couldn't wait. She ran, squealing with excitement, all the way to where he waited.

Jacinta and Hakeem were hard put to keep up. Hector only had time to shout out a greeting before she threw herself into his arms, heedless of any around. He hugged the young elf princess, who had dissolved in tears.

"Hector, at last we meet!" Hectors arms were full of elf princess, so Hakeem strode around and simply clasped Hector's right hand between two large hands.

Hector was overwhelmed and his heart leapt. Usually known for his eloquence, all he was able to say at first was "Oh Elana!" over and over, kissing her hair.

She had dyed it black!

They had been told she was dead. Then came news of a vast hunt for her. It was thought she was trying to reach Karsh in disguise. He had come here hoping for news. So many were hunting her that he had no real hope that his niece would reach here alive.

No elves had travelled into these exotic lands before, and he was unsure of his welcome, but when he and his escort arrived at the city gate, travellers quickly made way for them. People were shouting excitedly, "A group of elves has come!"

There was a riot of citizens trying to catch a glimpse of them and shout out well wishes. The soldiers sprang to attention and bowed before them, greeting them with something like awe.

When he mentioned the name 'Hector', the effect was dramatic. The streets were cleared by soldiers shouting his name and the weary elves were hastened, somewhat bemused to the Palace. When he was told that the princess was in the Qaṣba itself, Hector could hardly hope it really was Elana.

He left his main escort of twelve men to be looked after by the Mayor of Karsh no less, and ran himself with only two of his bodyguards and an escort from the city guard trying to keep up. And now he had found her!

"Great Mother!" he managed eventually, "It's so good to see you. We thought you dead." The old warrior had tears in his eyes.

"Oh, Hector! You don't know what it's like to see you after all this time. You must meet my family!" said Elana excitedly.

She turned so she had him clutched tightly arm in arm, refusing to let go. She felt like laughing, hugging him and jumping up and down on the spot all at once! All of a sudden, despite everything, she realised how much she was missing home and Seléne. With a shock, she couldn't even find the anger toward her father, though she didn't know *how* she felt about him yet.

Family? Hector thought. He had heard Elana was under the great warlord's protection. Was this large man one of his senior men or was he the Warlord himself? And that Gypsy girl? Elana had said "family," but he was given no chance to ask anything.

"Hector, oh I'm so happy! Please meet my husband, Hakeem, and my daughter, Jacinta. We adopted her. Well, Hakeem has adopted her twice! Oh there is so much to tell." Elana was talking breathlessly.

Much indeed, thought Hector. Elana believed that she had married and adopted a daughter, but it was without approval of her father or the Elvish Court, and both of them humans. This was a great shock now, with their kingdom on the brink of civil war.

But the Warlord himself! She could certainly do worse! Amongst humans there couldn't be many who were greater, and think of the alliance! But many elves would not stand for it.

He didn't need this complication just now, but his heart melted for the sad elven princess that he loved so much. He had never seen her so happy, and so in love! And who is this pretty Gypsy girl? And since when had Elana become so physically strong?

Just then, Hector made his decision. He was with Elana, whom he loved no matter what. He would support her against all, even to his death if needed. Even, if need be, against his Lord and brother. Somehow it seemed long overdue. Elana and Seléne would always hold his heart.

He pushed her back a little and fell to one knee. Elana shouted, "Hector, don't you dare! Stop that, this instant!"

But he ignored it with a smile, drew his sword and presented it hilt forward. "My Lady," his voice rang out clearly. "You will become my Queen. I, this day, swear allegiance to you before all others. I will hold none before you, I will serve and protect you until my death. Let all here, and the Great Earth Mother, bear witness that I am so bound!"

His personal bodyguards, two elven warriors, hurried up with a clatter of armour and fell to their knees before repeating the same oath. Elana had tears in her eyes. He couldn't be doing this.

The meaning was clear, he was swearing allegiance to her above his allegiance to his half-brother. For her to accept this would be treason. She had no idea why Hector would do such a thing, but she didn't ask. This was her beloved uncle, the greatest elvish general for centuries, perhaps the greatest of all time.

It might be treason, but without hesitation her voice rang out. "And I, Elana, princess of the elves, accept your pledge and those of your men here. I will give love for love, loyalty for loyalty, honour for honour. May the Great Mother and all here see that I am so bound!"

Oh, Uncle, what have you done? I hope you know what you are doing.

Hakeem and Jacinta as well did not miss the significance of what had transpired. Hector had sworn a sovereign oath to Elana, but she was only the heir, not yet Queen.

Did this mean war, elf against elf? Hakeem had only just become the Warlord. Must he now lead the tribesmen against the invulnerable fortress of the elves? Last time that happened the tribesmen had been virtually wiped out. Well, perhaps he would become the most famous, but possibly the shortest-reigning warlord.

One part of Hakeem's mind, as always, was racing through possible strategies; the other part was in shock. He wanted Hector's explanation, preferably immediately.

As the host, he spoke formally.

"So, uncle of Elana and hence my uncle, if you permit, please feel welcome in my house, Lord. Anything I have is yours. Can we withdraw to talk and have some food and drink? Please do not be offended that our daughter Jacinta will be included. The reasons will be made clear. There is much to discuss and I see you have much to tell us.

"You must refresh yourself first, as you have been travelling hard. Do you need rest?"

Hector bowed formally. "My great Lord of the Desert Tribes, I am honoured to meet you. I apologise for any rudeness. You see I thought Elana dead, and that had broken my heart. Now I am overjoyed.

"As you guessed, there is much to talk about and some news that burdens my heart greatly. I will rest and refresh myself later if someone could attend to my men. We are all very hungry, as we came in great haste.

"As to you calling me either uncle or Hector, I would be proud to have this from one such as you." Hector laughed a little self-consciously.

Such fair speech from an elf to a human! So this is Elana's beloved Hector. Hakeem had studied all his campaigns and longed to discuss them with him as soon as there was a chance.

He smiled. He knew that Elana's uncle and he would become fast friends. But rebellion? What had he and Elana done?

Hector's heart was heavy. The last thing he expected to be able to do was laugh. But first he chuckled and then he laughed out loud and it did his heart good.

Hector dreaded starting, and insisted that Elana tell her story first. He marvelled at what she had gone through since he had last seen her. She was not the same unhappy elf closeted in the court. She had lived in a world of experience: humiliation, terror, anguish.

She had found love, and more, where she had least expected it. She would be a queen that very few could match in understanding. She would be, as the common elves had already started to call her, "the people's princess".

She was excitedly describing some of her adventures, with the enthusiastic help of Jacinta. For the benefit of her weary guest, she focused on what was amusing. She didn't detail the death of Djorn, she skirted around many facts, and even made some dangerous parts sound amusing. One of her favourites seemed to be the leaky barn, when it started to rain heavily in the cold of the night. Imagine, she said, the others snoring snugly in dry comfort crowded in with the horses. And her, drenched to the skin, trying to push a reluctant cow out to give up its dry spot for her.

This was not the Elana he had seen before, and with a twinge, he was reminded of Seléne and *her* amusing tales. It was as if all the hurt, all the cares of many years, had fallen away from Elana. She was blooming with confidence and love, yet her eyes held a wisdom born of all that pain.

And Jacinta! He was thoroughly charmed by this bright and gorgeous young girl. It was obvious the two were as thick as thieves, more like fast friends than mother and daughter.

Hakeem was more reserved. He took their teasing in good humour, and looked at the pair with such pride and love that it warmed Hector's heart. He knew that this was indeed Elana's family, and he would not let anything on heaven or earth rob her of this.

Now, he was hearing something astounding, and it shook him to his very soul. "Did you not think of this when you agreed to adopt her?"

"No! And that's the thing! Jacinta was already the daughter of my heart, and she was the daughter of the man I love." Elana gave a look of pure love to the pair who were busy eating. "We didn't realise, till we had agreed. When we found out, we almost fainted ... I did faint!"

"I only found out about this filthy barbarian *after* I had agreed to marry him." She gave Hakeem a well-aimed kick under the table; he almost dropped his chicken leg. Hakeem gave Hector a self-conscious smile as he massaged his ankle.

"Oh, that he was to be the Warlord?" Hector replied. "How on earth could that be a secret?"

"How, indeed!" said Elana with some of her residual outrage. Hakeem carefully moved his feet away from hers. "But it gets worse."

After she had finished, Hector sat with his mouth literally dropped open. How was this possible? Hector had always taken it as a given truth that the other two who had been prophesised would be elves.

What a shock! If he didn't know Elana better ... Hector knew about paladins and knew Hakeem would not be lying.

It had to be true. The three of Prophecy were to be sent by the Great Goddess. And it matched: the Shantawi believed their paladins were sent by their God and it included this delightful young girl!

"People, even your allies, will think this is contrived," he cautioned. "They will say you have picked up a barbarian and a Gypsy stray from the streets." Hector was aghast at what he had just said, but it was out before he could stop it. He was too tired and too worn.

But Hakeem just looked amused, and the girls just laughed gleefully at the prospect.

"Of course they will! That's the very point, don't you see?" Elana exclaimed. She didn't seem to know how much trouble this could cause. Wait, Hector thought, never underestimate Elana. There were some who had, and they had come to regret it. She couldn't really be relishing the possible reaction he had just described, could she? But she was.

Of course, he reminded himself, still trying to come to terms with it all. If she was right … no, if she was the one foretold, she would be right in this matter. Whatever happened was destined to occur in the way it did! Well, some stuffy elves would certainly have their noses rubbed in their prejudices!

It was then that Elana asked him his news. The smile dropped from his face and he was silent a moment, dreading telling the news. Elana went pale and waited in anguish, all laughter forgotten. "It's not … not my father? He's not dead is he?" She sounded like a lost and frightened child.

Jacinta moved over and climbed into Elana's lap. She pressed her head against Elana's chest and put her arms around her mother's neck. Hakeem took Elana's hand and clutched it with both hands, bracing himself and her as they looked at Hector and waited.

Hector proceeded in a rush to get the main facts out.

"My Lady, I don't know. I left Elgard many weeks ago, we were told Cyron was gravely ill and dying, but no one is given access to him. It's a strange illness that seems to go on and on. Xanthe has assumed control as Regent and Nikan has returned from exile!

"They are replacing the palace guard with those loyal to them. I think Cyron's a prisoner but they'll keep him alive until they have a firm grip on power."

Elana looked pale and tears were in her eyes, "Seléne, tell me is she alright!"

"Elana, I don't know. You know she will oppose them, and Nikan would love to get his hands on his baby sister. I hope Xanthe will be able to protect her.

"But Lady, Nikan may have found out you are alive. If he has, it will force his hand. Cyron and Seléne will be in great danger."

"What help can I expect?" Elana asked, her face grim.

"My Lady, against Nikan the whole people will rise up as one, but he holds the palace, our King and Seléne hostage. If people think you fight against your father, or if Nikan spreads a lie that you are dead, it would be terrible. We will have elf against elf, father against son, brother against brother. There will be such destruction that I doubt the kingdom will ever recover."

Elana was frightened. She looked to Hakeem in shock, but Hakeem had a smile that conveyed no humour. "If you permit, Uncle, I may have some ideas," he said very softly.

Hakeem looked intensely at his wife's uncle.

"Hector, they don't fully suspect you are working against them yet. Send a message back that the Elana here is an imposter. It's some strange plot of the new warlord. That will be easy enough.

"That will make Nikan feel safe, but off balance, turning his eyes away from his enemies amongst the elves. He will be looking towards Karsh and wondering.

"I doubt Xanthe, from all I have heard, is clever enough to be behind what's happening. She is being controlled by Nikan.

"Now here is what I would suggest might work …"

* * *

Hector looked at Hakeem in astonishment. He had only just heard the problem and he already had the beginnings of a plan! There was danger, of course. They would have to move very quickly, but this was brilliant! He is legendary as a fighter but he also thinks strategy as easily as he breathes.

"So we really need to get to Cyron and Seléne and protect them somehow. Only then are we free to act," Hector finished, Hakeem nodded.

Elana was pouring some of the best wine. She had honoured Hector by serving him herself.

"But we need Omar!" Elana said looking at Hakeem. "He left a few days ago."

Hakeem looked puzzled. "He's an old man, though still strong. He's a monk and prefers peace. Besides, it would be hard to get him anywhere he can be of use."

"But if my father is still alive and sick, or if Seléne is injured, we may need Omar to heal them. We can't do that without him."

"No," Jacinta coughed, trying unsuccessfully to keep a straight face. "How could we heal them without Omar?" She gave Hakeem an innocent smile.

Elana flashed a look of intense suspicion at her husband. Then her face registered shock and her mouth opened in an 'O'. Hakeem was stuttering incoherently, and going crimson under his tan.

Elana stalked closer to Hakeem, jug in hand while she thought it through.

She had thought it was Hakeem that helped her at first, but everyone seemed to think it was Omar. She assumed what she remembered was a lovely fever dream.

And his leg! Hakeem's leg healed so remarkably.

And Garran! It was all coming back to her. Hakeem was *in* the tent behind her. Omar was outside. She couldn't believe she managed to save him. Of course she couldn't believe it .... because it wasn't *her*!

She had taken the arrow out and sewed the outside of the wound, but she couldn't reach the source of the bleeding. It had stopped and his breathing eased. It seemed impossible. Why didn't she see this at the time?

Hakeem was desperately looking around for a means of escape, but Elana had taken up a position firmly behind his chair. Could he fit between his chair and the table? He twisted round to peer anxiously at her.

She fixed him with a piercing gaze, her eyes flashing. "You lying dog!"

"Elana! Please, I never lied to you," Hakeem begged, frantically trying to squeeze into the narrow space.

"Elana!" She echoed in a nasty tone. "Elana! I never lied to you!

"Of course, you don't lie. You pig! You just don't tell the truth."

* * *

Assassins! The two guards looked up in alarm.

They heard the sound of shouting from the dining room and the unmistakable clash of metal. Then there was a shriek of terror from Hakeem. The stronghold was under attack! What under heaven could make their leader sound so frightened?

They had been playing cards with the elf companions of Hector. All four sprang up, overturning the small table and the cards in their haste. They drew their weapons and burst into the room together, ready for whatever lay beyond.

Ready for anything, anything except perhaps one thing.

There was the greatest warrior of his time, the fearsome Warlord.

He was still sitting at the table, trying to cower away from his furious wife who was standing over him menacingly, ready to strike. His clothes were soaked in red wine, it was dripping from the black ringlets of his hair and beard, and there was a growing pool at his feet

Elana had upended a fruit bowl over him for good measure, and there was a large bunch of grapes on his head he was peering through. There was fruit all around where he sat.

She had also tried to hit him with the wine jug. He had used his goblet to defend himself. Just as well she didn't connect, as the expensive items were dinted beyond repair. No one could have guessed, looking at Elana, that she was so strong, but that is the way of elves, they say!

Elana still held the useless battered wine jug in her hands and was studying the wine dripping off her husband with immense satisfaction. It looked like she briefly considered throwing the jug at him, but then placed it on the table carefully.

It flopped on its side, unable to stand upright.

The four warriors struggled to maintain neutral faces. They hopelessly tried to restrain their amusement. Perhaps he had done something to upset her!

This was such a shock.

It was said the Warlord had married a lady gentle and sweet to all who met her. She was enduringly patient and thoughtful even with servants, there was none of the spoiled petty demands, or careless arrogance expected of an elf or a royal. She had captured the hearts of the fierce people her husband commanded.

But now, it appeared that in the Great Princess of the Elves, their mighty leader had found a worthy and really formidable wife! They didn't know, just then, which of the two was to be most feared by their enemies. The elf princess was currently putting in a very good showing!

Hector and Jacinta could barely stand for laughing.

"I asked you not to do that, Elana." Hakeem managed in an injured tone. "That wine was expensive!"

"Oh, Hakeem, I am *so* sorry!" said Elana, regarding him in mock contrition. Then she grabbed her own goblet. "Oh dear, I missed some!" She slowly and very carefully poured the remainder over his head.

"You have a strange way of showing your gratitude to me, I must say!" Hakeem said, as he tried to bend forward to keep the wine out of his eyes. Seeing his men, he tried to draw himself up. The steady stream of wine from his wife's goblet, a soggy squelching noise and wine going everywhere spoiled any attempt at dignity.

"That was the last of it and you know how much I liked it," he said in a plaintive voice.

"What a pity," Elana smiled at him, with considerable satisfaction. "Here! I'm sure you can still save some!"

She passed him a small cloth. "And don't you dare call Nura to clean this up. ... Coming, Jacinta?"

As the two swept out giggling, Hakeem called, "Elana?"

Elana paused at the door, "Yes, dear?" She asked sweetly.

"It just occurred to me I might take our three guests, and show them those baths nearby, will that be alright?" Hakeem enquired.

"Of course dear, do be back for dinner, though."

"Yes dear ... I somehow thought it might be best to ask you, I'm sure you understand."

"Of course, you can, dear. And, Hakeem?"

"Yes dear?"

"Don't get the impression I'm not grateful, I certainly am. It's just I would really prefer that you tell me these things, that's all." She finished with a sweet smile at him.

"Well," said Hakeem, dabbing at his face and neck with the totally inadequate cloth. "I'll try to remember that in future."

"I can always remind you, if you like," Elana offered, back to being the sweet and helpful wife.

"No I don't really think you will need to do that. I'm beginning to understand how you feel about such things."

"Well, I'm glad we have that sorted out," she said with satisfaction. "Before we leave, is there anything else you want to tell me?"

"Is there?" Hakeem looked fearfully at Jacinta.

Jacinta's face broke out in an expression of pure mischief. "One thing, perhaps," she said, considering.

"And what's that?" Hakeem and Elana demanded in unison. Hakeem was looking panicked again.

"Well you know that meditation we do in the morning?"

"Yes…" said Elana glaring at Hakeem, who had got up and was starting to back away, looking not only thoroughly frightened but miserable, dripping and sticky.

No, Hakeem had *not* told her that he could use it to meet and communicate with his God!

"And you didn't think to show it to me!" Elana rounded on him.

"No, er ... really. It's not like, really it isn't! It's really not really at all that ... really. You really could, really, if I just, really." Hakeem tried.

"And you didn't! I could talk to a God, and you didn't think to mention it? Is it forbidden because I am not a Shayvist?"

Hakeem and Jacinta spoke together "Communicate, not talk."

Hakeem added, "Of course not, anyone is allowed. It's really easy." Then he realised he was digging himself in deeper. "I'll show you as soon as we have time. Jacinta, do not discuss this further!" he finished, with a note of command in his voice.

"Elana! Darling! Can you forgive me? You know I love you more than anything. You know there is a very good reason for this. It's just that I can't think what it is, at the moment."

"Forgive you?" Elana considered, trying to resist a smile "Let me see. Ask me after dinner. Jacinta and I will be removing those tiles I don't like. They are stuck. I suppose you don't mind me using that lovely new sword of yours do you? I think it will be perfect for that. Coming, Jacinta?"

Hakeem was busy mouthing, "Traitor! I'll get you for this!" to his Gypsy daughter, who was spreading her hands, in a helpless shrug and mouthing back "What could I do? I just couldn't resist." She was laughing uncontrollably, along with Hector and the four impromptu witnesses.

Hakeem prayed Elana was joking about his sword.

As the men were cleaning up and finding a robe and towels for Hakeem, Hector turned to Hakeem. "Did she really mean it, Jacinta I mean, about you meeting and talking to your God."

"Communicate! And don't you start. I'm still badly bruised from the last elf attack! Just ask and I'll show you."

Hector laughed, "I must say it's not something that usually occurs to me to ask my host. So there's no problem with me serving the Earth Mother?"

Then it hit Hakeem. Damn that Jacinta! That vixen! She knew!

"It's what you elves do all the time with the Great Earth Mother!"

"Oh you mean that … we do that all the time."

Meanwhile Hakeem was shaking his head from side to side and smiling in admiration. "Yes, she tricked me and she knew she did. She knew!"

He paused for a minute and then laughed. Many people seemed to be in awe of his abilities, but Jacinta seemed to be able to outwit him whenever she wished. He'd have to be much quicker off the mark to keep up with his twelve-year-old daughter, it was lucky he could find anything at all to teach her!

No, he chuckled, he was lucky to have her as a daughter. He would have to get his revenge, somehow of course. It was an awful shame, wasn't it, that Jacinta was *so* ticklish.

"Has your niece always had this problem with anger?" he inquired of Hector.

Hector looked at him, a bit puzzled. "Elana?... Oh, I don't think she was particularly angry." He looked thoughtful and then became very serious. "Believe me; you never, ever want to see her *really* angry."

Hakeem looked chastened and frightened. "That bad, huh?"

"Really, my friend, you have no idea. You just have *no* idea!" Hector shook his head in wonderment at the recollection.

Chapter 29: Seléne, her Torturer, and a Dying King

Seléne felt dead. Deep down inside she was dead.

She lay in listless misery in her cell.

Her sister was dead. Her father was dead or dying. Those of her friends who were not powerful and had not fled would be dead by now.

She didn't know where Hector was, but he couldn't raise an army to storm Elgard for her. Besides, a civil war was the last thing she wanted.

Day merged with night in the dank place. She prayed that she could die, and yet, she breathed in and out. She ate her meagre portion and drank such foul water as they would give her. Her body wouldn't die.

Nikan wanted something from her and he would keep her alive until he got it. Her half-brother wished to break her. It gave him the greatest pleasure to have girls helpless and in his power.

He still had her restrained and naked at times and came to touch her in his loathsome way. She no longer resisted, just lay limply not reacting, but this gave him no pleasure.

He wanted her to struggle, be frightened, or appalled, or at least pretending to be willing out of desperation. Would it really mean better treatment if she just gave him what he wanted? But that was impossible for her. Why she resisted when there was no hope, she couldn't say.

In just two weeks she would be sixteen. There would be no ball in her honour. She would wear no fine dress, and no handsome young men would be waiting to dance with her.

Her mother had warned her to keep away from Nikan, and for a while was able to protect her. But Nikan wouldn't keep away from her.

More than three weeks ago, they came and dragged her, filled with terror, to the dungeon. She hadn't had a bath and was given no blanket since.

Nikan had told her he had hired a torturer. He taunted her with what would be done to her. She should be terrified, but was too sunk into despair to react, and now the loathsome creature had come. He was huge! A great brute of a human, no elf would do such horrible work.

She heard him murmuring to the two guards, asking questions. Then he came into her cell, knelt down and turned her face towards him. He studied her with pitiless eyes.

"I am called Dumaya, are you sick?" he said in surprisingly good Elvish.

"Answer! I *said*, are you sick?" He shouted, his voice was cold.

She was like a specimen to him!

She listlessly shook her head. He placed her back down in a strangely gentle way, which only made her shiver uncontrollably.

Then he leapt up in a rage! He kicked the food bowl hard against the wall. It shattered.

The fat guard, Henron, the one that hurt her, started to protest. In a flash, Dumaya had a knife at his throat. How could one so big move so fast? He backed Henron up against the wall and pressed the knife till Heron was on his toes, with the tip of the knife resting over the pulsation in his neck. Dumaya twisted the knife gently back and forwards with a smile that didn't touch his eyes.

"I don't think Nikan will miss one jail guard. What do *you* think?" he asked softly, as if curious to find the answer. "Or do you think I would mind killing you?"

He caressed Heron's neck with the knife point gently, as if lovingly. Dumaya's eyes were crinkled in pleasure. Then he raised his voice angrily.

"Understand what I say! This Lady is in my care now, and you will do exactly as I tell you!"

The older, fat man was pale and shaking. Within seconds Dumaya had reduced the fat bully to terror.

"You!" He addressed the younger guard, Corin.

Corin had tried to be nicer to her, but could do nothing; he had a wife and mother to protect.

"You are now in charge of her care. This one," he gestured to the thoroughly cowed Henron, "will answer to you." He stared hard at both. "Am I understood?

"Good! Corin, bring your wife and mother to attend to the prisoner. Do you think I care what other tasks they may need to perform? Any who objects, arrest them and bring them to me. I will enjoy … the *discussion*.

"Well, do you have a more important prisoner? No, I thought not.

"I want clean clothes, I want blankets, I want her bathed by your women and no man is to look! I want good food, I want clean water! I want comfortable bedding. There will be no rats, no lice! Do you want to make her sick?" he yelled.

He was clearly tempted to tip over her latrine bucket, which hadn't been emptied for days.

"You!" He pointed in disgust to Henron. "Clean this filth up!

"And I want the keys. Do you have to chain a fifteen year old girl, for the sake of the Mother?

"What's she going to do, do you think? Attack me with her bare hands perhaps? Oh! I may be scratched! Oh!" He finished in a falsetto voice and then laughed at his own joke.

As he started to leave, he turned back. "Oh .... and, Henron." He paused, smiling.

"I look forward to returning and not finding things to my satisfaction. Do you wish to find yourself in that cell over there, with me giving you my personal attention?" He turned and finally swept out.

Suddenly, Seléne felt more alive and awake than she did in weeks! That man was a total monster! She was badly frightened of him. Soon she would face this appalling man.

He wanted her healthy for one reason only. She dreaded what would come next but for the moment, she couldn't help enjoying how he had reduced the big fat bully in just seconds and it sounded like one part of her treatment would be better at least ... a bath, clean clothes and proper food! The thought of a bath and clean clothes sounded like heaven.

* * *

Nikan didn't recognise his two guards, though one of the veterans looked vaguely familiar. There had been a massive influx of new troops in the last few days, recruited from his Duchy and elsewhere. Jason, the recruiting sergeant was doing wonders. This would allow them to take over the palace completely.

His next meeting was going to be with his tiresome mother, Xanthe. He kept her waiting deliberately, before nodding for her to be shown in.

"I want to see Seléne!" Xanthe demanded angrily as she stalked in.

"Dear mother! Surely you know I had to remove Seléne. She was spreading sedition! She threatened both of us! But don't worry. She is still my sister, I am looking after her, really I am. You will see."

Xanthe almost snarled at him, "You promised you wouldn't touch her. If I helped you, you wouldn't hurt Seléne. Take me to see her, now!"

Nikan gave his mother a cold smile, "Or what, mother? You will expose us perhaps? I didn't think so.

"Soon you will have the power you lost because of that bitch, Elana. Or would you rather hang?"

He softened his voice, trying to sound more reasonable.

"Mother, dearest, trust me. I am looking after Seléne. She is no longer in the palace, so I can't take you to her. I can't say where, as she might become a hostage to a rebellion.

"Now, leave me, I have many things to do."

Xanthe looked at him with horrified suspicion but there was nothing she could do. She left without another word.

Xanthe was becoming a problem. He smiled. Time to deal with *mother* soon. Soon, he thought, very soon.

The next meeting was doubly sweet. Belamus had been one of Hector's most trusted men. He was sent from a nearby fortress by Hector, but Belamus was no fool. On arrival he immediately offered his services to Nikan and he was already proving invaluable.

"Great Lord," Belamus bowed. "I have wonderful news. The recruiting is going well. With the peace, we have been able to get some veterans, not the green recruits of before.

"I've stocked the palace with some of the newer men, so you and they can learn who is who, and to keep them away from troops loyal to Cyron. I have put your most trusted troops on the outside walls of the city, to watch the others. I think we are now free to act as we wish within the palace.

"And the warlord? That was pathetic. The man has married a woman who looks no more than quarter elf, and he claims her to be Elana. That may impress some unwashed sheep herders, but the man is laughable!"

Nikan smiled broadly. "Belamus, you will be richly rewarded for your loyalty. Carry on."

* * *

Nikan was greatly pleased that the huge hooded figure of the torturer exuded such menace.

"So, they tell me you're the best."

"Without any doubt, Great lord," the big man murmured.

"Have you had a chance to meet the prisoner?" It was a rhetorical question. In reply the torturer simply smiled and nodded.

"I want her to be grateful for anything," Nikan demanded. "Any small thing I do for her. I want her to be ready to do anything, and I mean absolutely anything, to please me. Do you understand? I don't want her to be too damaged, but I want you to break her spirit."

The torturer laughed, "My Lord, this is a very simple manner. That bumbling fool you had in charge deserves death! I will give her to you broken and compliant very soon, and not in the dirty woeful condition I found her. I will hardly have to touch her. The terror will be enough."

Nikan felt a chill, which only made him feel aroused.

"Please," he said, with a smile of pleasure. "Tell me what you plan for my dear sister."

"Well," the torturer started with relish. "Some believe that torture is a physical process, it is not. It is a psychic process. It involves a battle of wits between the torturer and the prisoner. These, I always win. Sometimes my weapon is terror, sometimes humiliation, sometimes despair … and pain yes, but pain is the most crude of all.

"I am faced with a fifteen year old girl.

"At present she resists. Not because she has hope, but because she has none. I plan to give her full hope, and then to yank it away at the last possible moment. And then I will have her. After that, it will be a simple matter.

"With your permission Lord, I have heard of your problem with the King and your Mother. Belamus tells me the time is right. If you agree, I will pretend I am here to rescue her. I will take her to the chamber in which her father lies poisoned. Xanthe can meet us there.

"Of course there will be no escape.

"You and Belamus and a few trusted guards will be in the next room, so you can see her face when she realises she is trapped again. She will be just in time to see her father breathe his last, and her mother arrested.

"At that point of despair, after she had been most alive with hope, she will be yours simply for a promise to protect her mother. I promise, you will have all you want and Seléne in your bed, perhaps by this evening!"

Nikan laughed, and this evil man laughed with him. So simple. After weeks of frustration. He had considered executing this man later, but now he realised just how useful he could be.

"I suppose you are not too fond of Henron, are you?" Dumaya said with an evil chuckle. "I might have need of him, it will make it more convincing, and besides, I dislike the man."

"You wear a sword." Nikan observed.

"My lord, ever my best work is as an executioner. I consider myself as a bit of a scientist. I would like to see if a royal elf neck is any different to any other."

Nikan smiled, the man was so depraved that he had to be admired.

"Well, keep it handy, then. Perhaps I can supply a use for it very soon."

Dumaya gave a laugh. "I would like that, Lord! I would like that very much. Now, Lord, I understand Belamus was organising a big celebration in honour of you tonight. I guarantee great cause to celebrate."

The torturer bowed and smiled again. It pleased Nikan to dismiss the frightful man with a gesture, who would now go back to attend to Seléne. How much more terrifying it must be to be in his power.

For a time, Nikan found it hard to concentrate. His sister had insulted and frustrated him. He looked forward to her helpless, frightened, and reluctantly doing *all* his bidding. His mind kept turning to pleasurable thoughts about his little sister. The delicious full feeling in his groin grew.

It wouldn't be long now.

The big man was in a good mood as he marched back to the dungeon. He hummed slightly. What would be happening to Seléne and her family would be delightful. What a happy little reunion it would be! It would be in the latter part of the feast, to give time for Nikan to be in a good position and anticipating all the fun.

And now, to work on Seléne. As he came in, he was pleased with what had been done. She was out of the cell and in a larger room for those who had agreed to 'talk'. This would do splendidly! They had washed her, her dark hair was combed and trimmed and tied in a simple pony tail. She was dressed in a simple but neat dress. She was a pretty girl, very attractive, no doubt about it.

"I am pleased," he nodded to the women waiting. "You will make yourselves available to me and the prisoner. You are relieved of all other duties."

He gestured to the old woman. "Bring her one of her cloaks, the night is cold. She won't need her cell for the moment. If anyone protests, let me know immediately. I doubt anyone will. Nikan has told his staff to be wary of me." He smiled and chuckled to himself. "… very wary."

He was carrying a huge heavy leather sack by a strap over his shoulder. It was obviously very heavy: stout leather reinforced with wide metal bands. It clanked when he lowered it carefully into a corner. "No one touch this!" he instructed.

Seléne found she was looking at the sack in terrified fascination. She imagined what this torturer might carry in a sack. With difficulty she averted her gaze.

The food was brought in, and set up on a small table.

"Haven't you got a knife for her? How will she cut her meat … with a spoon?" Dumaya demanded irritably to no one in particular.

He very carefully cleaned one of his knives with water. Holding the blade by some clean cloth he presented it handle first to Seléne with a welcoming smile. Seléne just shuddered, not willing to touch it. It was an exquisitely decorated elf blade, razor sharp.

"My young lady," he smiled coldly at her. "You do well to fear me, but I assure you the blade has touched nothing unwholesome. I have no interest in you becoming sick. And…"

He smiled as she snatched it. "I know what you are thinking, now. That knife is very beautiful, it is long and very sharp! But you see it will do you no good against me. You are welcome to try to use it on me anytime you like. I will try very hard not to hurt you if you do.

"For the moment, all we will do is talk. I want us to get acquainted. Are you comfortable?"

Despite his attempt at conversation, he was getting very little back from Seléne.

She was watching him as a small bird watches a snake. Nonetheless, she started to eat quickly, in case the food was removed in some trick to taunt her.

He picked up a stool and placed it on the other side of the desk, to watch her eat. She flinched, but he didn't attack her, so she kept eating. She was very hungry, and it tasted possibly the best meal of her life.

He sat enjoying watching her eat for a moment, then leaned forward and reached his hand towards her. Quick as a flash, she stabbed down with the knife. He was lightning fast and caught her hand in a painful grip as he removed the knife. She flinched back, but all he did was to laugh and offer her the knife again. Her heart was thundering, and her breath was coming rapidly.

"You're truly fast," he said.

He seemed pleased with her speed. Seléne found this even more frightening. While he had only treated her well so far, everything about him emanated evil purpose: his smile, his apparent kindnesses. The most horrifying thing about him was his supreme confidence. She wouldn't be able to resist him long. Already she was almost petrified with fear to be in his company, and he had done nothing.

"Leave us!" Dumaya commanded of Corin's wife. When she hesitated, Dumaya laughed to her face. "Well, well woman, do you hope to protect her?" He smiled coldly, looking at her speculatively up and down.

"And who do you think will protect you? Leave now!"

The woman fled.

As soon as they were gone he leaned forward urgently. Seléne flinched back as far as she could in the chair. "Seléne, listen to me." He whispered. "Keep very quiet! I have come to rescue you and it will happen tonight. You must trust me; I give you my solemn promise, I won't let anyone hurt you."

Seléne's heart leaped with joy. Now this! He seemed a different person now. Could she trust this terrifying stranger?

"Now," he continued. "I can't tell you much. It's too dangerous. I will tell you some surprising things. You mustn't make a sound when I do." Seléne jumped a little as he came closer and then she tried to relax.

* * *

Nikan saw the entertainers and caterers bustling back and forward. It was going to be a great night, he could hardly wait! The large audience hall was not too far from the royal apartments, where Cyron was being 'helped' by Nikan's physicians. He could watch the feast and its entertainments, and then it would be only have a short distance to enjoy the best part of the evening!

* * *

"Relax!" Seléne thought. "He said, relax!" He had given her a sip of wine but Seléne couldn't sleep! Elana alive! Her father alive! And she would be smuggled in to meet with her family tonight.

* * *

Nikan was really enjoying himself! This was a special night and he was allowing himself to relax for the first time in a long while. He didn't want to drink too much, but a few glasses wouldn't hurt. These Gypsies really know how to put on a great show. Belamus must have hired a whole troop of them. It was juggling, singing, dancing, music, comedy … it went on and on.

* * *

It was Henron's turn to sleep in the cells that night. He wasn't happy when Dumaya returned to the dungeon. He looked at the torturer suspiciously. "You seem to be a little too nice to that girl for my liking. I think you want something *very* special from her. Will you share her with me? If you don't, I will tell our master about you!" He chuckled wickedly.

Dumaya smiled back, "I doubt you will." He moved closer. "Did you like hurting Seléne, Herron? Because I must tell you something that you will find interesting about her."

He held his hands out, empty, in a gesture of peace. He moved forward, giving Heron a conspiratorial smile. When he was close, he struck with lightning speed.

He hit Herron hard on the jaw. The man fell, as if hit by an axe. He was likely dead, but Dumaya bent over him and took the time to strangle him and make sure, smiling and humming to himself as he did. He dragged the body into one of the cells and carefully closed the door.

"Some people, it seems, can't take a hint. Too late now, I suppose!" Dumaya thought, with pretended regret and then he moved to where Seléne was kept imprisoned.

The big man knocked on Seléne's door and whispered urgently to her before he opened it. She was ready and brimming with hope and excitement. He passed her the dagger again, and took her hand. He lugged the sack with a strap over his shoulder very carefully, using his hand to steady it as he lifted it. It was obviously tremendously heavy and clunked a little. What was that for?

Henron was missing. Seléne was too horrified to ask what had happened to him. The big stranger had taken off his cloak, and was dressed like one of the guards, except he was obviously human … it would have to do.

"Now remember, Seléne, the guards are new and won't really know who you are," Dumaya explained carefully. "You go in front, like the noble you are, and I'm your escort following behind. Act confident, don't look frightened or guilty, it's as simple as that. Walk at a normal pace, not too fast, not too slow, can you remember that? Try to look happy.

"Get ready to move fast, if anything goes wrong!"

She was so frightened she could hardly remember what he had said. Dumaya took her arm, and smiled, not unkindly and looked searchingly into her face. "You have been through a lot. Not much longer, I promise! In the meantime … do not forget, you are a *Royal Princess!*"

That somehow did it.

For a big man, carrying a heavy load, he moved like a cat. At every step she was terrified. She expected a shout of discovery at any time. He said try to look relaxed! She tried valiantly to imagine it was a normal walk. She didn't feel she was acting naturally at all. Couldn't everyone around hear the loud hammering of her heart? But none of the servants and guards seemed to notice her, as they bustled back and forward on errands of their own.

The most dangerous part was near the entrance to the great hall, she realised. If someone came out from the feast and recognised her, all was lost. There seemed to be entertainers coming and going everywhere, even guards but no one she knew. Some glanced at her but did not seem to be curious about her.

Her big companion ignored them. He carefully placed the sack, with difficulty, on the ground and casually walked away, not even glancing back. Men came from behind and picked it up.

Then Dumaya and Seléne hurried down the corridor and passed through a large room and finally into another room, beyond which, he said, the King lay. There were no servants, but one of the physicians was there. He looked up in surprise. "You are early. I haven't given him the last dose yet. I can't get him awake enough to swallow."

Seléne rounded on Dumaya with a look of intense suspicion. He smiled and shrugged, self-consciously. "I'll see what I can do," he offered as he walked up to the physician.

Seléne felt like fainting with fright, Dumaya was about to kill her father.

As he got close to the man, he whipped forward, grabbing the man roughly and rammed him hard against the stone wall, his skull making a crunching noise.

He held him up by his throat his hand pressed against the jaw while he snatched for his knife and jerked it hard across the man's neck, almost in one movement. It was all so quick, Seléne barely had time to gasp.

He held the body against the wall firmly keeping the jaw closed till it finally stopped twitching, and then he carefully, almost lovingly lowered it to the ground, smiling in satisfaction.

Then he wiped his hands on the man's clothes. There was a patch of blood on his tunic which he brushed at ineffectually.

Seléne backed away from him in terror. The knife was pointed at him, her eyes were wide, her knuckles white from clutching it so hard.

"You're a monster! You're a murderer!" she hissed trying to keep her voice down.

"Seléne," Dumaya said patiently. "That was one of the men poisoning your father. He was about to kill him. Did you expect me to *kiss* him? He would have raised the alarm and now he can't.

"Just like Henron, I had to kill him ... and so I did.

"What else do you want me to do? Or do you *like* these people? What I did was quick and almost painless. Can you imagine what your father or your uncle Hector would do to them? Now, you must give me a few moments alone with your father."

Seléne poked her nose in the door. "He hardly breathes! He is so pale! He is dying!" She looked at her father in anguish.

"Seléne, we don't have much time," Dumaya said, gently pushing her out. "I *must* say something to your father, and I must say it now. I won't hurt him, I promise you. Just wait outside for a few moments. I will be as quick as I can."

Seléne felt a moment of anguish. Would this man kill her father, but if he wanted to kill her or her father, she could hardly stop him. She only prayed he was telling her the truth. Was it all a trick?

She waited outside her father's room with her fists clenched in an agony of indecision. She didn't think she could stand the anguish of having her hopes raised only to see them dashed now. Well, he wasn't acting like she was his prisoner. On the other hand, maybe he didn't need to.

It seemed ages till he called her in. "I know something of poison. Your father will live, but we came not a moment too soon." He looked very grim. "He's conscious now, but very weak. He has been poisoned for a long time."

She saw his face as he turned to her. While he spoke calmly, his face failed to conceal his fury. Seléne felt a thrill of fear. Perhaps her father had refused this man whatever it was he wanted.

Then she turned to her father. "Father!"

She wanted to shriek and clutch at him and just sob and sob, but there was no time.

"Seléne, trust him!" her father said in a faint voice.

Seléne was puzzled. "Do you know him?"

"Just met..." was all Cyron could say, before he fell deeply asleep.

"How are we going to get him out of here?" Seléne whispered urgently to Dumaya, who had joined her now.

Dumaya smiled. "Leaving was never part of the plan. Now, keep quiet. We will hide until your mother gets here, after which it's time to meet the rest of your family."

She looked at him quizzically, but he just looked smug and motioned her to silence.

* * *

Nikan was excited at the thought of surprising Seléne, Cyron and Xanthe all together. Then they would find out there was nothing they could do against him. Cyron would die of his poison, dear Mother would be imprisoned, and he would finally have Seléne desperate to please him in any way he wished.

He felt the thrill pass through him again and again while he waited with Belamus and four of his most trusted guards. There was the pleasant fullness in his groin and his body was tingling in anticipation.

He and the others had come the long way around. Xanthe had entered, they had given her a few minutes, and now they moved into the room before the King's chamber. In the next room, they could hear excited voices. At a nod to Belamus, they all burst in together.

"My lord!" said his torturer. "As you can see, it is all ready for you."

Xanthe looked shocked. She looked exhausted and had been crying, Seléne was in her arms. They were standing, in front of the King who was unconscious.

"Traitor!" Seléne screamed at Dumaya in impotent rage.

"Oh," said Dumaya with a broad smile and a small bow. "That all depends on your point of view. Seléne, aren't you pleased to see your brother? He is paying me a lot of money to get you into his bed."

Xanthe was hot with rage "Serpent! I should have had you drowned at birth! You are no son of mine, you hateful toad."

"Oh dear! Oh dear," said Dumaya, affecting the manner of a prissy teacher. "That's not very nice at all, is it? But, what's this I see? The King still breathes. Must I do everything myself?"

He looked at Nikan who smiled and nodded. Dumaya turned to advance on the unconscious king. Seléne and Xanthe threw themselves in his path. Dumaya was forced to step back and blood started to drip from his arm.

"That's much better, Seléne. You really are fast." Seléne was shaking in terror and rage, as she kept the bloodied knife pointing at him. "But my dear lady Xanthe, wasn't it *your* idea to poison Cyron?"

Seléne spun to look at her mother in horror.

"Not anymore!" shouted Xanthe angrily. "I deserve death for what I have already done, but I will give my life to stop you. You and that toad you serve."

"Such a touching family scene," Dumaya said. "One is missing, but of course dear Elana is dead." He sighed pretentiously, and shook his head. "You organised that didn't you, Nikan?"

Nikan smiled and nodded. "I was pleased to take care of that bitch."

"Indeed, but who is this, then?" Dumaya said as he turned to look to the door behind.

"Hello brother," Elana said as she walked in behind Dumaya, as if on cue. She was disguised as a Gypsy.

Her voice rang out clearly "Did you really think you could kill me so easily, brother? Did you forget *who* I am? Did you forget all about the Prophecy?"

"Arrest her!" Nikan screamed to his guards. They drew their swords, but they surrounded Nikan instead, disarming him.

In the confusion Seléne lunged at Dumaya again.

"Will you stop doing that Seléne? I already told you that you're fast."

He had succeeded in disarming her, but only after she had managed to stab him a second time. He sidled up and gave Elana a lingering kiss, trying not to get his blood on her. Then he looked across and nodded to Nikan, who was looking stunned.

"Meli, I'll give Seléne her knife back if you make her promise to stop cutting pieces off me."

Seléne threw herself into Elana's arms. She was trembling and sobbing uncontrollably.

"Oh, Seléne! Dear Seléne! Did you really think I wouldn't come for you?" Elana asked gently, her own tears starting. "Didn't you know I would come for you, no matter what or wherever you were? I love you, Seléne I would do anything for you." She was softly stroking and kissing her sister's hair as she hugged her.

"And as for you, Hakeem!" said Elana over her sister's shoulder. "It serves you right, you great big monster! You scared her half to death."

Hakeem looked abashed.

Then it hit Nikan. "You!" he pointed an accusatory finger at Hakeem, as the men were binding his arms. "You are the Warlord! Elana was in disguise all this time!"

"Yes, and you were involved with those trying to kill her," Hakeem reminded him coldly.

He turned to Xanthe, "Did you know anything of that?" Xanthe merely shook her head. She looked completely defeated.

Hakeem turned back to Nikan with a chilling smile. "Well, Nikan, you are about to find out what I do to people who try to kill my wife. I promise you won't like it, you won't like it at all.

"Care to tell me who the others are? No? Well, we will have plenty of time to talk about it later. No matter what you think now, you *will* be cooperative."

Wife? This was news to Seléne and Xanthe. They looked at Hakeem and Elana in astonishment. Seléne recalled in horror how she had attacked her new brother-in-law, injuring him twice, all within a few hours of their very first meeting. All this when he was risking his life to rescue her.

Hakeem passed the dagger back to Seléne. "Seléne, please forgive me. I would never hurt you, and would never let anyone else hurt you, but I had to keep you in the dark for your safety. If anything went wrong in the early part, it could still be Dumaya and his prisoner. We would have had a chance to get away. I couldn't ask you to act that! I also hoped to trick some information out of Nikan, but my act was mainly for your mother." He turned to address Xanthe.

"Xanthe, you are Nikan's mother and have a mother's love for her son. This has led you into appalling folly. You needed to see him for what he is."

He gave Xanthe a look of compassion. "While you hid yourself away from Cyron, you could pretend. You needed to come face to face with the murder and the monster you were unleashing. I wanted to give you one final chance at redemption. I find you are worthy of that chance.

"In the end, you were willing to give your life for Cyron's."

Xanthe held her hands to her face in shock. Much of the burden she had been carrying for such a long while fell away. Tears ran heedless down her cheeks.

She looked at Hakeem in wonder. "Hakeem, you have saved my husband and daughter. You have also saved me, I was at the brink of some waking horror, some damnation that I could not escape from. I will gladly pay with my life to make amends, as I must. At least I have a chance to repent and see a great evil prevented. Thank you!

"Elana, I have caused you great hurt, none of which you deserved. It was for my son, but please know that I go to my death regretting that, more than anything else I have done."

"Oh this is so touching!" snarled Nikan struggling with the guards, "None of you will get out of here alive!"

"Including, your own mother," Hakeem added. "You planned to kill her, because she was getting in your way. Would you save her now?"

Nikan simply laughed.

Just then, a young Gypsy girl strode in confidently, carrying two bows and quivers. She looked at Elana efficiently binding Hakeem's wounds as she laid Elana's weapons close to her. "Father, did you have to fight him? I didn't know there was someone good enough to do that to you."

Hakeem looked embarrassed. "No, it was the girl I was sent to rescue. You can tell she's related to your mother!"

Seléne's head was spinning. This is Elana's daughter? What did it mean for the Prophecy? She looked in surprise at Jacinta, and finally looked gravely at her new brother-in-law. She tiptoed over and reached up and kissed him on the lips. "Thank you, Hakeem for rescuing me. Thank you for everything," she said softly, eyes moist with gratitude.

Hakeem turned crimson under his tan, and looked infinitely pleased.

"Thanks Seléne, did you know you are so much nicer to rescue than your big sister? You may stab a man a few times, sure, but at least you don't swear at him like she did, and rescuing Elana was really hard. This has been easy so far."

Seléne was starting to wonder about her brother-in-law. He had seemed so terrifying, now he seemed, well ...

"My lord," one of the Gypsies burst in carrying a sword he had either smuggled in or taken from Hakeem's supply. "We have a serious problem!"

Hakeem had spoken too soon. Apparently the rescue was going to get very hard, very quickly. Hakeem, Belamus, Elana and Jacinta went hurriedly to the outer room to talk to the Gypsy lookout.

Nikan yelled out in glee after them. "It's not over yet! You can't get out of here!"

Hakeem shook his head. "What is this 'getting out of here'? That was never the plan."

But now he needed to find a way to keep his little group alive.

"It's messy out there, my Lord."

The Gypsies had been able to maintain communications and scout the enemy. That advantage was lost when the fighting had started.

Hector was now in control of the city itself, and easily outnumbered Nikan's followers. The problem was inside the palace. Belamus had positioned the few he could sneak in close to the King, and he hid what men he could amongst the servants. These were supplemented by the Gypsies but they were still outnumbered until Hector and his men could fight their way in.

Whether the rescuers were careless, betrayed or simply unlucky, forty or more of Nikan's men had managed to get into the inner sanctum and were rushing their way. The rest of the rescuers already in the palace were fighting for their lives against uneven odds, and couldn't help.

In the distance, they could hear the sounds of fighting and the clash of weapons. Hector had taken the armoury at least, so no shields and no bowmen.

Hakeem had Elana, Jacinta, four men and a Gypsy scout all up to protect the royals and guard one prisoner ... against forty men.

Hakeem wished he had brought a bow for Seléne. He wondered if she could she use it. He called them all out of Cyron's room to explain the situation. Cyron was deeply asleep, so Hakeem ordered them to leave him alone for the moment.

"Bar that door!" Hakeem shouted.

Not a moment too soon! Nikan's men were carrying a heavy bench to use as a battering ram and immediately started to pound the door. While it was a solid wooden door, it was not reinforced. There were only two doors between them and the seriously ill King.

"We can't keep them out!" Hakeem yelled loudly to the others. "We must negotiate!" He raised his voice higher and shouted, "We have Nikan!"

The noise outside the door stopped. A gruff voice replied, "Let him go!"

Hakeem asked "We have women and children. Will you spare them?"

"Yes, let him go!"

Hakeem looked at Nikan anxiously, "Do you promise them safe passage?"

Nikan looked smug. If he got to his men, he could win. "Of course!" he said, trying to look sincere.

There were howls of protests. Xanthe, Seléne, Belamus and his men were all shouting. Jacinta and Elana stared at Hakeem, frozen in horror.

"Can't you see? We can't hold them! We will all die," Hakeem said, facing Elana. "At least he will let the women and children live."

Elana looked bleakly back at Hakeem. "Do you really have to do this thing?" she said very softly.

"I'm sorry, my love, it has come to this," Hakeem said quietly, he looked miserable, defeated, his shoulders slumped. Elana nodded almost imperceptibly, her face very grim.

Hakeem stood between Nikan and the door, facing Nikan. He had his sword raised to prevent an escape. The others were back against the wall.

Jacinta tiptoed across to Seléne, took her hand and led her back to Elana. Elana rested her bow against a chair and pulled her sister close, then turned her so Seléne was facing her. She bent over and was talking very quietly to her, looking deep into her eyes.

Then Elana straightened up, her voice rang out, "Unbind him! Give him his sword!" she shouted over the protests. "You will obey me! Now! Stand well back from him!" She looked at Nikan. "Tell them!"

Nikan laughed. "Thank you so much, my dear sister. It's been such a pleasure to best you once again. You and your barbarian have lost." Then Nikan shouted to those beyond. "They are letting me go!"

The men inside cleared a table that was hastily pulled against the door and then moved back to the others. Hakeem yelled out in a loud voice. "Stand well back from the door, right against the wall. He's about to head out!"

He turned to Nikan. "Are you ready?" Nikan smiled broadly and gave a mock salute with his sword.

It all happened at once.

Elana grabbed Seléne and pulled her savagely towards her and bent over, smothering her face and covering her ears with her Gypsy dress. Jacinta nocked an arrow and raised it, her body completely relaxed as she had been taught. Nikan looked at Hakeem's implacable expression in sudden horrified understanding and desperately lunged.

Hakeem moved with impossible speed and power. He dodged back in a precise move to induce Nikan into a full extension, his sword blocking Nikan's as he did so.

Hakeem's body moved so quickly it was hard to follow. He rocked down and twisted away in one smooth motion, then instantly rebounded in perfect balance and control. He needed power for what he wanted to do. He deliberately twisted his powerful body as if winding it up. Then he struck like a cobra.

Grunting with the effort and picking up speed and power, he put his full power into the counter. Mir whistled through the air. There was a horrible soggy thump. Blood sprayed everywhere, Nikan's body dropped.

Nikan was known as an excellent swordsman; Hakeem had taken his head in two quick, precise movements.

Hakeem then put his boot on Nikan's head and hacked awkwardly at the remaining tissues, then he lifted the dripping head left-handed and ran to the door. Mir was held out, ready.

He unlatched the door, his left hand slippery with blood, and then booted the door hard open and charged through.

The men were pressed against the far wall when the warlord burst in on them. He was huge, wild and *very* angry. He was covered in dripping blood. His eyes looked crazed, he was snarling; his sword left a bloody trail on the floor underneath. He swung the dripping head like a sling. It flew, striking one of Nikan's men hard. The man fell with a cry and then, to the horror of the rest, the head bounced and rolled across the floor.

The bloody warlord screamed at them. "This is your Nikan! Throw down your weapons now! Or by all the Gods I will kill every one of you!"

He stalked halfway towards them and waited, arms wide, grinning hungrily. His face was changing in front of their eyes. It was as if a daimôn had possessed his body!

He crouched there drooling, mad and laughing. His face was distorted in an inhuman growl. His neck and body was red and bulging with muscle and tendons. He was terrifyingly strong, and he moved with impossible speed! He snarled and howled in evil glee!

Jacinta had run, just behind her father, bringing an arrow to bear. Elana threw Seléne roughly at Xanthe in haste. The girl tripped and would have dashed her head against the wall if Xanthe hadn't caught her.

Before Seléne recovered, Elana had snatched her bow and quiver and was halfway to the door, running hard. For an instant, the others were frozen in shock and then they all charged out, weapons ready and screaming for all to surrender in the King's name.

* * *

From a distance he heard Elana calling, "Hakeem, it's over."

Jacinta was somewhere there as if he heard her from the bottom of a well. "Father, let go of your sword."

He concentrated. It seemed so hard to open his hand. Then he heard the clatter of a weapon.

He was coming back to himself. While the guards were looking after the prisoners, the two women he loved led him back towards the room where Cyron lay.

"Can you bring my sword, Meli? It's not dinted is it?" he said through a haze. "Don't let people see me like this. I need to wash. What will they think of me?" he pleaded, distressed.

Jacinta laughed out loud, "What will they think of you? I think you had better ask the ones who saw you in action. Looking like you do now, you look just the part. Don't worry we'll get you cleaned up. I'm glad you are out of it.

"Berserker! Perhaps this was another small thing you forgot to tell us.

"I heard about the Berserkers but I thought it was just a legend, I never believed it. There were forty of them and they begged us to protect them from you. Does this happen often?"

"Only once before … I think it was because you and Elana were threatened."

"Well," Elana laughed. "I suppose that should make us feel safe, but you had us absolutely terrified as well. Some of the men wet themselves in fear. They were happy to surrender to us."

"Elana, Jacinta, please forgive me!"

"Forgive you! Well, let me see … I think I can!" Elana exclaimed, clutching fondly at her man. "You rescued my sister and father, you killed Nikan, you saved our kingdom, you prevented a civil war, you even did something good but weird to Xanthe!

"I love you so much. I know you don't mean to ... but just don't you dare not tell me these sorts of things again!"

"Speak for yourself, mother!" Jacinta said with a wicked grin. "There's something Hakeem did that I don't think I will ever be able to forgive as long as I live."

"What?" Elana and Hakeem both turned to her, seriously concerned.

Jacinta looked at her father fondly and laughed. "When you said 'he's about to head out!'... that is the worst joke, I've ever heard."

Soon the three were laughing and hugging each other, mindless of the mess. They all needed a bath. Elana reflected how bloodthirsty they had become under Hakeem's influence. The society women of her stepmother's court would not approve of her now, of course, they never really had.

Chapter 30: An Unexpected Return, Apologies, and Monsters

Hakeem took extra time to bathe and wash his hair and scrub each part of himself clean. He was just drying himself when Belamus came to see them in Elana's quarters. Elana very cautiously checked, before letting him in. Her hand was on her bow which was still strung and the quiver in easy reach. Hakeem cautiously peaked from the other room. He had Mir in one hand but was otherwise naked.

"Now there's a strange sight!" commented Belamus conversationally. "Does he do that in battle too?"

"Oh," Hakeem groaned loudly from the other room. "Don't you start on me! I don't think I'll ever live that down. I'll be out in a minute."

"How is he?" Belamus whispered.

"Really, he's just his old self, though he's *so* embarrassed. If he apologises one more time, I'll hit him myself! It was terrifying, like some sort of wild animal, but now I think it's almost sweet. This thing came out because I was in danger with Jacinta."

"Well he would only have got himself killed."

"You're so wrong!" Elana laughed. "They were carrying short swords. He had Mir. No one had a shield. He had them on the back foot.

"Jacinta and I could have easily taken three each, maybe more. Then the others were coming, but I suspect they would only have had what Hakeem and we left for them."

Belamus looked at Elana in amazement, "Forty men! You have got to be joking!"

Elana softly replied. "You haven't seen him fight! I have, and that was without any Berserker thing."

Belamus looked considerably chastened. "Oh," was all he could manage.

"How's Seléne?" Hakeem emerged in a tunic, towelling his hair. He had brought Mir in and propped it up against the wall.

"Surprisingly good, I think she's asleep now. Did you know Jacinta has moved in with her? Jacinta is her self-appointed bodyguard. There are no other young girls in the palace. No one would trust Nikan with their daughter.

"She keeps her bow strung and handy. It's not necessary. Hector and his men must have been over the palace a dozen times. They are so apologetic that they let Nikan get away with this."

"I think today we have forgotten to tell Jacinta just how much we love her," Elana said to Hakeem and they shared a tender smile.

"I certainly hope she has her bow strung!" Hakeem said firmly. "It's how she was trained. She's not to relax her guard too soon. I need to apologise to Seléne," he added.

"Hadn't you done that already, Hakeem, several times?" Elana enquired, carrying her bow and quiver with her as she moved around.

"Yes, well er," Hakeem said, in some confusion.

"Cyron is feeling a bit better already. He's had quite a large helping of broth and some water and he's calling for both of you," Belamus announced.

"You had better take your weapons," he added. "I saw a scullery maid lurking around earlier. I thought she looked suspicious and rather dangerous. She was carrying a large dish of suds!"

* * *

Cyron had been moved to the royal quarters. He was attended by two maids at all times. No one had thought to ban Xanthe, and she was keeping a bedside vigil.

"He is asleep again," Xanthe said, "He was asking for you earlier." She couldn't bring herself to say more. She looked tired and drawn.

Elana looked at her father.

"Oh, Hakeem! He looks so old and sick," she said shaking her head slowly. "I never thought my father would look so old."

Hakeem kept silent. He knew how desperately close Cyron had come to dying. The old King had been drifting into a coma from which he was unlikely to emerge. It was not surprising that he still looked ill. What was surprising was that he hadn't succumbed several weeks ago.

Elana bent over to look down on her father as he slept. She covered her mouth, to stifle a sob. A tear fell to wet her father's face. At that Cyron awoke, his voice was faint and scratchy.

"Elana? Is it really you? Please tell me this isn't a dream."

"Yes father, I have returned," Elana said softly. "Though not in the way anyone expected."

"Oh, Elana! Dear Elana!" The old man said, tears streaming down his cheeks. "They said you were dead. My heart was broken. I couldn't eat, I couldn't sleep. Now that I see your face I can die in peace."

"Not so fast you old fool!" Elana rebuked him, and then bent to kiss him tenderly on his cheek, smiling. "You need my permission to do that, and I certainly don't give it! Not at all! I have need of you, father!"

"Yes, I am an old fool," said Cyron. He relaxed back against the pillow with a contented smile, his tears still coming. "I'm glad, if you need my help. Can you ever forgive me?"

"Well, about that we'll just have to see, won't we?" said Elana, laying her head on his chest and hugging him. She gave him a firm kiss on the cheek. "You have to be on your best behaviour for a change, but first, you must get better."

"Hakeem," Cyron called. "Where is Hakeem?"

"I am here, Great Lord!" Hakeem announced. "But I never gave you my name."

"Hakeem," Cyron said. "You were there with me!

"You are the one foretold, of dark complexion but filled with great love. I am honoured to meet you. To think it has come. It has really come, and in my lifetime!

"And Jacinta, she is the third, is she not? Where is she?"

"Great King!" Hakeem was overcome. He fell to his knees, by the side of the bed. "You give me too much honour. It is I who is honoured to appear before the great King of the Eastern Elves, and the father of Elana and Seléne. As to Jacinta, she guards Seléne who has had a bad time, some of which I added to."

At the last remark, Cyron smiled. "I see you already love Seléne. Hakeem you are such a good man. You and Elana have my blessings on your marriage, let none say different! To have all three here … and two are human. Well, this will do some stuffy elves a great deal of good."

Cyron would need lots of sleep. Any food he ate would be tested till he recovered. They planned to find his old servants and healers whom Xanthe had dismissed.

"What will you do with Xanthe?" Hakeem asked as they walked back.

"You think I should pardon her, don't you?" Elana asked.

"My Lady, do you ask for advice, or what I might do were it my decision?" Hakeem asked. "If you ask me to judge your decision, I cannot. I am not you, nor am I in your position."

"I have already talked to Jacinta." Elana said with a small smile, "She told me what I have to do. Xanthe has plotted against the life of the King. The law is clear. Her life is forfeit, and she will be hanged!"

Hakeem nodded solemnly. "I will go to this, when will this be?"

"Well, that's the problem as Jacinta explained to me. You see, I have to set the date. Well, I am likely to be too busy to get around to it, at least for the next few years. In the meantime, she will live in exile on her estates. I will see she is well looked after. That is of course until the day ... damn! What was it I was supposed to do?"

Hakeem threw his head back and laughed and laughed, hugging Elana to him.

"Jacinta, Jacinta!" was all he could say.

Trust Jacinta to find a solution.

* * *

It took a few days to convince Hakeem to stop apologising. It was when Hakeem and Elana were visiting Seléne in her room. She was waiting with Jacinta who was her constant companion.

"Oh, Seléne!" Hakeem said as he walked in. "I hope you're better, you look better. You know how sorry I am for what happened."

Seléne looked at him in frustration. To everyone but Hakeem, it was obvious she had developed a slight crush on her new brother-in-law.

"Stop apologising! You come to visit; you say 'please forgive me!'" She said mimicking Hakeem's deep voice.

"I see you in the hall: 'please forgive me'. Everywhere I go 'please forgive me' What do I have to forgive? You have rescued me and my family, you wonderful idiot! No more 'please forgive me' or I'll hit you.

"You faced a hundred men with nothing but a chicken bone."

"Don't forget, as naked as the day he was born." Elana added, laughing. The three girls were in hysterics.

Hakeem gave a shy smile, "I'm sorr.....I mean, I ....thanks, Seléne that really means a lot to me. I'll try. I do feel a little embarrassed."

"Do you?" Jacinta enquired, seeming surprised. "We hadn't noticed! But 'Dumaya'?... Why is that name familiar?"

Jacinta looked thoughtful.

"Well, er. It's Aramaic for the... er ... angel of death ... I really think 'Dumaya' was one of my better creations, don't you think?" Hakeem finished brightly, and smiled hopefully at the three 'women'.

"Angel of death? Angel of death! That's a bit fancy for you isn't it, father?" Jacinta replied in mock astonishment. "Isn't the Paladin, the mighty Warlord, the scourge of the desert and the greatest fighter ever born enough for you? Angel of death, indeed!" This set the three girls again to laughing, and got a gentle chuckle from Hakeem.

* * *

Elana had joined Seléne in her room to chat, and catch up with the latest events. It was now two weeks since the rescue. The priestess had confirmed that Elana, Hakeem and Jacinta were indeed the three mentioned in Prophecy. The marriage of Elana to Hakeem and her adoption of Jacinta was confirmed by royal proclamation.

Xanthe had officially abdicated, and Elana was announced as the new Queen. It was an exceptionally low-key event for an elvish succession! A grand ceremony was planned for when Cyron was sufficiently recovered.

As Hakeem guessed, Cyron was recovering quickly. He would soon be well enough to travel to his country estate, where he wanted to recuperate. Seléne, Hector and Belamus would accompany him, so Elana would be left in charge in Elgard.

"At least it makes Hector's oath to me legal," Elana was saying. "As Queen I'm allowed a small number sworn to me above all others, and then I swear loyalty to Father. I really wish Father wasn't going, though.

"He is too weak to help, but at least I can ask his advice, and borrow his authority. Once he goes, I have to deal with the court myself.

"Many don't accept that the other two prophesised are human. They see it as an insult. It will be me that has to face the backlash and frankly I'm scared of it. I have to get the elves to see humans and elves as equals. How can I ever do that?

"Father thinks he's doing me a favour by getting out of my way! I don't need the old fool's favours, I need him. And you and Hector are going, you traitors. I *know* ... Father really needs both of you." She sighed.

"Father is recovering so rapidly," Seléne smiled. "We'll be back within a moon and you're *so* wrong about not being popular. Even before you left you were popular and now the story of your flight from assassins and return to rescue me and father is exactly the sort of tale that delights elves, you must know that. They are writing stories and songs about it already.

"That you returned with two humans instead of two elves was a shock, even to me. But Hakeem and Jacinta! None could be better! Give people time, your remaining enemies are very much in a minority, believe me."

"I hope you're right," Elana said pensively. "I didn't want to be a princess then, and I certainly don't want to be a queen now. Did you know that I wished I never had to return?

"All I really wanted was be Hakeem's wife and give him children and never see this place again. I had so much pain and unhappiness here. The further away I got from this place the happier I became.

"Then I heard you and father were in danger. I was so frightened! Hector didn't know what to do. I know Hakeem would ride to his death unconcerned, but he seemed so sure of himself. He actually seemed to be looking forward to it, bless him.

"Everything seemed so complicated and difficult but Hakeem just asked his questions and made it seem simple. Hector idealises him and you know Hector's reputation.

"He knew the only way to guarantee your safety was to have us all together and have Nikan and, if need be, Xanthe, captive. He can be lightning fast and accurate in his thinking in a battle. He says it just seems obvious to him. It's in contrast to his thinking about relationships." Elana smiled fondly. "Nikan was a dead man as soon as Hakeem found out what he was doing."

"Thank you for sparing me from seeing what happened to Nikan," Seléne continued to her sister. "I really thought for a moment you planned to smother me, so Nikan couldn't get me again, then you tried to dash my brains against a wall! Luckily mother caught me. You don't know how strong you have become."

Elana laughed. "I really had to move quickly, to cover those men. I wasn't trying to kill you. I was trying to rescue you."

Seléne laughed. "Well try to remember that next time, dear sister!

"I don't know why I thought Hakeem would ever let Nikan go. It seems ridiculous now. Why would he let Nikan go and join his men? But it was all happening so fast, and Hakeem made it seem inevitable. How did you and Jacinta know?"

Elana thought for a moment. "It just seemed obvious. Perhaps because we know Hakeem so well, but more likely, we are starting to think like him. Jacinta went to fetch you to me, without being told. She knew exactly what was going to happen.

"Hakeem and I may have *seemed* to be discussing releasing Nikan, but we were really talking of the need to execute him on the spot. Hakeem wanted to shock those men into surrender. Cutting off Nikan's head and throwing it at them was part of his plan as soon as he heard they were coming.

"He didn't want all those men to die just because they were loyal. That's how he thinks. He says once he killed Nikan, those men were definitely going to surrender and he had Xanthe, if need be, so having to fight them was most unlikely."

"You could have fooled me," Seléne said. "I thought he was ready to attack those men with his bare hands if necessary." She shuddered at the memory.

Elana nodded, "Well, not with his bare hands. Sometimes you have to kill to defend those you love, even if those you kill aren't bad people. That is the evil of war, Hakeem says. He can't recall anything beyond starting the counter to Nikan's lunge, so we'll never know for sure. Apparently that's an effect of the Berserker rage."

"So he would have killed my mother too, if he thought he had to? If she was a danger and there was no other way. Even though she was unarmed?" Seléne shivered.

"With shocking abruptness," Elana nodded. "He doesn't kill innocents and only kills when there is no other way but Xanthe could hardly be seen as an innocent, whether she carried a weapon or not. If she was a danger to us and there was no other way, she would be dead already.

"I know it makes him sound like a cold monster. I have come to the same attitude, so I guess I'm a monster too, and your darling Gypsy friend, Jacinta, is another cruel monster.

"Try to understand it from their point of view, and it's my view too. People don't die. They are simply reborn into the next life. If you *truly* believe this, you do not fear death."

"Oh, my dear sister!" Seléne complained. "You're giving me a headache!"

"I know," Elana chuckled. "Hakeem loves to talk about tactics and philosophy. Ask him sometime if you have a very great deal of time and want to be bored through the floor.

"Well he isn't that bad, I guess, but he can talk endlessly, about his religion and he really gets carried away unless you ask him to stop. Did you know he wanted to become a religious monk?"

"Hakeem … a monk?" Seléne snorted in surprise.

Elana nodded. "It's easy to get the wrong impression about Hakeem when you first meet him. I certainly did. Then you realise that he is a warrior, yes, but he lives and breathes his beliefs. He really cares for people and hates war."

"I certainly got the wrong impression at first. I didn't think it was possible to be so frightened of someone," Seléne volunteered. "Was there a real torturer?"

Elana nodded, "Belamus found out about it, it was supposed to be Nikan's secret."

"Let me guess," Seléne said. "He met Hakeem."

Elana actually laughed and nodded, smiling. "It was a very brief meeting."

Seléne smiled, shaking her head. "I think Hakeem's making me a little bloodthirsty too. I can't feel sorry for people who enjoy torturing people ... especially if they were going to torture me.

"Dear sister, apart from being more bloodthirsty, you are different: more confident, happier than I have ever seen you. It warms my heart to see you like this."

Elana's eyes became moist and she smiled gently with a distant look on her face.

"It's not just Hakeem and Jacinta, though I love them both deeply. After getting away from the palace I found in common people, and in being a common person, so much love and happiness." Elana started to cry and Seléne hugged her sister with tears in her own eyes, tears of happiness.

Chapter 31: A Catastrophe only a Woman Could Understand

It was before Seléne and Cyron left, that the new Queen faced the first crisis of her rule. It was a catastrophe any fellow woman could understand!

"Arrgh! ..." Elana screamed in horror. "My hair is *ruined*."

She began to cry.

Seléne and Jacinta sat on either side and tried to comfort the young Queen. Her hair was still wet, from her latest attempt to remove the dye with a vinegar wash and ... it was still *black*. The skin dye they had used had gone at last. So Elana at least looked like an elf again, but the hair dye couldn't be washed out, no matter what she tried.

Seléne's hair was full-bodied and black, which was unusual for one of the Eastern Elves, but it still had the gorgeous lustre of elvish hair. Elana's hair on the other hand was typically elvish: soft and silky but very fine and it grew slowly. If she couldn't remove the dye, she would be doomed to almost a year of blond roots and black tips, or she would have to shave her head, usually a severe punishment for young elves.

"What am I to do?" she asked the two girls tearfully. "Hakeem loves my hair, and my job as Queen will be hard enough without me looking stupid."

Her mouth formed a wicked smile, through her tears. For an instant she was dreaming of Omar chained in her dungeon, and introducing him to Dumaya.

"Mother!" Jacinta caught the look and read her mind. "Whatever evil thoughts you are having about Abbā Omar, you will stop them right now, he saved our lives. Besides, he is a bachelor, he probably didn't know about the hair dye."

Elana slumped, despondent. Hakeem was unlikely to torture his friend.

He would if he *really* loved her!

"Perhaps you could try Anaxagoras," Seléne said considering.

Elana looked up with red rimmed eyes. "What's that?"

"You really didn't get around a lot, before, did you, sister?" Seléne said, "Not what, but who. Anaxagoras is the Royal Chemist. He is very clever, if rather unusual. He will help .. if he finds the problem interesting."

"He'll help if he finds keeping his head on his shoulders interesting," Elana growled.

Desperate matters required desperate measures!

"Mother!" Jacinta scolded Elana. "We just got rid of one bad Queen. You're not allowed to become another. You will need to learn to rule with more than just threats. Besides, I have met Anaxagoras and he wouldn't understand threats.

"He is, well, *unusual*. All you have to do is flatter him about his knowledge and pretend you're interested in whatever he wants to talk about and he will do anything for you."

Seléne looked at Jacinta in surprise. She was right. She hadn't thought of it before, but that was exactly how to get Anaxagoras to do something for you.

Seléne was starting to notice just how clever her Gypsy friend could be.

* * *

Unusual was a good description when Elana went to see her Royal Chemist. Anaxagoras was a hunched, untidy elf of uncertain age. He had untidy red hair and penetrating green eyes that burned with unusual intelligence. His work area was cluttered by very odd bits of half-completed experiments. Elana didn't expect him, despite seeming to know about almost everything about everything, to know anything about hair.

When she did ask, she almost wished she hadn't.

He was delighted to have an interested audience, and it started a seemingly endless monologue. As he talked, he carefully examined Elana's hair and showed his apprentices. He looked at it, separated it, looked at its roots and the scalp, felt it, and combed it back and forward. He took a few strands and examined them, saw how strong they were. Burnt some, and then added chemicals to others. All the time he was lecturing not only his apprentices, but Elana!

After more than an hour of this, Elana had a dazed look on her face. She just wanted her hair fixed. She didn't want a year's course on the philosophy of hair, but all elf scientists tended to be the same. Sometimes, they even forgot to eat.

What were these people called in Greek? Megalofyias! It was after *Megalofyia* ("big head") the small but especially annoying Karian sprite of knowledge and philosophy.

He tried washing it, nothing happened. Elana could have told him that already.

He was intrigued as to how Omar managed a permanent effect. Without really wanting to, Elana learned that the colour of the hair was at the core, in Eastern Elves it was blond or reddish.

The outer protective coat resulted in the hair's silky and lustrous feel. Most the common dyes that were gentle enough to use on the hair, would only coat the outside. The result was uneven and obvious, and would wash off, sometimes in a single wash.

"My Lady," the chemist finally concluded. "I simply can't bring back the natural colour of your hair!"

Elana's gasped in horror. "Omar!" she said through gritted teeth.

The chemist held up his hand. "I'm sure Father Omar didn't know. It wouldn't be of his invention. Humans discover lots of things through trial and error, but this is truly marvellous. I didn't know it could be done."

"I intend to do some things to Omar when I next meet him that he won't see as marvellous!" Elana said bleakly.

"My lady, be fair. The Lord Abbot saved your life by your disguise. Any other dye would not make you look like a Gypsy. He even managed to add a bit of bounce to your hair. This is wonderful!"

Elana wasn't finding it at all wonderful, and was getting images of tipping some of his more toxic chemicals over the head of this particular 'big head'.

"What I can do … is give you something *close* to your normal hair colour, and then you will have to wait till it grows out. I have never done this before, but I'm sure I can do it.

"It is only fair to warn you, though, that there may be some dangers. To get at the inner core of the hair, where the pigment is, I will have to damage the outer protective coat that gives the hair its shine and silky feel. That's what must have been done.

"Did Omar use several steps? … Yes, that makes sense.

"After I dye your hair I will have to repair it. You know the feel of greasy wool? Nothing like that, but your scalp still produces oils to repair your hair, and I will have to produce something to do the same job.

"Mmm. They have damaged the hair, dyed it and then repaired it! Now I understand … that's marvellous!"

To damage then repair something that was not living didn't sound marvellous to Elana. It sounded like the height of recklessness.

And she didn't want to be left with something like greasy wool. At least, he could help her, if only he would get to the point.

"Now where was I? Oh, yes, I can make a substance that can damage the outer layer and remove the dye but it will remove your natural pigment altogether. Your hair will not be golden, but more of a white. Then I can try to copy the process that was used for the dark dye, but instead use a golden colour, and finally, I will repair the outer layer!

"Damaging the outer layer has already been done, so I have to be more careful. I'll use warm water so we don't have to use as much chemical, but we mustn't scald your scalp, that wouldn't be so healthy, now would it?" He permitted himself a small chuckle over his joke.

No off course not! Elana thought, as she gritted her teeth. Burning your Queen's scalp would not be at all healthy for you, would it now, Anaxagoras?

But he was going on.

"We will bring your hair back to its colour over two or three treatments. The danger would be that you will be left with thin and dry hair, or the colour won't be as I wish. I will have to purify some chemicals I have. Was one of them the one that blew up last time? Er, let me think!"

Great! That's reassuring, Elana thought. He'd never done this before. She might be left with thin and dry hair, or even be blown up, or scalded!

Perhaps Hakeem would remove this megalofyia's head for her, if he made a mess of her hair. Elana smiled at the thought. Oh, well. If she didn't let him try, she'd have to cut most of her hair off anyway.

She gathered her courage, "Let's do it! Can Jacinta and Seléne come with me?"

* * *

"Aaah!" Elana wailed in horror, throwing her mirror on the table. "I look like a mouse!"

It was the afternoon following the first treatment. The three girls were in Seléne's room. Jacinta and Seléne had continued sharing, though there were plenty of rooms at the Palace.

"It's not too bad," Seléne and Jacinta said in unison, trying desperately not to giggle.

Poor Elana! A mouse was a perfect description! It was exactly that colour: light brown with faint silver-grey hues!

"Oh, Mother," said Jacinta, putting her arm on her mother's shoulder and trying to comfort her. "It's only for one week, or two at the most, you heard Anaxagoras. He was delighted with the result. I'm sure he really didn't mean to say it could go green."

Elana started to cry. It was going to be an impossible task of breaking down millennia of elvish prejudice against humans. She had the incident at her coming of age and her trip to Djorn. Now, to make it completely impossible for her when she first appeared as Queen, she would look like freak.

"No one can see me!" Elana decided firmly, putting on her *diklo*.

"Mother!" Jacinta laughed. "Get rid of that ridiculous hat!"

Jacinta made a lunge and grabbed the hat, but Elana jumped on her, pinning her to the bed. Jacinta made an awkward one-handed pass to Seléne who retreated to the other end of the room with the prize.

Should they play piggy in the middle? Seléne wondered. Elana used to like that game.

Just now though, Elana looked like she would offer violence!

Then they heard Hakeem approaching.

"Hakeem! ... He can't see me like this!" Elana cried, in a panic.

"Now, how do you propose to prevent that, sister of mine?" Seléne asked, incredulous.

Elana made another desperate attempt to retrieve her ridiculous hat, but Seléne held it firmly out of her reach.

"Mother! Listen to me!" Jacinta whispered urgently. "With you in that gorgeous dress, Hakeem will hardly notice!"

"No, Jacinta, you are wrong," Elana said. "Your father is a master tracker. You've been with him in the forest."

"*Mother*, he's a male!" Jacinta said, surprised at her mother's ignorance. "Women have to cook, clean, look after two or three children and boss their man around; all the while they are chatting with their best friends and family as well.

"Inside the house, men can only focus on one thing at a time. They simply don't register all the details women do, trust me. In the presence of beautiful women, their focus becomes narrowed.

They notice the tone of her voice, a general impression of her body and … well … her breasts, and then her mood."

Elana snorted, "Mostly her breasts, I think."

Jacinta nodded, "Now if you promise not to get angry with father, I'll show you, just be nice."

Elana looked at Jacinta sceptically, and then she looked resentful. Finally, reluctantly, she nodded. It was going to be hard not to get angry, but she would try.

"Well hello, girls! Hello Elana!" Hakeem burst in a little breathlessly, giving Elana an absent-minded kiss.

He was as excited as a small boy. He could hardly contain himself. "Guess who I just met, of all people? Anaxagoras! And you know what? He's agreed to help me."

Hakeem paused, triumphant, waiting for their reaction. The three girls looked at him blankly.

"You must know, surely you remember. The fireworks at Kassie's wedding of course! I want to see if they can be used to make a weapon."

Elana almost swore at him, couldn't he focus on something important for a change? Like her hair? But she had promised to keep her temper; so she smiled pleasantly around gritted teeth. Jacinta flashed a smirk at her mother.

"Oh, I *do* like that dress!" Hakeem smiled in obvious appreciation. That was better, Elana thought.

"Would you like it better, if it were the colour of the night-dress mum wore to bed the night before?" Jacinta enquired innocently.

All three girls were looking at him with seemingly innocent interest, Hakeem found it very disconcerting. He screwed up his face in an effort to remember what Elana wore. He remembered how wonderful she looked, and the feel of her body under the silky fabric, but which one was it?

He started to feel nervous. His palms were starting to sweat. He carefully watched the girls' expressions. No, he didn't seem to be in trouble … yet.

"Er… red?" he suggested.

"No, Honey," Elana gave him a serene smile. "I wore that the night before. It was the dark green, you remember?"

Hakeem's mind was completely blank. He remembered the feel of her arms around him, her putting her hand on his chest, kissing her and her body, the gorgeous feeling of her breasts, making love afterwards.

Hakeem laughed nervously, "I'm sorry honey, it was too dark."

"No it wasn't, darling." Elana replied, still smiling, "We sat by the fire talking, surely you remember that?"

Hakeem dabbed at his forehead, and eyed his wife nervously, he was sweating freely now and his breath felt constricted.

Elana twirled around "What about the rest of me? What do you think?"

Hakeem rarely felt he was being watched so intensely.

He scanned his wife rapidly: feet, bare … no ankle chain; the pendant, earrings, bangles were the same. "Oh yes, you've cut your hair. And … changed the colour!" he added triumphantly. "No I haven't cut it darling, it's just been washed. Do you like it?" Elana enquired.

Hakeem considered. They could almost see the wheels turning slowly in his mind. "Sorry darling, I prefer your original colour. You still look lovely and I really like that dress!"

"Thanks darling, why don't you go off to see Anaxagoras? Of course it's alright if we miss you for lunch, we'll just see you at dinner."

Hakeem left quickly, retreating while he could.

He would have to try to memorise what Elana wore but he loved his wife, he loved to watch her: standing, talking, sleeping, how she moved, almost anything. He still felt flushed at times by her presence; he loved her feel, her touch, her scent and making love.

The other day, she asked him if he thought she had put on weight. How would he know something like that? Why didn't she ask one of the girls? She looked great, that's all he knew!

As he left, he heard the three girls laughing. Now what was that all about? Soon he was giving it no more thought.

Chapter 32: Hakeem, Other Mad Scientists, and the Holy Mother

Kaboom! There was a loud explosion and a small wooden box flew two feet in the air to land upside down, smoking. It left a great cloud of smelly black smoke hanging in the air. Elana was treated to the strange sight of Hakeem (in trousers and a short-sleeved shirt) and Anaxagoras in his laboratory smock hugging each other and dancing up and down. Anaxagoras' students were cheering from a safe distance.

"We did it, we did it!" the two very oddly matched friends were shouting excitedly.

Both men's faces were blackened, their clothes looked filthy. Anaxagoras's hair was dishevelled and dusty with cinders, his eyebrows and lashes were singed. Hakeem was not much better, with his beard was singed in several places.

Elana had come to see why Hakeem had missed an official lunch, as if she didn't know.

She was wearing an exquisite gown. Her hair was blond, well ahead of schedule, and was very prettily done up with sparkles like stars. In truth, it looked more like human blond than elf blond, but the effect was stunning. She hadn't managed to convince Anaxagoras that women would kill for the chance to change the colour of their hair at will.

Now Hakeem and Anaxagoras were acting like two small boys who triumphantly found a patch of dirt in which to play. It had only been a week since Hakeem and Anaxagoras had met, and yet they acted as if they had known each other all their lives.

"My Lady! Your husband is brilliant! Did you see that box lift?" Anaxagoras called out breathlessly.

Indeed, Elana thought, no one's lifted a box before!

Hakeem was thrilled that she arrived just in time to see their experiment. He almost ran over to hug her excitedly with his filthy black hands. Elana danced skilfully out of the hug, with a small squeal.

Then Hakeem realised, and held his hands behind him and offered his black face to be kissed. Again Elana had to duck and weave so her elegant gown and subtle face-paint weren't spoiled.

"Look at what we have made," Anaxagoras held up a long thin scrap of paper. "You know what it is?"

Elana smiled. She, too, sometimes screwed up small scraps of paper. It was just before she threw them out, but she was given no chance to reply.

"A wick!" Anaxagoras claimed excitedly.

A candle with such a wick would not do very well now would it? Perhaps she was missing the point.

"It's thin paper twisted around and around with fire powder inside. We can use it to light the fire powder and we can put the fire power in a small space and cause an explosion. Surely you can see how important this is!"

We can move more boxes around! Elana decided. "Hakeem, haven't you forgotten something?" she enquired mildly.

"Oh Lord, sorry! The Persian Ambassador! When is lunch?" Hakeem asked, attempting to lift his coat up with his elbows and forearms, so he didn't get it dirty. Elana picked it up and then realised, belatedly, it was filthy.

She passed it to one of the students, while she cleaned her hands in a bowl. The man she gave it to looked at her and at the coat with a puzzled expression.

Give it to be washed, you fool! Elana thought at him, as she turned to her husband.

Lunch was over two hours ago, Elana had never known Hakeem to miss a meal before.

Relations between the Shantawi and Persians were strained after the Persians invaded the Shantawi lands with a large force decades ago. They were only beaten back by a hair. As a result, the Shantawi had acquired a small string of Oases and some grazing land from the Persian Empire, which the Persians wanted back, now that peace was finally declared.

They had no hope whatsoever.

Of course the Ambassador of the powerful Persian Empire wouldn't be upset by a deliberate snub! Elana had to admit he was an insufferable boor and wished she could have forgotten the meeting herself.

She wasn't as angry as she had been two hours ago, but this had to be brought under control.

"Hakeem, you're going to wash up, you've played enough! Now say goodbye to your friend, you won't be able to play with him again for a few days. The ambassador has invited us for afternoon tea." And I have a double dose of him, thanks to you, she thought grimly.

"That's fine, honey, that's all we had to do," Hakeem replied happily, as he came along with her. "Anaxagoras can do the rest."

Elana tried to understand why he was so excited and pleased with what they had done. Noise, black smoke and lifting boxes were all she could see. Just like small boys at play, she thought.

Hakeem seemed like a child in a toy shop when he was introduced to the elven scientists and philosophers. They immediately accepted Hakeem as a member of their strange group and engaged him in their completely incomprehensible discussions.

Jacinta would join them when she could bear to separate herself from Seléne. She never would have dreamed it possible, but the signs were unmistakable, Hakeem was a 'big head'!

In an instant, her husband had transformed into a perfect big head. He had been recognised and warmly welcomed by the members of the elvish 'big head' society. Anaxagoras didn't seem to consider it strange that his new friend was a trained killer. He would sometimes come to the training field in search of Hakeem to resume some obscure conversation.

Would she ever understand the whole of the man she loved?

Then a very dark thought occurred to her: Hakeem had always had been a thoroughgoing megalofyia but his specialty was being an efficient killer. No, that wasn't at all fair: his specialty was being a paladin, whatever that was. Elana smiled. She had married a megalofyia, without realising it. Elana just wished the other elves would accept Hakeem as readily as the megalofyias and the Priestesses of the Holy Mother.

Elana had grown up around the holy priestesses when she was sent to them for religious instruction. They had given her the training that helped her cope with the treatment she had at the hands of Xanthe.

She loved the Great Mother, Astrior and she respected her, partly for who she was and what she was, and also partly from long training as a child, but it was tempered by familiarity.

It was hard to reconcile this with the attitude her husband and daughter had towards her. When they were told the old lady wished to see them, Hakeem became very sober and serious and Jacinta went very quiet.

When Hakeem, Jacinta and Elana arrived together at the temple of the Great Earth Mother they almost caused a riot! They were the three mentioned in the Prophecy! Everyone wanted to see them and talk to them, even touch them, from the most humble novice to the most senior of the sisters.

It took some time before the three could be ushered in to an audience with Astrior. Instead of the half-bow Elana was used to giving Astrior, Hakeem and Jacinta hurried forward and fell prostrate to kiss the ground before her.

Astrior accepted this without any surprise. Hakeem and Jacinta continued to call her 'Holy One' as if it were a title, but the three of them started talking in front of Elana as if they had known each other all their lives. The instant connection between the Shayvists paladins and the Holy Mother should have surprised Elana, but somehow it didn't.

When she asked Jacinta about it, Jacinta got a faraway look on her face and took a while to reply. Eventually she sighed, "Astrior has returned to our level of existence after ascending. There are very few of those. In her presence, we both felt it very strongly."

* * *

Elfriede, Anaxagoras's wife, looked at her new Queen in surprise. "Do we really need *all* this sugar?"

Elana nodded. She had come to talk to Elfriede but was delighted to find the older woman preparing to make biscuits for the late festival of winter. The wonderful elvish winter solstice and Jacinta's thirteenth birthday celebrations had been ruined by Nikan's coup and the aftermath.

Elana could not get anywhere near the royal kitchen without causing a scandal. Elfriede watched her energetically kneading small lumps of butter into the mixture of sugar and oatmeal flour. "If this becomes popular, we will have to plant more sugar beet," Elfriede suggested, chuckling. It was obviously a human recipe.

"Then we will have to plant more sugar beet," Elana laughed, as she hefted a large ceramic jar of oatmeal flour onto the bench. "I'll send you some more sugar, but you can only make this for festivals, it's too expensive otherwise, but you know how we elves love sweet things."

Her new Queen was talking as if she were a peasant, careful about her money.

Elfriede couldn't believe that Elana was not merely visiting her, but cooking in her kitchen as if it was the most natural thing in the world, and she was so obviously enjoying herself and enjoying the company.

Elfriede, as the wife of Anaxagoras, had no more status at the court than a wife of a simple artisan. She was trying to work out what it was that caused her to feel such powerful affection for the young Queen. Elana had not simply survived what would have been poverty and hardship for any other royal, she had liked it.

Why, she is one of us! Elfriede realised. She is not just a spoiled product of the court. She really is one of us.

"Now, where was I?" Elana was saying. "I explained all this to Anaxagoras and I don't think he understood."

"With just a little more work, this could make the two of you both fabulously wealthy. Women could change their hair to black, blond, red or brown whenever they wished, maybe even shades in between or they could have the main body of their hair one colour and the tips another.

"When I told him, he just nodded politely and smiled and then went back to working on something else."

"My Lady," Elfriede said gently. "Anaxagoras understood."

Elana paused, looking at her in surprise. "I don't understand."

"In that way, he'll never be rich. I knew what it would be like when I married him," Elfriede smiled fondly, her eyes looking into the distance. "In his own way, though, he is rich.

"I swear the man would never eat if I didn't see to it. Give him time alone and a problem and he is rich. I hear you never wanted to return here, my Queen, do you know what I mean now?"

Elana had her mouth open for a moment before she remembered to close it. "I see," she said in a husky voice with her eyes moist. "You're right, your husband is rich."

Elana still intended to raise his salary and insist he hire a maid to help his long-suffering wife, even if she didn't feel she was long-suffering.

* * *

It was just after Cyron had left that Elana and Jacinta were invited to see the results of what Hakeem and Anaxagoras had been working on. They knew they would have to seem duly impressed, no matter what the men had done.

Elana invited Elfriede, but she firmly refused. It was a secret of her successful marriage, she said. She never went into his workshop, except sometimes to remind him to eat.

Anaxagoras and Hakeem had set the apprentices, aided by two blacksmiths, to all sorts of last minute clanging and hammering before the main show started.

Elana winced as she entered, her hands over her ears. If dust and noise was all that were needed for success, the results were assured.

Then, bang, bang! Hakeem lit the wicks of two small paper cylinders and threw them into the middle of the courtyard. They made an alarming noise for objects so small. It was obviously the fire powder. Alright, good for scaring horses but wouldn't it scare our horses too?

The bronze cylinder that shot a metal bolt a short distance with a terrible loud noise was mildly impressive but it couldn't replace *ballista*, those massive siege crossbows taller than a man. Hakeem said his device could fire faster than a ballista but its power was limited. They needed to find a way to improve the power and to prevent the barrels cracking.

The noise, fire and smoke might be enough to impress their enemies, but what was the use of something that could blow up in their faces?

The fire-liquid Anaxagoras showed … now that was something else entirely! It was a dark liquid that could be pumped into a jet, which could be lit. So, it could shoot out a jet of flame, like dragon breath. It could even float on water, for naval use.

As soon as she saw it, Elana knew that this secret must be guarded above all else. How it was made, even very existence!

Much to the disappointment of Anaxagoras, she stopped him from enthusiastically explaining it to all nearby who would listen.

Anaxagoras said he had some ideas to make it safer but he wouldn't permit anyone else but himself to use it because it was too dangerous. Elana would certainly put a stop to this habit. By royal decree if need be!

Elana realised as she watched, that she was looking at one of the most valuable elves in her kingdom, perhaps even *the* most valuable elf alive.

No one could completely stop Anaxagoras from trying to blow himself up, but she was going to appoint him some 'minders' from the palace guard. A certain friend of Seléne who was a junior officer but a clever diplomat would be just the one to put in charge.

Anaxagoras would be bothered, but his wife would be overjoyed. Perhaps Elana would enlist Elfriede in explaining to Anaxagoras just exactly how things were going to be from now on!

Chapter 33: Jacinta's Clever Parents

Elana was bored and falling asleep. The fat landowner seemed to drone on endlessly. Her audience room today only had a few nobles assembled to watch her dispense justice. Interest in what she did was waning. It didn't surprise her, nothing she attended to was interesting and nothing she did was particularly exciting.

She had heard that her father was recovering rapidly, which was good news. She longed for his return so she could spend time with her family again.

The Prophecy suggested that she was destined to be a great queen, but she knew she was showing no signs of that so far.

Added to this, the court was distinctly unsettled. Many of those chosen by Nikan who were not already in prison felt insecure, and those who suffered under Nikan's court held serious grudges against those who didn't.

Nikan had replaced many who were loyal to Cyron with his own nominees, so Elana had the court stacked against her. Cyron would sort this out when he had returned to health, but in the meantime Elana didn't even know who her enemies were.

At first, Elana was grateful to have Dimitrios, the adviser to Xanthe. He was a mine of information about who was whom and the intricacies of elf politics.

More recently, though, she suspected he was manipulating her. He packed her day full of trivial matters. She was so exhausted that she had taken to sleeping on a bed just off the audience room. She was getting no exercise. He always found a pressing reason to stretch her day longer.

Important promises had been made that couldn't now be cancelled, and new 'emergencies' were coming up every day.

She found that he was making the really important decisions, and he kept information from her. Whatever decision she made, he seemed to find reason why she was wrong on the basis of some supposedly superior knowledge. And now she was almost falling asleep hearing some silly dispute over maybe three score of cattle that had wandered.

Before that, she had to sit through an argument over whether crockery was of sufficient standard for the maker to be paid. All because Dimitrios said one of the parties was an important man!

She was tired and sick of all this. She had already decided to rein in the process and had been arguing with Dimitrios increasingly in the last few days. She wanted it to be obvious to all that he was at fault, yet she was finding him too subtle so far. The battle of wills had started, and a showdown was brewing.

Her thoughts which were starting to drift but they were brought back by a disturbance near the door. Her heart leapt with joy to see Hakeem and Jacinta outside. She realised with a shock that she hadn't seen them for a couple of weeks, and not much before that.

How could so much time pass so quickly? Suddenly, two guards were thrown roughly aside and others were running up to help.

"Let my husband pass!" Elana shouted indignantly.

She had left orders that her family could get free access to her. Why were the guards trying to stop them? The guards looked to Dimitrios who nodded before they finally stood aside.

"I gave orders that you are not to be disturbed by anyone whom I have not authorised, your majesty," Dimitrios whispered. "You know how busy you are and how tired you are," he added with apparent reasonableness. "All I asked was that my Lord Hakeem make an appointment like everyone else."

"Do you presume to correct my order?" Elana asked coldly.

"Your Highness," whispered Dimitrios urgently. "You don't understand. You are in audience in the Elven Court. You will offend the nobles waiting. You don't want people to think you just let them barge in, do you?"

Elana felt uncertain, the audience was watching her intently.

"My Lady Elana," Hakeem called out as he approached. "For three full days I have sent messages through this buffoon that I need to see you in a matter most urgent.

"There have been promises, but each time I have received a last-minute apology. The guards won't let me pass in many areas of the palace, including seeing you. I am openly insulted, and I have found even the lowest servant has been instructed not to follow my orders. Is this how I am to be treated?"

Elana turned to Dimitrios, furious. "Is this true?"

Dimitrios was unrepentant. The Queen was in a weak position about her treatment of these humans. "Well, he demands your time when you are so busy with your father away. He won't tell me the reason. So I must assume it's not important, mustn't I?"

"Why should I explain myself to a *servant*?" Hakeem said, disdainfully. "I am treated this way because I'm not an elf. Elana, do you remember what you promised in front of the Gypsies about the treatment of humans? Or is it different now that you are home?"

"I'm sorry. I just haven't time to get to everything," Elana said, feeling distressed and overwhelmed, including the time needed to sort out Dimitrios! "I'll make it up to both of you, and sort this out, I promise. But you must understand: I've been so busy, I scarcely have time to think."

"And you *let* this happen! You let this mongrel of a stray dog keep you too busy with foolish work to do the important work of ruling your kingdom!" Hakeem replied loudly.

"How dare you!" Elana felt pierced with shame. Hakeem was right. She was becoming an unpopular and incompetent ruler. It seemed to be happening no matter how hard she tried to please!

"I am the Queen! I will decide how I rule!"

Jacinta looked at the point of tears.

Hakeem smiled bitterly. "At last you see your task! The little time I had to speak to you has been used in waiting. Can you talk to me now?"

"My Lady!" said the fat landowner, the original owner of the cattle. "Doesn't he understand? He spreads the private business of Her Majesty in public view! We have waited for this audience. Do we have to talk in front of this horseman and a Gypsy?"

Dimitrios was talking at the same time. "Madam you cannot! You will be late for your meeting with the Duke as it is!"

Oh dear, the Duke! Elana felt swamped with anxiety and guilt. She was giving offence to everyone.

She now had to be in three places at once! "Sorry, Hakeem, I *will* see you later. That's a promise. Now, let me finish the work I have first, please."

Hakeem nodded coldly. "In the meantime, you must hear about a dozen cattle and a handful of plates. Do you think I don't know? But it's about elves. They are much more important than humans, even family, even if I say it's urgent and no matter what else might be happening.

"Perhaps there will be time for a husband to talk to his wife later. I don't know when that will be." He spun to leave.

Jacinta desperately grabbed at Hakeem to stop him. "Hakeem, you can't! It can't happen like this. Not this way! She doesn't know!"

"Jacinta!" Hakeem shouted angrily. "You will obey me! Did you not hear it yourself?

"I said it was most urgent and I have already waited more than I can afford. What answer do I receive? Another vague promise. Even trivial elf affairs are more important than we are. I can wait no longer, I have told her that and we have been asked to leave. Well, let it be so."

Jacinta looked like she had been hit. She cast a devastated look at her mother and then Hakeem forced her to the door.

Elana was thrown into confusion and anguish. She had let this snake contrive grave insult to Hakeem and Jacinta. She couldn't concentrate on this nonsense over cattle.

"Is it true that he has been asking to see me for days and said it was urgent?" Elana demanded. "Is it true that the guards blocked access? Who else have you prevented from seeing me? What else have you kept from me?" she demanded of Dimitrios.

She felt she was waking from a dream.

"My Lady, he doesn't respect your work, can't you see? He refused to tell me what it was about. So it can't be important. These humans forget themselves. He even tried to order me around! As for whom else, there was a ragtag Gypsy. He even claimed he was a king."

Elana had suddenly gone very quiet. Elvish arrogance against humans can be so entrenched that they fail to see it. Completely unaware, it had led Dimitrios into a disastrous miscalculation. Many were secretly observing his game, but none had grasped his peril.

The fat landowner took this opportunity to protest. "My Lady! You allow this Gypsy waif and the barbarian to intrude. I must protest! I'll be glad when they're gone!"

Elana turned horrified to Dimitrios, who appeared almost pleased. "They are leaving? And when were you going to tell me?" Suddenly Jacinta's behaviour was horrifyingly clear.

Dimitrios tried to laugh it off. "My Lady, you seriously don't expect me to keep track of these humans for you, do you?" He gestured to the open door. As he turned back, his eyes widened to find Elana's knife at his throat.

"Guards!" Elana yelled loudly. The four guards at the door looked startled and then they sprung to obey.

"You two," Elana pointed. "Arrest this man and take him to the dungeon. The charge is treason. I don't care how he is treated," she continued, shouting over Dimitrios' protest. "Just keep him alive and able to answer questions. See that he gets no visitors. After that, get half a dozen men. I expect to be in my husband's quarters."

A now thoroughly frightened and pale Dimitrios was being manhandled by the guards.

She looked at him coldly. "You have been very clever but you have made a final mistake. You will have enough time to find out just how seriously you have miscalculated."

She turned to the fat landowner, "Were you involved in this?"

He was trembling and shaking his head.

"I will give you the benefit of the doubt, just once. Never cross me again. Do you understand that? Now when are they to leave and why?"

Elana almost fainted ... Today!

It had only become common knowledge, since yesterday. The Makedónes had taken Byzántion. They had crossed the straits and would threaten Troia! All Aiolía was mobilising to come to Troia's aid.

She felt a moment of white-hot rage! And Dimitrios fooled her with wandering cattle. He planned to tell her after Hakeem left. He foolishly thought four guards could prevent Hakeem from walking where he wished.

Who else was involved in these plots against Cyron ... and now her? She would preside over his hanging, but time for that later!

She shouted at the remaining elf nobles, who looked chastened and quickly disappeared. The Queen had awoken! And she was one to be reckoned with!

Elana couldn't breathe from mounting panic. Had they already left? She couldn't see through her tears. "Find them and tell them to wait till I talk to them!" she cried, but it was her guards who could scarcely keep up with her as she ran to the quarters.

* * *

Hakeem's anger was gone. The horses were saddled and the escort was ready. The need was most urgent but Hakeem hadn't left.

He was sitting on his couch receiving a decidedly thorough dressing down from his young daughter.

"So, you are going to part in this fashion!" she said angrily, pacing back and forward in front of him.

"Jacinta be reasonable! I am beside myself. I have received an urgent summons. Troia and Aiolía are in great danger. The Macedonians have landed 10,000 infantry and 3,000 of their own horse. They can bring five times that number from Makedonía alone, more if they wished to issue a call on the Hellas. You know how impossible to beat the Makedónes have proven to be, and how cleverly they are led. Then there is the Athēnai to think about.

"I have called a muster of the all tribesmen that can be mobilised at short notice. I don't even know how I will pay them and supply them, but even then I don't think it will be enough. I really think we will lose this one.

"My delay here has only been useless torture for me. I cannot put my personal problems before duty even a moment longer." He stood up resolutely.

"My King is in desperate need. I must leave."

As he said this, Elana rushed in and threw herself at Hakeem's feet "No! You can't be going! Hakeem, I'm sorry, I was a fool!" Tears were running down her cheeks, as she clutched at his ankles.

Hakeem stood impassively. "My Lady, there is no choice. I have delayed my departure beyond what is wise, to the very point of breaking my vows, just so I could speak to you. What time we could have had is now spent in whatever way you have chosen. You always knew that your time with Jacinta and me was limited.

"I've hardly seen you in the last moon. I am insulted, no human is allowed to talk to you because you are the Elf Queen, even when my King Helios rides to war, even for me to say goodbye. I, at least, never forget who my friends are, no matter what way the wind blows."

Elana felt as if he had slapped her with the last remark. She looked up in a haze of tears. "Can't you at least stay tonight?" she pleaded.

"I'm sure you can see that I cannot." Hakeem sounded so hard and so cold.

Well, Elana knew she deserved it!

"I'll come with you!" she said desperately.

"Elana you cannot. You are the Queen of the Elves, you have a kingdom to look after. This battle will be a desperate one, but it is one for humans, not elves. Your father is old and not yet strong, your place is here amongst the elves. Our time of travelling together, I will always cherish deep in my heart, but that time is over."

"But you'll come back, won't you?" Elana pleaded through her tears. "I'll see you again, won't I?"

"Lady, I will try. The odds are heavy. Assuming we win, assuming I don't fall." He melted a little, pulling her up and gently hugging her. "I'm sorry to distress you, Elana. But in truth, I can wait no longer."

Elana pushed herself back and forced herself to stand.

She was the Queen. She gathered her dignity with an effort.

"I see. You are bitter and you have a right to be. I am seriously at fault and now it is too late. Excuse me a few moments, I wish to get ready. I will fare you well. It's the least I can do, as I may not see you again. I apologise for my distress.

"Please don't leave till I can be there."

Hakeem's heart ached to see her so. "Elana, I'm not angry. I tried. I love you, but it is just how it must be."

At that, Elana fled. It would have been easier if he hadn't said he loved her.

As she went, Jacinta slammed the door. "Did you have to do that? Elana made a mistake. Must you break her heart in revenge?"

"Jacinta," Hakeem said wearily sitting down on his couch. "I have no choice. These elves have driven me mad, I cannot do more. Now, I will have to gallop most of the way, only stopping for a change of horses. I have to leave now. I didn't want it to be this way, but it is.

"I am not angry, I am sad. It was something Elana herself allowed to happen. It is her Karma. I just pray she learns from this."

"Oh, so you say you're *not* angry! You can't see it, you are *so* angry," Jacinta replied, glaring at her father. "Search your heart for your feelings towards Elana and you will find them cold. You have been hurt. A cold hard wall has come between yourself and your feelings."

She turned and angrily left.

Hakeem plonked down on his couch and took his head in his hands. He looked deep inside himself. He didn't feel anger at Elana. She was simply facing the consequences of the elvish disregard for humans. She became the Queen and then immediately became caught up in elvish concerns, giving no thought to her human friends. He hoped she learned from this or the love they had was finished.

Yes, it seemed like logic, but it was an unusually hard and cold. He had every right to be angry, but it was his anger that was so hard and cold, not his logic.

He thought of a wall inside himself and how it was so familiar and what it had cost.

Then he thought of Elana, of all she had been through, and the reason she had fallen into this trap. When he thought of the love they had shared and what it would do to her if he left like this, his heart ached for her.

Curse these difficult elves! He thought angrily, not for the first time. He got up and told the six men who would escort Jacinta and himself that he was not leaving yet. He would stay the night.

At the same time Hakeem was doing this, Jacinta was giving her elvish mother a piece of her mind. Elana was reminded by the furious Gypsy girl what her task was, and she was given a scorecard of her dreadful failures.

Elana agreed she bowed her head, deeply miserable; her role was to change thousands of years of elvish prejudice.

Not so simple a task, Jacinta admitted.

And what happened? She wanted to please everyone. She thought she was winning people over so they would come around to her view later. In fact, she was only making a fool of herself. Sensing it was not going well, she lost her courage and began to fear everyone's bad opinion.

After Hector and Seléne left, Jacinta and Hakeem had been treated with contempt by their enemies. Hakeem didn't want to resort to violence, and Elana wasn't there to support him.

"I made a real mess of being Queen, didn't I? I lost my courage and stopped standing up to people. Well, unfortunately Dimitrios and others will pay the price of my failure. It's as much my fault for letting him get away with it. If I had been stronger, he never would have tried. I am a poor learner."

She sighed as she reflected back on her behaviour. "I have fallen for the same trick twice. Someone pretends to be my friend and I become a fool. Maybe Xanthe even trained him. I've let that wonderful man down and now he hates me!"

"No he doesn't, leave Hakeem to me, "Jacinta said grimly.

Just then Hakeem was at the door. Tears were welling in his eyes as he walked stiffly into the room, his arms hesitantly stretched out to her. "Elana! Jacinta, forgive me! I almost let an awful thing happen. I can stay till the morning. It's the least I can do, but it's all I can do. I love you too much to let us part with such an argument."

Soon the three of them were crying in each other's arms.

Jacinta, you're a wonder, Elana thought with fierce love for her daughter. No sooner had Jacinta said she would deal with Hakeem, than it was done!

Hakeem looked over at Jacinta with a broad smile. "Jacinta, if I ever give you a direct order, what must you do?"

"Ignore it," Jacinta laughed, "I hadn't forgotten."

She felt happy again for the first time in many weeks. As they were talking quietly to one another, they heard yelling and the clatter of horse's hooves. The Elvish King and his party had returned and they were in desperate haste!

Cyron was near collapse when he arrived, so Seléne stayed with him. Hector had urgent things that required immediate attention, so they would all meet as soon as the King had rested.

It was just over two turns of the glass when they were summoned to an audience. Cyron looked almost normal again. Seléne and Hector were hovered protectively on either side.

Hakeem, Elana and Jacinta crowded in together, pleased to see Cyron but anxious to see what had brought him back with such haste.

"I'm not as recovered as I thought, it seems." Cyron admitted breathlessly, with a rueful smile. "A fast ride back here almost finished me."

"We told you to take the carriage," Seléne said tartly, sniffing a little. "And perhaps acting more your age wouldn't hurt either!"

Elana and her uncle Hector traded a meaningful look. Her father wouldn't have been the easiest of patients.

"And what were you three looking so pleased about?" Cyron asked, changing the topic. "Oh yes: Dimitrios. I just heard. That was very well done, and it flushed out his supporters too!

"I knew others were involved in Nikan's plot. Dimitrios was an obvious suspect, as I'm sure you both realised from the very first. I had to keep him at the court rather than send him away, in the hope we could find evidence against him.

"We were kept informed about what was happening. When he started to plot against you and Hakeem, I thought to warn you, but then I wanted to see how you would handle him.

"You had to make people think he had you fooled, until all could see what he was doing. You did it perfectly! Then just when he seemed about to win, you sprung your trap dramatically in front of an audience. Many here won't realise you were acting a part. I'm so proud of both of you.

"Apparently, he has been very cooperative. You really must have scared him, Elana. Don't worry about the Gypsy King. He and some of his family were my guests for a few days, and I explained to them all that has been happening. I would hardly forget what the Gypsies did, would I? Old Djordji tries to pretend he is a complete rogue of course, but he's a delightful fellow.

"It must have been hard for Hakeem! To be insulted so! But he never once lost his temper, I'm really impressed."

Jacinta called King Cyron 'grandfather', at his insistence. "Grandfather," she said, smiling ever so sweetly at her two parents. "What has happened here has convinced me *just* how clever my two parents can be! I will certainly watch them more closely in the future. But you couldn't possibly think Elana and Hakeem would be silly enough to let something like this come between them, could you?"

No, no! Of course not! Hakeem and Elana looked at each other sheepishly.

"I'm so glad to catch Hakeem here," the King continued. "I was afraid you might have left.

"Elana, do you plan to travel with Hakeem and Jacinta, or will you come with the rest of the army?"

The three looked back at him in amazement. Army? From Elgard?

"Well," Hakeem took a deep breath "I delayed, hoping Elana could come." What had he told Jacinta about lying?

"Of course," said the King. "I'm surprised and pleased you waited for me. In your place, I would have been tempted to take to horse immediately. I must say, you are a cool one.

"The delay lets us plan. I'm sure you understand why I can only give you two and a half thousand elvish bowmen, under Hector, but they are all veterans. I should be able to assist with supplies, and I will send advisors and craftsmen to help with fortifications around Karsh. I hope we don't need them too soon."

Hakeem beamed! Cyron was taking it for granted that the elves would be joining this fight. He made a mental note to take back all he had been thinking about ungrateful elves. He had been talking to the wrong elves.

Two and a half thousand veteran elven bowmen ... and he said *only!* Two and a half thousand ... Hakeem thought he must be dreaming. The Macedonian Hoplitai were in for a great surprise.

What fortifications in the desert?

"We need to fix your role with the elvish forces here, Hakeem" Cyron said, continuing.

"I have talked to Hector, and we have decided to appoint you as *our* warlord. The elves will report to Hector, but technically you will be second only to me." Cyron indicated his half-brother and Hector nodded, grinning broadly.

Hakeem was stunned.

It would be an honorary title obviously, but what an honour. This would stop anyone giving Hakeem the type of problems he had just experienced.

Cyron had resumed talking. "Now, it's really good that you caught Dimitrios. This goes back to the attacks on Elana and me. It's obvious now who was helping him." Cyron saw their completely blank expressions.

"The Hun of course!" he added as if it were completely obvious.

Jacinta and Hakeem almost interjected, "Who?" Elana and Hakeem and Jacinta exchanged confused glances. What Hun?

But Cyron only nodded to himself, as he continued. "That's why we can't send more help. That's why we have to get Karsh ready for a siege. They have moved into central Asia, the lands of the Aryans, and they are moving through that powerful and wealthy Oasis region in a way that I find frankly terrifying.

"They have crushed the main army of Sogdianē already. Or did Dimitrios manage to keep this from you too?"

"Grandfather," Jacinta interrupted, giving Cyron a respectful bow. "I can see from my parents' expressions that this is news to them, as it is to me. I know little of Sogdianē and thought it was a long way from here. Would it be possible for you to instruct me on the Hun and Sogdianē?" she asked politely.

Cyron nodded and smiled bleakly. "That's a good idea. I don't think Seléne has heard the full story either, though she knows part of it.

"It's a long and grim tale, we will eat first. I need some music and light talk before we discuss something like that. I suspect we will be hearing more than we ever want to about the Athēnai, the Makedónes, and the Hun in the future. They can certainly wait till we have eaten!"

Hakeem didn't know much about the Hun. Cyron would say no more for fear of upsetting his family's appetite. That didn't seem a good sign.

* * *

They had lain on couches in the Greek style, to eat, with a musician playing the beautiful elf-harp softly in the background. Cyron preferred chairs for serious business, so he had led them to one of his favourite sitting rooms after lunch.

The room was surprisingly small and modest for the Great King of the Western elves. The floor had a beautiful Mosaic of a hunting scene and on the roof was a scene from the sack of Elvish Troia.

Out of consideration, Cyron insisted Hakeem and Jacinta sit closest to the fire. The elves, didn't feel the cold nearly as much as humans, it would soon be spring, but it was still decidedly chilly in Elgard.

The walnut chairs with their embroidered black silk cushions were even more comfortable than they looked. Between them was a low cedar table, oiled to a deep colour and with a picture of a great dragon carved into it, outlined in black but Jacinta could hardly take her eyes off the life-sized statue of an elf maiden. She was desperately straining forward with a look of pure anguish on her face. She was held back by two faceless soldiers.

It was a copy of a favourite elf statue, 'Helénē's Agony'. The Greek soldiers were holding her back as they murdered her two young children.

How would it have been so long ago for the elf princess, when all that she loved was destroyed and something as wondrous and beautiful as Elvish Troia was to be no more?

With difficulty, she brought her attention back to Cyron, who was beginning his explanation.

"Jacinta, I will first explain how barbarians can have such power that they can destroy *all* of civilisation as has happened once before," Cyron started. When Cyron was in the mood, he was an excellent teacher. "Civilisation starts with farmers producing more food than they need; a staple food, something like wheat or rice that can be produced in great quantities and stored. Then you need trade between the countryside and cities and towns."

Jacinta nodded, it was simplified, but it made sense. Civilisation enabled people to specialise. A city with surrounding farms is more efficient, so the population can be many times greater and wealthier than a group of hunter-gatherers on the same land.

A city needs trade and a source of food to live. It was the dilemma the Athēnai faced. Athēnai is the greatest city in the Western world but much of the local land is poor and limited, so they need to import most of their food.

If Philippos took Troia, he could cut them off from the Black Sea grain shipments and they would be forever at his mercy.

Cyron was continuing, "Now I must explain about the barbarians.

"There are some lands where life is particularly harsh and difficult. There, only the toughest men and animals can survive. We call the men barbarians. Only two regions of our world have barbarians in large enough numbers to trouble civilisation.

"The first region is the land of frost and snow. Most of this is too dry and sparsely settled to be a threat, but in the northwest of our world there is a region where the sea makes the climate kinder. They keep animals, they fish, they trade, and of course they raid their neighbours.

"Even these people, the 'Norrœnir' as they call themselves, don't have the numbers to cause the scale of catastrophe that devastated this world a millennium ago.

"The barbarians behind that devastation came from the Great Steppe, a huge region of dry grasslands. It is unimaginably vast, lying in a wide band starting north and a little west of the Hellas and reaching almost to where the land ends in the east."

"Stretching three quarters of the known world!" Jacinta murmured. It *was* huge!

Cyron nodded. "It is the land of the great horse nomads. They live mainly on meat and milk, they grow large and tough, and they are very savage in war. We believe the Aryans came from the Volga river area and the Steppe to the east of that.

"They became clever herders and horsemen and began to spread east a thousand years ago. They invented new ways of fighting, new bows and faster chariots with spoked wheels. They bred bigger and stronger horses to pull them. No one could stand against them, and they began conquering those around them, including the wealthy oasis regions of middle Asia, what we now call Sogdianē, Bactria and Xvairizem. They have held that area ever since.

"The climate has cycles, both great and small, and at first there was a long period when that climate was kind. The Aryans could graze bigger herds, many could live well in lands that previously could only support few people and so they became numerous.

"Then there came a drought like no other.

"Deprived of their grazing lands, the nomads began to raid farms and trade caravans, so trade stopped and starvation stalked their own cities. The starving people of all these lands began to move in great numbers. Any in their path had to join them or perish. Finally, there were a whole people on the move, in wave after wave, in numbers too vast to count, with weapons and techniques beyond all others of the time."

"The Aryan hordes," Elana said softly.

Cyron nodded, "This was the time of the famous Aryan hordes. They spread like a grass fire, destroying all in their path."

"It was the end of the Western Elves," Jacinta added.

Cyron nodded. "Not just the Western Elves. The light of civilisation was extinguished throughout the world. Much that was great and fair was no more. Mighty cities, kingdoms and empires, some of which had stood for thousands of years, lay in ruins. Stores of knowledge were lost forever. Due to the damage to farms and trade, a great famine followed, which killed even more than the Aryan spears and bows."

Jacinta nodded. There would be chaos if the land could suddenly support only a small fraction of what it could before.

"Pockets of civilisation remained, but only few. There was a long time of darkness before the survivors started to build again."

"The Bronze Age Collapse and the Great Dark Age," Elana said, wondering what this would mean for them.

Cyron looked at his daughter. "That's what the Greek scholars call it now?" he smiled, amused.

"The Aryans did not disappear. They remained as the great nomadic horsemen who live across the vast grasslands of the Great Steppe. And now there are many civilised Aryans, along the Volga and similar rivers, the Black Sea coast, Northern India, Central Asia (Sogdianē, Bactria, and Xvairizem) and the Great Empire of Persia. Being a Gypsy, Jacinta, you are part Aryan and part Indoi.

"The Aryans have dominated the East and the Steppe for the last thousand years."

Hector spoke softly. "Until now."

Everyone felt a chill at these words.

Cyron nodded grimly. "Long ago, the Aryans had crossed the Tiān Shān Mountains into the region near Cīna. For almost a thousand years, they were the greatest of the barbarians of the grasslands to the north and west of the Chin. They also merged with the Yuezhi (Yu-chi), the other fair race in this region, who held the rich trade city of Kashgar in the west and the other wealthy oasis cities of the Taklimakan desert.

"It was to the north of this place that they first met a new and even more dangerous barbarian."

"The Hun," Jacinta said, her voice hushed. "Grandfather, I don't know those places. They seem so far away."

"It is half a world away," Cyron said softly. "But not far enough. The Chinese call them 'Hun zhu' or 'Xiōngnú'. Greeks call them 'Turks' and we elves call them 'Hun', which means 'people' in their language.

"They are like the Shantawi, in some ways at least. They are horse archers. The Shantawi are a grimmer people in war, better trained and equipped. The tradition of the warrior is a deeper and greater thing with the Shantawi, though the Hun have their own traditions of war.

"The Shantawi, however, will never be a great people. They don't have the area and they don't have the numbers."

Hakeem's eyes glinted in the firelight. "And we met the elves," he smiled. "We are not sorry. I am not sorry."

He took Elana's hand. Meanwhile Cyron reached for a papyrus map from under his chair and unrolled it on the table, holding it open with exquisitely moulded lead weights.

Eurasia and the Lands of the Aryans

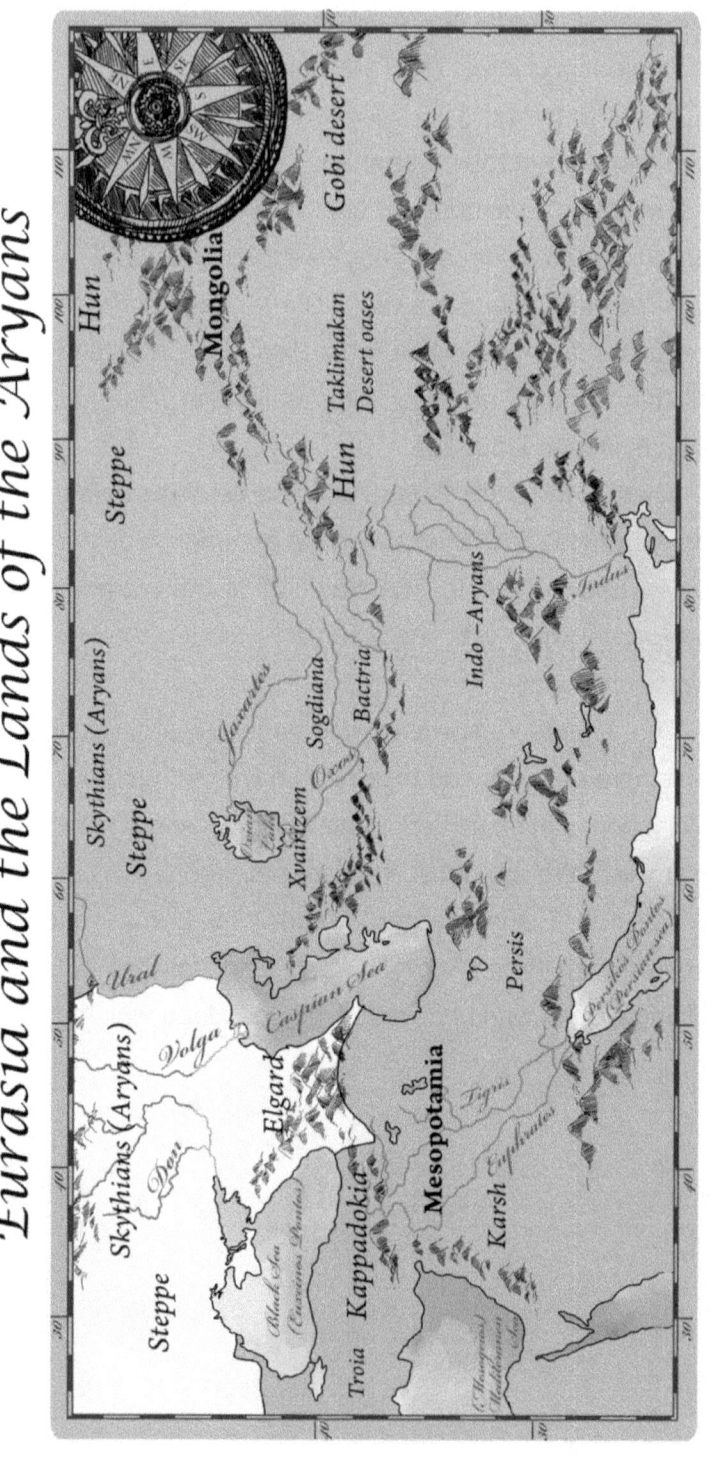

"The Hun *have* become a great people," he continued and pointed to the map.

"They have seized the Tarim region from the Yuezhi and have taken all that part of the great Steppe near the land of the Chin.

"The Chin tried building walls and fortifications against them but it did them no good. The Hun have conquered a great deal of land and built a great empire. They are wealthy and numerous, and have learned many of the secrets of the Chin who are known to be a clever race.

"For reasons we don't know, they suddenly stopped their conquest of the Chin, and offered treaties and demanded tribute instead. For two years, we heard nothing, and then a huge army suddenly appeared near the wealthy kingdom of Sogdianē. They have defeated the army sent against them. They will threaten the capital at Samarkand if no one comes to their aide.

"If they conquer the rich lands of Sogdianē and then Bactria, they can move on the greatest of these Oasis lands, Xvairizem which your father would call 'Khwārizm'. "

Jacinta and Hakeem craned forward as Cyron pointed to each place.

"Then they will control all the steppe and oases east of the Volga and the Caspian Sea," Cyron continued. "If they cross the Volga and they are strong enough to do so, there will be nothing left between them and us apart from Scythian horse nomads. Or they could turn south and come up against the *Parsua* (Persians)." Cyron pointed and then lay back resting.

"And now," Hector said, "After a long period of plenty, a time of great hardship has come again to the Steppes and the arid lands."

"It is happening again!" Seléne said in horror. Hector stretched across and took her hand in both of his.

"Yes, it begins again." Hakeem agreed grimly as he traced the line the Turks must have followed to cross the mountains.

"They are still far away, but for reasons we don't know, they plan to come here," Hector added, almost in a whisper. "We know this because they paid for the attempts on the life of Elana and they helped Nikan. There is no doubt, they are the great tide that the Prophecy warns of. It's not that bad, yet!" he said, seeing their expressions. "We have time to deal with the Makedónes before any Hun come knocking on our door. Then we will be glad to have a union of Human-kind and Elfkin!"

Hakeem had lost his smile. He felt he could hardly breathe. "How many … how many are there?"

Hector's face was unreadable. He already knew. The women looked badly frightened. Hector kissed Seléne's hand.

"Too many to count, I'm afraid. Not as many as the Aryans were, but more than enough for us. Elves were far stronger back then." Cyron leaned forward. "You know how you can't get proper numbers unless you have spies at the very top. I think they might have as many as four armies of fifty thousand warriors each that they can send and still cover their strong points. Two of these are already in Sogdianē, but they pick up more fighters as they go. If you're scared of 13,000 Makedónes, this will make all that has ever threatened our peoples in the last thousand years seem like practice."

Two hundred thousand and growing! Who can fight such odds? It wasn't an army. It was an elemental force of nature!

Hakeem thought back to his youth and living through a locust plague. They devoured all that stood in their path and nothing could be done.

"And," Cyron added looking into the far distance, "they build siege weapons, good ones!"

So, not even the best fortress could hold out against them. They had easily swept aside the strong and populous Chin and then destroyed one of the mightiest armies in Central Asia.

Hakeem wasn't sure they could stop the Makedónes, but this? He clutched at the hands of the Jacinta and Elana and held them fiercely. Would this be the fall of the remaining elves and all that stood with them?

And so, my God, this is the task you give me! It cannot be done!

But I am asked. So, we will see, Hakeem continued thinking grimly. We will see.

Book 2 of The Paladin Chronicles

The Defence of Troia

The Makedóne army under Parmenion has crossed the Bósporos and is carving its way through the Greek Maritime cities of Bithynia with ridiculous ease.

The Greek city of Troia is now an ally of Aiolía but has been seriously weakened after losing the last war. Of the cities of Anatolē that line the entrance to the Black Sea, Troia is the great prize and now it stands in desperate peril.

Philippos the Makedóne King plans to increase his army in Anatolē several fold and when he does he will surely overwhelm all possible resistance. The Athēnai navy is likely to attack even before that.

Hakeem, his wife (the Elf Queen Elana), and their adopted daughter Jacinta ride in haste to join the city as it prepares for a siege.

The large armies headed to Troia are not the only danger for the pitifully few defenders. As something seems to go wrong with the preparations, the mood of the city turns dangerous; if the populace revolts, the small city garrison will be unable to maintain order and all will be lost. Also while the *elves* have lost most of their magic, pitted against them are those whose dark powers are undiminished.

Meanwhile, Elana begins to get premonitions that a great catastrophe is approaching the beleaguered city.

If they can survive the coming siege, Elana and Jacinta must then find a way to search for the lost items of elvish magic, but how can they find things that were lost for over a thousand of years even before the destruction of Elvish Troia?

The defence of Troia, Book 2 of the Paladin Chronicles, continues the story of the struggle to save the elves and their human allies. Now read on:

Excerpt: Book 2
The Paladin Chronicles.
The Defence of Troia

Chapter 1: A Desperate Race, a City in Peril, the Elf Queen

For Elana and Jacinta, the next two weeks were a blur of pain and misery.

The allies had set up a fast courier service from Elgard to Troia. Every ten miles there was a station with fresh horses and a small escort. The Makedónes had taken Byzántion and had crossed the Bósporos straits into Anatolē. Now Hakeem, Elana and their daughter followed this route in a desperate dash from Elgard to Troia.

Hakeem at first kept offering them rest, but the girls angrily refused and pushed on till they were drooping in the saddles. It took an awful lot to worry Hakeem, and they had never seen him so worried.

Hakeem forced them to eat and drink, but as soon as they lay down, they were asleep ... only to be woken in a daze to ride again. The weather was appalling, blizzards and cold stinging rain.

Jacinta and Elana were young and healthy and had been training like elite athletes. Now they were called on to give all they could give, and then they were asked to give more ... and then more again.

The girls no longer knew where they travelled or for how long.

It was the night of the sixteenth day and Elana could feel her horse carrying her up a long steep slope. Through a fog of exhaustion, she realised she could see the walls of Troia outlined by rows of torches flaming in their sconces.

She heard the challenge and the proud reply. "My name is Hakeem. I am a commander for King Helios, the warlord of the desert people and now of the elves. King Helios and I have given our oaths to assist you in danger. We are proud to call the brave men and women of Troia friends, and prouder yet to stand with them in their hour of need!

"With me is Elana, Queen of the Eastern Elves and Jacinta the daughter of our heart! Be assured: armies of Helios, my tribesmen and the elves will follow and more will come from the cities to the south. Now, let us pass, and show the way, so we may give honour to your King!"

A great cry went up! Never, since Troia was an elf city more a millennium ago, had it faced such peril! People were in despair. Suddenly, out of this darkness rode hope! Old foes came, not to gloat, but out of love. They came to stand shoulder to shoulder with the people of Troia.

The Warlord himself came! And the great Elven Queen! And look at them. They have spent themselves to come so far.

They rode, by some feat of great endurance to aid us. Hope has returned.

Troia had been defeated, yes, but now they were treated with great honour by the victors. Oaths were taken, yes. Yet now they were honoured beyond hope. Troia had formidable and determined friends, whatever it faced! With them, it was stronger than before.

Never, ever, would this gesture, this act of honour, this kindness be forgotten!

The weary, travel-stained trio were given greater honour than if they had arrived with pomp and finery at the head of a mighty host. Their ragged unkempt appearance showed their willingness to give their all for the people of Troia.

While only three came, with a small escort, it had an effect never equalled in the history of the city.

Hakeem and Jacinta fell to their knees before King Leandros of Troia, Jacinta sagging. Elana bowed but was swaying on her feet. The King himself leapt up before all his court to hug and kiss them before sending them to rest. And while their guests slept, the Troians celebrated with glad heart.

No greater token could be sent! The Queen of Elves herself! And the Warlord, wearied to the limit of endurance. They even brought their young adopted child to share the danger of the imperilled city

But elves! It was a miracle!

Elves had always avoided the new Troia, haunted as they saw it, by their ancient dead. They never involved themselves in the affairs of humans. Now in Troia's most desperate hour, the mighty elves themselves heeded the call and returned again to defend the site of their ancient holy city!

www.ingramcontent.com/pod-product-compliance
Lightning Source LLC
Chambersburg PA
CBHW052345020726
47503CB00001B/111